DEFIANCE
THE PROTECTORS #9

SLOANE KENNEDY

CONTENTS

Copyright v
Defiance vii
Trademark Acknowledgements ix
Acknowledgments xi
Series Reading Order xiii
Series Crossover Chart xvii
defiance xix

Prologue 1
Chapter 1 9
Chapter 2 19
Chapter 3 28
Chapter 4 36
Chapter 5 43
Chapter 6 54
Chapter 7 64
Chapter 8 73
Chapter 9 82
Chapter 10 87
Chapter 11 93
Chapter 12 105
Chapter 13 115
Chapter 14 123
Chapter 15 131
Chapter 16 139
Chapter 17 146
Chapter 18 152
Chapter 19 157
Chapter 20 172
Chapter 21 183
Chapter 22 194

Chapter 23	207
Chapter 24	214
Chapter 25	225
Chapter 26	231
Chapter 27	239
Chapter 28	246
Chapter 29	256
Chapter 30	261
Chapter 31	266
Epilogue	277
Sneak Peek	283
Prologue	285
Chapter 1	291
About the Author	303
Also by Sloane Kennedy	305

Defiance is a work of fiction. Names, characters, businesses, places, events and incidents are either the products of the author's imagination or used in a fictitious manner. Any resemblance to actual persons, living or dead, or actual events is purely coincidental.

Copyright © 2017 by Sloane Kennedy

Published in the United States by Sloane Kennedy
All rights reserved. This book or any portion thereof may not be reproduced or used in any manner whatsoever without the express written permission of the publisher except for the use of brief quotations in a book review.

Cover Images: © Wander Aguiar

Cover Design: © Jay Aheer, Simply Defined Art

Copyediting by Courtney Bassett

ISBN-13:
978-1548184223

ISBN-10:
1548184225

DEFIANCE

Sloane Kennedy

TRADEMARK ACKNOWLEDGEMENTS

The author acknowledges the trademarked status and trademark owners of the following trademarks mentioned in this work of fiction:

Sig
Boy Scouts of America
Band-Aid
Disney's Thumper
Hardy Boys
Nancy Drew
The Black Stallion

ACKNOWLEDGMENTS

A big thank you to Susan Wells for providing the perfect inspiration picture and name for Vincent's character!

Thank you to Claudia, Kylee, Lucy and Courtney for the quick and thorough beta reads!

As always, thank you to my soul sisters, Claudia, Kylee and Mari for your love and support!

SERIES READING ORDER

All of my series cross over with one another so I've provided a couple of recommended reading orders for you. If you want to start with the Protectors books, use the first list. If you want to follow the books according to timing, use the second list. Note that you can skip any of the books (including M/F) as each was written to be a standalone story.

Note that some books may not be readily available on all retail sites

Recommended Reading Order (Use this list if you want to start with "The Protectors" series)
1. Absolution (m/m/m) (The Protectors, #1)
2. Salvation (m/m) (The Protectors, #2)
3. Retribution (m/m) (The Protectors, #3)
4. Gabriel's Rule (m/f) (The Escort Series, #1)
5. Shane's Fall (m/f) (The Escort Series, #2)
6. Logan's Need (m/m) (The Escort Series, #3)
7. Finding Home (m/m/m) (Finding Series, #1)
8. Finding Trust (m/m) (Finding Series, #2)

9. Loving Vin (m/f) (Barretti Security Series, #1)
10. Redeeming Rafe (m/m) (Barretti Security Series, #2)
11. Saving Ren (m/m/m) (Barretti Security Series, #3)
12. Freeing Zane (m/m) (Barretti Security Series, #4)
13. Finding Peace (m/m) (Finding Series, #3)
14. Finding Forgiveness (m/m) (Finding Series, #4)
15. Forsaken (m/m) (The Protectors, #4)
16. Vengeance (m/m/m) (The Protectors, #5)
17. A Protectors Family Christmas (The Protectors, #5.5)
18. Atonement (m/m) (The Protectors, #6)
19. Revelation (m/m) (The Protectors, #7)
20. Redemption (m/m) (The Protectors, #8)
21. Finding Hope (m/m/m) (Finding Series, #5)
22. Defiance (m/m) (The Protectors, #9)

Recommended Reading Order *(Use this list if you want to follow according to timing)*
1. Gabriel's Rule (m/f) (The Escort Series, #1)
2. Shane's Fall (m/f) (The Escort Series, #2)
3. Logan's Need (m/m) (The Escort Series, #3)
4. Finding Home (m/m/m) (Finding Series, #1)
5. Finding Trust (m/m) (Finding Series, #2)
6. Loving Vin (m/f) (Barretti Security Series, #1)
7. Redeeming Rafe (m/m) (Barretti Security Series, #2)
8. Saving Ren (m/m/m) (Barretti Security Series, #3)
9. Freeing Zane (m/m) (Barretti Security Series, #4)
10. Finding Peace (m/m) (Finding Series, #3)
11. Finding Forgiveness (m/m) (Finding Series, #4)
12. Absolution (m/m/m) (The Protectors, #1)
13. Salvation (m/m) (The Protectors, #2)
14. Retribution (m/m) (The Protectors, #3)
15. Forsaken (m/m) (The Protectors, #4)
16. Vengeance (m/m/m) (The Protectors, #5)
17. A Protectors Family Christmas (The Protectors, #5.5)

18. Atonement (m/m) (The Protectors, #6)
19. Revelation (m/m) (The Protectors, #7)
20. Redemption (m/m) (The Protectors, #8)
21. Finding Hope (m/m/m) (Finding Series, #5)
22. Defiance (m/m) (The Protectors, #9)

SERIES CROSSOVER CHART

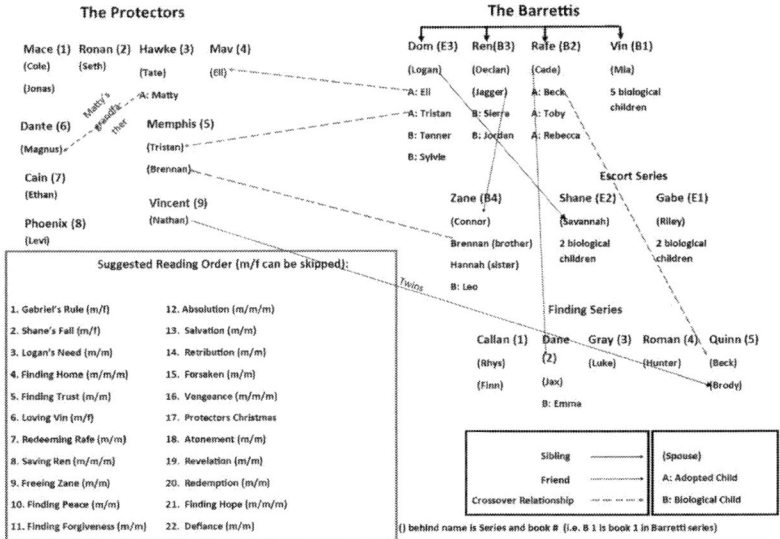

DEFIANCE

də'fīəns\

Open disregard; contempt

PROLOGUE

VINCENT

"No," I said without hesitation as I studied the men before me. I'd talked to Ronan Grisham on the phone a couple of times, but Memphis was new. Of course, I already knew as much about him as I needed to, though, since I'd done my homework on him as soon as Ronan had asked me to fly to Seattle for a meeting. I could have told them before I'd even left my place in West Virginia that I had no interest in taking on any job they might offer me, but truth be told, the little group Ronan had going on here had intrigued me. I suppose I had Ethan Rhodes to thank, or blame, for that, depending on how you looked at it.

I'd met Ethan Rhodes six months earlier when Ronan had asked me to take a look at a damaged phone in Ethan's possession, which had had evidence of a murder on it. From the moment I'd met the doctor, I'd been transported back to a time in my life that I'd had no wish to return to. It wasn't that Ethan had necessarily looked like David; it was more about the way he'd carried himself. He'd had an air of vulnerability about him, but there'd been a fierceness in him as well. It was the reason I'd helped Ethan go after his lover, Cain Jensen, when he'd feared the man's life was in danger.

For all the struggles David had gone through in our final year together, he'd been unfailingly loyal...and protective. He hadn't always been able to find the strength to fight for himself, but if there'd been even the slimmest chance I was in danger, he'd been ready to stand by my side, guns blazing.

It was that memory that Ethan had stirred in me that'd had me doing something I hadn't done since I'd lost David to his demons.

I'd given a shit.

And that wasn't a good thing.

Not in my line of work.

But I'd done it anyway, and I'd started wondering about the kind of work Ronan and his men did. I'd never actually met Ronan - our relationship had been more of a friend-of-a-friend kind of thing. He'd cashed in a favor and I'd paid one off.

It should have been a simple transaction.

I should have held up my end of the deal and been done. But then Cain Jensen had called me and asked me to stay with Ethan while he took care of the man's vengeful ex once and for all. I'd been on the cusp of saying no, but I'd heard that thread of desperation in the young man's voice.

And I'd known what he was feeling.

That need to do anything and everything to protect that one person in your life who completed you...who was your reason for everything you did. Every breath you took, every battle you fought... going on day after endless day, even after you lost them, because without you, there was no one left to keep their memory alive.

It was the only reason I'd been able to get up every morning after David had been taken from me.

And despite the bullet he'd put in his own brain, he had been *taken*. The man I'd fallen in love with when I'd still been in my teens had started to disappear before my very eyes the moment he'd gotten that notice from the army that'd said his service to his country was no longer valued.

The same notice I'd gotten.

And all because David and I had made the grievous error of falling in love with each other.

"You're not even going to hear us out?" Memphis asked.

We were sitting in his living room. A white cat had taken up residence on my lap the second I'd sat down. When Memphis had gone to move her, I'd waved him off. I'd take the presence of an animal over a human any day of the week.

I had no interest in hearing him out, but I decided to humor him and merely nodded my head at him. I would still be telling him no, though. Because I had absolutely no interest in playing bodyguard to anyone, since that would mean having to spend more than five minutes in another person's company.

Yeah, no thanks.

"His name is Nathan Wilder. His brother is in a relationship with the son of a friend of ours and another man," Ronan said.

I remained quiet, though I was intrigued by the concept of three men in an equal relationship with one another. Memphis, himself, was in the same kind of relationship, though I hadn't met either of his young lovers. The research I'd done on him had just been the basics including financials, employment, and family history, but I could tell from the handful of pictures I'd seen of him and two good-looking young men in their twenties, that what they had between them was the real deal. As someone who was pushing fifty, I'd seen a lot in my time, but a ménage relationship that appeared to be about more than just sex was a new one, even for me.

"He's received some threatening emails and it sounds like there's a chance the assailant has taken it to the next level. Brody, that's Nathan's twin, was mentioned in some of the emails, but we suspect that was more to rattle Nathan than anything else," Memphis explained.

The assailant sounded like a smart individual…psychological warfare made a man an easier target. The stress alone of knowing his twin might be at risk would have had a lasting impact on this Nathan guy. Wear a guy down enough mentally, and he'd be an easy target in the long run.

"We were hoping you could check it out…sit on him for a bit and see what you can find," Memphis continued.

Curiosity got the best of me and I said, "Why me? From what I've seen, your little operation here has plenty of qualified muscle."

Ronan and Memphis exchanged a brief glance. Ronan finally said, "We think your skill-set and contacts would give you unique access and insight."

If Ronan hadn't said the words with a measure of hesitation, I would have thought he was sucking up to me. But the fact that he'd almost seemed reluctant to voice his reasoning had me straightening from where I'd been leaning back against the couch. "How so?"

The men looked at each other again. It was almost comical…like they were afraid to say whatever it was that was on their minds.

"Nathan is running for Senate-"

"No," I said simply, and then I gently pushed the cat off my lap.

As I climbed to my feet, Ronan murmured, "He needs help, Vincent."

"Not my problem," I responded as I stepped past him. Irritation went through me as I thought about how hesitant both men had been.

Which meant they knew about my hatred of all things government.

Everett.

Fucking busybody. He'd known exactly what he was sending me into when he'd encouraged me to take the meeting. No, I hadn't made the decision to meet Ronan based solely on him, but between him and my curiosity about what kind of group would go to such lengths to protect a complete stranger like Ethan Rhodes for no other reason than it was the right thing to do, I'd climbed onto the private jet Ronan had sent for me with the expectation that at the very least, I'd get Everett off my back about the whole damn thing.

"Vincent-"

"I don't give a fuck what Everett told you about me," I snapped as I turned to look at both men. "You want to protect this guy, *you* go right ahead. But you sure as shit don't want me doing it, because one less politician is a win in my book!"

"Memphis?"

The sound of a man's voice, along with a rhythmic knock on the front door, had me stopping my forward movement.

"In here," Memphis called.

"Sorry, I heard voices, but I figured maybe you didn't hear me knocking," a man said as he rounded the corner from the front hallway. He was heavily built and in his early forties with a bald head. I stilled as I realized I knew him.

"No problem, Dom. We were just finishing up," Memphis said.

"Tristan forgot some sheet music at our apartment…"

The man's voice dropped off as his eyes fell on me.

"Major St. James?"

"Dominic Barretti," I murmured.

I felt my heart constrict painfully in my chest as Dom saluted me. It was something he'd done the few times I'd seen him after my discharge from the army. And it was something he *shouldn't* be doing based on the type of discharge I'd received. While I knew it was a sign of respect on his part, it still cut me to the core.

I couldn't bring myself to salute him back, but luckily, he didn't maintain the position long. He strode forward and held out his hand. As soon as I took it, he leaned in and clapped his hand on my back. I wasn't one for hugs, but Dom wasn't just some guy off the street.

Not even close.

There weren't a lot of people who'd stood by me after the shit that had gone down with the army, but Dom had.

And he'd taken it a step further.

He'd offered me something that I hadn't had after the army had shattered my entire world.

I just wished like hell I'd taken him up on it.

"What are you doing here?" he asked as a wide smile passed over his lips.

I had no idea how to answer him. I knew enough about Dom to know he ran his business legit, and I was anything but.

"We asked Vincent to help us out on the Wilder case," Ronan announced without hesitation.

Dom nodded and walked farther into the room, handing Memphis a folder, presumably the sheet music he'd mentioned.

"How do you guys know each other?" I asked, still completely caught off guard that Ronan's group of vigilantes would have ties to Dom's aboveboard security business.

"My husband and I met Ronan last year when one of his men began seeing our oldest son, Eli. And we met Memphis right after that. He's in a relationship with Logan's and my son and our nephew," Dom explained.

"Tristan and Brennan aren't actually related," Memphis clarified. "Brennan's brother and his husband are friends of Dom and Logan's family."

"I'll take your word for it," I said, smiling despite myself.

"Cade will be so glad to know you're helping out Nathan," Dom said. "Beck is worried sick about Brody who's worried about Nathan…"

God, I needed a fucking whiteboard to keep up. "Wait, Cade… Cade Gamble?" I asked.

Dom smiled. "Yep…except it's Barretti now. He's married to my brother."

"Cade Gamble is married?"

I couldn't wrap my head around that. While I'd known Cade was gay when I'd met him and Dom while we were stationed in the Middle East, I'd also known him to be a player…to the extreme. The fact that he was married, and with a kid no less, was blowing my mind.

"Yep. Five kids, too," Dom said with a laugh. "You should stop by and say hi."

Part of me actually wanted to take him up on the offer, but the other part…the part that still mourned David even after all the years that had gone by, sent silent warnings to my brain not to get involved. I'd had the chance for a different life, but I'd blown it.

I'd chosen wrong.

And it was too fucking late to do anything about it.

But I couldn't discount what Dom had said. "Tell me about Cade's son," I said.

Dom sobered and then he glanced at Ronan and Memphis. "May I?" he asked as he motioned to the couch. Both men nodded. I went to sit in an armchair because I could tell just by looking at the expression on Dom's face that whatever he had to tell me was not going to be easy.

"Beck is nineteen…almost twenty, actually," Dom began. "Cade and my brother, Rafe, adopted Beck and his brother and sister when Beck was twelve. Beck has struggled with some mental health issues over the years, but we didn't know until this past summer what was driving some of the behavior. He's finally in a good place, but with the threat against Brody's brother, Beck and both his men are feeling the strain. The mention of Brody in some of the emails Nathan received has made things even harder, especially on Beck."

My eyes shifted to Memphis and Ronan briefly before they fell back on Dom. When his eyes met mine, I felt anger settle over me.

But it wasn't directed at him.

It was directed at myself.

I'd had a chance to have a man like Dom in my corner, but I'd been naïve enough back then to think that the country David and I had served would step up and make things right.

Now David was dead and I'd served my country in a different way.

A way that would have shamed David.

I got up and went to Dom and extended my hand. He immediately stood up and shook it, though he looked both confused and surprised.

"You had my back when no one else did," I said. "I've got your nephew's."

As much as the idea of going back to the world that I'd fought so long and hard to escape sickened me, I knew that was no longer a factor in any of this. I didn't give a shit about Nathan Wilder or whatever bullshit he wanted to sell to the American people so they'd give him the power he needed to push his own personal agenda, but I did want to do something that might have David looking down on me with pride instead of shame.

I turned to look at Ronan and Memphis. "If I do this, I'm doing it my way."

Both men nodded. I turned to leave, but then thought better of it and paused long enough to say, "After this, lose my number. It'll be better for all of you that way."

CHAPTER 1

NATHAN

Hey Nathan, it's me. I know you don't want to hear from me so I'll stop bothering you after this. I just wanted to wish you a happy birthday...

My brother's voice dropped off, but the voicemail message didn't stop. My gut clenched as I heard his voice become more uneven.

I really miss you, big brother. I just...I...

Another pause had me dashing at the tears that threatened to fall. I'd made the mistake of hitting the play button on the voicemail message while still sitting in my car after parking it in my driveway. I'd had two new messages and had accidentally hit Brody's message instead of my campaign manager's, and the mistake was like a punch to the gut.

Because I always needed to steel myself before I let myself listen to my twin's voice, which was so much like my own.

Brody's voice lost its luster as he blurted, *I hope you're okay.* And with that, the message ended.

I wasn't okay. Not even close.

But Brody didn't need to know that. And he most definitely didn't need to know how badly I wanted to hit that call back button and tell him how fucking sorry I was.

"Fuck," I muttered to myself as I reached for the door handle. The message from my campaign manager could wait, because I needed a drink.

Or ten.

I climbed out of my car and wiped at my eyes. Luckily, it was late and there weren't any stray reporters lingering today. Because I wasn't sure I could paste the smile on my face that was a requirement for the camera that inevitably got shoved in your face, along with the microphone or tape recorder that was thrust so close to your mouth that you wondered if it shouldn't have been required to buy you a drink first.

I loved coming home. It was one of the few places where I could just be Nathan instead of the various titles that I'd somehow managed to accrue, despite how very little I'd actually done with my life.

Candidate for Senator.

Son of Chandler Wilder, governor and political scion.

Former poster boy for the right-wing movement to *Bring God Back to America*.

Fuck the damn titles tonight. I'd turned thirty today, and the only person I would have even considered celebrating that milestone with was over two thousand miles away.

Because I'd driven him away.

I managed to remember to lock my car as I made my way up the path leading to my front door. I would have liked to park my car in the garage, but it was full of campaign paraphernalia that I hadn't been able to find the time to get moved to my new campaign headquarters in the heart of Charleston.

I'd bought the little Cape Cod home earlier in the year after I'd escaped the stronghold of the right-wing movement my father had begun building in Columbia, the capital of South Carolina. I'd left my law practice, too, which had pissed my father's former General Counsel off to no end, since he'd gotten me the job at the prestigious firm shortly after I'd graduated from law school. Yeah, the plan had always been for me to get into politics, but I'd kind of fucked those plans up when I'd abruptly turned my back on my father and his constituents to run as a Democrat instead. To this day, I received countless calls from endless high-ranking officials in the Southern Baptist community who were trying to usher me back into the fold. They'd even suggested how I could spin my explanation for the sudden, albeit temporary, switch in my political affiliations.

Blame it on Brody.

I'd told them what they could do with that idea, and for a good ol' Southern boy, I'd chosen some pretty colorful language to get my point across. Didn't mean they didn't stop trying, though.

And they'd stepped up their game.

The emails had started over six months ago. They'd been a nuisance at first, and I'd dismissed them as just another incensed member of my father's constituency. But they'd taken a dark turn when they'd mentioned Brody.

And an even darker one when things had gone beyond just veiled threats in writing.

I shot a glance over my shoulder at my car and reminded myself that I really did need to get my garage cleared out. I'd already had to spend thousands of dollars in body work and new tires to fix the damage that my apparent stalker had inflicted upon the vehicle a few weeks ago. Luckily, the damage had occurred while my car had been parked overnight at a parking garage near my campaign office, so I had no reason to believe the asshole had my address.

Even the possibility that he did had me hurrying my step. I was a big guy and could handle myself well enough if push came to shove, but I knew unbalanced guys brought guns and knives to fistfights. Whoever he was, he wasn't going to play fair, and I needed to remember that.

It wouldn't stop me, like he was clearly so intent on doing, but it would make me more vigilant.

The night air was quiet around me as I unlocked the front door. I lived on a quiet street in a family-friendly neighborhood, and by the looks of things, most of my neighbors were already asleep. Not surprising, considering it was well after eleven.

I'd been thirty for almost twenty-four hours and I hadn't even realized it until I'd heard Brody's message. If I was any kind of brother, I'd at least text him to tell him happy birthday.

But I'd lost that privilege a long time ago. Even if the circumstances surrounding my life didn't pose a threat to Brody, I still wouldn't have called him. Yeah, he'd hinted at wanting to try to rebuild our relationship when I'd gone up to Dare, Montana to warn him about the potential threat against him, but it wasn't something I was even considering.

For many reasons.

But mostly because I'd fucked up any chance I had at being a brother to Brody when I'd betrayed him twelve years ago.

Despair lurched through me as I remembered that night, and I quickly shoved open the door. I needed that damn drink. I hurried to the alarm panel in the front hallway and was already punching in my code when I realized it hadn't sounded.

Fuck, I'd forgotten to set it. That was what week after week of eighteen-hour days got you.

A shitty memory, a refrigerator with a couple of Chinese takeout cartons and a bottle of ketchup in it, and a house that relied on others like a gardener and housekeeper to take care of it so the press wouldn't start writing articles speculating your body was rotting away inside because the grass was more than ankle high.

I returned to the front door and locked it, then went straight for the small bar in my living room. The only light I turned on was the one above the bar. I searched out the whiskey and grabbed a glass before heading to my favorite leather chair. It was ridiculous that I had such an ornate living room setup when all I did was sit in the single chair which was pointed at the flat screen TV on the wall. But I'd let Virginia do the decorating, and my only condition had been that the furniture had to be masculine.

She hadn't liked that, of course, since she'd fully expected to share the house with me someday, at least for as long as it took to buy something bigger and fancier.

She hadn't liked a lot of things.

But the game changer had been the day I'd done the unthinkable and stood before God and much of America and denounced my father's stance on gay marriage, the very thing that had made him a household name and catapulted him, and me by extension, to the forefront of the right-wing movement. Virginia had been certain it was some kind of joke or temporary act of rebellion, but when she'd placed the blame on Brody, saying he'd somehow used the devil to influence me, I'd kicked her ass to the curb, not caring one whit about what the press would say about it.

I dropped down into the chair, but didn't bother with the TV. I got enough of the news during my daily briefings with my campaign manager, Preston Bell. He wanted to make sure I had answers to any and every controversy that cropped up. The man was a slave to talking points, while I had no problem with veering off topic if the situation called for it. I'd told Preston that from the beginning when he'd approached me with an offer to run my newly founded campaign. I'd been a joke at the time, so it wasn't like I'd had a lot of offers. Democrats had been suspicious of my switch in positions, and I'd become a pariah within even the most liberal of Republican circles. Preston had claimed the whole thing would be his crowning glory in a long-running career of getting people into office. But I'd suspected the truth…the man liked what I stood for. Because, despite all the things I did to drive him crazy, he never balked when it came to making it clear to voters what I stood for. He never tried to have me compromise in order to save face with one group of voters at the sacrifice of another. Simply put, he let me show people who I really was, which was all I'd ever wanted.

And since I was leading in the polls, I must have gotten something right.

I downed the whiskey in one shot and then filled the glass with two fingers of the amber liquid. I wasn't a big drinker, but tonight I was happy enough to get shit-faced. Not enough that I wouldn't be able to get up at five in the morning for my usual run and then head to the office, but enough that I didn't have to worry about looking bleary-eyed on camera, since I'd told Preston not to schedule me for any interviews.

After just a few sips, the alcohol began to warm my insides, and I set the glass down on the table next to the chair. I had a bad habit of falling asleep in the chair and was determined not to tonight. I forced myself to my feet, grabbed the glass and headed towards the kitchen. Ida, my housekeeper, was kind enough to cook for me a couple times a week and would stash the food in the freezer. She only worked part-time, so I didn't get her home-cooked meals every night, but they usually got me through a few days out of the week. Take-out took care of the rest…or I simply didn't eat. Most nights I was too tired to care, anyway.

I flicked on the overhead light in the kitchen and went to the fridge. Ida had thrown out the Chinese food, no doubt because if it had stayed in there any longer, it would have grown feet and walked away on its own. But in its place were two plastic containers. I opened the first and sent Ida a prayer of thanks for the huge helping of lasagna, one of my all-time favorite meals. Curiosity had me reaching for the second container. It was taller than the first, but not as wide. I stilled when I saw the sight of a single cupcake sitting inside. There was even a candle stuck in it.

As grateful as I was for the gesture, it made me feel even shittier.

Thirty years old, and the only ones who'd taken the time to even remember my birthday were my twin brother and my too-kind housekeeper.

And I had no one but myself to blame.

I stuck the container of lasagna back into the fridge and then took the cupcake over to the table and sat down. I didn't have any matches or lighters in the house, so I set the candle aside. It would have been too depressing to light the damn thing anyway. I reached for my phone and let my thumb hover over the play button on Brody's message.

"Don't," I whispered to myself.

But I did it anyway. I played the message again.

The second I heard that crack in Brody's voice, I shoved the cupcake away and reached for the whiskey. I downed the rest and then heaved the glass at the wall, relishing in the sound of it breaking.

No, I didn't feel any better, but at least I got to show the rage I couldn't show in the real world.

I wasn't sure how long I sat there before I lifted my eyes and stared out the picture window, which faced the front yard. If the alcohol had had more time to work, my reflexes wouldn't have been fast enough. I barely understood what I was seeing in the reflection of the window, but there was no mistaking the glint of a knife just above my left shoulder, along with a figure dressed in black standing right behind me. I instinctively threw myself to the right and hit the floor hard as my attacker plunged the knife down. It hit the table, sinking deep into the wood. As the man, and I had no doubt it was a man based on the heavy build, tried to yank the knife out, I kicked out at him, catching him behind the knee. An ordinary man would have hit the ground where I could have continued the attack. But this guy had either seen my blow coming, or he'd expected it, because he twisted at the last minute and my foot glanced off the fleshy part of his leg right below the knee joint...not enough to disable him.

He grabbed the knife as he threw himself down on top of me and I barely managed to catch his wrist as he plunged his arm in a downward arc. At 6'3, I wasn't a small guy and I worked out enough to keep fit, but I wasn't at my fighting weight. The stress of the campaign trail, among other things, had caused me to lose a good forty pounds, and this guy had that much on me at least, and all in muscle.

I tried swinging my legs out to knock him loose, but he'd pinned me in a way that I couldn't move. My eyes fell on the remnants of the glass I'd thrown against the wall. The top part had broken into several small pieces, but the bottom piece hadn't completely shattered. It had broken enough so that it was jagged along the top and bottom edges, and it was only about a foot away. It might be my only hope, but if I had to release him with one hand long enough to reach for it, I'd be giving him an advantage and he could easily plunge the knife into my throat long before I managed to grab the piece of glass.

But I didn't have a choice because even now, my arms were burning under the strain of holding him back. The man suddenly used his right hand to punch me in the side. I gasped as he knocked the wind from me, but instinct had me holding onto his arm. When he went to hit me again, I used his momentary distraction to release his arm with one hand and snag the piece of glass. I ignored the pain in my hand as the glass sliced my palm open and punctured the skin on a couple of my fingers. I used all my strength to slash at the man's face. He was wearing a ski mask, but the glass easily sliced through it and ripped into his flesh. Shouting, he fell back, grabbing his cheek. I used both hands to knock him backwards. I managed to scramble to my feet, but I'd just barely managed to stand when he was on me again and shoved me back against the wall. The knife was gone, but it didn't slow him down because he slammed his fist into my jaw and then smacked my head against the wall. I managed to stay upright, but I was dazed, so I couldn't move as he stepped back and pulled out a gun.

I'd watched enough TV to know it had a silencer on it.

I wanted to laugh at the irony of it all. I'd been morosely thinking about the press starting rumors about my dead body going undiscovered in my house based on an unkempt yard, but that was exactly what was about to happen. Even Preston wouldn't miss me for a while, since he was in D.C. meeting with the power players to try and get more endorsements for me.

In that split second as I waited for the bullet to pierce my body, I thought about Brody. We'd had that twin thing early on in our lives where we could feel each other's emotions when they were heightened enough, but I doubted that link remained, at least for him. I still had the occasional sensation of happiness come over me at the strangest of times, and since my life wasn't exactly the epitome of joyful, I'd had an idea of where that feeling had come from. It had been confirmed when I'd seen my brother with his men.

If he was listening, I tried to convey something other than the fear I was feeling, along with the regret of knowing I'd never be able to make things right with him.

The man aimed the gun at me. "You're getting off easy," was all he said. I watched as his finger settled over the trigger. I could have begged for my life, but I wasn't about to give him the satisfaction. Not with the dead look in his eyes, and most certainly not after everything he'd said to me in the emails…I just hoped like hell my death would satisfy whatever insanity was driving him and he'd stay away from Brody.

"Fuck you," I whispered.

The man's mouth pulled into a sneer, but before he could pull the trigger, there was a loud crashing sound as the kitchen window suddenly exploded. I instinctively turned my head away as glass went flying, but I didn't feel any of it penetrating my body. I heard a popping sound, but didn't know what it was at first. But when the guy threw himself past me and towards the hallway that led to the main part of the house, I realized I was, in fact, hearing gunfire.

Just not from his gun.

I turned in the direction the shots were coming from and watched in amazement as a man calmly stepped through what was left of the large picture window. He had a huge gun in his hand and it, too, had a silencer on it.

"Get down!" he ordered, his voice loud, but not panicked.

I instantly dropped to my ass as bullets flew over my head, and I realized the guy was still trying to shoot the man as he escaped the kitchen. The guy stepped past me and disappeared down the same hallway. My gut was telling me to run, but I was in a state of shock at the close call. I had no idea who the guy who'd just shot out my window was, but I had to assume, since he hadn't blown my head off when he'd had the chance, he wasn't my enemy.

I heard more popping sounds, and then a few seconds later, a heavy tread as footsteps came my way. I knew I should try to hide in case it was the first guy coming back, but I couldn't find the strength to move. My hand hurt like hell, as did my jaw. My side also hurt and I wondered if some of my ribs were fractured.

I dropped my head back against the wall as I tried to catch my breath. But within seconds, the second guy reappeared and he dragged me to my feet. He was huge…bigger than me, even. I suspected he was older than me by at least fifteen years, putting him well over forty. His short hair was a mix of black and silver and barely looked ruffled, considering everything that had just happened. He was wearing military-style clothes, all black. His upper arms were huge, with muscles bulging beneath the fabric of his T-shirt. I finally noticed that, in addition to the huge handgun he was carrying, he had a second gun hanging by a strap at his hip. It was considerably bigger than the handgun, but not quite as big as a rifle. It also had a silencer on it, and I wondered if he'd used that gun to shoot out my window.

"We need to go," he said. He may as well have been telling me about the weather because, despite his declaration, he was utterly calm. I felt sensation spark to life just beneath the surface of my skin where he was holding me by the upper arm.

"What?" I asked. Was he serious? Go? I wasn't fucking going anywhere. Not until I got some answers.

And that was exactly what I told him.

CHAPTER 2

VINCENT

"I'm not going anywhere until you tell me what the hell is going on!"

Figured the guy would be an ungrateful asshole. I shoved him back against the wall and said, "In case you missed it, you stupid fuck, you almost got your ass blown off. When that happens, you typically don't want to stick around to give them a SECOND FUCKING CHANCE!"

I forced myself to calm down, though by most people's standards, I probably appeared completely calm and in complete control. Yeah, I was in control, but I wasn't calm. I hadn't been from the second I'd seen the assailant standing behind Nathan, knife poised to strike. I'd still been in my car, so I hadn't bothered to shout a warning to him. By the time I'd grabbed my guns and darted across the yard, the man and Nathan had disappeared from view, and it hadn't been until I'd gotten closer to the house that I'd seen them in a death match on the floor. Nathan had managed to break free from his attacker, but he'd been seconds away from death when I'd grabbed my Sig short-barreled rifle and started firing through the window, knowing full well the rounds wouldn't reach the attacker, but the breaking window would sure as hell distract him long enough for me to get inside.

The whole thing had been too damn close. And while I didn't

particularly give a shit what happened to the man myself, I did care about the impact it would have on Dom's nephew. I'd been curious about Beck Barretti after the way Dom had talked about him, so I'd done a little research just to appease that curiosity.

I hadn't been appeased.

At all.

The mental issues Dom had alluded to had included a suicide attempt. I'd hacked the computers of the psychiatric hospital the young man had been admitted to and learned that Cade had been the one to find Beck and had managed to cut him down just in time. I hadn't gone digging beyond that, because even the little bit of research I'd done had felt like a violation, not to mention it had brought back some pretty shitty memories for me. I'd had what I'd needed, anyway. Beck Barretti needed a shot at a better life and he was going to get it, even if I had to keep this ungrateful ass in one piece to do it.

But as soon as I grabbed Nathan by the arm again, he jerked away from me.

And immediately stumbled.

I managed to catch him around the waist before he fell, and I *really* did not like the feeling of awareness that went through me at the sensation of his body pressed up against mine. I quickly reached out with my foot to grab the leg of one of the kitchen chairs and jerked it over. Nathan wasn't much shorter than me and I figured when he was at his normal weight, he'd give me a run for my money in the overall size department. The fact that he'd managed to survive the brief, albeit intense, attack from his assailant was proof that he had some decent muscle built up, along with the instincts to fight back against someone with better training than him.

"Sit," I murmured as he continued to resist me.

"We have to call the police," he said, even as he sat down and put his uninjured hand up against his head.

"So you know who attacked you?" I asked as I went around to the kitchen and snagged a clean-looking hand towel that was draped over the oven door handle.

"No," Nathan murmured as he lowered his arm so it was resting against his leg. The move allowed him to keep holding his head without having to keep his arm in the air. It was testament to how quickly he was crashing after the adrenaline rush.

I tore a wide strip off the hand towel and knelt down in front of him. He winced as I wrapped the strip around his hand and used enough force to stop the bleeding. The wounds on his palm and possibly the ones on some of his fingers would need stitches, but I didn't have time to deal with it now. "Hold pressure on that," I said as I motioned to the binding. I climbed to my feet and went to the window. The frame was still intact, so I pulled the large retractable blind down in the hopes passersby wouldn't notice the window was actually missing. Although both the assailant and I had used suppressors on our weapons, the sound of shattering glass would have been hard to miss. I could only hope like hell this was one of those neighborhoods where everyone assumed someone else was calling for help.

"Then you have an idea of who attacked you?" I asked, knowing full well what the answer was.

Nathan, predictably, remained mute.

"Let me tell you how this is going to go," I bit out as I stood before him. I expected him to look up at me, but when he didn't, I bent down so I could look him in the eye. Because I was giving him one shot at this. Dom or no Dom, I couldn't help someone who was too stupid to help himself.

"You call the cops and the first thing they'll do is start digging into every aspect of your life. And considering who you are, I don't think you want that. Because you know what happens the second even one cop talks to a reporter to confirm Nathan Wilder was attacked in his own home by a gun-wielding fanatic."

Nathan's eyes lifted enough so he could look me in the eye, but he still didn't say anything.

"You really think when the press gets wind of that story, they're going to have any interest in your political views? You think voters will?"

Nathan finally reacted by looking away. There was a slight hardening of his jaw. God, he was so fucking predictable. Threaten his life and he wanted to argue, threaten his career and he couldn't shut up fast enough.

"So what, I'm just supposed to go with you?" he finally asked. "I don't fucking know you, man."

"You don't need to know me," I ground out, hating that my irritation was starting to get the better of me. "All you need to know is that you stay here, you die. You come with me, you might have a chance. That's assuming I don't shoot your ass myself for being such a pain in mine."

Before Nathan could respond, there was a knock at the front door.

"Fuck," I muttered, because I knew exactly who it was. "One of your worried neighbors coming to check on you, no doubt," I groused as I left the kitchen and went to the front door to confirm my suspicions. There was a small window next to the door and I could see a man through it, dressed in pajamas, a red bathrobe, and slip-on shoes. Nathan appeared beside me.

"Your choice," I said. "You've got two minutes to either get rid of him or tell him to call the cops. I'm going to go check the rest of the house."

I pulled my gun from my waistband and began sweeping the rest of the house. Not for the assailant, but for clues. But having seen the guy's moves and the hardware he'd been carrying, I doubted he'd been careless enough to leave anything behind that would offer up any clue to his identity.

Nathan's house wasn't big, so it didn't take me long to check it out. I heard his muffled voice as he spoke to his neighbor, but had no clue what he was saying. I almost wanted him to choose the cops because then I'd be rid of him.

I tried to reassure myself it was because I hated politicians and everything they stood for, but the sensation of Nathan's body pressed up against mine for those brief seconds as he'd stumbled was peppering my mind. It wasn't so much that I was surprised that I was attracted to him, since he was a good-looking guy; it was that the physical stirring I was feeling was driving my thinking.

That just wasn't acceptable.

People who made decisions based on emotion or lust didn't survive long in my business. And I hadn't come this far, put down so many men and even a few women who'd come after me, just to give it all up because I'd liked the way a guy had felt in my arms.

I made my way into what I could only assume was the master bedroom. It wasn't a huge room, but it was comfortably decorated with neutral colors and masculine furniture and bedding. But there was very little in the house that spoke to the man himself. The pictures on the walls were all generic-looking paintings and art prints. There were no knick-knacks or photos, save one on the nightstand. The light on the nightstand was on, so I moved closer to the bed and picked up the framed picture. It was of Nathan and his brother. They were standing in front of a small lake and there was a little boat behind them. One twin had his arm around the other. My gut was telling me the one putting his arm around the other was Nathan. I didn't know how I knew, I just did...there was something in his eyes that was just a little bit different than the other boy's.

Pride, maybe?

The other boy, Brody, was smiling wide and holding up a decent-sized fish. I guessed the twins to be around ten in the picture.

I knew from my research that Nathan was the older twin, and looking at the picture, I could see that. There was a certain protectiveness in the way he held onto his brother. I felt a shimmer of pain go through me. I'd had that once...the weight of an arm around me that said, *I'm here for you.*

I sensed rather than heard that I was no longer alone. I turned to see Nathan standing in the doorway, his eyes on me. I silently cursed the awareness that went through me.

"I told Mr. Deville that I accidentally broke the window when I was trying to move some furniture around."

His statement should have irritated me, since I knew what it meant.

It didn't.

And that just pissed me off.

I didn't want to be stuck with him. Didn't matter why.

I returned the picture to the nightstand. "You have two minutes to pack a bag," I said as I strode past him. When he grabbed my arm, I instinctively reacted and shoved him back against the doorjamb. He sucked in a sharp breath, but didn't try to get away from me.

"Don't," I muttered, feeling stupid for my reaction. I released him and pushed back. I had to force myself not to move away from him like I wanted. Mostly to prove to myself that I didn't need to. That his proximity to me didn't bother me.

Fuck, when the hell had I decided it would be a good idea to start lying to myself?

"I can't just leave," Nathan finally said. "I have responsibilities, commitments."

"What you have is a target on your back," I returned. "I know your job is to lie to people, but don't pull that shit on yourself. It'll just get you killed."

Nathan stiffened at my words, but didn't say anything. He hung there for a moment, and then he did the damndest thing.

He checked me out.

Not in an obvious way.

No, his eyes quickly swept my body from head to toe.

And my body reacted in a big way.

"You have a minute and thirty seconds left," I snapped before I stepped past him and went back downstairs. I returned to the kitchen and pulled out my phone.

I dialed and smiled to myself when a groggy voice said, "Yeah."

"Jesus, Ev, it's only eleven. How fucking old are you?"

"Fuck you," he murmured. "We can't all be GI Joe."

I snorted at that. "Whatever you say, Grandpa. You're not even sixty yet, Ev. Next thing you know, you'll be eating dinner at five and trying to stay up late enough to watch that reality dancing show you like so much."

"Hey, that show kicks ass. Speaking of…"

I shook my head. "He's alive," I said.

Everett chuckled. "I should hope so. But if you're calling this late, it's not just to give me shit for my television viewing choices."

"Need you to take care of something for me."

"Fuck, Vincent, how many?"

"None, you asshole," I responded, knowing he'd assumed the worst. That I'd left bodies in my wake as usual.

Okay, so maybe it hadn't been such a stretch of the imagination.

"The only casualty is a window. Can you get someone over here to fix it…and ignore the bullet holes all over the kitchen?"

"Yeah," Everett sighed, and I heard him moving around. "Address?"

"624 Birch Street."

Everett paused, presumably so he could write the address down. "So I take it no bodies means the threat's still out there?"

"Yeah," I murmured.

"You taking him to your place?"

God, the last place I wanted to take Nathan to was my house. But it was the safest place, so I'd just have to get past the idea of having someone I despised in my private sanctuary. When I didn't answer, Everett said, "Give him a chance, Vincent. He might surprise you. I did."

I smiled at that. Yeah, Everett had been a big surprise, in more ways than one.

"You're the exception, not the rule," I said. "I gotta go," I added when I saw Nathan enter the kitchen, small bag in hand. "Talk to you later."

"Later," Everett said just before he hung up. As I was tucking my phone into my pocket, I saw Nathan grab his off the floor.

When he went to put it in his shirt pocket, I shook my head and said, "No, that stays here."

"I need my phone," Nathan said.

"You need it more than you need to breathe?" I asked impatiently. "Because it's traceable." I reached for it to take it away from him, but he stepped back. I got into his space and ripped the phone from his hand. "Is your career really more important than your life?" I ground out. "Because it sure as shit isn't more important than mine." I dropped the phone to the floor and made a move to crush it under my heel, but Nathan suddenly lunged forward.

"Don't!" he yelled. My instincts took over and I grabbed him by the arms and swept his legs from underneath him, taking us both to the floor. He let out a whoosh of air as my body crashed down on his. Too late, I remembered the way he'd been holding his side after the earlier attack.

But I didn't apologize.

"You lay your hands on me one more time-"

"My brother's messages!" Nathan shouted, his voice thick with emotion.

"What?" I asked, startled.

Nathan drew in several breaths. "I want the phone because it has my brother's voicemail messages on it," he whispered. His whiskey-colored eyes met mine. "Please," he murmured.

I suddenly became very aware of his hard body sprawled beneath mine. During the scuffle, one of my legs had gotten wedged between his, putting our cocks precariously close to one another. I had his hands pinned to the floor and I could feel his body trembling beneath mine.

I knew it was likely just the lingering shock, but I couldn't deny what having him completely at my mercy was doing to me. Especially since he wasn't fighting me. I hadn't given much thought to whether or not Nathan was gay like his brother, but I sure as shit was thinking about it now.

"Please," Nathan repeated, and a perverse part of me wondered what he was actually asking me for. I knew I needed to get off him, but I found myself reluctant to move. Nathan's fingers flexed, drawing my gaze to them. It would be so easy to move my hands up to link my fingers with his. I shifted slightly to take the pressure off the knee that I had wedged between his legs, but the move caused my dick to brush his. I jerked my eyes to Nathan's when I heard him let out the tiniest of whimpers.

"Let me up," he suddenly said, and then he was pushing at me. I could have easily kept him there on the floor like that and taken what I wanted...a taste of him. But I shifted off him instead and then snatched his phone off the floor. Nathan struggled to his feet, but didn't try to grab the phone again.

My brain told my fingers to drop the damn thing so I could crush it, because anything less wasn't safe. But my body disobeyed the order and instead, I turned the phone off and handed it to Nathan. "Leave it off."

I turned to head towards the hallway leading to the front door, but stopped when Nathan said, "Wait."

I forced myself to turn around. "What?"

"I don't even know your name."

There were a million things I could have said to him, none of which included actually giving him my name. Just like with the phone, it wasn't safe for him to know who I was.

"Vincent," I said.

"Vincent," Nathan murmured, more to himself than anything else. "Thank you, Vincent."

I didn't want his thanks. I didn't want anything from him except to eliminate the threat against him and then get the hell away from him.

"Let's go," was all I said, though, and then I turned away, not really caring if he followed.

CHAPTER 3

NATHAN

I could feel blood trickling down my wrist, despite the pressure I continued to put on my hand. Strangely, though, there was no pain. The interior of the car was too dark to see how badly my hand was bleeding again, but I wasn't about to ask Vincent to turn the lights on. Truth was, I didn't want to know.

Then this could all be some fucked-up nightmare that I would wake up from any second now.

Wake the fuck up, Nathan!

We'd walked out my front door thirty minutes earlier and I hadn't thought to ask where Vincent was taking me. I hadn't really cared, either.

Probably due to the shock of it all.

"Keep pressure on it," I heard Vincent say, and I glanced over at him to see that he wasn't even looking at me. How the hell did he know about my hand?

It was a stupid question, considering all the questions I should have been asking him.

Who the hell are you?
What were you doing at my house?
Why the fuck didn't I just call the cops?

I knew the answer to that last one. Vincent had hit the nail on the proverbial head when he'd mentioned the cops leaking their report about the attack to the press. It was a risk I just couldn't take.

Even if it meant I was destined to spend more time with the man next to me than I would have liked.

And not just because he intimidated the hell out of me.

No, I had much bigger problems than that.

Like how it had felt to have his weight pressing down on my body, pushing me against the cold, hard granite tiles of my kitchen floor. Or the way his calloused fingers had dug into my skin as he'd held my hands down. Or that gravelly voice that had washed over me as he'd warned me not to touch him for the second time in nearly as many minutes.

I shrugged off the thoughts that threatened to take over. I needed to focus on the here and now, not the odd sensations the man had stirred in me as he'd manhandled me into submission.

"What were you doing at my house?" I managed to ask. My body felt hot and cold at the same time, and I had to wonder if it was from the blood loss. In theory, I hadn't lost very much blood, but between my hand, my aching jaw, and the reminder that I'd had a knife poised just inches above my jugular less than an hour ago, that was enough to leave me feeling excessively queasy.

"Watching it."

"Watching it?" I asked. "Seriously?"

Vincent didn't respond, and I bit back the curse word that threatened to spill forth. "You weren't there by coincidence," I said. "Are you a cop or something? Did Preston talk to you?"

"You mean that weasely little campaign manager of yours?"

While the description might fit Preston in the sense that he was short, thin, and had beady eyes and a receding hairline, he was anything but.

"Preston Bell is one of the most respected men in the business. He's run more successful campaigns-"

I stopped short when I saw Vincent shake his head. "What?"

"That supposed to impress me?" he asked. "That the guy's good at helping you people spout your bullshit to unsuspecting Americans?"

It was the second time he'd taken a dig at my profession. But as much as I wanted to tell him to fuck off, I was currently at his mercy since we were speeding away from Charleston into the dead of night like a bat out of hell.

In a muscle car that had my jaw vibrating with the powerful engine's hum.

"Who are you?" I repeated. "And where are we going?"

"My place," he responded, though from his tone, I suspected he thought he was doing me a favor by even answering the question at all.

What an asshole.

"Stop the car," I muttered.

He ignored me.

"Stop the goddamn car!"

Still nothing.

It wasn't until I reached for the door handle that I got a reaction.

A dangerous one.

I'd been bluffing, but Vincent clearly wasn't because in one swift move, he yanked the steering wheel to the right, sending the car skidding along the shoulder of the highway until it came to a jarring stop, all while his arm came up to slam against my neck, causing my head to jerk backwards.

"Now either you sit there and shut the fuck up, or I will do it for you, do you understand me?"

In my gut, I knew what my answer should have been. But when that part of me that had always kowtowed to others reared its ugly head, I grabbed his arm with both my hands, not caring that I was probably getting blood on him, and said, "Fuck you."

I didn't yell it.

Didn't shed tears with the words.

And I didn't give a shit if it meant he'd follow through on his threat. I couldn't remove his arm from my neck; he was just too strong, even with me using both my hands.

I couldn't see his eyes in the darkness, but I could sense them on me. I gasped for air when his arm suddenly disappeared and his fingers wrapped around my throat. I knew what he wanted.

No way in hell was I giving it to him.

Just like with the guy who'd been about to shoot me, I wasn't going to beg.

Several long seconds passed, but just as I was on the verge of passing out, Vincent released me. I sagged forward and sucked in some air, and then I reached for the door handle and climbed out of the car. I didn't even care that my bag was still in the car. I had my phone and that was all I really cared about.

So I just started walking.

"Brody."

I stopped dead in my tracks at the sound of my brother's name. There was no traffic on the road around us, and dense forest was creeping in on us from both sides. Moonlight filtering in through the sparse clouds was the only thing lighting the ground in front of me.

I turned around and saw Vincent leaning against the trunk of the car. There wasn't enough light to make out his face, but I could see his stance. Arms folded, one foot crossed over the other.

Like he didn't have a care in the world.

He probably didn't.

"What about Brody?" I asked.

"You want to do something stupid, that's on you. But your brother is the one who's going to have to pay for it."

That had me moving.

"You don't know what the fuck you're talking about! Brody's safe! I stayed away from him to keep him safe!"

Despite the fact that I was once again in Vincent's space, he seemed unfazed, and I briefly wondered if the man had ice running through his veins instead of something boringly human like blood.

"I'm talking about the fact that he'll have to live with your death."

His simple and calmly spoken statement had me deflating just like that. I took a few steps back because I found that standing too close to him left me feeling wholly unsettled.

Though I wasn't sure why.

You know why.

I cursed the voice in my head and asked, "How do you know my brother's name? I didn't say it back at the house."

Vincent straightened, and then he was the one to move forward. "Nathan, at the rate you're crashing, you're going to be out really soon. You really want to be out here in the middle of nowhere when that happens?"

"I have my phone," I said mutinously, though all the words did was make me feel like a whiny child.

"Yeah, and the second you turn it on, you might as well hang a neon sign around your neck that says *Come Shoot My Ass Because I'm Too Much Of An Idiot To Know Any Better*. You'll be like that stupid girl in the creepy house that always insists on going to check out the basement full of sharp tools to make sure it's empty."

While the comparison pissed me off, I knew he was right.

"In a storm," I muttered.

"What?"

"She always goes down there when it's lightning out. And the power is out, of course."

I couldn't see if he was smiling, but it sure sounded like it when he said, "And her boyfriend and other friends have all mysteriously disappeared."

"I can't just get in that car with you, Vincent. Not without some kind of explanation."

He sighed.

Actually sighed.

Instead of grabbing me and ordering me into the car or just ditching my ass.

It was progress.

Sort of.

"Give me a couple hours to get some more distance between us and them," he murmured. I was stunned when he reached out for my hand. I barely managed to stifle a gasp when he tightened the strip of towel around my palm to stem the bleeding.

And it wasn't because it hurt.

Well, not *just* because it hurt, anyway.

"When we stop for the night, I'll fix this and answer your questions." Before I could say anything, he added, "*Some* of your questions."

Fuck, I'd take it.

And not because I didn't have any other options.

Okay, that *was* exactly why I was going to take it, but he didn't need to know that. With that in mind, I stepped past him and went back to the car. Within minutes of him getting us back on the road, I leaned my head back against the headrest and then I was out.

~

"No fucking way," I said as I shook my head vigorously.

"If I don't stitch it, it will keep tearing open," Vincent explained, his voice mildly irritated as he began threading a wicked-looking curved needle.

I glanced down at my palm and sure enough, the two-inch-long cut was oozing fresh blood. My problem wasn't with getting stitches, it was with *how* I'd be getting those stitches.

Without the benefit of any kind of anesthetic.

Or medical professional.

It had been well after three in the morning when Vincent had none too gently shaken me awake and declared we'd arrived at our destination, which had turned out to be a rundown-looking motel that was a throwback to the disco era. Worse, it had once been some kind of honeymoon destination, since it was located near the Cherokee National Forest. I hadn't known whether to laugh or cry at the sight of the heart-shaped mattress when Vincent had unlocked the door. When I'd declared the whole thing to be some kind of joke, he'd asked me if anyone would ever think to look for me in a place like this.

That was an unequivocal no.

But if they happened to see me in it, with a man no less, I could kiss my political career goodbye. When Vincent's answer had failed to satisfy me and I'd told him as much, he'd rightly pointed out that the chances of someone recognizing me in a place like this were zero to none, especially since I could count on one hand how many cars I'd seen parked in the lot. And I highly suspected the few other guests had the same goal in mind as us.

To remain invisible.

I jumped when Vincent took a hold of my hand. My whole body hurt like hell, though I wasn't sure why since it should only be my side, my jaw and, of course, my hand that had been injured.

"Lay your hand flat and don't move it," Vincent said as he settled my hand palm up on the small table we were sitting at. My eyes kept straying to the hideous bed covered in red satin.

"What the hell do people even see in a place like this?" I wondered as I looked around the room which, in addition to the god-awful bed, sported an outdated-looking jetted tub in the corner. "I mean… FUCK!" I yelled as cool liquid splashed over my hand, sending searing flashes of pain coursing up my arm. The burn didn't last long, but it was enough that I was breathing hard to keep myself from yelling any more obscenities. If Vincent hadn't been holding onto my wrist with an iron grip, I most certainly would have yanked my hand away.

"What was that?" I asked once I could manage to talk again. My eyes settled on a small bottle of scotch next to Vincent's elbow.

"Poor man's antiseptic," he said calmly. "Anesthetic, too," he added as he reached for the bottle with his free hand and handed it to me.

I grabbed the bottle and took a healthy swig.

"Thought Southern Baptists frowned on alcohol," Vincent murmured as he reached for the needle. I downed another swallow of the cheap scotch and hoped like hell it would work sooner rather than later.

It didn't.

I bit into my lip as Vincent pressed the tip of the needle into my skin. "You've been doing your homework on me," I said once he'd pulled the needle all the way through.

"Not like there isn't a trove of information out there to be found," he said as he inserted the needle again.

I took another drink, but eased back on the urge to take a big swallow.

"Is that how this is going to go?" I asked.

"How what's going to go?"

"You answer with non-answers."

"You didn't actually ask me a question," he observed.

I barely refrained from rolling my eyes at him. "Who are you?"

"Next question."

I shook my head and put the bottle down so that I wouldn't be tempted to drink anymore. I needed to have my full faculties for this conversation. "Were you following me?"

"Yes."

"How long?"

"Three days."

"Why?" I asked.

"Because you're payback."

"Payback?" His answer made no sense to me.

"A mutual friend wants to see that you keep breathing."

"Who? How is that payback?"

"What's with the drinking?" Vincent asked as he motioned to the bottle with his head. "Won't Daddy be mad?"

If the mention of my father hadn't put me on edge, the sarcasm in his tone would have for sure.

"You know what, Vincent?" I said, before waiting until he looked up at me. "Cut the bullshit you keep accusing me of spewing and tell me what the fuck is going on. Before I'm tempted to let my would-be assassin find me just so I don't have to spend another second with you. Because you're a real dick."

CHAPTER 4

VINCENT

I had to admit, the guy had balls. He hadn't even bothered to wait until I was done jabbing a needle through his skin to call me out on my behavior.

Yeah, I knew I was being a dick. I just didn't really care. I'd been tasked with keeping the man alive, not catering to his inflated ego or handling him with kid gloves. He had a rich family and countless kiss-asses on his staff to do that.

Okay, so maybe the dig about his father had been a bit much, but I'd done my homework on the man, and he was the epitome of everything I hated. I'd had little interest in Chandler Wilder's take on gay rights when he'd been governor, because I'd already known what so many gay men and women in our country had yet to accept.

We'd never be equal.

And we'd never be seen as anything beyond our sexual preference. There wouldn't be a time where one guy marrying another would be referred to as anything other than *gay* marriage, and even then, it would be seen as an oddity, not the norm. The government could say all the right things and it still wouldn't change shit.

I was a gay man first. I'd learned that lesson a long time ago, and it wasn't one that I needed to repeat. The fact that the leaders of the very country David and I had sacrificed so much for only saw the fact that I preferred dick to pussy once they'd learned I'd had the audacity to hold my boyfriend's hand for a few minutes so many years ago was proof of that. I hadn't been Major St. James, dedicated soldier who'd saved the lives of his entire platoon more than once anymore. I'd no longer been the son of Fallon St. James, one of the most respected generals in the army, or brother to Pierce St. James, recipient of every conceivable military medal known to man. I'd been a fag first and foremost.

And only.

Until I'd had to make a name for myself in a whole different way.

"Beck Barretti," I murmured as I kept my attention on the remaining stitches I had left. Nathan was handling the pain better than I'd expected. I'd had stitches more times than I could count, and while they were never fun, I'd gotten used to them. But the first time I'd gotten them without the benefit of anesthetic when I'd been a fresh-faced cadet, I'd barely managed not to cry.

And I'd consumed a lot more alcohol than the measly three swigs Nathan had swallowed.

"Beck? My brother's boyfriend?" Nathan asked in surprise.

"*One* of your brother's boyfriends," I reminded him, just to gauge his reaction.

But he seemed unfazed as he said, "You know Beck?"

"I know his father and his uncle," I clarified. "Seems your little visit to Montana a while back caused quite the stir."

When he didn't respond, I looked up from my work. His eyes were downcast and he was worrying his lower lip with his teeth.

"I needed to make sure he was safe," Nathan said softly. "I didn't think he'd worry…not after…" His voice dropped off.

"Why didn't you think your own brother would worry that your life was in danger?" I asked as I went back to work.

"My life wasn't…wasn't in danger then. It was just a few nasty emails…"

Since I'd hacked his email account, I knew it was more than just a few, and nasty didn't even begin to cover it. I'd also seen the police report about his vandalized car. Since he was so paranoid about things being leaked to the press, I had to wonder if there were things that had happened that he hadn't told the cops. He certainly hadn't let them know about the emails.

Which was why they'd attributed the car to a simple act of teenagers being assholes.

"So, you figured Brody wouldn't be upset about you being the target, just that his name had come up?" I probed.

Nathan didn't respond, so I finished up the stitches and then dug around in my bag for the stuff I'd need to treat the small puncture wounds on his fingers.

"You said we were going to your place," Nathan said after several minutes of silence. "Where is that?"

"West Virginia…near the George Washington and Jefferson National Forest."

"West Virginia? I can't go that far away from home. I have meetings, interviews…I need to be near Charleston."

I held onto Nathan's hand when he tried to pull it free. I could sense a major blowup in the making, but I wasn't in the mood. Between the close call tonight and the fact that I hadn't gotten much sleep in the past three days, I was wiped.

"You're going to have to make other arrangements," I said simply.

"No, I-"

"Listen," I bit out. "I'm not going to keep having this argument with you. Until we figure out who wants you dead – and make no mistake about it, because that guy with the knife sure as shit meant business – you and I are joined at the hip, only my hip's in charge, got it? You do what I say, when I say. You don't like it, there's the door," I said as I jerked my head over my shoulder.

Nathan hardened his jaw. Before he could respond I said, "Believe me, you're the last guy I want to be spending the foreseeable future with, so I'm more than motivated to figure out who the fucker is that tried to skewer you tonight like a shish kabob…but if you think you can do better on your own, by all means."

I forced myself to calm down, which wasn't something I had to do often. The fact that this man brought out such strong emotions in me wasn't a good thing.

Not by a long shot.

I quickly wrapped Nathan's hand with a bandage to keep the smaller wounds clean, and then I slapped a bottle of ibuprofen on the table. I stood up and grabbed the revolver from my ankle holster and placed it on the table. "I'm going to take a shower. Someone comes through that door, pull the trigger…or don't," I snapped. "I don't give a fuck."

I pushed back my chair and stepped past him and went to the bathroom, stopping only long enough to grab my overnight kit from my bag. Not only were my emotions raging, my dick was, too.

Another oddity for me. Not because my sexual appetites had waned as I'd gotten older, but because I usually had more control over myself when I was working.

I hurriedly stripped off my clothes and climbed into the shower. I'd purposefully left the water on cool in the hopes it would drive down my libido, but even as a chill swept through my body, my dick bounced against my abdomen, demanding attention.

"Fuck," I muttered as I reached for the knob and turned it up so that hot water began to sluice down my back. I slapped one hand against the tile wall and went for my dick with the other. I pulled up the image of the final time David and I had made love. He'd been in rare form that night, considering how much he'd been struggling in the previous months. I'd thought that moment had been about renewing our relationship after all the strain losing our careers had put on us and our commitment to one another.

I hadn't realized it had been goodbye.

David had ridden me for the better part of an hour that night. It'd been like he'd never wanted that moment to end.

Because he hadn't.

Our demons hadn't found us when we'd been lost in one another's bodies.

I closed my eyes as David's hands settled on my chest to brace himself.

So perfect, Vincent. Love this...you.

I'd let him roll his hips above mine over and over again as he'd brought us both to the edge countless times, but when my impeding orgasm had become too much to ignore, I'd sat upright and wrapped my arm around his waist. David had shifted enough so he could curl his legs behind me, forcing my dick even deeper into his body. His arms had locked around my neck as he'd held on to me and we'd moved as one.

I'd told him to promise me it would always be like that.

He hadn't answered me.

Two days later I'd realized why he hadn't when I'd found him dead in our bathroom.

My dick started to deflate as an image of David's body jumped into my head. I let out a string of curses and released my cock. Well, I'd wanted the inconvenient erection to go away.

Mission accomplished.

I turned so that I was facing the water and began washing myself with the small, heart-shaped soap that I had to pry free of the plastic film protecting it. I let my thoughts wander to what I knew about Nathan and how I'd find the guy who was out to silence him.

While I'd read all of the emails his would-be stalker had sent him, I hadn't found any clues as to the man's motive or identity. But he wasn't your run-of-the-mill fanatic. If I hadn't seen the hardware he'd been carrying tonight, I would have known that just from the steps he'd taken to cover his tracks with the emails. He'd used dozens of ISPs all over the world to mask his true IP address, which meant it would be next to impossible to figure out his location. The emails themselves had spewed a lot of filth about Nathan's change in political positions, so in theory, it could be a disgruntled former constituent who'd expected him to follow through with the conservative values he'd grown up with. While Nathan hadn't actually run as a Republican, there'd been a lot of money spent by his father's political backers to get the ball rolling.

Chandler Wilder was the epitome of right-winged conservatism, and it wasn't unusual for that faction to have some fanatics mixed in. From everything I'd seen, Chandler had stayed out of the public eye in recent months after lambasting his oldest son for his unexpected and uncharacteristic change in party loyalty. The deluded man had gone on to spout a bunch of scripture shit to whoever would listen about the devil luring his child away from the side of the good and righteous. So it wasn't unreasonable to think that someone loyal to the senior Wilder would take it upon themselves to get vengeance for dear old dad. Hell, Chandler could even be pulling the strings…wouldn't be the first time I'd seen blood turn on blood.

I let my thoughts drift to the man I'd seen attacking Nathan, hoping some small detail in my mind would stand out. I hadn't seen much through the window once the pair had hit the floor, but as I'd raised my gun to shoot out the glass, I'd seen Nathan say something to his attacker as he'd stood against the wall, blood dripping from his hand and the bruise on his jaw already forming.

He'd looked pissed, not scared.

I'd admired that.

Not that I'd ever admit that to him.

I'd seen pictures of Nathan during my research, but they hadn't done him justice. Maybe because they'd all been props. Perfect hair, bright smile, tailored suit…empty eyes. But tonight, he'd looked…human.

Not to mention the vulnerability I'd seen and heard whenever he mentioned his brother…

I realized my mistake as my dick began to harden again. My plan had been to try and ferret out useful information that would help me be rid of Nathan Wilder sooner rather than later, but my cock was only interested in the memory of Nathan's hard body beneath mine… his smell…his ticked up breathing that could have been from fear…or something else.

I ignored my dick and quickly washed my hair with the little bottle of shampoo the motel provided, but this time there was no settling it. I leaned back against the wall and began stroking myself eagerly, this time calling up a different image of David…one from a particularly raunchy encounter we'd had in the dirty bathroom of a nightclub we'd visited in Germany while on leave. But the image wouldn't stick.

"No," I muttered as Nathan's smell tickled my nose and his thick fingers teased my cock before wrapping around it. I willed my brain to go back to David, but like my dick, it refused to listen and before I knew it, I was eagerly thrusting into Nathan's hand. Then it was his ass gripping my flesh in unbearable heat and pressure. It felt too good to ignore, so I pressed on.

Full steam ahead.

I fucked him hard and fast, and I drank down his throaty moans as he pushed his ass back to meet every powerful thrust. Lust shimmered in my belly and my balls drew up tight when he began whimpering my name and begging for more.

Harder.

Faster.

Deeper.

I gave him everything he wanted. And when I leaned over him and bit down on his shoulder right after ordering him to come, he did.

So did I.

With my release deep inside of him, bathing my cock in its own juices, I continued to pound him. It was only when I opened my eyes to look down at his beautiful ass still holding me in the tightest, hottest grip I'd ever known, that I realized it was my own hand wrapped around my too-sensitive flesh. Horror gripped me as I grappled with how real the fantasy had been.

No fucking way.

I released my dick and stuck my hand under the water to get rid of the ropes and ropes of cum I'd spewed on myself.

And the wall.

Disgust tore through me as I angled the shower head to clean off the wall, and then I quickly rinsed. And as I dried off and pulled on just my briefs, pants, and nothing else, I kept hoping Nathan wouldn't be waiting for me once I got out of the bathroom.

But luck just wasn't on my side tonight.

CHAPTER 5

NATHAN

I jerked awake at the sound of the bathroom door opening and quickly straightened against the headboard, though I wasn't sure why I didn't want Vincent to know I'd dozed off. I was surprised I'd managed to drift off myself, considering how on edge I'd been the second Vincent had gone into the bathroom. I'd sat and stared at the gun for a while before I'd forced myself to pick it up and go to the door to double-check it was locked. I'd then quickly changed into a pair of sweats and a T-shirt before crawling onto the bed and turning on the television in the hopes that it would serve as a distraction. Without my phone, I had no way of checking the news to see if my neighbor hadn't bought my story about the broken window and called the cops or the press. Mr. Deville had once complained about reporters waiting outside my house at all hours of the day, so I had to hope that fact would have kept him from calling anyone about what had happened tonight.

I'd put the TV on a 24-hour news program, but there'd been no mention of anything. Of course, it wasn't like a broken window at my house would make national news, but if the cops had shown up and found the place riddled with bullets and me missing, that sure as hell would have been breaking news. I'd thought about using the motel room phone to call Preston, but the fear of the call somehow being tracked, not to mention I had no clue how to explain to Preston what had happened, had kept me from reaching for it.

It was torture to be out of the know. I wouldn't label myself a control freak, but I definitely liked knowing what was happening around me. I wasn't someone who easily "turned off" at the end of the day. I was hoping that quality would serve me well in D.C., but right now it was basically torture.

So the fact that I'd fallen asleep while so much shit was happening that I had absolutely no control over was practically a miracle in itself.

As Vincent entered the main part of the room, I carefully took the gun off my lap and placed it on the nightstand. I'd never been a fan of guns, even though my father had taken me and Brody hunting often enough. I'd been twelve when I'd made my first kill. We'd been going hunting with my father a lot longer than that, but I'd been purposely missing my shots for all that time. I'd finally broken down and killed a young buck after my father had railed at me and Brody for being sissies. He'd been particularly hard on Brody because my brother had cried when my father had handed him a rifle and told him we were going hunting for the first time. Brody had always been the softer-hearted of the two of us. Even when we'd gone fishing whenever we spent the summer at my maternal grandfather's cabin in northern Minnesota, Brody had insisted that we use artificial bait instead of real worms, and we'd always thrown back whatever we'd caught. As much as I'd hated killing that deer, I'd needed to protect Brody from our father's cruelty more.

So I'd pulled the trigger.

My father had slapped my back with pride and then he'd told me to finish off the poor creature with a kill shot. I'd done it, and I'd suffered through every second of him sharing the story with the guy we'd taken the deer to so that its body could be processed for meat… and, of course, the actual trophy…its head.

As soon as I'd gotten home that night, I'd gone to the bathroom and thrown up. Then I'd climbed into the shower and cried until my brother had found me and helped me out. He'd crawled into bed with me and held me while I'd sobbed uncontrollably.

Then he'd thanked me.

Because he'd known what I'd done.

It had always been that way with me and Brody. Us watching out for each other.

Until the night I'd stopped having his back when I'd realized I couldn't protect him from what was to come. I'd let my fear and uncertainty take over at that point, and I'd driven Brody away.

I was jolted from my thoughts by Vincent's close proximity to me as he removed the gun from the nightstand. His eyes landed on me briefly, but he didn't say anything. He looked pissed.

Though I had no idea how I could have pissed him off by just sitting there.

I watched as he went to his bag and rifled through it. I saw him take out a small cylinder of some kind, along with a roll of string. He went to the door and stuck the container to the doorframe. I had to assume it had some kind of adhesive on it that kept it mounted to the door. He tied a piece of string around a ring on the end of the cylinder and then attached the other piece of the string to the doorknob.

"What is that?" I asked.

"Homemade security system."

"What do you mean?"

Vincent glanced over his shoulder at me and I couldn't help the shiver that ran down my spine. He was a good-looking guy. I wasn't sure exactly how old he was, but I knew he was in better shape than a lot of men his age. His muscles along his back rippled every time he moved and his tanned skin still had a sheen of moisture on it. My belly was fluttering and I felt an uncomfortable tightening in my pants. I willed it away, but unlike all the other times, this time my head was not so successful in overruling my body.

It's not real...it's the stress, I assured myself.

"This is a stun grenade. You've probably heard it called a flash bomb. Police use it for crowd control, and for when they're storming a house or building where there's an armed suspect inside."

"I've seen those on TV. They emit a loud sound, right?"

Vincent nodded. "Light, too. They disorient a person long enough for the police to take them down."

"So if someone opens the door…"

"I'll have the time to disarm them and put them down."

"Won't it disorient you, too?" I asked.

He sent me a smirk over his shoulder and I felt that flutter in my belly turn into a full-on parade of butterflies.

"I'll be expecting it," he said. "An intruder won't. And since all I need is a few seconds of the advantage…"

He let the statement hang and stepped back to check his work. "Needless to say, if you decide to make a run for it, let me know first. Not like I'm going to stop you."

I ground my teeth at that.

"Those guys must be good friends," I muttered.

"What guys?"

"Beck's father and uncle."

Vincent was silent for a moment before saying, "They understand loyalty."

It wasn't the words themselves, but the way he said them that made me feel like he was definitely taking a dig at me. Which made no sense, because he didn't know the first thing about me.

"Is it just me or all politicians?" I asked as Vincent moved to the opposite side of the bed…the side closer to the door.

"Since I don't know you from Adam, what do you think?" he asked.

"I think you're a judgmental son of a bitch," I said.

"I call it like I see it."

I was about to make a snide retort when I saw Vincent reach for the button on his pants. "What are you doing?" I squeaked.

Yeah…squeaked.

Nathan Wilder, thirty-year-old candidate for senator, just squeaked like a girl.

"I'm going to bed," he said simply. My throat went dry as the button popped open. The sound of the zipper was like a gunshot going off. I knew I needed to move, but all I could do was sit there and watch Vincent's thick fingers maneuver his pants down his hips. "You didn't think this was one of those scenarios, did you?"

I had no clue what he was talking about. Was he even talking? I heard sound coming from his mouth, but my brain was focused on the sight of his cock nestled in his black briefs.

His very large cock, if the bulge was anything to go by.

"What?" I managed to ask. It wasn't until Vincent stopped pushing his pants any farther down his legs that I realized I'd been staring. I jerked my eyes up to his and saw a gleam of satisfaction in them. "What?" I asked again, completely lost.

"I'm not giving up the bed to the injured damsel in distress, if that's what you're thinking."

"You want to share?" I asked stupidly. Was he kidding?

"What I *want* is irrelevant," Vincent returned as his eyes slid over my body. Jesus, was he…was he checking me out? I barely heard him say, "What I'm *doing* is getting ready for bed. What you do is up to you. Take the other side, the floor, no skin off my nose."

"We can't share a bed," I said as I quickly climbed to my feet. "It's not…appropriate."

"Fine," Vincent said easily as he shucked his pants and tossed them over the end of the bed. He snagged one of the pillows and threw it at me. "Enjoy the floor, Nate."

Nate?

No one ever called me Nate.

I ignored his attempt to irritate me further and reached for the top blanket.

"Nuh-uh," Vincent said as he put his hand on the blanket to stop me from moving it. "I get cold at night in just my skivvies."

Ass.

I knew he was just messing with me, but I wasn't in the mood to deal with his shit. Mostly because it was exactly what he wanted.

"By the way," Vincent began as he got settled underneath the covers. "Not all of us fudge-packers are interested in every hot piece of ass we see…especially straight, uptight asses that already have sticks shoved so far up them that they could probably spit up a decent amount of lumber."

There were so many parts of that statement that warranted a response, but I was still stuck on the beginning of it.

"You're gay?" I asked in disbelief.

"Yep." He cast me a glance and said, "But I'm sure you don't have a problem with that, seeing how *progressive* you are." His snide tone had me stiffening my spine. "I mean, you're all for equal rights and all that shit now, right? Gay pride, love is love," he added, pumping his fist slightly.

"You really think daring me like a ten-year-old is going to work?" I asked.

"Yeah, you just proved my point," he said before reaching over to turn off the light next to the bed. He hit the button that controlled both the lamps on either side of the bed so we were pitched into darkness. Part of me told myself to leave it alone, but I told that part to fuck off and hit the switch to turn the lights back on.

"What point?"

Vincent sighed and rolled on his back. His hand came up to absently stroke over his chest. At least, it looked like just a casual move, but as I watched his fingers glide over his pecs and down his muscled abdomen before moving back up, I had to wonder if he wasn't doing it on purpose.

"Don't worry, Nate, people will buy it," he said as he turned to look at me. That damn hand kept up its movements and I struggled to keep my attention on him and not those calloused fingers.

"Buy what?"

"Your story. Good ol' Southern boy goes against the grain and stands up to his rich, conservative daddy. You spout off all the right bullshit to get the votes you need…gays, minorities, immigrants… promise them exactly what they want to hear, and then fuck 'em the second you sit down in that fancy office on Capitol Hill."

"You think that's what I'm doing?" I asked in disbelief. His words had done what my brain hadn't been able to do and taken my attention off his roving hand. I was completely focused on him now.

"That's what *you* do," he said simply. The inflection as he said "you" had me realizing he really wasn't talking about me at all.

"So, it really *is* all politicians, then," I murmured.

I barely noticed him stiffen. He reached back over to flip the lights off. Before I could even think to turn them back on, he growled, "Turn them back on and see what happens."

God, the guy really was an ass.

I went to drop the pillow on the floor, but then thought better of it and tossed it on the bed. Fuck him if he thought he had me all figured out. And why the hell should I be uncomfortable all night long? He'd already made it clear that he had no interest in me sexually.

Which didn't bother me, by the way.

No, not in the least.

Right.

I let out an internal curse as I crawled under the blanket. Yeah, when I'd been younger I'd believed that bullshit I'd been fed about gay people trying to lead good Christians astray with the lure of their bodies, but I most certainly didn't believe that crap now. And contrary to what the asshole next to me thought, I did believe in equal rights for everyone. Sure, it had taken me time to figure that out, but it wasn't just some elaborate scheme to get votes. Hell, I'd practically been assured of the Senate seat under my father's tutelage. After all, South Carolina was and had been a red state for a long time, which meant I was fighting an uphill battle as a Democrat. I'd managed to win the primary in a surprise landslide, but the general election was a whole different thing. I was going up against the incumbent who'd held his seat for more than thirty years. His original plan had been to retire so I could take over the reins, but when I'd changed parties, he'd decided to run for another term.

As I lay there waiting for sleep to come find me and get me the hell away from Vincent for a few hours, my thoughts inevitably drew me to the exact subject I was trying to escape. I'd met plenty of people who were skeptical of politicians and I couldn't really say I blamed them, but Vincent was downright hostile about the subject. Of course, he didn't seem like the most open-minded of guys. Hell, what did I know? The man was a complete enigma, and I knew next to nothing about him.

Except that he was dangerous.

And moody.

Unpredictable.

Disinterested.

I could have gone on with the negative characteristics, but I kept going back to one thing.

He was also the reason I was still breathing.

Because Vincent felt a certain loyalty to his friends. Enough that he'd risked his life to save someone who wasn't even directly linked to them. He'd saved me for Beck Barretti so that the young man wouldn't have to watch my brother suffer through losing me.

I'd met Beck only once, but I'd found myself drawn to the young man, especially after I'd seen him with my brother and their other lover, Quinn. To discover that my brother was in a threesome had been a shock, to say the least. As I'd made my way to Montana to talk to Brody, I'd fully prepared myself to find him with a boyfriend. But two? No, there'd been no preparing for that.

I hadn't even known that was a thing...I'd heard of polygamy as part of those weird religions where a guy had multiple wives, but from what I'd seen of Brody's relationship with Beck and Quinn, it wasn't anything like that. For starters, I hadn't seen even a wisp of jealousy between the three. While my knowledge of men with multiple wives was limited to some news articles and shows I'd seen, I'd always gotten the sense that the relationship revolved around the husband. The wives were there to serve him and give him children, but they weren't in a relationship with each other, at least not a romantic one. And I certainly never saw stories about a woman having multiple husbands in the same context. I couldn't throw my support behind a relationship that was based on the needs of one member of the family being met while the needs of the remaining ones were ignored.

I could get behind Brody's relationship, though, because he'd finally found what he'd been looking for his entire life.

He finally fit.

I'd seen that in the few minutes I'd spent with my brother. I'd felt it in the way Beck had hugged me when he'd thought I was Brody. I'd seen it when Beck and Quinn had looked at Brody with concern and fear in their eyes.

I was happy for my brother.

Beyond words.

But inside, deep down where it wasn't dangerous to acknowledge, I was envious, too. I'd never have what he had.

I'd accepted that a long time ago.

But I could make sure that my brother and people like him had the right to love whoever they wanted. Vincent could believe whatever the hell he wanted, but I knew the truth.

Thoughts of my brother had me wishing I could hear his voice again.

"Vincent," I said quietly as I stared at the ceiling above me...the ceiling that had a fucking mirror on it. I would have laughed if it didn't feel like my heart was bleeding inside of my chest.

There was enough light coming from the parking lot through the gap in the curtains to see the outline of Vincent's body in the mirror above us. He was lying on his side, his back to me.

"What?"

"Never mind," I muttered when I heard the grumpiness in his voice. No way he wouldn't be a dick about what I wanted to ask him.

"What?" he repeated. I wanted to believe his voice held a slightly gentler edge to it, but I knew it was wishful thinking.

"Is there a way to get my brother's messages off my phone without risking it being tracked?"

Vincent was silent for so long, I was certain he wasn't going to answer. But he surprised me by flipping onto his back. I couldn't actually see his eyes in the reflection, but I sensed them watching me via the mirror just the same.

"Does your phone sync to a cloud account?"

I shook my head. "No. Preston said it wasn't a good idea to keep recordings on those kinds of sites…leaves them open to hacking by rivals."

"Of course it does," Vincent responded snidely.

I shook my head. "Just forget it," I muttered, and flipped onto my side so I wouldn't have to look at him anymore.

I felt the bed shift and assumed it was him turning over again, but to my surprise, I felt his hand on my shoulder. Even through the fabric of my shirt, the contact burned and I tried to quell my fluttering stomach.

God, this could not be happening to me.

Not now.

Vincent pushed me onto my back and I held my breath in anticipation of what was coming. I had no idea why I wasn't getting my ass out of the bed.

Except I did know.

I just wasn't brave enough to admit it.

Even here, in the darkness of this room.

Vincent stared at me for the longest time and I had to wonder if his night vision was somehow better than mine, because I had no clue what he was thinking. He just hovered there, braced on one elbow.

Not touching me in any way at all.

Even though it felt like he was.

All over.

"We can't turn the phone on, Nate," he finally said. "Not even long enough to get the messages off."

I nodded in understanding, even as disappointment and humiliation went through me. I began rolling back over, but Vincent put his big hand on my shoulder again, and this time he held it there. The weight of it felt so fucking…good.

"Most phone providers store their customer's voicemails and texts on their servers, sometimes for up to six months. I can't let you access the account the normal way, but I can probably get the messages for you without anyone knowing."

I felt Vincent's fingers press into me for the briefest of moments before he said, "Tomorrow, okay?"

I nodded. "Thank you," I whispered. "I know it doesn't make sense…"

I was shocked into stupefied silence when Vincent's thumb came up to press against my lips to silence me. "Get some sleep, Nate."

I could barely breathe as he caressed my mouth briefly. Then he was pulling away and turning back over. I couldn't move as I tried to make sense of what had just happened.

"Good night, Vincent."

He didn't respond.

Not for several long seconds.

And when he did, it was simply to stun me with a few quiet words.

"Happy Birthday, Nathan."

CHAPTER 6

VINCENT

*A*t the least, the heavy weight pressing down on my chest should have had me shoving the offending object away, since being trapped in any kind of way was a danger, but even as my brain teetered back and forth between sleep and awareness, I knew what – or who, rather – was pinning me to the bed. And I also knew why I was actually reluctant to do anything about my predicament, despite the inherent danger of it.

He's not David, I reminded myself as the warm breath skittering across my nipple had shivers of excitement flickering just beneath the surface of my skin. As I forced my eyes to open and acknowledge the truth of the situation instead of the hopeful wish that I was once again lying in bed with David splayed across my chest, I fisted my left hand into the bedding so I wouldn't be tempted to reach for Nathan, either to push him away…or pull him closer.

Because despite the familiar pain that came racing back every time I remembered David really was gone, I still liked that feeling of warm skin against mine. I liked the fingers that were pressing into my skin just beneath my armpit. I liked how the soft blond hair tickled my chin.

Once my vision cleared, I looked up at the mirror above the bed and felt my throat constrict at the sight that greeted me.

At some point Nathan had kicked the covers away and his sweats had slid up enough to reveal his calves, one of which he'd tossed over my right leg. The blanket had stayed put enough to keep our lower bodies from actually touching, but Nathan's shirt had ridden up so that his muscled abdomen was pressed against mine and I could see the gentle slope of his lower back. His ass was just gorgeous, even in the loose sweatpants, and if my right arm hadn't been pinned beneath his body, I probably would have been reaching for it before I could have stopped myself. I was gripping the blanket with my other hand to keep from doing exactly that.

Nathan's head was tucked up just beneath my chin and his arm was thrown over my chest. His other hand…

Fuck, his other hand was beneath his body. And I didn't need to see it to know what it was doing.

Because I could damn well feel it and I just couldn't believe it.

His hand was linked with mine. It was a crazy position for him because it couldn't have been a comfortable angle for his arm, but that clearly hadn't stopped him.

But the part that still had me floored was that I'd completely missed the moment he'd turned into me. As light a sleeper as I was, I should have noticed the move. The only thing I could think was that my traitorous body had somehow mistaken Nathan for David. But I knew it was a stretch. David had been gone for more years than we'd been together. Just like the night before when I'd wanted it to be David in the shower with me, my brain had chosen reality instead of memory.

Nathan stirred against me, but didn't wake up. I inwardly cursed when his lips briefly pressed against my skin as he adjusted his head.

I suspected Nathan was gay, but either in complete denial about it or so deep in the closet he'd need a compass to find his way out. I had a feeling it was the former because of the way he'd reacted to my touch the night before when he'd asked about getting to the messages on his phone.

I had no clue what had possessed me to touch him like I had, but he'd made it a hell of a lot easier when he hadn't moved away. A straight man would have been making a run for it the second I'd hovered my body over his. And touching his lips...instead of pushing me away, he'd held his breath.

And waited.

It had taken every ounce of control I possessed to pull away from him. Everything about Nathan Wilder turned me on. Just because I hated what he did for a living didn't mean I couldn't fuck him. God knew I'd fucked guys for all kinds of reasons. But I'd heard that damn vulnerability in his voice as he'd mentioned his brother, and that had sealed the deal for me. As interesting as it would have been to show the guy he was most definitely into cock instead of pussy, I wasn't going to take advantage of someone who was struggling emotionally.

Even I had my limits.

Nathan shifted again, but when his hand suddenly began skimming down my side, I was done and I pushed him none too gently off me. By the time he woke up, I was already pulling my pants on. I glanced over at him just in time to see him looking at my side of the bed in confusion. His eyes shifted to me and I could see the question there. But I didn't say anything as I went to the bathroom to piss and brush my teeth. By the time I returned to the main room, Nathan was sitting on the edge of his side of the bed, his head in his hands. I was glad to see his bandage didn't have any blood seeping through it, meaning my stitches had held. When he lifted his gaze, I saw a slight discoloration on his jaw, but it wasn't bad.

"We're leaving in five minutes," I said as I went to the door to remove the stun grenade.

"Good morning to you, too," he muttered as he stood. I watched him long enough to see that his movements weren't hampered, which meant his side was likely bruised, but his ribs probably weren't fractured.

Nathan grabbed his bag on the way to the bathroom. I began packing up my own bag and within the five minutes I'd allotted him, Nathan was out of the bathroom and heading for the door. I stepped in front of him to keep him from leaving first. Energy charged the air around us as my arm brushed his chest briefly.

Fuck, how the hell was I going to keep my hands off him for however long it took to figure out who was after him?

I unlocked the door and left the room first, holding out my arm to Nathan to make sure he understood to wait behind me. Once I was sure there was no threat, I motioned him outside and went to my car.

"Wait here," I said as I pointed to the front of the car. I quickly walked around the car and then dropped to the ground to check the undercarriage. The engine was next.

"What are you doing?" Nathan asked.

"Checking to make sure it wasn't tampered with."

"Tampered with?"

"Brake line cut, explosive or tracking device attached," I said simply.

"Jesus," Nathan whispered. I glanced at him long enough to see his eyes had gone wide. If he only knew this was my normal.

"Get in," I said, motioning to the passenger door. He moved reluctantly, but I didn't say anything. He'd either learn to trust me or he wouldn't.

Once we were on the road, I found a fast food place with a drive-thru window.

"Tell me about the emails," I said once Nathan was done inhaling the first of two breakfast sandwiches he'd ordered.

"What do you want to know?" he asked.

"How many were there, what was in them…"

I already knew the answer, but I was interested in what he had to tell me about them.

"It started a few months ago, I guess. A lot of people reached out after I denounced my father's stance on gay marriage. Some of them commended me, others didn't," he hedged.

"Were there any people from your father's constituency that contacted you?"

"Dozens," he said quietly. "Even people I'd thought were friends began calling and telling me the same thing. That I was confused about Brody…that I was letting the fact that he was my brother overpower my loyalty to God. Said it was the devil's lure." Nathan laughed, but there was no humor in it. "That was always my father's answer to anything that didn't go his way. Devil's lure. It was as common a phrase in our house as *Praise the Lord* and *Amen*."

"Did any of the people threaten you with bodily harm?" I asked.

"My girlfriend at the time chucked a vase at my head after I told her to get the fuck out of my house. Does that count?"

I smiled despite myself. "She didn't like the new Nathan Wilder?" I asked.

"Not sure she even liked the old Nathan," he said.

"What do you mean?"

Nathan shook his head. "She was a prop," he said. "Just like everything else in my life at the time." He went quiet for a moment before saying, "Anyway, when she jumped on the "Blame it on Brody" bandwagon, I told her we were done. She tried to brain me with the vase, called me all sorts of very un-Southern-Belle-like names and stormed out of my house. Haven't seen her since."

"What about once the furor died down?"

"After a few weeks, there was just one left. GodWillJudgeYou@mail.com," Nathan murmured.

"Tell me about the emails."

He turned his head to look out the window. "It seemed like the typical stuff at first. Ranting about how I was going to hell if I didn't repent. After a while I didn't even read the whole message."

"Did you ever respond?"

He shook his head. "Figured that would just encourage him."

"Did you tell anyone?"

"No."

"What about your campaign manager?"

"Preston would have freaked," Nathan responded. "He's seen a lot of shit in this business, so I knew he'd figure it was one of my rivals and insist we retaliate in some way."

"So much for running a clean campaign," I said.

"Hey," Nathan said, his voice carrying an edge to it. I looked over at him.

"Any chance you can wait until after I finish my coffee before you start bashing me and my entire profession?" The anger glittering in his eyes had my dick tightening in my pants. God, I was so fucked.

"I make no promises," I replied, but kept my voice light. The effect was devastating because I saw Nathan's lips inch up just a little before he dropped his gaze.

Hell, what would he look like when he full-on smiled? And not that fake smile he wore in his campaign photographs or whenever there was a camera pointed in his direction.

"I'm not interested in running a campaign that's based on mudslinging, even if that's the norm. So I didn't tell Preston about the emails. Besides, those emails were sent to my personal email address, not my campaign one."

"Who has your personal email address?" I asked.

"Preston, a few trusted staffers, my mother."

"Your mother? What about your father?"

If I hadn't looked over at him at the exact right time, I would have missed the stiffness in his frame. When he saw me looking at him, he forced his body to relax and said, "My father's not big on technology...devil's lure, remember?"

"You're lying," I said without preamble. "None of this works if you lie to me, Nate."

He held my gaze briefly and then hardened his jaw before looking away. "I don't even know what *this* is."

"This is me trying to keep you alive so you can-"

"Vincent, I swear to God, if you make one more crack about me lying to people to get votes..."

He shook his head and put his hand to his mouth as if to stop himself from continuing the sentence.

"I was going to say see your brother again," I remarked.

His eyes shifted briefly to me before returning to look out the window. Several minutes passed before he said, "My father is in the early stages of dementia. He isn't lucid for long enough periods to do something like email me, and I doubt he checks my mother's email account for anything."

His declaration surprised me, since I hadn't seen any stories about Chandler Wilder's declining mental health in the news. And something like that would have made the news. After all, the man had etched his name into history by defying the Supreme Court's ruling making gay marriage legal. He'd gone so far as to order the county clerks in his state not to issue marriage licenses. He'd eventually caved, but the high-profile nature of the case had made him a household name and he'd become a political lightning rod. The fact that his mental health was on a rapid decline would have been a significant story.

"It's being kept secret?" I asked.

Nathan nodded. "My mother moved him to Louisiana. Her sister lives there. The few people in his inner circle who know have convinced his supporters that he's chosen an early retirement so he can reaffirm his commitment to God. People are convinced Brody's and my defection have him seeking solace in his faith."

"Would your mother give out your email?" I asked.

He was silent for a moment before saying, "I'd like to believe she wouldn't, but I can't be sure."

The words were enough to tell me there was more to the story there, but I didn't press him. It was irrelevant anyway. If the guy emailing Nathan had enough skill to mask his IP address, he sure as shit had enough skill to find his personal email without any help.

"When did the emails start mentioning Brody?" I asked.

"About a month after they started. The first one said if I continued on the course I was on, I'd burn in hell like my...like Brody."

"That's not what it said," I said.

Nathan's eyes jerked to mine. "What?"

"Beck's uncle told me what the emails said," I lied, since I wasn't ready to tell him I'd read the email myself. "It said you'd burn in hell like your faggot brother."

Nathan closed his eyes and swallowed hard. "Don't," he whispered.

"Don't what?" I asked.

"Don't use that word. Please."

I knew which word he was talking about, of course. What I didn't know was why it bothered him so much. Yeah, it was ugly and cruel, but it was reality. I'd been called that very word more times than I could count, and I had no doubt Nathan's brother had, too.

"It's just a word, Nathan."

"It's not," he said harshly as he fisted his hands on his thighs. His reaction was over the top. I considered him for a moment before understanding dawned.

"You called him that, didn't you?" I asked gently.

"I can't," he whispered. I saw him dash at his eyes just before he turned away to look out the window. Before I could stop myself, I reached out to cover one of his fisted hands with mine.

"I won't say it again, okay?"

He nodded, but it took several long seconds of me rubbing his clenched fingers before he relaxed his hand until it was spread palm down on his thigh. I'd already settled my hand on top of his before I realized what I was doing and jerked it away from him. Luckily, he didn't seem to notice.

"What did you do when you saw that first email?"

"I panicked," he said. "I didn't know where Brody was. After he... after he came out to our family, he moved away. We didn't keep in touch, so I didn't know where he'd gone at first. Some reporters eventually found him in Florida when the shit with my father and the Supreme Court ruling happened, but I didn't reach out to him at the time. After the email, I hired a private investigator to find him."

"And when you got the second email?" I probed.

"I freaked because the guy talked about going to talk to Brody. I knew if I could find him using a private investigator, he could too."

"So you went to Dare to warn him."

He nodded. "I knew it was a risk, but I had to take it."

"Risk?" I asked.

"That the guy would follow me there. I did my best to cover my tracks...I didn't use my email or anything to make the reservation for the flight. I just went to the airport and got a ticket for the flight to Montana. My assistant put the rental car in her name, stuff like that."

"Were there any other emails referencing Brody?"

"A couple, but just more of the same stuff. Warnings about me being on the wrong path and that it was Brody's fault."

"Was it ever more than just the emails?" I asked.

I only knew about the vandalized car, but when Nathan paled, I knew there was more.

"Tell me," I murmured as I put my hand on his again. I was stunned when he wrapped his fingers around mine briefly before moving his hand away.

"I'm not sure about some of the stuff," he hedged.

"Tell me anyway. Every little bit helps."

"Um, I started noticing little things around the house every now and then. A book on the bookshelf pulled out just a little bit farther than the rest, a glass left out on the counter on days when my housekeeper wasn't scheduled to stop by, a favorite tie clip or cufflinks going missing…I just thought it was me being forgetful."

"What else?"

"A flat tire now and again, missing mail and packages…all things that could be explained away."

"When did you know something had changed?"

Nathan hesitated before saying, "I came home one night and found…I found the body of this stray cat I used to sometimes feed just outside my patio door. Its neck had been broken."

I stiffened at that.

"Did you tell someone?" I asked.

He shook his head. "No."

"Why the fuck not?" I snapped. When he didn't answer me, I said, "Did the cat happen before or after you went to Dare?"

"Before…I left the very next day. The second email about the guy going after Brody had come that morning."

"You didn't tell Brody about the cat, did you? Or the other stuff?"

Nathan shook his head.

"Why not?"

"Because I knew what he would have done if I had. As much as he hated me, I knew he'd still have my back. He was always a better man than me."

"And you didn't want to risk putting him in further danger," I murmured.

"Of course not. I don't…I don't get a pass on what I did to him because of all this," Nathan snapped as he motioned between us. "I could see it in his eyes when I left," he murmured.

"See what?"

"That he was going to forgive me."

"And that's so bad why?" I asked.

"Because what I did was unforgivable." His voice was so thick with regret I felt my own throat tighten in response.

"Nate-"

"It's Nathan!" Nathan snapped, his voice raw. "Are we done?" he asked as his pain-filled eyes turned to meet mine.

I wasn't done, but I knew *he* was. "We're done," I acknowledged.

He didn't say anything; he just turned his gaze back out the window. We didn't speak again until I pulled the car past the heavy iron gate at the end of my driveway.

CHAPTER 7

NATHAN

Vincent's house wasn't anything like I expected. For starters, I'd expected a log cabin or something since the house was located deep in the woods. But the structure looked quite modern and although it wasn't huge, it was a decent size and had two stories from what I could see. The iron gate at the end of the driveway was actually the first of two gates, and I noticed they were timed so that the second gate didn't open until the first one closed. I had to wonder if it was some kind of additional security measure. There were keypads and security cameras for both gates and I could see that, like with the gates, there were two fences running along the front of the property. The fences were made of the same iron as the gates.

Vincent pulled the car into one of the stalls in the attached three-car garage and immediately closed the door behind us. Lights came on above us as the door closed so I could easily see a big SUV parked in the second stall. The third stall had a motorcycle in it.

"Do you…do you live alone?" I asked.

Vincent merely nodded and got out of the car. As I grabbed my bag from the back seat, Vincent pulled his own bag plus a much larger one from the trunk. Up a short flight of stairs were several wooden workbenches along the front of the garage. I followed

Vincent and watched him set the bag on one of the workbenches next to a large metal cabinet. The bag was open enough that I could see it was filled with all sorts of guns. Vincent went to the cabinet, placed his finger on a small keypad next to the handle, and waited. Seconds later, the entire front of the cabinet slid up to reveal a slew of guns, knives, and other weapons I couldn't identify hanging from brackets on the wall.

What the hell?

Vincent put the bag in the cabinet and then pressed a button on the inside of it which caused the door to slide back down again.

I glanced at the two identical cabinets next to the first one, but kept from asking if they were filled to the brim with weapons too. I kind of didn't want to know.

I followed Vincent to the only door in the garage. He used his finger on the keypad to open that door, too, and then he motioned me inside.

"What, no alarm?" I asked jokingly once I stepped inside and was met with silence.

Vincent shot me a glance and then pulled out his phone and showed me the screen. The phone was vibrating as my image appeared on the screen. I automatically looked up to try and find the security camera that was watching me, but I couldn't see it.

"Alarms that make a lot of noise are meant to scare an intruder off. Where's the fun in that?" he asked. I noticed Vincent's watch was flashing and I could hear the slightest vibration emanating from it. There was a letter and number flashing on the watch's digital screen.

"What does it mean?" I asked as I pointed to the watch.

"Tells me where my guest – wanted or unwanted – is."

"Doesn't that get old?" I asked. "Having it go off every time you move?"

"It knows I belong here," was all he said, and then he was leading me down a short hallway. We entered a large kitchen with white granite countertops, white cabinets, and black appliances.

No sooner had Vincent put his bag down than a large orange tabby cat jumped up on the counter and immediately put his paws against

Vincent's chest. The sight of the man's big fingers affectionately rubbing the animal's cheeks had my insides warming.

"Mickey," Vincent said as he motioned to the cat. "And Minnie," he added as he glanced to our right. Sure enough, a second cat that looked almost identical to the first except for a small patch of white on its forehead was watching us from the entryway that appeared to lead to the rest of the house.

"Mickey and Minnie?" I asked with a smile.

"My boyfriend had a thing for all things Disney when we got them," he said simply. The mention of a boyfriend caught me off guard, especially since he'd said he lived alone. But the dark look that flashed in his eyes for the briefest of moments had me keeping silent.

"Outer fence is electrified 24/7, inner fence is only at night," Vincent began as he grabbed his bag and headed towards the doorway where the cat was still sitting. He stopped long enough to run his fingers over the cat's head. I reached for my own bag and followed. The kitchen opened into a large, open floor concept living room with black leather furniture, and a flat screen TV hung above the huge fireplace. Light streamed in through the large windows facing the back of the property as well as through the skylights in the vaulted ceiling. "Glass is bulletproof," Vincent continued as we walked. He stepped into a room just past the living room. It was a spacious office with several computer monitors on the wall along one desk, and a single monitor and desktop computer on the other side of the desk. Vincent went to one of the drawers and pulled something out. He tapped some keys on the keyboard of the computer, then did something with his phone before coming to me. I finally realized it was a watch similar to the one he was wearing.

"Leave this on. It's waterproof," he said as he handed it to me. "It has a tracking device in it so I'll know where you are even when you're not in the house."

"I'm allowed outside?" I asked snidely.

He sent me a dark look. "If there's a threat from the air or along the perimeter, the watch will notify you. Get your ass back in the house if that happens. I'll show you the entry points once we're outside."

I shook my head in disbelief. "Is all this really necessary?" I asked. "Surely he can't find me here."

But Vincent didn't respond, and it occurred to me why. "It's not about me, is it?" I asked as I once again looked at the monitors.

"The bedrooms are upstairs. If something happens, we go into lockdown mode."

"Lockdown?" I asked, but before I could even ask what he meant, he hit a button on his watch and I jumped as a heavy piece of metal slid over the only window in the room as well as the skylight above us, pitching us into darkness. Similar sounds rattled outside the room and when I followed Vincent out the door, I saw the house was almost completely dark except for lights along the floorboards that came on and turned off as we moved, illuminating only a few feet in front of and behind us at a time.

"Jesus," I muttered. "Who the hell are you?"

"The only way out of the house during lockdown mode is through this door," Vincent explained as we reached what looked like an ordinary closet at first. He pushed the jackets aside and then took my hand and put it near the back wall and the panel instantly slid open. "The watch controls the door." Vincent took me by the wrist and led me into the small space that was barely big enough for the two of us. The panel slid closed behind us and dim lights illuminated a narrow walkway that led to some stairs. "See that ladder?" I followed his finger to my right and nodded. "The closet upstairs is identical to this one," – he motioned over his shoulder to the closet behind us – "except you have to climb down the ladder to get here. Follow this corridor and down those stairs, through the hall to another set of stairs. You'll end up in the garage. There's a trapdoor beneath the SUV. There's an extra set of keys to the SUV and a gun taped to the trapdoor. The garage door won't open in lockdown mode, but as soon as you open the trapdoor, the locks on the door will silently disengage so you'll be able to use the SUV to break the door down-"

"Why are you telling me this?" I interjected.

"In case I'm not around to get you out," he said simply. "If the house is breached, your only goal is to get to this door or the one upstairs, do you understand me?"

There was barely enough light to see the firm set of his jaw. "What about you?" I asked, as even the thought of leaving him behind had my mind crying foul.

Vincent maneuvered me backwards until my back hit the wall. His hand came up to clasp the back of my neck. "This is not Q&A time, Nate. This is shut up and listen time."

"So what, I'm just supposed to leave you behind?" I asked.

"God, you're so..." He dropped his head briefly as if trying to control himself. When he lifted his head again, I expected him to continue, but he didn't. I didn't need to see him to know he was looking at my mouth. And I knew why.

I couldn't let him, though.

I just couldn't. It was a line I wouldn't...couldn't cross.

But I didn't move. I didn't ask him to release me. I didn't do anything except wish for the impossible.

He let out something that sounded like a mix between a curse and growl, and then he was dragging me back through the panel after waving his arm in front of it. By the time I stepped through the closet, the metal covers over the windows and doors had started to recede and I finally noticed how the house had been cleverly designed to hide their presence.

So this wasn't just some safe house or something. It was really where he lived. Why the hell would someone have to live like this? I remembered how he'd crawled on the ground to check beneath his car for a bomb at the motel. And I started to wonder if I was really any safer with him.

Vincent didn't speak as he led me to a set of stairs that led to the second floor. Both cats had joined us, though the boy, Mickey, was walking in front of Vincent while Minnie was trailing behind me. Brody and I hadn't been allowed to have pets as children and I hadn't had the time in recent years to get one, but I'd grown stupidly fond of the stray cat that had shown up night after night at my patio door

DEFIANCE

looking for food. Just the thought of the poor creature's fate had my throat swelling with sadness.

"Your room," Vincent motioned to an open doorway. Mickey was already sitting on the middle of the bed when I walked into the bedroom. Like the living room downstairs, it had a stunning view of the backyard, which had a little bit of a nicely landscaped yard before opening up into a clearing surrounded by dense forest. I saw a small pond on the far side of the clearing. In the distance, I could see the double line of fencing and I could only assume that meant it stretched around the entire property.

I turned to ask Vincent if that were the case, but he was gone. I went to the hallway and peered down it, but all I saw was an open doorway at the end. I wasn't ballsy enough to enter his private domain, so I returned to my room and looked around. It wasn't overly extravagant, but it was definitely set up for comfort. Generous bedding in neutral tones, a huge bathroom with a whirlpool tub and separate shower, and a small sitting area by the floor-to-ceiling window. I put my hand against the glass to see if I could tell it was bulletproof, but it felt no different than regular glass, at least not to my inexperienced hand.

I took a few minutes to unpack my bag. I'd brought the picture taken of me and Brody at our grandfather's cabin when we'd been kids, but somehow seeing it was a reminder of things I wasn't ready to deal with. My conversation with Vincent in the car had brought back some ugly memories that I'd worked very hard to bury. It wasn't that I'd forgotten them, I was just really good at compartmentalizing them so that I only had to deal with them when I was ready to. And I most certainly couldn't handle them around Vincent. I was already feeling too vulnerable around him as it was.

My thoughts drifted to earlier that morning. I hadn't missed the fact that I'd woken up on his side of the bed. I could only hope he hadn't been in it when I'd migrated in that direction. I'd slept surprisingly well considering everything that had happened, but I was still wiped out. I waited a few minutes for Vincent to come and collect me so he could explain what was going to happen next, but when he didn't show I decided to take a quick shower since I hadn't had the chance to do it the night before. I closed the bedroom door and then went into the bathroom. As inviting as the tub looked, I didn't have the time to make use of it, so I stripped off my clothes and got the shower going. My side was bruised, but it wasn't hurting as bad as the night before. Since I didn't have anything to cover the bandage on my hand with, I removed it, but left the small Band-Aids Vincent had used to cover the puncture wounds on my fingers. My palm felt like it was on fire, but I ignored the pain and climbed into the shower, closing the glass door behind me. The hot water felt amazing, and I found myself standing underneath the spray for a good ten minutes before I even started the process of washing myself.

Everything took a lot longer since I was pretty much one-handed, but now that I was benefitting from the relaxing spray of the shower, I took my time. I let my thoughts drift and tried not to stress about everything I should have been doing today. Even though I'd planned to take it easy today and just focus on administrative tasks like following up on emails and phone calls with constituents and party leaders, it still felt like I was slacking off.

And I never slacked off.

Even as a kid, it had been hard for me to get into the rhythm of summer vacations at my grandfather's cabin. Brody hadn't had that problem. Nor had he minded missing church every Sunday, or lying to our parents about not attending or not doing our nightly bible study. My mother's father hadn't been big on church, so he'd never enforced my parent's rules about attending Sunday services or reading our bible every night before bed instead of watching television. I'd done both anyway because doing any different had felt wrong. But there'd been many times I'd wanted to break the rules like my brother. I just hadn't been wired that way.

I wanted to believe that was why I'd turned on Brody after I'd discovered him in tears the night of our prom and he'd admitted he'd had sex with his girlfriend and had hated it. I myself hadn't ever had sex at that point, so I'd been certain that it was just the newness of it all, but then Brody had uttered those few words that had changed our lives forever.

I think I'm gay, Nathan.

"Fuck," I muttered to myself as I felt the tears sting my eyes. I hadn't meant to let my mind go back to that night. But now that I was there, my subconscious refused to let me walk away from it.

"No, you're not, Brody," I said as the reality of his words crashed over me.

Tears continued to slip from his eyes. "I'm sorry, Nathan. I've...I've tried to be normal..."

"You can't!" I shouted. "You can't be a...a fag," I said, completely horrified as I realized I couldn't protect Brody from something like that. *"You'll go to hell,"* I whispered as even the thought of my brother burning in eternal damnation threatened to send me to my knees.

"I'm sorry," he repeated as he wrapped his arms around his waist. I'd gotten home from the prom hours earlier after saying goodnight to my own date with a simple kiss on the cheek right outside her front door. I'd been studying my bible when I'd heard Brody enter his room, which was right next to mine. I'd gone in to see how things had gone and had found him curled up on his bed, still in his tux, and sobbing uncontrollably.

"It's a mistake," I said as I shook my head.

"It's not!" Brody cried as he settled his eyes on me. "I'm gay, Nathan."

The certainty in his voice was my undoing, and I jumped off the bed. In that moment, he wasn't my brother. He was all the things my father had said.

An abomination.

The devil.

I nodded my head. Yes, it was the devil talking through him. That had to be it. "You're a sick pervert," I snarled at him, and then I did the only thing I could think of to save my brother from the evilness that had taken him over. I went to find my father.

It wasn't until my body began to feel cold all over that I came out of my daze and remembered where I was. I'd somehow ended up sitting on the shower floor, my arms around my raised knees and my head resting on them as tears streaked down my cheeks. The water was quickly turning cooler and I managed to reach up and turn it off before it became ice-cold. I carefully climbed to my feet and got out of the shower. I hadn't thought to find a towel before getting in, but luckily there was a stack of clean towels on the edge of the vanity and I quickly grabbed one and began drying off. I avoided the mirror because I didn't want to see the proof of what had just happened.

It wasn't often that I lost time like that, but when I did, it usually had to do with the memories of that night, the weeks that had followed, or the night three years earlier when I'd cast Brody out of my life for good.

Since I'd worn the same clothes this morning that I'd been wearing the night before, I decided to put on the jeans I'd packed at the last minute the night before when Vincent had given me ninety seconds to figure out what to bring with me. But when I reached the bedroom to get them from my bag, I stilled at the sight of something sitting on the foot of the bed.

I realized what it was as soon as I picked it up.

A digital tape player. I glanced up and saw the bedroom door was still closed, but the player's presence was an obvious sign that Vincent had come into the room at some point. And since I hadn't thought to close the bathroom door while I'd showered, it was very possible he'd seen...or heard me.

I let out a harsh laugh as I sat down on the bed. The man was just destined to see me at my worst. I hit the button on the player.

Hey, it's me.

I immediately turned the player back off, because I was just too raw to listen to Brody's voice at the moment. I knew I should get dressed and go talk to Vincent about whatever the plan was, because I couldn't *not* know what was going on. But I didn't have the energy to do anything more than lay down on the bed and pull the coverlet over me, not caring about the damp towel wrapped around my hips. I clutched the tape player against my chest as more tears threatened to fall. But luckily, exhaustion beat the tears and darkness stole me away before I had to relive the nightmare all over again.

CHAPTER 8

VINCENT

"Yeah, might not hurt, Ronan," I said as I felt my watch vibrating. I glanced at it and saw the location pop up. Nathan was up and leaving his room. "Keep me posted," I said as I glanced at the monitor that would show Nathan. I hung up the phone and watched him head towards my bedroom. He knocked and waited a few seconds, but I was glad when he didn't just walk into the room. I didn't have anything to hide, but I was already struggling to deal with having him in my house. Knowing he'd been in my bedroom would have felt like my last sanctuary had been breached.

When he turned around and began walking down the hallway towards the stairs, I got up and left the office. I still had no clue what to say to him. I shouldn't have left the damn digital player on the bed. But I'd been so lost in the sounds of his sobs and the sight of him sitting broken in that shower stall, that I hadn't given much thought to how he might feel knowing I'd heard him. Hell, I didn't even know how *I* felt. What I did know was that it had taken everything in me not to walk into that shower and pull him up off the floor, his nakedness be damned, and demand he tell me what was wrong. I supposed it could have been the lingering shock from the attack, but I doubted it. I suspected the issue was much closer to home, and it was the very reason I wasn't going to tell him that I'd told Ronan he might want to put some guys on Brody and his men. Ronan had agreed, but his guys would be shadowing the men so they wouldn't know they were being watched. Anything else would just cause them to worry about each other and Nathan. And if Nathan knew the failed attack could potentially be putting his brother at greater risk, he'd never be able to relax and help me figure out who was behind all of this.

And I really needed to figure it out, because I wanted him out of my house and out of my life. I'd been in his physical presence for less than twenty-four hours and it was already becoming a serious distraction. The way he'd stood up to me after I'd told him his only job was to get himself out of the house if we came under attack had been too much. I'd been pissed, yes, but I'd been a lot more than that.

I met him at the bottom of the stairs. My perpetual shadow, Mickey, sat down next to me and I saw Nathan smile when his eyes fell on the cat. It wasn't the carefree, natural smile I really wanted to see someday, but it still had my insides dancing. When his gaze returned to me, he shuttered whatever emotion he'd been feeling and I saw his cheeks color.

"Sorry, didn't mean to sleep so late," he murmured.

"It's fine," I said.

He stopped a few steps above me and shook his head. "Fuck," he whispered.

"What?" I asked.

He shook his head and pushed past me. "What?" I asked, grabbing his arm.

"You heard me, didn't you?" he asked.

When I didn't answer quickly enough, he pulled free of my hold and headed towards the kitchen. I followed him and watched him go to the fridge. Before he opened it, he looked at me and I nodded. He yanked it open and scanned the contents.

"Hard shit's in there," I said as I motioned to the lower cabinet next to the fridge.

He closed the refrigerator and began rifling through the cabinet until he found what he wanted.

Whiskey.

A man after my own heart.

He plunked the bottle down on the island between us. "Up there," I said when he looked at me questioningly. He followed my gaze to the upper cabinet right behind him. He pulled out two glasses and splashed a generous amount of the alcohol into each one before reaching for one and downing a healthy swallow.

"Don't fucking feel sorry for me," he snapped, and then he pushed the second glass towards me. "Go back to being a dick."

I chuckled and said, "You got it...you drunken asshole."

A smile tugged at the edge of his mouth. "Prick," he muttered and then he took another drink.

"Food's in the microwave," I said.

"Not hungry."

"It wasn't an offer," I responded. Nathan's eyes went dark. God, he'd be such a hot piece of ass in bed. I just knew he'd give as good as he got. The image of fighting him for control in my huge bed had me growing hard just like that, and I went to sit down at the kitchen table so I could hide my predicament.

Nathan went to examine the contents of the plate I'd prepared for him and then began the process of heating it up. He didn't ask where the silverware was and instead, began searching through my drawers. I supposed it was his way of rebelling, so I held my tongue and focused on him. He still looked tired, but he was moving easily. He'd unwrapped his hand and he was definitely favoring it, but I didn't see any signs of fresh blood. I should have berated him for getting the stitches wet, but I held my tongue. I'd save the comment for when he needed a reason to get pissed at me.

My eyes fell to his ass when I realized what it was about him that looked so different. He was wearing jeans. Not particularly loose ones, either. The man looked damn good in dress pants, but the casual look was working for him too. His hair looked deliciously rumpled and the gray T-shirt he was wearing stretched tight across his chest.

I took another swig of my drink as I watched Nathan grab the plate from the microwave and carry it, the silverware, and his drink over to the table to sit across from me. When I'd built the house, I knew I'd have no need for a big dining area, so the table only seated four people and I'd removed two of the chairs altogether and slid the table up against the window. On the occasions that Everett would join me for dinner, we often ate in the living room in front of the TV. I hadn't given much thought about how close I'd be to Nathan at the table. As it was, if I moved my foot just a little, I'd be able to reach his beneath the table. I was surprised our knees weren't knocking, considering we were both so tall.

I watched him pick at the food at first, and then slowly start to dig into it with a little more gusto. I generally ate pretty light fare, but I'd purposely made something a little higher in the fat department since Nathan looked like he could use all the calories he could get.

"It's good," he murmured between bites. "Thank you."

I didn't comment. His eyes lifted to mine and I saw a little bit of pesto sauce on his lower lip. I was half-tempted to reach out and wipe it away, but his own tongue beat me to it and I felt my dick tighten even more in my pants. Thank God I'd had the foresight to wear jeans after I'd finished my workout this afternoon and showered while Nathan had been sleeping.

As the silence grew between us, Nathan seemed to get more and more tense. His eyes kept shifting to mine, and finally he put his fork down and sat back. "Can you just tell me something embarrassing so I can pretend we're on even ground again?" he asked. "Even though I know we never really will be."

I hid my smile at that. I knew he was smarting over what I'd heard in the shower. I leaned back and studied him for a moment and said, "Rabbits."

"Rabbits?" he asked, shaking his head in confusion.

"I'm fucking terrified of rabbits," I admitted.

"Shut up," he muttered in irritation. He reached for his fork.

"God's honest truth," I said as I raised my hand. "Scout's honor," I said.

"Were you even a Boy Scout?" he asked.

"I was. So you know I have to respect the Boy Scout pledge."

His lips quirked up before he said, "Rabbits."

I nodded.

"Why?"

"My brother had a rabbit when we were kids. It was a mean little shit…used to bite me all the time. Anyway, Pierce made me watch this scary movie once about giant rabbits that ate people."

"How old were you?"

"Six or seven, I guess."

"And your brother? How old was he?"

"Fourteen." Even the brief mention of Pierce had my stomach cramping, but I pushed the sensation aside and focused on the man in front of me. "So that night after I went to bed, I couldn't sleep, of course, because that movie had scared the hell out of me. So I'm lying there, debating whether or not I should get up and go ask Pierce if I can sleep with him, when I see this shadow on my wall. I'd left a light on in the bathroom," I added. "The shadow was of this big-ass rabbit and it was moving towards my bed. I started screaming and then Pierce is there, standing in the doorway, laughing his ass off with his goddamn rabbit in hand."

Nathan laughed and I felt it ripple through my entire body, easing the sting that had accompanied the brief memory of my brother.

"Oh, wow," he said.

"Yeah…I got him back, though."

"How?"

"I snuck into his bed every night for three months. I even accidentally wet it once or twice when that fucking rabbit of his would move around in its cage."

"No you didn't," Nathan scoffed.

I held my hand up again in silent deference to my time in the Boy Scouts.

The sight of Nathan's lingering smile did something to me I didn't want to think too hard about, and I reached for my drink to swallow the rest down in a healthy gulp. The burn in my belly had nothing on how hot I felt all over as I watched Nathan resume his meal.

"Better?" I asked.

"It's no crying like a baby in the shower, but I'll take it," he said.

I chuckled at that and watched him eat the rest of his food. When he was done, he pushed the plate away. "There's more in the fridge," I said.

"No, thank you," he responded. "That's more than I've eaten in a while. It was delicious."

He could use a lot more meals like that, but I kept that thought to myself.

"So, what's the plan?" he asked.

It was a question I'd been waiting for, but I was reluctant to answer. Maybe because I knew what would happen as soon as I did. Whatever these few minutes had been between us would be gone. It shouldn't have bothered me as much as it did.

"I try to figure out who wants you dead, I find them, take them out, you keep breathing," I said simply.

"That easy, huh?" he said doubtfully.

"Never said it would be easy. I just told you what's going to happen."

"And what am I supposed to do in the meantime?" he asked.

"Whatever I tell you."

Predictably, the answer had all the tension leeching back into his system.

"So, I just put my life on hold? Give up everything I worked for?"

"Would that be so bad?" I asked. "After all, one less politician-"

"Fuck you, Vincent," he snapped. "You have no idea how hard I've worked-"

"I don't care," I cut in. "Spare me your speeches about how you just want to make this world a better place. You want your brother's forgiveness for whatever you did to him, be a fucking man and ask him for it! While you still have the chance."

The last words left my mouth before I could call them back, and I quickly reached across the table to snatch Nathan's plate just so I'd have something to keep my hands busy.

"What does that mean?" Nathan asked, and I wasn't surprised when he followed me to the sink where I began rinsing the plate.

"Nothing," I bit out.

Nathan's voice quieted as he said, "You don't know a thing about me."

I laughed at that as I quickly put the plate and silverware into the dishwasher and then wiped my hands on a dishtowel. "You're such a fucking cliché, Nathan. And the fact that you're working so hard to prove to yourself you're doing all this just for Brody and other people like him makes the whole thing that much more pathetic."

"What thing?"

"Nothing, never mind," I said as I turned away from him, since I had no desire to get into this with him.

Not surprisingly, Nathan forgot all my previous warnings about not touching me and grabbed my arm. I spun him until his back hit the fridge.

"I told you-"

"Tell me what you're talking about!" he interrupted. His voice had jumped several octaves and I actually felt sorry for him. God, how far in the fucking closet was he really?

"This," I said as I pressed my lower body against his and felt his hardness graze mine.

Nathan gasped and then struggled to get away from me. I used my heavier weight to keep him pressed up against the refrigerator. Our bodies were flush and he was breathing hard.

So was I, for that matter. What had started off as a lesson in reality was quickly turning into something else.

"You're wrong," he whispered. "I'm not…I'm not…"

"Can't even say it," I murmured as I shook my head. The fact that he was blatantly lying to me and himself had me moving his arms above his head so I could pin his wrists to the refrigerator with just one hand. I slid my free hand down his body and felt a violent shudder wrack his entire body, even as he tried to seek out more of my touch.

"So this," – I slid my hand over his groin and squeezed his erection – "doesn't mean anything to you?" I asked. My lips were just inches from his.

He didn't say anything, and I felt a moment of guilt when his eyes slid shut, and not from pleasure. I removed my hand and lifted it so I could clasp the side of his face. "Open your eyes," I commanded.

He did as I said. His amber eyes were heavy with confusion, lust, and shame. "Lie to me, lie to your brother, lie to the whole goddamn world, but stop lying to your fucking self, Nathan."

I released him and stepped back, putting a good foot between us.

"You should take your own advice," he said just as I began to turn away. He straightened and whispered, "Was all this really about teaching me a lesson? Or was it you wanting to make sure I knew you were in control…that you have all the power here?"

He was the one to close the distance between us this time and I held my breath as he got in my space, but didn't touch me. "Or maybe you're trying to convince *yourself* you're still in control," he murmured. His eyes fell briefly to my lips before lifting again. "Maybe it isn't about me at all," he ventured.

His words hit just a little too close to home. I stepped forward, forcing him backwards until his back once again hit the fridge.

"It's most certainly about you," I said coolly. "And that control you're so worried about is the only thing keeping me from bending you over that table" – I pointed to the kitchen table – "and fucking you so long and so hard that once I'm finished, you'll be shouting to anyone and everyone who will listen that you're all about dick now."

I could see it on the tip of his tongue…his pride getting ready to force my hand. "Don't," I whispered right before he opened his mouth. "I'm too close," I said huskily. "Do you really want your first time with a guy to be on a fucking table, Nate?"

I knew I was making an assumption about him never having been with a guy before, but everything was telling me he wasn't the kind of closet case who'd come out long enough to test the waters at any point in his life.

It took an inordinate amount of time for him to shake his head. We were so close I could feel his chest rising and falling against mine. At some point, his hands had come up to settle on my waist while I'd plastered mine on the fridge along either side of his head. I needed to step back. I needed to tell him to go to bed. I needed to escape to the safety of my room so I could call up an image of David and ease the painful throb in my cock with my own hand. But I didn't move.

"Go," I managed to get out.

But he didn't move. His eyes held mine and then I saw it. The slightest shake of his head.

"Jesus," I whispered and then I was closing my mouth over his.

CHAPTER 9

NATHAN

Even though I'd known it was coming, had asked for it even, I couldn't have begun to fathom my reaction to it. I'd kissed a few women in my time, but I'd passed off my lack of interest in the act as just not being *that* guy.

But even if Vincent hadn't forced me to confront the lie head-on a few minutes earlier, the feel of his mouth slanting over mine certainly would have done it.

I most definitely *was* that guy.

Because kissing Vincent, or being kissed by him, rather, since I wasn't doing anything but trying to survive the onslaught, was unlike anything I could have even perceived. My entire body came alive the second his hard lips ground over mine, and I felt tears stinging my eyes as an emotion I never would have ever considered bombarded me.

Relief.

Humiliation went through me as Vincent gentled his kiss and then pulled back just a little. "Nate?" he whispered, and then the rough pad of his thumb was swiping through the silent tears that were skimming down my face.

I shook my head and tried to keep myself from completely

breaking down. Because I really wanted his mouth back on mine. "I'm sorry," I said as I shook my head.

"Why are you sorry?"

He tipped my head up, forcing me to look at him. I felt like a foolish child instead of a grown man. I shook my head again. No way I could tell him.

His lips brushed over mine tenderly. "Tell me," he urged.

I laughed as he held me there like that, and I knew he was going to strip me raw without even trying. I didn't recognize my own voice as I whispered, "It's like I can finally breathe." I released one of my hands from his waist long enough to wipe at my eyes. He didn't move his own hand away. "I know that doesn't make sense," I stammered as I struggled to keep looking at him. When he didn't say anything, I tried to pull away so I could escape the humiliating moment.

But he held me firmly in place and then his mouth brushed over mine again. "It makes perfect sense," he said softly, and then he was kissing me again. The onslaught was devastating and all I could do was cling to him. When his tongue sought entry into my mouth, a voice in my head told me I needed to stop this, that I had already crossed a line that would be hard enough to come back from, but I didn't listen. I opened for him and eagerly let him angle my head however he wanted.

I nearly stopped breathing when his tongue stroked over mine in greeting. I'd hated kissing girls like this. But I could never explain why.

Now I knew.

The texture of their lips, the softness of their mouths, the hesitation as they'd demurely returned my kisses – it had all been wrong.

This…this was right. And at the moment, it was the only right thing in my whole goddamned life.

Vincent wasn't just kissing me. He was taking, he was owning, he was consuming. I had no control, but I also had no fear as I tried to kiss him back. My body was thrumming with excitement and need and I quickly wrapped my arms around his back and tucked them over his shoulders, ignoring the pain in my injured hand. I couldn't stop shaking as I began rubbing up against him like a cat in heat. Whimpers were falling from my throat and when he pulled his mouth from mine, I tried to follow. Instead, his hand slid into my hair and tightened so his hold was bordering on painful. But even that just stoked my lust instead of easing it. Teeth scraped over my exposed throat as he forced my head back.

"Oh, God," I grated out as he gently bit down on the sensitive skin where my neck met my shoulder. His tongue was sliding over the spot a second later, soothing it. He took his time working up the other side of my neck, licking, biting and kissing as he went. At some point, he'd wrapped his free arm around my waist and pulled me so tight against him, there wasn't room for even a wisp of air between us.

When his mouth covered mine again, all bets were off and I knew he was done gently easing me into my first kiss with a man. And I'd never been more grateful for anything in my life. I was also done being a passive participant. I sifted my fingers into his hair and held on as I pushed my tongue into his mouth. I didn't care how awkward it probably was. All I cared about was getting as close to him as I could. All I wanted was more of his hands everywhere.

"Touch me!" I demanded as I kissed him with no finesse. In theory, I knew what I was asking for, I just didn't know how to ask it.

But luckily, Vincent knew what I wanted, and the second his hand closed over my cock through my pants, I began humping his palm. I couldn't breathe, so I had to stop kissing him. His mouth latched onto my ear as he began murmuring things into it. How hot I was, how good I felt. Didn't matter what he was saying. All I cared about was his voice urging me on and his hand giving me the pressure I needed. But it wasn't enough and when I told him so, he kissed me again as his fingers fumbled with my pants.

The sound of my zipper being drawn down set off warning bells in my head, but my body was too far gone to care.

"Nate-"

"Don't stop!" I demanded as I searched out his mouth again. I knew that even if he gave me the chance to stop, I wouldn't take it, despite my brain trying to remind me how wrong all of this was.

"I don't care," I told myself, unconcerned that I'd said the words out loud.

As soon as Vincent's hand closed around my shaft, I could feel my orgasm taking over.

Although it wasn't like any orgasm I'd ever known. I wrapped my arms around Vincent's neck and buried my face against his shoulder as I ruthlessly fucked his hand. My body was in complete control and my mind was only along for the ride. The pleasure began rolling over me in building waves that weren't quite enough.

"Vincent," I cried out desperately, willing him to fix this...to fix me.

"I've got you, baby," he whispered, and then his hand began stroking me in earnest, the roughness of his skin heightening the sensation. Definitely a man's hand...no mistaking it for anything else.

I was being jacked off by a man.

And I couldn't think of any place I'd rather be in this moment. I felt Vincent's heat seeping into my body as he held me tight against him, his free hand splayed across my back. I couldn't even imagine the picture we made...locked in a tight embrace, me humping his hand as I clung to him like he was my lifeline.

Because that was exactly what he was.

I was thirty years old with a successful career, money in the bank, and a future most men my age could only dream of, but I'd never felt more small and insignificant than I did in that moment. The only thing holding me together was this man.

This man who made no effort to hide how he really felt about me.

This man who'd been so certain he could make me admit something to myself I'd been denying for years.

God, he was right. He was so very, very right.

That was my last cohesive thought as the orgasm shot like a rocket from my balls. Explosions cascaded throughout my body as the pressure in my dick came to a head and I began shooting into Vincent's hot, tight grip. I wept with joy as the insurmountable relief washed through me and my whole body began to float. I absently wondered if I'd died in that moment because everything I was seeing, feeling, had to be inspired by something greater than myself, than the man in my arms.

I felt wrung out as my knees threatened to buckle. The euphoria continued to blanket me in heat and tingling pleasure as awareness began to return. Vincent was practically the only thing holding me upright and I was having trouble catching my breath. I could feel warm lips pressed against my neck. I felt hot and sweaty all over, but all I really wanted to do was lie down.

That lasted only until I felt my dick being released from a warm, wet grip. Reality returned and I locked my knees so I wouldn't fall. I felt the moment Vincent either returned to reality himself or realized I had, because he stiffened in my hold and then he was putting space between us. I almost didn't want to look down at myself, but the temptation was too great. Sure enough, my softening dick was covered in cum, as was Vincent's tanned hand. All the pleasure leeched out of my system as I realized what I'd done. I let my eyes slide up Vincent's body. He was still fully clothed, but I could see a wet stain on the front of his jeans and another one on the lower part of his shirt.

Shame crashed over me as I realized I'd come all over him like some teenage boy. I'd had no control, while that was all he'd had.

I didn't say anything…I couldn't. I merely tucked my dick back into my pants and then I pushed past him. He might have called my name as I left the kitchen, but I couldn't be sure. I didn't care, either.

Because that crippling weight that I'd carried on my shoulders my entire life was back, and heavier than ever. And I had no one but myself to blame.

CHAPTER 10

VINCENT

My body ached, and definitely not in a good way. But I refused to let up on the weight bag as memories from the night before kept bombarding me, despite my best efforts to will them away.

Twelve hours.

Twelve hours ago, I'd done something I hadn't done since I'd met the boy who'd become my entire world.

I'd come in my pants like I had when I'd been fifteen and David and I had fooled around for the first time.

Since then, I'd learned to control my body and its reactions. Even with David, I'd always been in control of pleasure…his and mine. There were times he'd even joked about it and had made a game of getting me to try and lose it. And while there'd been times I'd come close, I'd never once been in a position where my body had controlled me and not the other way around.

But that was exactly what had happened last night. Nathan hadn't even been anywhere near my dick. Neither had my own hand, since I'd been using one to get Nathan off and the other to hold him close to me. All it had taken was the feel of his arms around my neck as he'd clung to me, whimpers bubbling up from his throat as he'd whispered my name, and the sensation of his cum hitting my body as he'd shattered into a million pieces. I'd come at virtually the same time, though I doubted he'd noticed since he'd been so caught up in his own orgasm. A fact I was grateful for.

What I wasn't grateful for was the look of shame I'd seen in his eyes. I might have forced him to face the truth about himself last night, but he certainly hadn't accepted it.

After he'd left the kitchen, I'd started to follow him…to do what, I had no idea. But then my common sense had returned, and I'd quickly gotten the house secured before I'd gone to my own bedroom to clean up. Once I'd showered, I'd climbed into my bed and pulled the single picture I kept of David from my nightstand drawer, and I'd done what I hadn't done in years.

I'd talked to him.

And I'd started with an apology. Because despite how incredible that moment with Nathan had felt, that was exactly what I'd felt the need to apologize for. I'd been with plenty of men since I'd lost David, but none had held a candle to him. I'd used most as a stand-in for him. But David hadn't been anywhere in my mind the night before…not from the moment I'd pressed Nathan back against that refrigerator.

My watch vibrated, distracting me from my thoughts, and I checked the display. Nathan was up, which was a surprise. I'd expected him to hide out in his room all day. He certainly had every right to. Truth be told, I didn't want to see him because I was clueless as to what to say. Not to mention, I was afraid I'd want a repeat. Only this time, I'd want it in my bed and I'd want to be deep inside of him when his gorgeous eyes went dark with passion.

"Fuck," I muttered as I slammed my fist against the bag one last time and then grabbed it to stop its movement. I leaned against it for a moment as I tried to catch my breath. My watch continued to vibrate, indicating Nathan's movement throughout the house. I stepped away from the bag and began removing my gloves and wraps. The vibrating on my watch stopped and I glanced at it to see there was no number. Which meant Nathan had left the house. A ripple of worry went through me, and I quickly grabbed a towel and my bottle of water and hurried up the stairs.

I found him standing on the back porch, staring off into the distance, fully dressed.

"Morning," I said when I stopped at his side. He didn't look at me.

"Morning. I need to contact my office today," he said, his voice surprisingly even, though it had a certain emptiness to it.

"What for?" I asked.

"It's not normal for me not to check in with them every day. They'll start to worry. My assistant or Preston will go to my house at some point and when I don't answer the door…"

"I told them you were sick."

It took him a full five seconds to register what I'd said and then he was turning to look at me. "What?"

"I told them you had the stomach flu and would be out for at least a few days."

"You talked to them?"

"Not exactly," I hedged as I wiped at the sweat clinging to me. "You did."

"What?"

Fuck, this was going to be bad. "Go change," I said as I motioned to his jeans. "Let's go for a run and then I'll explain everything."

"Explain it now," he said, his eyes glittering with anger.

Which, of course, only served to turn me on. "You have three minutes to change," I said.

"Go to hell."

I hid my smile. I definitely preferred a pissed-off Nathan to an emotionless Nathan.

"Okay, I'll be back in thirty. Don't leave the house," I said as I began to walk towards the few steps that would take me down to the grass.

"Wait!"

I paused and glanced over my shoulder. He was definitely pissed, and I could see he was debating what to do next. "You have two minutes and forty-five seconds."

I swore I heard him mutter "asshole" under his breath, but then he was turning and going back into the house. He was back within two minutes wearing sweats, running shoes, and a white T-shirt.

Probably because the gray one he'd been wearing last night had cum on it.

I cursed the errant thought and began striding towards the side of the property. I hadn't had a chance to explain the outside of the property to Nathan the day before so I said, "Your watch will unlock the gates and turn off the electricity to that section of the fence. You'll know the fence is off because that light" – I pointed to a small indicator light near the security camera attached to the top of the fence – "will be green."

I showed Nathan that the fence was indeed off and then walked through the gate. "There are eight gates total, one on each section of the fence. Reentering the perimeter is the same as leaving…the watch controls it."

"What if you lose power?" he asked as I opened the gate on the second line of fencing.

"I have redundant generators. Two of them. They kick in automatically if the power goes out. The generators can only be accessed from within the perimeter, so even if someone manages to cut the power to the fence, the house will still go into lockdown mode."

I saw him shake his head, but he didn't say anything.

"Try to keep up," I quipped as I started off with a simple jog. The run was a cooldown for me, but I knew Nathan needed to warm up.

As we ran, I enjoyed the quiet of the forest around us. I'd bought nearly a hundred acres of the land surrounding the piece of property I'd built my house on, so I was assured that I wouldn't be stuck with any nosy neighbors anytime soon. I'd see signs of the occasional hiker, but it wasn't often since there weren't any public access points nearby.

Nathan managed to keep up with me, but I could tell he was struggling, so I slowed my pace and shortened the run so that we were heading back to the house after a mile. By the time we reached the deck, Nathan was breathing hard and covered in sweat.

And I wanted him more than fucking ever.

I wasn't surprised when he grabbed my arm, though he didn't hang on to it for long. I was learning to temper my instinctive reaction to him touching me.

"Now tell me what you meant earlier!"

"Go shower and change and meet me in my office. Coffee is in the kitchen."

"No! You tell me now!" he snapped, and then he was in my face.

"You really want to do this again, Nate?" I breathed as my body reacted to his nearness.

My words were like dumping ice water on him. He quickly let go of me and took several steps back. I was moving forward before I even realized it, and I barely managed to stop myself from snagging him around the back of the neck and pulling his mouth to mine.

"Shower, change, coffee, my office," I bit out. "In that order."

I didn't wait to see what he would say in response, because I suspected it would just piss me off and I'd either hit him or kiss him.

Although I knew it was the latter and not the former.

I went to my own room and quickly showered and predictably jerked off to images of Nathan coming apart in my arms. I cursed the fact that I had so little control that I'd even had to do it in the first place, but it was better than being tempted to bend him over my desk.

Who the fuck was I kidding? I was going to be imagining that anyway.

My watch told me Nathan had beat me and was already in my office, so I took my time getting some coffee and willed my still-raging dick to settle down. The little shit would have to just get used to my hand because Nathan's gorgeous ass was definitely off limits. It was one thing to jerk the guy off in the heat of the moment, but to fuck him…no way. Hell, he was a fucking virgin.

Even the idea of me being the first man to touch Nathan like that, to bury myself inside of his luscious body, had my cock twitching in excitement. Fuck, at this rate, I'd be spending most of my waking hours in the gym or the damn shower.

I was pleased to see Nathan had grabbed himself a coffee. I went around my desk and tried to ignore the sight of him with damp hair and those damnably tight jeans. I absently wondered if he'd had to clean the proof of his release the night before off the jeans in the sink or something. I took a sip of coffee and then set the mug down on the desk as I began mentally preparing myself for yet another battle with the man.

CHAPTER 11

NATHAN

*E*ven being this close to him was bringing back all the feelings from the night before that I'd been trying to convince myself hadn't been real. From the moment I'd gotten to my room, ripped off my clothes and climbed into my shower, I'd been letting myself fall back on my father's teachings.

That I'd somehow been lured by the devil.

But I knew it wasn't true. Yeah, Vincent was a lot of things, but he hadn't been responsible for what had happened the night before. I'd had the chance to walk away...several chances. I'd just wanted him more. If anyone was the devil in this scenario, it was me.

Because I was the one standing in front of crowds and going on TV saying one thing and believing another. I'd been telling people for months now that I didn't see my brother and people like him as anything but equal, but I'd refused to acknowledge that I was one of those very people. Somewhere along the way, I'd decided it was better to be someone with some sexual hang-ups and a poor track record with women than face the truth.

I didn't want to dwell on why that was.

So I focused on the man in front of me. I didn't even bother telling him to explain himself. He knew what we were here for and I was tired of being on unequal footing with him. Which meant I had to force myself to be patient as Vincent messed around with his computer. When he finally did look at me, the stern expression had me struggling not to squirm in my seat. Because I knew what that look meant. I wasn't going to like what he had to say, and worse, he expected me not to argue with him about it.

Well, he was in for a big-ass surprise because I was tired of all of it – the orders, the secrecy, him always being a step ahead. I was on the cusp of losing everything, and I'd be damned if I let him take anything else from me.

"After Beck's uncle asked me to help you, I began tracking your movements. I also hacked your accounts."

I stiffened, but managed to stay calm as I said, "Which ones?"

"All of them."

The way he said it, like it was an everyday thing, had me grinding my teeth together. "Why?"

"Because I needed to know what I was up against. Subjects often withhold information because they think it isn't of value or they're too embarrassed to share it. Or they have something to hide…"

"What gives you the right-" I began, but not surprisingly, he cut me off.

"Your life," he said. "Your life gives me the right, Nathan. Because it means something to someone else, even if you take it for granted."

"That's bullshit," I snapped.

I saw only the slightest narrowing of his eyes, but he didn't respond to my outburst.

"So you read my emails…"

He nodded.

I shook my head in disbelief. "And all that crap about asking me about them yesterday?" I asked. "Why bother if you knew what they already said?"

"I needed to see if you were going to tell me the truth about them."

I was surprised by the hurt that lanced through me. I knew it was ridiculous to be upset by something as insignificant as him trusting me, but I was. Maybe if last night hadn't happened…

I shook myself free of the errant thought. Last night had been about sex and nothing more. I needed to remember that.

"So, you took it upon yourself to email my office? Preston? As me?"

"I've seen enough of your email habits to see you're in regular communication with your assistant and Preston. Which means they would have noticed if you hadn't checked in. I emailed them that you were sick yesterday while you were sleeping. I told them you'd be in touch via email, but you wouldn't be answering your phone. Your assistant hopes you feel better soon, by the way."

His nonchalant attitude ate at my insides, and I found that I no longer cared what he had to say to me. All I felt was numb. I'd let this man do things to me that I'd spent a lifetime avoiding. I'd told him things…

I barely managed to stifle a sob as I climbed to my feet. As I left the room, I had only one thought.

Escape. I just needed to fucking escape.

I began walking, not even caring where my feet were taking me or if Vincent followed.

He didn't.

My feet bypassed the stairs that led to the second floor and took me right out the front door. I quickened my pace once I got outside and quickly spotted the gate Vincent had mentioned. Once I reached it, the watch unlocked it, as well as the next gate on the second fence. As soon as I reached the driveway that wound through the dense trees, I took the watch off and dropped it on the ground. I didn't care that I didn't have my phone. I didn't care that no one knew where I was. I didn't care about anything except keeping moving.

Anything to escape the man in the house behind me.

To escape those few moments last night where I'd finally been allowed to be the real me.

Where I hadn't needed to be the perfect Nathan Wilder anymore.

I'd been Nate. *His* Nate.

Now…now I had no clue who I was. I didn't know if I could go back to being the man I'd been. I didn't know if I even wanted to.

I heard the roar of an engine coming up fast behind me, but I made no effort to escape it since I knew who it was. But it wasn't Vincent's car that flew past me and then rolled to a stop a half dozen feet in front of me.

I watched Vincent lean back on the motorcycle after turning it off. He wasn't wearing a helmet, though I could see one dangling from one of the handles on the bike. I knew nothing about motorcycles, but I suspected whatever model it was, it was designed for one thing and one thing only.

Speed.

And Vincent looked perfectly at home sitting on it.

"Let's go for a ride."

Was he fucking kidding?

"No. You said I could leave whenever I wanted."

"And you can," he said. "I'm not here to stop you. When we get back, if you still want to leave, I'll give you a ride wherever you want to go."

Wherever I wanted to go.

Where the hell *was* I supposed to go? Back to my old life? Even if by some miracle I could get it back to where it had been before Vincent had stepped through my shattered window, was that even what I wanted?

Neither of us moved as we stared each other down. And then he did it. He held out his fucking hand.

His touch...it was like a goddamn magnet. I didn't understand it.

But I was also too tired to fight it. There was no logic to what I was doing. Not in going with him. Not in continuing on my own. But I kept going back to that moment the night before when I'd wrapped my arms around him and finally felt safe...and free. Would it be so wrong to have a little more of that?

I stepped forward and put my right hand in his. His grip was gentle on my injured hand as he helped me settle on the back of the bike. He reached behind my left thigh and pulled a helmet free from some kind of clip and handed it to me. I worked it over my head, mindful of my hand, and waited until he put his own helmet on. Then he was reaching behind him to grab my arms and wrap them around his waist. Logically, I'd known I'd probably have to hang onto him like this, but actually doing it was causing a maelstrom of emotions to go through me. I wanted to both jump off the bike and lean into him at the same time. I settled for in between and held myself stiff as I gripped his hips. But as soon as the bike got moving and picked up speed, I knew it wasn't going to work, and I gave up and leaned against Vincent's back. I tried to tell myself it was purely for safety purposes, but I was tired of lying to myself. There would be plenty of time for that later.

The ride took about an hour, and by the time we reached our destination, I found that I didn't really care anymore where we were going. It wasn't until Vincent turned off the bike and rubbed his hand over where mine were joined together on his abdomen that I snapped out of my daze and straightened. I'd been admiring the view during the entire drive and hadn't realized at first that we were going higher up in elevation until we'd gotten out of a particularly heavy section of forest and I'd seen the valley below us. The place Vincent had stopped was an overlook of some kind. I climbed off the bike and set my helmet on the seat after Vincent dismounted.

I watched Vincent loop his helmet over one of the handlebars of the bike, and then he was moving towards several large rocks that were just a few feet from the edge of the overlook. There were no other people around, so I didn't have to worry about being recognized. I followed Vincent, but when he leaned against the rocks and just studied our surroundings, I held back. It would have been easy to move to his side and pretend we were there for different reasons than we were.

"The bike belonged to my boyfriend," he said as he glanced at me and then looked at the bike. "One of his favorite things to do was come up to these mountains when we were on leave."

"You were in the military?" I asked, despite my promise to myself to let him do the talking.

He nodded. "I enlisted first. David joined up a year later when he graduated high school."

"You were together in high school?"

"We grew up together. Both military brats. Our parents were friends. There were a few times our fathers were stationed at different bases, but by the time we were fifteen, they were both working for the Department of Defense, so we lived in Virginia. Went to the same high school. It was the most natural thing for us to end up together."

I couldn't help myself. I ended up moving closer to Vincent so I could see his expressions as he spoke. I didn't even really care why he was telling me this.

"We weren't out to our families back then...those times were a lot different. So we had to sneak around. I think my father knew, but it was one of those things everyone just pretended wasn't really happening. I finally came out to my parents when I was eighteen."

"What happened?"

Vincent shrugged. "My mother cried a lot, my father said I was ruining my life. Said I'd never amount to anything if the military found out I was a fag."

I flinched at the word. "Why was that important?" I asked. "The military part."

He smiled, but it wasn't a real smile. "Because the military and the St. James family went together like peanut butter and jelly. You couldn't have one without the other."

I settled on the rock next to him. "I hate peanut butter," I murmured, which earned me another smile, this one genuine. "Did you want that? To be in the military, I mean?"

He nodded. "Only thing I ever wanted more was David."

I didn't like the sliver of jealousy that went through me. It was unexpected and troubling.

"So what did you do?"

"I did what my father said. I never mentioned it again. Not to him, not to the army."

"And David?"

"Things didn't go as well for him. His parents kicked him out when he told them he was gay. I begged my parents to take him in since he was only seventeen and still had a year of school left. I told them if they didn't, I wouldn't enlist."

"Did they?"

Vincent nodded. "Peanut butter and jelly, remember?"

I nodded. I knew that feeling all too well. I admired Vincent for having the guts to use it to get what he wanted.

"David enlisted, but we weren't in the same unit. He was a great soldier, but he didn't have the leadership skills needed to move up the ranks. By the time I'd worked my way up to Major, he was still a Private First Class."

I had no clue what any of that meant, but gathered it meant the two men hadn't been on equal ground, professionally speaking.

"Did that cause problems between you?"

"No," he said. "He was just so fucking happy," Vincent murmured. "All he'd ever wanted to do was serve his country. If that meant cleaning the base bathrooms, he would have done it, as long as it meant he was giving back."

"What about you?"

"What about me?" he asked as he looked at me.

"Was that what you wanted? To serve your country?"

His eyes shifted back to the view and then he nodded. "I loved everything this country stood for. Freedom, equality, justice…I would have laid down my very life for it."

The heaviness in his voice had me reaching for him, but I realized what I was doing at the last moment and clenched my hand in my lap instead.

"Something happened," I observed. "Something changed."

"Everything changed," he responded. "David and I were stationed at the same base. We didn't see each other often, but every once in a while we'd find a way to meet up." He looked at me and said, "Don't Ask, Don't Tell was still in effect at that time."

I stilled because I realized what he was telling me…and what it meant. "You were discovered."

Vincent nodded. "Someone saw us holding hands one night. A few seconds of giving in to that need to touch one another, and that was it."

"What happened?"

"We were both discharged. Other than honorable."

"What does that mean?"

"It's a step above a dishonorable discharge. It was the military saying we'd never been soldiers. We lost our benefits. It was like we'd never been…that none of the sacrifices we'd made had mattered."

"Vincent…" I began, but he shook his head.

"I lost David after that. Not all at once, but that was when it started."

"What do you mean?"

"David had always been someone who went full throttle at things. When he lost his parents, his home, I think the military became that for him. Besides me, it was all he had. Without purpose, he just…he didn't know who to be, I guess."

"I'm sorry," I whispered.

"I had some money saved up, so when we were discharged, I bought us a little house in Maryland. I guess I still thought something would change at that point…that someone would stand up and do the right thing. They'd see that all David and I had wanted to do was serve the country we loved. I reached out to the military asking them to reconsider. Especially the type of discharge."

"Why that?"

"Because it was like a stain on our careers. Potential employers wanted to know what we'd been doing all those years, but as soon as they discovered the OTH, they looked at us like we were nothing. No one cared *why* we'd gotten discharged…they made up their minds about us as soon as they found out it wasn't an honorable discharge."

My heart broke for him, but I didn't know what to say.

"I tried reaching out to every branch of government I could think of. No one gave a shit. We were less than nothing to them. For every person who refused to help us, I lost another piece of David. He'd already been struggling with PTSD as a result of the combat he'd seen.

The depression that followed made everything so much worse. We were struggling financially..."

"What about your parents? Couldn't they have helped you?"

"My mother died a few years after I enlisted, and my father had no interest in me after I was discharged. The last time I spoke to him, he asked me if I was happy that my deviant ways had brought shame to my entire family. I wasn't even notified of his death. I had to hear it from my brother, even though he was overseas at the time."

"Was your brother...was he supportive?"

Vincent nodded and I felt a sliver of relief. "Pierce was a colonel when I was discharged, but even he couldn't stop it. He managed to find me some work with a private contractor about nine months after David and I were discharged. The work mostly had to do with protecting U.S. contractors who worked in hostile countries...like the guys who worked for energy companies. I was basically hired muscle. But it meant I had to travel a lot, and I was away from David more and more. About a year after we were discharged, I was home for a few weeks of vacation. David wasn't doing well and I begged him to get some help. He agreed, and within a week of seeing a psychiatrist to get on antidepressants, he was better. I thought it was a fucking miracle," Vincent said with a hoarse laugh.

"I thought we'd finally turned a corner. I was hoping I'd be able to get David a job with the same company I worked for. Three days before I was set to leave, I found him dead in our bathroom. He'd shot himself in the head."

I'd known from the way Vincent had been talking that his story wouldn't have a good outcome, but he still caught me off guard.

"Vincent-"

"They wouldn't even let me bury him at Arlington," he whispered, and I felt my throat tighten as he wiped at his eyes.

I knew he was talking about Arlington National Cemetery. I reached out to cover Vincent's hand with mine, not caring what it meant. He squeezed my fingers briefly, and then he was pulling his hand away. He got up and stepped closer to the edge of the cliff. There was a small guardrail, but it wasn't much, and somehow seeing him standing so close to the edge after everything he'd told me had my heart leaping in my throat.

"I can't tell you the details of what happened next, but I was approached by someone who'd been my commanding officer at one time in the army. He worked for the Department of Defense. He offered me a job." Vincent turned to face me. "I said no at first, because I wanted nothing to do with the government that had betrayed us. You want to know why I hate politicians?" he practically snarled.

"Because they sat in judgement of me and decided I wasn't good enough to serve this country. Not because I botched up a mission or I let men die on my watch. But because I fucking held my boyfriend's hand for thirty seconds! Because I dared to allow myself those few seconds to feel! To remember what I was fighting for."

I understood his anger and did nothing to try to stem the tide of it as he practically screamed at me. He seemed to catch himself, and he took several deep breaths.

"I eventually accepted the job because there was this part of me that wanted to show the fuckers that they hadn't broken me." His voice went particularly quiet as he said, "I guess David wasn't the only one who'd found purpose in serving our country."

Vincent shook his head. "The fucked-up thing is that I had a chance for something different. Beck's uncle, Dom Barretti, had been stationed at the same base as me when I was discharged. He reached out to me right after I'd accepted the other job, and asked me to join the security company he and his brother were starting. I would have been a full partner." Vincent's eyes pinned mine. "I chose wrong," he said cryptically, and then he fell silent.

When he didn't speak again, I said, "Why are you telling me all this?"

"You were upset that I implied I didn't trust you to tell me the truth," he said as he turned and walked towards me. He stopped just a couple feet from me. "I think if last night hadn't happened, you wouldn't have been so quick to leave."

The fact that he could read me so well bothered me more than I wanted to admit. "Would you have been so quick to follow me if last night hadn't happened?" I asked, though I wasn't sure why. Maybe I needed to know I hadn't been the only one feeling things I shouldn't have. But did I really want the truth? Assuming he would even be honest with me.

Vincent studied me for a long time, and I held my breath as he stepped even closer to me. I actually separated my legs in anticipation of him needing to be even closer. I hadn't meant to do it, but like last night, my body was overruling my head. Vincent's eyes fell to my legs and his jaw tightened almost imperceptibly. But just as I began to sit up and draw my legs back together, he stepped between them and then he was leaning over me, his hands coming to rest on the rock next to my hips.

"No," he said softly, finally answering my question, though it took me a moment to even remember what it was. I didn't dwell on the impact of the admission, because then his mouth was covering mine. I knew I should stop the kiss, but I didn't even try. Knowing and doing were two so very different things. And wanting was a whole other animal.

Because I wanted Vincent more than I'd ever wanted anything else in my life. I didn't understand it and knew it wasn't right, considering I was so fucked up in the head right now that every interaction I had with this man was just making things worse, but I didn't care.

I wanted.

That was all it came down to as his mouth danced with mine.

I opened in invitation for him, but he only let his tongue graze mine before he pulled away. Then he was stepping back. "Last night was a mistake," he muttered. "We both know that."

Yeah, there was that damn knowing thing again.

But I nodded anyway. Because at some point I would need to let reason return, and my brain would need to start making the decisions again.

"I can't do this if you don't trust me," I admitted. "I can't be someone you hate just because of my career."

"I don't hate you."

I barely kept from laughing at that. Yeah, he wanted me, but that didn't mean he liked me.

"If you want to know something about me, you ask me. Contrary to what you think, I don't want to die," I said.

"And you need to remember that everything I do has a reason behind it…last night notwithstanding," he retorted. "My ability to protect you depends on understanding *you*."

This time I did laugh. "God, this is never going to fucking work."

CHAPTER 12

VINCENT

I couldn't exactly disagree with him. After all, nothing about this case was turning out the way it should have. Starting with the fact that I'd not only followed Nathan, I'd fucking talked to him.

Not just talked. *Talked.*

I'd told him things I'd never told another living soul and that shouldn't have mattered, since my past had absolutely nothing to do with my ability to protect him. But as soon as I'd muttered those words in the office, I'd known that I was going to lose him.

I needed to see if you were going to tell me the truth...

I'd had the chance to clarify things as soon as I'd admitted the underlying issue between us was about trust, but instead, I'd poked the bear and made the crass comment about his assistant hoping he was feeling better. I'd done it for one reason and one reason only.

Because I'd needed to get us back to where we'd been before last night had happened. I needed him to just be another job…another subject.

I'd failed miserably.

Just like I'd failed when I'd told myself I didn't give a shit if he left. With every vibration I'd felt as my watch had tracked his movements,

I'd felt like the asshole he'd accused me of being from the moment we'd met. When my watch had stopped vibrating, I'd switched to watching him on the security monitors, and I'd told myself to let him go…that he wasn't my problem. But the second he'd been out of view of the cameras and the tracking signal had come to a stop, I'd been moving.

And not just because I owed Dominic Barretti.

It would have been simple enough just to get in my car and go get him, but I'd known the damage I'd done wouldn't be undone so easily. I'd known I'd have to give him something, and it would come at a heavy price. Especially since I'd stopped apologizing to people a long time ago. And no, I hadn't actually apologized to him, but telling him about my past *was* an apology of sorts.

Because that was shit I never told anyone. Everett was the only one who knew about that part of my life and that wasn't even because I'd told him about it.

"We should go," I said as I moved farther away from him so I didn't risk taking another taste of his mouth. I had no doubt he'd give me that taste, either.

Nathan straightened, and then he was climbing to his feet. I almost dreaded the fact that he'd have to be pressed up against my back on the ride back to the house.

Almost.

But deep down, it was one of the reasons I'd grabbed the bike instead of the car. Yes, I'd decided to tell him about David, but I could have done that without the benefit of the motorcycle or the trip to David's and my special spot.

Like when we'd left the house, Nathan initially tried to hold himself back from me, but it didn't last, and by the time I rolled the bike through the first gate, he was once again plastered to my back, his strong arms wrapped around my waist.

After parking the bike in the garage, I reached into my pocket and pulled out my keys. I removed the key for the SUV and handed it to him. "It has a tracking device in it. Leave it wherever you want and I'll pick it up."

Nathan took the key and I resisted the urge to snatch it back from him. I moved past him and into the house. Mickey was waiting for me as usual, and I went to the kitchen to search out the bag of cat food I kept there. The cat's happy meows greeted me as he waited by his bowl. Minnie appeared a moment later, but she held back, her yellow eyes on me. David had been her favorite, and while she'd warmed up to me eventually, I suspected she still mourned her true owner. My thoughts drifted to the day David had brought both kittens home. It had been two months before his death, and he'd been so excited about having something to care for in my absence, that I hadn't even considered arguing about the new additions. And I'd never even once thought about giving them up after his death, even though owning pets hadn't been conducive to my new lifestyle. It had been nearly fifteen years since I'd lost David, and I knew that although the cats were both healthy considering their age, I'd be losing them at some point in the near future.

Which meant I'd be losing one of my final links to David.

"If I stay, I need to know it's as an equal participant in all this."

I turned to see Nathan standing inside the entryway to the kitchen. I straightened from where I'd been petting Mickey and said, "Within reason."

"Vincent-"

"There are things I can't tell you, Nathan," I interjected. "If you ask me how I know something or how I found out some piece of information, I might not be able to tell you. It's to keep you safe."

He studied me for a moment and then nodded. I watched as he walked towards me and then placed the SUV key on the kitchen island. Then he held out his hand. "The watch," he said.

I smiled at the fact that he'd known I'd picked it up. I pulled it out of my pocket and handed it to him, trying not to touch him as I did it.

"If you emailed Preston and my assistant, does that mean it's safe?"

"From my computers, it is," I said. "I'm using what the assailant used...fake IP addresses so he can't figure out our actual location."

"I don't want you to speak for me anymore," he said. "I want to email them myself, and anyone else I need to reach out to." He held up his hand when I opened my mouth to speak. "You can read every email I send, if that's what you want. I just...I need a little normalcy back."

"Fine," I said with a nod. It wasn't an unreasonable request. "But you limit yourself to only the people you need to talk to, and if you need to use the phone, you clear it through me first. I have a special secure line that isn't traceable."

"Okay." Nathan put the watch on. "What's next? How are we going to find this guy?"

His use of the word "we" sounded wrong to me, since I always worked alone, but I remembered his comment about needing to be a part of this...needing to be equal. "I have a couple of things I want to do to see if he's hacked any of your accounts or any of the people closest to you. If I don't find anything there, I'm going to set up a trap for him."

"What does that mean?"

"Chances are he's been watching you for a long time, and not just physically. Judging by the hardware he used the other night, he's not your average stalker," I hedged. "I'm probably not the only one who's been monitoring your email and phone. If I can't find him, I'll bring him to me by sending messages that will indicate your location, only it won't be your actual location."

"You'll bait him?" he asked.

I nodded. "He'll think you're holed up in a cheap motel somewhere. By now he's figured out that you didn't go to the cops to report the attack. And he's probably gone back to your house and discovered you haven't been back."

"Won't he figure it out? I mean, he must have sensed the same thing about you...that you weren't just some random guy."

"He was brazen enough to attack you in your home, Nathan. He wanted to send a message. Whatever his beef with you is, it's not going to go away anytime soon. Either he's getting paid a lot of money to take you out, or he's got more personal reasons. In any case, he's not going to let someone like me stand in his way. He'll just come better prepared next time. And he doesn't know what I'm capable of...

at the most, he'll assume I'm hired muscle and nothing more. I've been careful to make it look like the email you sent to Preston and your assistant came from a library in Charleston – he'll think we're still in the area but just lying low. And that we're not smart enough to realize he's monitoring you electronically."

"You're giving him a false sense of security," Nathan murmured with a nod of his head. "So you draw him out, and then what?"

"How about we make that subject one of the ones I get to veto," I offered.

He tensed, but didn't push the issue. Undoubtedly because I'd answered his question by not answering it.

"Why not just let me draw him out?"

"What do you mean?" I asked.

"Actually stick me in a motel room somewhere. Let him think I'm alone."

I began shaking my head before he even finished. "No."

"No? That's it? What happened to equal participant?"

"Putting yourself in a dangerous situation isn't equal participation," I snapped. "It's stupidity."

He shook his head and drummed his fingers on the island. "Not going to work," he muttered to himself.

I knew I was overreacting, but the idea of him back in that fucker's direct line of sight had me on edge. Especially since I didn't know who I was dealing with. "Look, let me see what I can figure out and we'll go from there," I conceded. "If I think that I can't draw the guy out on my own, I'll…I'll think about it, okay?" Even the words sounded wrong, but deep down, I knew Nathan was right. I needed the threat to him to be gone, and I needed it to happen soon.

And not just because I wanted to fulfill my commitment to Dom and his nephew.

Nathan nodded. "Can I take a look at my email now?"

I nodded and led him to my office to get him set up with a computer.

"Here," Nathan said as he set the laptop down on the kitchen island. I was in the midst of preparing dinner, so I put down the knife I'd been using to chop vegetables and pulled the laptop around so I could see it. Nathan came around the island and pointed at the screen. "These are the emails I worked on," he said as he put his finger on the tracking pad and moved the mouse to open the draft folder. "You can check the sent folder to see that I didn't send anything without letting you look at it first."

"Not necessary," I said. I only glanced at the emails in the draft folder before hitting the send button. It was a monumental effort on my part not to actually read them, but I'd had a lot of time to think about what Nathan had said. It wasn't that I didn't trust him…I didn't know how to trust, period. Even with Everett, it had taken me years to get to the point where I'd let him into my life. But there were things I still kept from him, and not just to protect him.

I felt Nathan's eyes on me as I turned the laptop back towards him and resumed cutting up the vegetables.

"I also worked on a speech I have to give later this month…did you want to see it?"

I shook my head. "Only if you need a second opinion on it." I lifted my gaze and said, "And since we both know I'm pretty much the worst one to ask for a second opinion on a political speech…."

Nathan smiled and I inwardly cursed the dreaded butterflies in my belly. Hadn't felt those damn things since I'd been with David.

"It's not a political speech," he said as he closed the computer.

When he didn't say anything else I said, "What kind of speech is it?"

"Nothing," he responded, shaking his head.

"Tell me," I urged.

His pretty eyes settled on mine and I could see the uncertainty in them. God, I really was an asshole if he was this afraid to tell me something that clearly seemed to be both personal and important to him.

"Tell me," I repeated, softening my voice and stopping what I was doing.

"It's this career day thing for a youth center in Charleston. It specializes in helping homeless kids get off the street. I've been volunteering there for a while and the director asked me to give a speech about government service."

"You volunteer there?" I asked softly. "I didn't see anything about that-" I stopped abruptly when I realized what I'd been about to say. I hadn't seen evidence of that when I'd been digging into his personal life.

"I don't want people to know because then the center becomes the focus of reporters. And my opponent will say I'm there just to boost my image."

I wasn't someone who surprised easily, but he'd managed it. "What kind of volunteering do you do?"

Nathan shrugged. "Whatever they need. Legal stuff mostly. Sometimes just sitting and listening to the kids."

I knew Nathan was a lawyer, but I'd assumed he'd gotten the degree just so he could use it to get into office. I'd assumed a lot of things.

"What are you making?"

His question pulled me from my thoughts, especially the questions of self-doubt that had begun to pop into my head. What else had I gotten wrong about him? I'd only viewed him through the lens of financial accounts, emails, news articles and interviews…how much had I missed about the real Nathan Wilder?

"Stir-fry," I said.

"Do you need help?"

I didn't, but something about this tiny moment of peace had me saying, "Would you mind emptying the dishwasher?"

He nodded, and then he was pulling the dishes out and setting them on the counter. As I worked, I told him where things went. I was so distracted by the sight of him moving so comfortably around my kitchen, I lost track of the knife and let out a harsh curse when I felt the sharp blade slice into my finger.

"Fuck," I muttered as blood began welling up from the cut. It wasn't overly deep, but I still felt foolish for even letting it happen. Especially considering *why* it had happened.

"Damn," Nathan said, and then he was grabbing my wrist and leading me to the sink. I barely noticed the cold water running over the wound as his warm fingers held onto my wrist to keep me from moving my hand.

"You have a first aid kit?" he asked. When his eyes met mine, we both stilled as electricity charged the air around us. He swallowed hard and then forced his eyes down. "If it needs stitches, you're on your own," he said with a nervous laugh.

But I couldn't find it in me to laugh. I didn't know why.

His eyes lifted to mine again, probably at my lack of response, and I watched his tongue dart out to wet his lips.

"First aid kit?" he said softly, distractedly.

"Second drawer," I said as I motioned to the cabinet behind him. I missed his touch when he released my hand to go get the kit. He grabbed it and then he was handing me a clean dishtowel. "Put pressure on it," he offered.

I certainly didn't need to be told how to treat the minor injury, nor did I need him to dress it, but when he told me to sit down at the table, I did it anyway. And when he brought the second chair around to face the chair I was sitting in, I held my breath. Sure enough, when he sat, his legs shifted until one was between my legs. I barely heard anything he said as he carefully cleaned and dressed the wound, which wasn't bad enough to warrant a stitch. It barely needed a Band-Aid, but something about him fussing over me was fucking with my head, and I found myself reluctant to tell him just to leave it alone.

"Feel okay?" he asked when he finished putting the bandage in place.

"Yeah," I said quietly.

Nathan was still holding onto my hand, even though he was finished, and I found myself reluctant to pull free of his hold. He was the one to move first, and I suspected that was because he was starting to feel the same charged energy surrounding us.

"I'll clean this up," he said as he stood and then motioned to the small pile of vegetables. My senses cleared once he was out of my immediate reach, and I quickly closed up the first aid kit and returned it to the drawer while Nathan threw out the ruined vegetables and began washing the knife and cutting board. I'd cut enough vegetables that I could get started on the cooking and I did my best to ignore Nathan, even though his body was just inches from mine.

It was strangely comforting to be working side by side with him. I was most definitely in lust with him, but even with the desire simmering between us like a live wire, I still found myself watching his movements as he cleaned the dishes and then began wiping down the sink. He kept casting me glances, but didn't say anything.

"You mind getting me the beef from the fridge?" I asked. Nathan nodded, and then he was moving to the refrigerator. I watched his eyes settle on the door for a moment and I knew what he was thinking. I was thinking it myself. How good it had been last night. I wondered if he was also thinking about how good it could be again. He cast me a glance over his shoulder, and I barely managed to hide my smile at the flush of color that stained his cheeks. When he returned to my side and handed me the bowl full of sliced beef, I had to remind myself why it would be a bad idea to let the bowl hit the floor and reach for him instead.

"Thanks."

"Should I set the table?"

The idea of being that close to him again had me shaking my head. If we ate at the table, he likely would end up bent over it this time around. But before I could suggest that we eat in the living room, which had enough furniture to ensure we didn't end up anywhere near one another, my watch vibrated and I heard my phone beep. I glanced at my watch and recognized the code immediately.

"Better set it for three," I said as I turned the stove off so I wouldn't burn the food while I greeted our unexpected guest.

"Someone's here?" Nathan asked, his voice carrying an edge of tension.

"A friend," I said. When he tilted his head at me, I knew what he was thinking. "Shut up, I have friends."

His lips curled into a smile and I wanted to curse the interruption.

"Just...don't freak out, okay?" I said as I went to the fridge and grabbed a bottle of beer.

"Freak out? Why would I-"

Nathan's words were cut off when the front door opened. "You here, Vincent?"

"In here, Ev."

I kept my eyes on Nathan and stifled a laugh when his mouth dropped open at the sight of our guest.

"Oh my God."

"Everett, this is Nathan Wilder. Nathan, I'm guessing you don't need the introduction, huh?"

But Nathan didn't respond to me, nor did he acknowledge I'd even spoken. I couldn't really blame him. After all, it wasn't every day the former president of the United States walked into your kitchen.

CHAPTER 13

NATHAN

"Oh my God," I repeated stupidly, even as I automatically held out my hand to the man across from me. "Mr. President, it's...it's an honor."

"Honor's all mine, Mr. Wilder."

I doubted that, but I was still too awestruck to say anything besides, "Call me Nathan, please."

"Nathan, it's a pleasure. Please, call me Everett."

There was no fucking way I could call him that. I watched in stunned disbelief as Vincent handed the man a bottle of beer.

The former leader of the free world drank beer. And he twisted the cap off like every other guy in America.

And he somehow knew Vincent.

"Mmmm, stir-fry?" Everett said as he eyed the stove.

"Yep," Vincent said, and then he was turning back to the stove and getting it going again.

"You're not putting any of that tofu shit in it, are you?" Everett asked as he took a long pull from the bottle.

Holy hell, the president swore.

"Why yes, Everett, you may join us for dinner. And no, it's beef."

"Beef?" Everett said before letting out a low whistle. His eyes shifted to me and he said, "You must be special."

His comment sent a rush of heat through me. Did he somehow know what had happened between me and Vincent? Fuck, had Vincent told him? My eyes shifted to the man next to me.

"He's talking about the fact that I rarely eat red meat," Vincent said calmly and then shot Everett a dark look. "Make yourself useful and set the table."

"The table?" the older man said. "Wow, really special," he quipped as he shot me a smile and then actually winked at me.

The former president of the fucking United States was taking orders from Vincent and he'd winked at me. What the hell alternate universe was I stuck in?

"You know the president?" I whispered to Vincent once Everett was out of immediate earshot.

"Clearly," he said, and I fought the urge to punch him in the arm.

"You know what I mean."

"It's a long story."

"Then tell me the abbreviated version."

"Later," he said. "Go talk politics – he loves that shit."

"I can't talk politics with the president," I said fiercely.

Vincent laughed, actually laughed, and shook his head. "Fine, then talk about reality dance competitions. You'll never get him to shut up."

"I heard that," Everett said.

"Should we set a place for Grady?" Vincent asked as he began sautéing the beef.

Everett let out something that sounded like a mix between a curse and a growl. "Bastard took an early retirement. Moved to Florida to be closer to his seven grandkids. Can you believe that?"

"That he moved to Florida?" Vincent drawled.

"No, smartass, that he's got seven grandkids." Everett began plunking silverware down next to the plates. "He must have been practically a baby when he started having kids."

"Isn't he like five years younger than you?" Vincent asked, a small smile flitting over his lips.

"Seven years, you asshole. Which means he's only a few years older than you. *Seven* grandkids."

It took me a moment to realize the men were grousing about their ages. From what Everett was saying, he was only ten years older than Vincent, which put him near the sixty mark. While the man might not be as built as Vincent, he was still gorgeous. Thick, glossy salt-and-pepper hair, a little bit of scruff on his wide jaw, stunningly bright blue eyes, and a fit body that filled out his dress pants and button-up shirt beautifully. It wasn't until I sensed Vincent's eyes on me that I realized I'd been staring at the older man. Vincent's knowing smile said he knew exactly what I'd been thinking.

"They assigned me a new one."

"A new what?" I asked, hoping I wasn't stepping on any toes. But I was completely clueless as to what they were talking about.

"Secret Service agent," Vincent responded.

"The snot-nosed little shit's turning the house upside down with all his security measures. He's convinced I'm the target of the next great terrorist plot."

"Was there a threat or something?" I asked.

Everett waved his hand as he returned to the island and took another swig of his beer. "He's looking to prove himself. He pissed off some muckety mucks somewhere along the way and he's doing time in purgatory."

"What did he do?" Vince asked.

"Rumor has it, he slept with the VP's daughter…the VP's barely-legal daughter."

Vincent laughed before saying, "Fuck purgatory. He's going to burn in suburbia until you send him into early retirement like you did Grady, or till you're six feet under."

I watched in astonishment as Everett punched Vincent's upper arm. "Nice," he said. "And I didn't drive Grady away. We had an understanding."

My belly did an insane flip-flop motion when Vincent cast his eyes in my direction and rolled his eyes.

"You know new guy probably put a tracker on your car."

"Yeah, I know. That ungrateful shit Grady probably warned him I liked my alone time."

"Alone time?" I asked.

"Everett has a habit of ditching his Secret Service detail. He ropes his household staff into helping him."

"Staff," Everett snorted. "It's Helga and Jeremiah," he said with a wave of his hand. "You're making me sound pretentious, Vincent."

"Shut up, old man," Vincent returned. "No one's buying your "aw, shucks" act." Vincent glanced at me as he began searching out a bowl in the cabinet next to the stove. "Everett's sharp as a tack, even for his advanced age. He pretends he's all about making pottery and babying his prize-winning roses, but it's complete shit. He could just as easily walk into the situation room at the White House and take control of whatever fucked-up shit's going on there."

I shifted my eyes to Everett, who winked at me as he finished his beer.

Before I could say anything, Vincent's phone was beeping.

"There's your man," Vincent said. "You tell him the rules?"

"Where's the fun in that?" Everett asked. Vincent shook his head which had Everett saying, "I told Grady to tell him."

Vincent turned the stove off, and then he walked over to a small monitor on the wall near the entrance to the kitchen. I followed him and saw him punch a button on a digital panel next to the monitor. I could see on the monitor that a dark sedan was sitting in the driveway. The first gate opened and the car immediately pulled in. The gate closed behind the car, but when the second gate didn't move, the driver began honking his horn and then an arm came out to hit a button on the small metal post just before the gate.

"Yes," Vincent said, his voice holding none of the mirth it had a moment ago.

"United States Secret Service," the voice said sternly. "Open the gate."

"What's his name?" Vincent asked Everett.

"Nash?" the other man said.

"Are you asking me or telling me?"

"It's either Nash or Bridges."

Vincent shook his head. "Where are you getting that from?"

"I remember thinking I miss that show when he introduced himself," Everett explained. He looked at me and said, "It was a good show, huh?"

Since I'd never seen it, I merely nodded in agreement.

"Ev, focus," Vincent said.

"Nash," Everett murmured with a nod.

"First name or last?"

"Not a clue," the older man said with a shrug.

I smiled to myself as I watched the byplay between the two. Whatever they were to one another, it was something they'd likely spent years building.

Vincent hit the button on the dial pad and said, "What's your name, Agent?"

"Special Agent Jonathan Nash," came the response, and then the man was holding up ID. "Open the gate, sir."

The man's tone left little doubt what he expected to happen, but seeing the way Vincent tensed up, I knew the fun had come to an end. "Agent Nash, I assume you're armed."

"That's none of your concern, Mr..."

"If you were any kind of agent, you'd already know my name."

"Fine, whether or not I'm armed is none of your concern, Mr. St. James. I'm here to collect President Shaw and if you don't open this gate immediately, I will be forced to break it down and you will be arrested for interfering with a federal officer."

Yep, the game was definitely over because Vincent straightened and then he was striding past the door.

"Bad move, Nash Bridges," Everett said to himself, and then he was rushing past me. I hurried after both men and caught up to them just in time to see Vincent pull a rifle from the trunk of his car in the garage. He slammed his hand against the garage door opener on the wall between the doors.

"Vincent," Everett called, but Vincent ignored him and strode out of the garage. "Fuck," Everett muttered, and then he was striding after

Vincent. By the time I caught up to them, Vincent had reached the gate.

"Get out of the fucking car!" Vincent snarled and then he pulled the lever back on the rifle.

"Put the weapon down!" the man in the car yelled. "Put it-"

Vincent shot out the front driver's side tire before the man could even finish talking.

"Jesus, fuck, Vincent," Everett yelled and then he was pushing between Vincent and the gate. I reached Vincent's other side and grabbed his arm, not caring what he'd likely do to me, considering how he normally reacted anytime I touched him.

"Don't," I said softly.

He didn't take his eyes off the man in the car who'd at least had the sense to put his hands up. But he also didn't throw off my hand.

"Get the fuck out of the car, Nash," Everett snapped and then he went to the side of the gate. I finally noticed he had a watch just like mine and Vincent's. He waved his wrist against a small metal panel on the gate post and it slid open. The car door slowly opened and the man got out. His arms were no longer raised, but he was careful about where he put his hands since Vincent hadn't lowered his gun.

The easygoing Everett I'd met just moments ago was gone, and in his place was the man I'd watched countless times on television as he'd talked to the American people. A man I'd hoped to be just like someday.

"Did or did Grady not explain to you who this man is?" Everett pointed to Vincent who had yet to take the gun off the man. Everett seemed completely unconcerned that the weapon was essentially now pointed at him.

"He did," Agent Nash said, his voice steady and even as his eyes remained on Vincent.

"And is it your habit to disrespect a man who is more of a brother to me than my own fucking flesh and blood?"

"No, sir," the man responded coolly.

"Yet you come onto this man's property, knowing what you know," – Everett's voice ticked up as he spoke – "knowing I'm safer with him than I am with ten of the likes of you, and you don't show him or me the courtesy of respecting his wishes. Do I have that correct, Agent?"

I was stunned when, instead of cowering, the man stepped forward, getting into Everett's face. "With all due respect, I am not Grady, and contrary to what you and everyone else thinks, I'm here to do my job and that includes keeping you safe from any threat." The man's eyes shifted briefly to Vincent, but he seemed unfazed that the gun was still trained on him. "If you'd shown *me* even an ounce of the very respect you're demanding, you would have allowed me to accompany you this evening instead of running off like an errant child, and I would have been given the opportunity to meet Mr. St. James under more appropriate circumstances. And only once I'd made sure you were safe in his care would I have respected his ridiculous rule about leaving all of my weapons in my trunk."

Agent Nash shifted his focus to Vincent. "If you care about him so much, you would let me do my damn job and keep him safe. Just because he's with you doesn't mean I'm off the clock," the man bit out. "I don't know what your deal about federal officials coming onto your property armed is, and frankly, I don't care. I'm here to do my job and I'll damn well do it, no matter how many of my fucking tires you blow out."

Vincent's jaw ticked a few times and then he lowered the weapon. "You get five minutes with me while I explain the perimeter's security, and you can wait out here until Everett is ready to leave. But you will *not* come armed into my house, and I will not be showing you the interior security."

Agent Nash held Vincent's gaze a moment before nodding. Everett was noticeably quiet, and I couldn't help but think that he seemed lost in thought as his eyes followed Agent Nash as he walked through the gate towards Vincent. I fully expected Vincent to comment on the fact that the man was still armed, since I could see a pistol sticking out from beneath his jacket in some kind of shoulder holster, but Vincent remained silent. I guessed Agent Nash to be a few years older than me. His hair was coal black and his skin had a slightly olive tone to it. Italian heritage maybe. He was almost as tall as Vincent and had a similar build, but whereas Vincent had a certain hardness about him, Agent Nash seemed stiffer. Like he was always on point.

Everett stopped by my side as we watched the men begin walking along the fence line. I noticed that Vincent kept his finger near the trigger of the rifle and while he wasn't holding it on Agent Nash, it wasn't exactly in a non-threatening position either.

"What happened to him?" I murmured before looking at Everett. I'd initially thought Vincent's reaction had been about Agent Nash being a federal agent, but I'd quickly realized the real issue – the only issue – had been that the agent had been unwilling to put his weapons away.

Everett patted my back and said, "Would you believe he's actually come a long way?" There was no humor in Everett's voice as he spoke, though, and I knew he too must have been rattled by the encounter. Though he didn't seem overly surprised by it…at least not by Vincent's reaction. Now Agent Nash's reaction…

As I followed Everett back into the house, I had to wonder if Agent Nash would still have a job come tomorrow…assuming he and Vincent even made it back to the house in one piece.

CHAPTER 14

VINCENT

"You sure do know how to throw a dinner party, Vincent St. James."

I looked up to see Nathan standing above me, two glasses of whiskey in hand. He handed one to me where I was sitting on the steps leading down the porch and into the backyard. Dusk was just starting to fall, so Mickey was chasing fireflies all around the grass while Minnie had taken up residence on a lounger by the patio door. We'd said our good nights to Everett twenty minutes earlier, but when I'd started helping Nathan clean up the kitchen, he'd waved me off with a comment about the cook not being on dish duty. I'd retreated to the patio to nurse the rest of my beer as I'd considered my behavior earlier in the evening.

And the fact that Nathan had been privy to all of it.

I knew my reaction had been over the top when Agent Nash had blatantly refused to follow my rule about not bringing any weapons into my house. I'd gotten used to Grady and Everett's other long-time agents following the rule without question. But I begrudgingly had to admit, Agent Nash had had a good point. If the roles had been reversed and I'd been charged with protecting Everett, nothing and no one would have gotten between me and that duty. I hadn't actually told the man that, but I'd allowed him more than the allotted five minutes when he'd asked in-depth questions about the security measures I'd taken to protect my property. Luckily, he hadn't asked me *why* I'd gone to such lengths. Once we'd returned to the front of the house, I'd helped him change his tire, though I hadn't invited him to join us for dinner. I still wasn't sure enough about the guy to risk having him in my house. And he'd seemed just as content to remain outside.

Everett had been quieter than usual after the encounter. If we'd been alone, I would have tried to figure out why. I'd thought maybe he was just thrown by how bluntly Agent Nash had spoken to him, but he'd seemed more and more distracted as the night wore on…restless, too. Yeah, he'd interacted with Nathan and they'd rambled on about all sorts of political happenings, but I'd tuned out that conversation and had just focused on my friend. There'd been no explanation for the sadness I'd seen lingering in his eyes. Yes, it was something he always carried with him, but he was usually better at hiding it, especially after all these years.

"Yeah," I murmured.

"Take a walk with me." His words caught me off guard and I looked up at him. "Come on, I need to walk off dinner. I don't remember the last time I've eaten this well."

"It's not safe to leave the grounds after dark," I automatically said.

"We won't," Nathan responded. "You've got this gorgeous backyard, Vincent. Come show me around it."

I nodded and climbed to my feet. I'd left myself a couple of acres on the inside of the fence and had had it professionally landscaped to include a small creek that fed into a larger pond in one corner of the yard. So it didn't surprise me when Nathan headed in that direction. I fell into step next to him and tried to ignore how damn good he smelled.

"Vincent, I need you to stay calm," Nathan said in a hushed voice.

"What? Why?" I asked. I immediately began scanning the property for some kind of threat and automatically reached for the gun in my ankle holster.

I was shocked when he put his hand on my arm. "Stay calm. The assailant is about twelve inches tall with buck teeth, but he's got a pretty sizeable set of ears on him so he can probably hear us."

I followed Nathan's gaze to the far side of the pond and then shoved at him hard. "Fucker," I said as the small rabbit spotted us and took off.

Nathan laughed and said, "Sorry, I had to. Didn't want you to go all commando on Thumper's ass."

"Asshole," I said, even as I smiled. Never in a million years would I have guessed the man had a sense of humor. We fell silent as we made our way closer to the pond. But it didn't last.

"So are you going to tell me?" he asked.

"Tell you what?"

"Oh, I don't know…how it is that you know the president of the fucking United States."

"Little starstruck, were you?" I asked.

"Yes, and don't deflect."

"I met him about a couple years before his term ended. But I can't tell you the how and the why." When Nathan opened his mouth to object, I added, "It's not my story to tell."

"Fine…then tell me why you need to live in Fort Knox," he said.

"Fort Knox might as well be made of toothpicks compared to this place," I said.

Nathan's voice softened as he said, "And you don't see anything wrong with that?" I glanced at him and couldn't help but think how beautiful he looked. At some point after Everett had arrived, Nathan had snuck up to his room to swap out his T-shirt for a white button-down shirt. He'd rolled up the sleeves to expose muscled forearms with just a smattering of blond hair on them.

"I'm not some paranoid Y2K fanatic, Nathan. I live like this out of necessity, not because I want to."

"Is that what you're doing, Vincent? Living?"

We'd reached the pond, but Nathan was looking at me instead of the water. His eyes were far too perceptive and I found myself looking away so he wouldn't see things he shouldn't.

"Just drop it," I murmured.

"Look, Vincent, I don't pretend to understand, but-"

"You're right, you don't understand," I bit out. "And frankly, it's none of your business."

"Vincent-"

"Just shut the fuck up, Nathan!" I snapped. The pain in my belly had grown to epic proportions, and I quickly downed the rest of my drink in the hopes it would stem the sensation. But it did nothing to quell the rage and agony that began to consume me. I'd had years to deal with it, but the wounds were as fresh today as they'd been that night.

I was dimly aware of pain in my right hand, but it wasn't until I heard Nathan say, "Fuck, Vincent," that I realized I'd gripped the glass in my hand so hard that it had broken. "Are you hurt?" Nathan immediately asked as he put his own glass down in the grass and reached for my fisted hand.

"It's fine," I said. There was a small cut on my palm, but it could barely be called a scratch.

"No, it's not. It's bleeding," he said, and then he was lifting the bottom of his shirt and pressing the hem against my hand, turning the bright white fabric dark red. "We should go back to the house."

My eyes fell on his hand which he'd bandaged again at some point. "We match," I said absently. It was a stupid thing to say, but I was finding that between the beers I'd had during dinner and the whiskey, my tongue was a little looser than normal.

"Yeah, I guess we do," he said as he grabbed my wrist and tried to pull me forward. With the amount he'd touched me in the last twenty-four hours, I had to wonder if he was just a touch-feely kind of guy or if there was something more going on.

I wanted it to be the latter.

Badly.

But I knew I shouldn't want that.

It was like wishing that night twelve years ago had never happened or that I hadn't lost David.

I couldn't undo either of those things, and I couldn't have this man even just for a night.

Nathan continued to try and tug me forward, presumably to get me to the house, but I resisted, and when he finally realized I wasn't moving anytime soon, he looked up at me with questioning eyes. I wished it were lighter out so I could see the unique mix of gold and brown in them.

"Vincent," he whispered. "Talk to me."

It figured he'd see it in my eyes…the need to give him something of myself. A part that no one else had.

"They killed my brother," I finally said.

"Pierce?"

When I nodded, Nathan asked, "Who?"

"Guys who came looking for me. Pierce was staying at my house because he'd just finished his last tour and was leaving the army. I wasn't home. They tortured him and then they slit his throat. Because he refused to give them what they wanted."

"What…what did they want?"

I dropped my eyes because Nathan had started rubbing little circles into my wrist with his thumb.

"They wanted him to tell me to come home. They used his phone to call me and tried to force him to tell me there was an emergency at the house. He warned me instead. Shouted at me not to come home. The call cut off right after that and by the time I got home, he was dead. Tied to a chair, covered in blood and bruises. They broke his fingers one by one, cut him, burned him." As Nathan's expression grew more and more horrified, I stopped talking and pulled my hand free of his. "You want to know why I live like this?" I said as I motioned to the house. "Because I don't have a fucking choice. Because even though I got vengeance for my brother, there are a dozen more guys waiting in the wings to get their shot at me."

"I'm sorry-"

"Don't be sorry," I snapped. "I don't need your pity. I don't want it."

"What do you want, Vincent?"

"That's the thirty-four-thousand-dollar question, isn't it?" I bit out.

I took a few more steps back because I needed some fucking space. I'd admitted more to him than I'd intended and it had left me feeling shaky and off balance.

But instead of leaving me be, Nathan stepped forward until he was practically pressed up against my chest. He didn't touch me, though. "What. Do. You. Want. Vincent?" he asked, punctuating each word with the tiniest of pauses.

He was fucking with me. He had to be. There was no way he wanted…not after last night. Not after everything I'd told him today about invading his privacy.

"Nathan-"

"Nate," he murmured. "I like when you call me-"

That was as far as he got before I slammed my mouth down on his. But unlike the night before, I didn't even try to ease Nathan into the kiss. I took what I wanted without question. Maybe I needed to give him a chance to back out, but I couldn't do it. I wrapped my arms around him and dragged him forward against me as I plunged my tongue into his waiting and very willing mouth. He kissed me back without any kind of hesitation whatsoever, and that proved to be my undoing.

I took him to the ground in one seamless move and then I was covering his body with mine. I expected some kind of resistance or fear, but there was nothing. We ate at each other's mouths and I felt his hands everywhere. My back, my sides, my ass. I wedged my knee between his legs and wrapped an arm around his back so I could pull him up against me while I kissed him. His tongue fought mine for control of the kiss, and I gladly handed him his victory and welcomed him into my mouth.

"God, you feel so good, Nate," I said as I tore my mouth from his and pressed kisses against his neck.

He let out a whimper, and I wondered if it was because I'd sucked his skin between my lips so I could leave my mark on him, or because I'd used the shortened version of his name. I didn't really care. All I cared about was him bucking beneath me in an attempt to get closer. I gave him what he wanted and ground my groin against his, and he let out a startled cry.

"Fuck," he whispered and then, to my surprise, he was rolling me onto my back. Though I was caught off guard by the change in position, once his mouth crashed back down on mine, I didn't give it much thought. Nor did I object when his hands closed over my wrists, pinning them to the cool ground. It wasn't often that I gave up control to my partners, but it was the last thing I'd expected from Nathan, and I was more than happy to indulge him. Except for David, all my other partners had been guys who'd carefully orchestrated their responses in ways they'd seemed to think I'd wanted.

But what I wanted was exactly what Nathan was giving me.

Wild, uncontrollable need.

Blind lust.

Even if he'd *wanted* to control his body's reactions, from his blown pupils and writhing body, I doubted he even could at this point.

And it had been mere minutes since I'd kissed him.

When Nathan's lips skimmed down my throat, I closed my eyes and reveled in how good his skin felt where it was touching mine. I loved the heavy weight of his body, and I couldn't get enough of the little moans and whimpers that began slipping unchecked from his throat. I felt his fingers pushing my shirt up and then his mouth was closing over one of my nipples. I let out a hoarse shout that startled him at first, but then a spark of energy lit up his gaze as his eyes searched out mine. After that, he was a man possessed. His mouth explored every bit of skin he could reach without moving off me, and his fingers sifted through my chest hair. It wasn't until his hand drifted over my abdomen that he showed the first signs of hesitation. He was still lying on top of me, but he'd shifted enough so he could watch what he was doing.

His gaze slid down to my groin and the bulge that was urgently pressing against the fabric of my jeans. It seemed to take him forever to finally take that last step and slide his hand down. I couldn't stop myself from bucking up against it when he began rubbing my cock through my pants. His eyes held mine as he continued to caress me with different levels of pressure.

Testing.

Learning.

The air around us grew heavy with something more intense than mere passion. And I was afraid to try to figure out what it was as I stared at Nathan and he stared at me.

I reached up to grab him by the back of the neck and dragged him down for a kiss. Then I was rolling him beneath me. I kissed him long and hard before I eased off and just sipped at his lips.

"Tell me what you want."

His dark eyes held mine. "Everything," was all he said.

My heart leapt into my throat. I knew this was a supremely bad idea, but I also knew I wasn't going to be the one to stop it. He'd have to do that.

I couldn't.

I wouldn't.

I needed this too badly…him. I needed *him* too badly.

"Let's go to my room," I said as I licked over his lower lip before sucking it between my own lips.

Nathan's hands were on the backs of my arms, so when I went to shift off him, he tightened his grip.

"No, here," he said. "I want it to be here."

"Nate-"

"Here, Vincent. Just like this. Please."

He'd had me at Vincent, but I didn't tell him that. Instead, I nodded and then I leaned down to seal my mouth over his.

CHAPTER 15

NATHAN

I was scared shitless. There was just no way around it. Because I knew what I was asking for. And there would be no coming back from it.

I hoped that Vincent couldn't feel the nerves that were threatening to consume me. It was humiliating enough to be the singular person in this encounter who had no clue what to expect. And if it turned out to be anything like the first time I'd had sex with a girl, I wasn't sure what I'd do.

"Tell me what you're thinking," Vincent murmured against my mouth.

"Noth...nothing," I stammered.

"You're shaking like a leaf. And while I'm good, I'm not *that* good," he said with a small smile as he placed soft kisses along my jaw.

I doubted that, because I knew part of the reason I was shaking so bad *was* because of what he was doing to me. Even the mere act of his heavy weight pressing me into the cool, soft grass had all my cylinders firing. Add in the drugging kisses and I was pretty much a goner. If I hadn't been clueless as to what to do next, I would have jumped him for sure.

His lightness caught me off guard, so I didn't have time to shore up my defenses.

"I was thinking about my first time." At his questioning look, I quickly said, "With a girl."

A light rumble of laughter went through him. "I'm definitely losing my touch."

It took me a moment to realize what he was saying, and I let out a bark of laughter as I realized what my statement must have sounded like. The humor helped ease some of the tension, and I flopped my head back on the grass and closed my eyes.

"Sorry," I muttered. "I'm messing this up."

Vincent suddenly ground his hips against mine, causing our cocks to slide over one another. I let out a sharp moan.

"Unless you tell me to fuck off, I'm not going anywhere." His fingers skirted through my hair and then he kissed me again. "Talk to me, Nate."

I sighed. This definitely wasn't the way I'd thought this would go. With me about to spill the details about one of the most humiliating nights of my life. "When Brody came out to me, he told me what losing his virginity to his girlfriend had been like. He was so upset about it." Since I didn't want to get into the details of that night, I bypassed the rest of the conversation I'd had with Brody and said, "What he said stuck with me for a long time. I kept putting off having sex with my high school girlfriend – I always had some excuse– I was too busy with football or some academic event or church obligations. I didn't actually go through with it until I was in college. Sophomore year. I thought once I got into it more, it would be okay…that my body would start acting…normal."

I could feel the heat rising in my cheeks. "Nothing she did got me…hard. So, she suggested we watch some porn."

As I spoke, Vincent lifted off me enough so he could put some of his weight on his bent arm. His finger kept stroking up and down my cheek, occasionally straying to my lips. It helped relax me, though I couldn't look him in the eye as I talked.

"The porn worked, but not for the right reasons."

"You were watching the guy, and not the girl."

I swallowed past the lump in my throat and nodded. "I made her leave the video running so I could watch...him. It was the only thing that made it bearable." Tears pricked the backs of my eyes as I said, "Afterwards I finally understood what Brody had been trying to tell me. It felt like I'd been..." I choked back a sob and then Vincent was leaning over me, pressing his forehead against mine.

"It's okay, baby," he said softly.

The endearment had me turning into him and burying my face against his chest. I felt his hand come up to cradle the back of my head. I managed to stifle the gut-wrenching sobs that were threatening to consume me, but when Vincent kissed my temple and said, "Let it out, Nate," I was helpless to stop any of it. I clutched his shirt between my fingers as I sobbed into the fabric, soaking it within a matter of seconds. Vincent kept murmuring things in my ear, but I couldn't really make out the words.

But it didn't matter. I had what I needed.

Permission.

To feel.

To rage.

To accept.

At some point after the worst had passed, Vincent eased me onto my back and used his fingers to skim my face. "What am I going to do with you?" he whispered, and then his mouth closed over mine. The kiss was sweet and tender and didn't last long. "Let's go inside. We don't have to do this tonight."

He was giving me an out that part of me wanted to take, but it was the part of me that was scared to take this final step. This step where I'd finally be admitting who I really was. It was something I couldn't come back from, and it would change my life forever. I'd hidden for so long because I hadn't been as strong and as brave as my brother. I wasn't sure that had changed. But looking up at Vincent, seeing the patience and tenderness in his normally hard eyes, feeling his weight pressing me into the hard earth...how could I not want this? How could I not want this feeling of rightness in my life? Yes, it would change everything, but the reality was, I'd already started to change. It had begun the night I'd cast the person I loved more than anything in this world out of my life.

"No," I whispered as I lifted my fingers to toy with his hair. "I've been waiting for this moment my whole life. I'm not going back."

He was breathing hard against me, despite the fact that our passion had cooled. It gave me hope that it meant he was feeling things that weren't just about sex. I knew it would just complicate the hell out of things, but I still wanted it.

Him.

I didn't give him a chance to answer. Instead, I reached up and clasped the back of his head and pulled him down for another kiss. As soon as his mouth touched mine, I let my tongue slide over his lips, asking for permission. He granted it, and then our tongues were stroking over each other in greeting. I groaned as he shifted his weight onto me completely, and when his knee pushed between my legs, I opened for him. I moaned into his mouth as he settled between my legs and his cock ground against mine. The position should have made me feel awkward and vulnerable, but it didn't.

It made me feel...wanted.

Like he couldn't get close enough.

I'd had this image in my head that as soon as I told him I wanted him, I'd end up on all fours with him shoving into me from behind. But this...this was...perfect.

Perfect, but not enough.

"More," I moaned as he began rolling his hips against mine and his mouth latched onto my ear.

"Gonna give you everything, baby," Vincent growled. "Just like you wanted."

He shifted up and moved his legs so he was straddling my hips, effectively pinning my lower half to the ground. He reached over his shoulder and tugged his T-shirt off. I'd already seen his chest in the motel room, but up close, it just took my breath away. Tanned skin, rigid muscles, chest hair...and it was all mine.

I surged up so I was in a sitting position, and Vincent shifted backwards enough to give me room. I wrapped my arms around him and then slid my hands up and down his back, losing myself in the feel of his hot skin. I didn't know what possessed me to do it, but I pressed my nose against the middle of his sternum and drew in a deep breath. He smelled of musk and sweat and man. I let my tongue flick out to taste his skin. Vincent's hand came up to capture my head and hold me to him. I pressed my fingers into the hard muscles of his back and then flicked my tongue over his nipple. His reaction was immediate and unmistakable. He moaned and his fingers tightened in my hair. I sucked on him gently and then played with the other nipple. He let me have my way, but then I felt his hand smoothing down my back. As his hand moved back up, he pulled my shirt with it and then suddenly he was pulling it over my head, forcing me to release my hold on him. Since it was a button-down shirt, the whole thing was awkward, but Vincent didn't seem to care, because he jerked it off and tossed it aside. Then he was grabbing my face and his tongue surged between my lips.

His hand slid down my back again, hot and heavy on my skin. He kept right on kissing me, even as his fingers slid beneath the waistband of my pants. It should have freaked me out to feel his hand so intimately pressed to me, but all it did was make me want more.

"Want you so bad," he breathed against my mouth.

I nodded, because I was panting too hard to actually speak. God, we'd barely done anything and I felt like I was going to come in my pants.

Vincent's weight pressed me back down into the grass and then he was sliding his lips down my body. I kept my hands on his shoulders, more to ground myself than anything else, as he worked his way down my chest, then my abdomen. His mouth was setting me on fire where he touched me. When he finally reached the button of my jeans, I held my breath. But instead of opening my pants, he began palming my cock through the fabric.

"Jesus," I whispered, and then I was covering my eyes with my hands because it just felt so damn good. I tried to think of anything else besides how badly I needed to come, but when Vincent called my name, all other thoughts disappeared and I dropped my hands so I could look at him.

"Keep your eyes on me," he ordered.

I would obey the order even if it killed me. It wasn't like I could have looked away, anyway. His dark eyes were so heavy with hunger that they were pulling me in, drowning me in their depths.

I did as Vincent said as he worked my pants open. I barely managed to keep my eyes on his when his big hand closed around my aching cock. I wanted to look down to see him holding me, but I was trapped in his gaze. So it was his eyes I followed down as he lowered his head. He didn't even break the connection when his mouth reached my dick, which he was still stroking with one hand.

I knew what he was going to do. I knew it and I wanted it and I was fucking terrified. I knew it wouldn't be like that night when Jennifer had taken me into her mouth in a last-ditch effort to get me in the mood. No, this time I was terrified because if he touched me with that sinful mouth, I'd blow.

"I won't last," I croaked when I felt his warm breath skitter over my crown.

"You don't need to," Vincent whispered. "Just feel, Nate."

I cried out when he ran the flat of his tongue over my crown and I fisted my fingers in the grass. Sensation rocketed throughout my entire body. "Please!" I shouted.

I wasn't sure what I was asking for. His tongue on more of me, his mouth…I just knew it wasn't enough. Pleasure crawled up my spine as he licked up the length of my shaft and then across the head again, but when his mouth closed over my dick, I was a goner. I shouted as my orgasm ripped into me, violent and unforgiving. Vincent sucked hard on me as I fed him my release. The added pressure had me bucking up into his mouth as I grabbed hold of his head to hold him in place as I ruthlessly fucked the hot, wet cavern of his mouth. The climax seemed to go on forever before I felt my muscles unlock and I sank back into the grass. I was dimly aware of Vincent's mouth releasing me with a pop, but I couldn't find the energy to look down. He climbed up my body, but I couldn't move. I couldn't even raise my arms so that I could touch him.

I opened my mouth to tell him I was sorry for my lack of control, but then his tongue was there and something else…something warm and salty and bitter. It was just a few drops, but I knew what it was.

It should have revolted me. I'd had blow jobs from exactly two women in my life and neither had kissed me afterwards. So the taste of myself was foreign and strange and very unexpected. But I didn't pull away, and I didn't feel disgusted. What I felt was unbelievable, considering what I'd just been through.

Desire.

Fast and hot.

And no, my body hadn't completely caught up yet, but I could already feel my dick stirring as Vincent kissed me, his sweetness mixed with the tang of my release. I somehow found the energy to return the kiss. He took his time kissing me and then he was exploring my neck again. Then every other part of my body. And all the while I could feel his hardness pressing against me.

But not once did I feel like he just wanted to turn me over and shove into me. I didn't know what to make of that. I'd expected fucking…or at the very least, sex. They were the only terms I could think of to describe the act of getting off with another person. I'd thought that was all Vincent had wanted, even if I'd secretly hoped it would be more. But how could I call what he was doing to me sex? It was so much more.

"Vincent," I murmured as I shook my head. His name sounded like a question more than anything else, and he returned to my mouth.

"Do you want to stop?" he asked. The question wasn't asked with anger or worry…it was asked with such gentleness that I felt something in my chest spark to life. But I was afraid to try and identify it, even if deep down, I knew what it was.

I shook my head.

"You sure?"

"I'm sure."

"Good," he said as he placed a soft kiss on my lips. "Because I need inside of you so badly right now…"

His words dropped off and I felt him stroking my hair. I nodded. "Yes."

I couldn't manage anything else, mostly because of what I might end up saying. And as gentle and as sweet as he was being, I needed to remember this really was still just sex.

Even if that little piece of my heart that I'd just lost to him wanted it to be so very much more than that.

CHAPTER 16

VINCENT

I should have been able to stop. I should have been able to climb off of him, take him by the hand, and lead him back to the house. I should have been able to leave him at his door with a few words about how what we'd done couldn't happen again…that things couldn't, no, shouldn't, go any further.

I didn't do any of that, of course. Not after the stunning man beneath me, eyes shining with a mix of satisfaction and renewed hunger, had spoken that one little word giving me permission to take everything he was offering. No, instead I began kissing him again because I just couldn't get enough of how his mouth moved perfectly beneath mine.

He gave.

He took.

He was with me one hundred percent and he put every part of himself into those kisses. I knew he was nervous; how could he not be? But it wasn't enough to stop him. I'd given him so many outs that he could have taken any one of them and I would have let him walk away.

But he was still here, his hard body pressing up against mine, trying to get closer.

I could feel his cock growing hard against mine and I cursed the fabric separating us. I reared back and quickly climbed to my feet so I could shuck the rest of my clothes. I half expected him to just lie there, but he shocked me when he quickly scrambled out of his pants. I nearly tripped in my eagerness to escape my clothing, but when I saw Nathan's hand move to his cock to begin stroking it as he watched me undress, I nearly came then and there.

Fuck, how the hell was I going to stay in control long enough to make this good for him?

I barely managed to remember to grab the condom and packet of lube from my wallet before I fell to my knees in front of him and just drank in the sight of him. Legs splayed, fingers gripping his rock-hard dick, chest rising and falling with heavy breaths, eyes twinkling with a mix of excitement and fear.

"Nathan-"

"Don't," he cut in, and then he was sitting up. "Don't you dare give me another out."

His fingers curled around the back of my head and then he was pulling me to his mouth for a searing kiss. "I'm so very ready, Vincent," he murmured against my lips. "I've been waiting so long for this…for you."

I knew I shouldn't put more behind the words than he'd meant, but that was exactly what I did as I pushed him down into the grass and settled my weight on top of him. He might have meant he'd been waiting for someone like me, but that dark, lonely part of my heart that had appeared after I'd lost David chose to believe he really did mean me.

I took my time kissing Nathan before I worked my way down his body. I let my fingers skim over the bruise on his side, but I didn't let them linger because I didn't want to be reminded of how close I'd come to losing him.

Losing him?

He wasn't fucking mine.

I needed to remember that.

"Vincent, please," Nathan cried out as I licked over the ridges of his abdomen, tasting both the remnants of his cum and the sweetness of the pre-cum that was streaming from the head of his dick. I looked up to see that he was on the verge of losing it. I wasn't doing much better.

"Turn over," I said as I used my hands to urge him onto his stomach. He hesitated for the briefest of moments, likely because his nerves were starting to take over. But he did it, and I sat back enough so I could take in the sight of his gorgeous back and perfectly-shaped ass. I wished like hell I'd managed to talk him into going back to the house for this encounter because the light was fading fast and I felt like I needed hours just to get my fill of him visually. But it wasn't like my dick was going to wait patiently in the wings.

I settled over his back, leaving no space between us, my cock nestled against his ass. As I nibbled on the back of his neck and along his collarbone, I shifted my hips until my dick was actually in his crease. Enough moisture was seeping from the head of my dick that it only took a few glides between his firm muscles to distribute the natural lubricant.

Nathan's arms were folded beneath him, supporting his head. I stole kisses now and then, but mostly focused on letting my shaft brush back and forth over his hole. Within a matter of minutes, Nathan was humping the ground beneath him. Since I knew he'd likely end up making himself come that way, I forced myself to sit up and straddled his muscular thighs as I searched out the packet of lube. My fingers shook as I got some of the cool substance on them. I braced myself so that my face was near Nathan's as I rubbed the pad of my thumb over his entrance. The position allowed me to see and hear the things he wasn't saying. Not that he needed to say anything, considering his whole body had locked up tight as soon as I'd placed my finger against him.

"Relax, baby. Just feel, okay?"

He nodded and I felt him take in a really deep breath. I kept my touch light as I played with his opening. I placed kisses along his shoulder, neck, and cheek as I gently massaged him. When he began pushing against my finger, I knew he was finally letting himself enjoy the sensation rather than getting hung up in the anticipation of what was coming.

I murmured inconsequential things in his ear, but it wasn't until he turned his head and hungrily sought out my mouth that I knew he was ready for more. I kissed him deeply just as I pushed my finger inside of him. He hissed into my mouth and squeezed his eyes shut.

"Just breathe, Nate," I whispered as I stilled my hand.

He nodded and did as I said. I'd only bottomed on a few occasions, but I still remembered my first time and everything it had entailed. David and I had still been incredibly young when we'd started having sex, so our inexperience had worked against us in a lot of ways. We hadn't understood the concept of taking it slow and preparing each other…we'd just been too eager to be together in every way.

As badly as I wanted Nathan, I wasn't that naïve, inexperienced kid. I waited until Nathan's body stopped fighting before I added a bit more pressure. Just as he tensed up again, I pulled my finger out a little and then pushed forward.

"Fuck," Nathan moaned.

My heart surged into my throat when Nathan's fingers suddenly closed around mine where I had my hand pressed against the ground by his head. I let him link our hands and then I leaned down and kissed him hard.

"So fucking beautiful, Nate," I said softly, and then I pushed my finger deep inside of him. Another guttural moan tore free of Nathan's throat, but he kissed me back without hesitation. I was deep enough to search out the bundle of nerves I knew would change the game entirely. The second I rubbed over his prostate, Nathan let out a ragged shout and bucked his hips up against my finger. I managed not to plunge any deeper into him. As I began massaging him, he let out little grunts and groans.

"Vincent, I need…I need…"

I kissed him. "I know what you need, baby," I said against his mouth, and then I pushed my finger all the way inside of him. He cried out, but not in pain. I pulled my finger out, then plunged it right back in.

"Yes! God, yes!" he shouted as he tried to push back against me. I'd settled more of my weight onto his back, so I was truly in control now. I nipped, licked, and sucked every piece of skin I could reach with my mouth as I began finger-fucking him in earnest. He barely seemed to notice when I added a second finger. The words falling from his lips made no sense, but I understood exactly what he was saying.

As much as I would have liked to make him come again just by using my fingers, my body wasn't patient enough. Nathan was young enough that he'd likely recover quickly enough that we could go for round three without too much preparation, but I wasn't as certain of my own libido.

Even though I was currently more turned on than I'd been in in a really long time.

Maybe ever.

I dropped my mouth to Nathan's ear as I stilled my fingers in his ass. "Tell me you still want it, Nate. I can make you come like this," I said as I pressed against his gland.

He let out a harsh curse. "No," he gasped. "You! It has to be you."

I understood what he was saying and was so damn glad that I gave him another hard press that had him stifling a cry of pleasure against his forearm. I eased off him and carefully pulled my fingers free of his body. It took just seconds to get the condom on and the rest of the lube slathered over my rock-hard shaft. I used my hands to split Nathan's ass open, but it was too damn dark for me to see anything. I gripped my cock in my hand and maneuvered it to his hole.

"Bear down on me, okay?"

Nathan had gone tense as soon as I'd pulled my fingers out of his body, but he nodded in agreement. As I began putting pressure on his entrance, I felt him push back against me. He let out a ragged gasp as my crown slipped past his outer muscles. I carefully laid down over his back, my body covering his like a blanket.

"So hot," I said as I sifted my fingers into his hair and pulled his head up so I could kiss him. It was an animalistic move, one of ownership and dominance, but I didn't care.

He was mine.

He'd been mine from the moment he'd told me yes.

I let his body adjust for several long seconds before I slid more of myself inside of him.

"Fuck," he ground out.

"Hurts so good, doesn't it?" I asked.

He nodded. "Need more."

I knew the sensations he was experiencing. Even as his body fought the intrusion, it wanted more. The stretch, the burn, even the pain to some degree.

I slid farther into him as I kissed him hard and deep. "So perfect, baby. Like you were made just for me," I whispered.

He nodded.

I wanted to believe it was agreement, but I knew I was reading too much into it. He was overwhelmed by what was happening to him. It could have been anyone doing this to him and he wouldn't have known the difference.

The thought made me unreasonably angry.

"Open your eyes, Nathan," I demanded.

He immediately did and they locked on mine.

"Whose body is this?" I growled as I bottomed out inside of him.

Nathan let out a harsh moan, and I had to repeat my question. I knew I was being too aggressive as I kept his head at an awkward angle so I could see his expression, but it was like I was battling some unseen force.

"Whose?" I repeated for a third time when I pulled nearly all the way out of his body.

"Yours, Vincent!" he cried. "It's yours!"

I rewarded him with a hard surge that had him screaming in ecstasy. I released his head, but to my surprise, he kept it elevated so he could look at me. Something deep inside of me cracked wide open at what this man was giving me.

So much more than just his body.

His trust.

His vulnerability.

Him.

God, I could see everything in his eyes.

"Christ," I whispered even as I began to thrust into him with hard, heavy drags. The pressure was so fucking intense that I was sure I wouldn't last long enough to get him off.

And those eyes.

I needed to look away.

This was supposed to be sex…fucking, damn it! Nothing more.

I shook my head as I kissed him. Who the hell did I think I was kidding?

"Need to see you," I snarled, and then I pulled out of him. I had him on his back in one swift move. I used my arms to lift his legs high and wide and shoved into him hard, my body desperate for relief. Nathan's body was splayed wide open as I began fucking him harder than I'd intended. But I saw no sign of pain or fear. His fingers were wrapped around my wrists where I had my hands planted on the ground next to his sides.

"Can't stop," I tried to explain.

He shook his head. "It's…it's not enough," he admitted.

The unexpected words surprised me.

"Need all of you, Vincent," he demanded, and then his hand was snaking up to grab the back of my head. He pulled me down for a kiss.

And just like that I gave up and stopped trying to keep the last vestiges of myself apart from him.

CHAPTER 17

NATHAN

I was so fucking scared.

By how good it felt. And not just the feel of Vincent's thickness rippling inside of me.

I'd known something was missing once I'd gotten past the pain of Vincent's entry into my body. Along with the pain, there'd been the uncomfortable burning and stretching as my body had tried to accept his, but once it had passed, the only thing that had kept going through my mind as he'd begun thrusting in and out of me had been a singular word.

More.

A small part of me had shattered when Vincent had turned me over so he could take me from behind. I'd had no idea why it had mattered, but it had. And now that he was facing me, I knew why.

Because face to face meant I could see everything. And I saw the exact moment Vincent stopped trying to hold himself apart from me. His gorgeous eyes had gone dark with more than just lust, and when I pulled him down for a kiss even as he continued to drive into me, I finally felt it.

That *more* I'd been seeking.

But not just more…everything.

"It's so good, Vincent," I whispered against his mouth as I wrapped my arms around his hot, sweaty back. I felt raw and vulnerable. Somehow, I'd lost all control...of my body, of my feelings. Maybe that was why I'd needed to see all of Vincent. Maybe I needed to know I wasn't the only one going through this.

Vincent's lips gently skimmed my jaw and then settled over the pulse point on my neck. He had to be feeling how rapidly my heart was beating. Like it was going to pound out of my chest at any moment.

His fingers tangled in my hair, gripping me hard as he continued to plunge in and out of my body in long, smooth glides. Every few strokes he'd shift his body just enough so he could hit that spot inside of me that had me seeing stars.

"Need to come," I whimpered. I was so close, my body hanging right over the precipice. I'd had orgasms before, but this...this was so much more. It was like my body was finally waiting to be set free after so many years of being locked away.

"Come, baby," Vincent growled as he settled his mouth against mine. "Need to see you."

He was there with me. All in. And I loved it. His words were giving me so much more than permission to let my body feel something that it had been denied for so long.

I could feel tears sliding from my eyes as Vincent slowed his movements and carefully slid the head of his dick against the spot. I began nodding frantically because my pleasure increased tenfold every time he did it. I locked my ankles around his ass, digging them into his flexing muscles as he surged in and out of me. My fingers scrambled for purchase along his hot, wet back.

And then it happened.

I screamed in relief as the coil of need inside of me snapped and flung me over the edge. I couldn't speak or breathe. All I could do was feel as wave after wave of agonizing sensation flayed my body alive in the best way. I was dimly aware of Vincent murmuring things into my ear, but I couldn't be sure of anything he actually said. His dick pulsed and throbbed inside of me as my body clamped down on his and then he was ramming into me hard, driving my pleasure higher in sharp, angry spikes.

It almost became too much.

Almost.

But as Vincent yelled my name, my nickname, I managed to open my eyes. I saw the muscles of his neck straining as he braced himself above me. His arms were once again holding his body above mine as he plowed into me, and I saw his eyes watching where our bodies were connected. I looked down long enough to see his dick spearing in and out of me. He let out an angry curse and then a shout of relief as he shoved into me hard. His body collapsed on mine and he wrapped his arms around my upper body, clinging to me like I was his lifeline. He jerked against me, his cock shoving into me in short, jerky thrusts over and over as he rode out his orgasm. Bursts of energy danced beneath my skin as my own orgasm continued to surge beneath my skin.

I lost all track of time as Vincent fucked into me over and over. By the time his body slowed and all his weight settled onto me, I couldn't move. I managed to hang onto him with my arms, but that was it. My breath was seesawing in and out of me, and I felt so hot I was sure I was going to burst into flames. Vincent's length still filled me and every once in a while he'd let out a little moan as his body jerked inside of mine. I eventually managed to regain my senses enough to lift one arm enough to cradle the back of his head. I pressed kisses against his temple, but didn't say anything.

What was I supposed to say?

Thank you?

Those words were hardly enough for what he'd just done to me...given me.

The sounds of the night returned slowly, as did the coolness of the ground beneath me and the mugginess of the air surrounding us. I knew we needed to go inside, but I was reluctant to move.

Because reality was returning like a vengeful bitch who'd decided she'd been gone just long enough that you got to see what life could be like without her.

Vincent shifted somewhat, and then he was using his arms to lift himself off me. He reached between our bodies and it was then that I realized I'd come without him or me even touching my dick. Vincent grabbed the edge of the condom and slowly pulled out of me.

I instantly felt empty.

And cold.

And not just from the cum that had pooled on my belly and chest.

God, I'd just let a man fuck me.

In his backyard.

On the ground.

I waited for Vincent to say something…anything, that would make those other facts irrelevant, but I knew no such words would be forthcoming when he said, "We should go inside and get cleaned up."

Humiliation coursed through me as I nodded and sat up. I grabbed for my jeans, bypassing my underwear, and began tugging them on, not watching as Vincent pulled the condom off. My throat was threatening to close off my breathing altogether, so I quickly stood and put my back to Vincent. My ass hurt like a son of a bitch, but despite the shame rolling through me, the lingering effects of the orgasm were making it hard for me to function. I managed to get my pants pulled up and my shirt on, though it ended up being inside out.

He didn't say a thing.

Not one goddamn thing.

My fingers shook as I tried to get the button closed on my pants, but I couldn't manage it. Even the zipper proved to be too much for me, and a humiliating sob tore free of my throat.

I felt him behind me, but he didn't touch me.

"Nathan," he said quietly as he came around me.

Nathan, not Nate.

Not *baby*.

I couldn't swallow, couldn't breathe. My heart felt like it was going to pound right out of my damn chest.

When he reached for my pants, presumably to help me fasten them, I jerked away from him. "Don't," I croaked, because that was all I could get out. And then I was pushing past him, wiping at the tears that had started to fall without my permission. I nearly tripped over Mickey as the cat raced past me towards the house. Minnie hopped off the lounger and headed for the door before I reached it, and both cats followed me up the stairs and to my room. I was oddly grateful for their company as I shut the door behind me and went to the bathroom. I got the shower going and began stripping my clothes off.

That was when I made the mistake of looking in the mirror.

I gasped at the sight of myself.

My hair was mussed, probably from the many times Vincent had grabbed me to demand I give him the answers he wanted. He'd been so dominant, forceful...

My body began to react to the memory and how much I'd loved the way he'd manhandled me. At the same time, he'd been so incredibly gentle.

I shook my head as I took in the rest of my appearance. My lips were glistening and swollen from all of Vincent's kisses, and there were grass stains covering my entire body. There was blood, too, but I knew it wasn't mine. At some point Vincent's injured hand had likely started to bleed again, and he hadn't noticed or cared. The sight should have sickened me, but it didn't.

Knowing how badly he'd wanted me...

Finger-sized bruises marred my skin, too, and I couldn't help but run my fingers over them. Who would have thought having such an aggressive, dominant lover would have made me feel so safe and wanted...needed?

My eyes fell to the streaks of cum that my clothes hadn't soaked up, and I was instantly reminded of the powerful orgasm that had held me in its grip for so long. Even now, I wanted it again. I wanted Vincent to walk into that bathroom and wrap his arms around me.

God, when had I become so needy?

Anger surged through me and I stepped towards the shower. I needed to just forget this night had ever happened. It had been a terrible mistake, and now it was over. This whole thing would be over soon and I could go back to my life. I'd spend however many days it took for Vincent to figure all this shit out and get rid of the guy trying to kill me, and then I'd go back to being Nathan Wilder, budding politician.

Yeah, that's what I'd do.

Fuck Vincent St. James, and fuck all this shit he'd made me feel.

Nothing had changed.

Nothing.

CHAPTER 18

VINCENT

Jesus, how the fuck had I let this happen?

I dropped my head against the tile wall as I tried to make sense of what I'd just done. I'd fucked a man…no, a goddamn virgin…in my backyard under the cover of falling darkness, not caring one whit about what had been going on around me. Hell, the whole world had ceased to exist the second I'd buried myself inside of Nathan's beautiful body.

And God, that orgasm…

I shook my head. I could still feel the aftereffects of the damn thing. I was physically exhausted, and the pleasurable sensation that lingered beneath my skin warred with my mind about how incredibly stupid the whole thing had been. Nathan was a client. A goddamn favor!

I winced as I remembered the sob that had torn free of his throat when I'd tried to help him do up his pants.

I'd been such an ass just to pull out of him like that and pretend the whole thing hadn't happened. Or that the orgasm hadn't done something to me I'd never felt before.

Not even with David.

Guilt tore through me at that, and I sent David yet another silent apology.

I'd never felt particularly guilty for sleeping with guys after losing David, because it had just been cheap sex that hadn't meant anything. Hell, it was the same thing as when I jacked off on my own. I'd been taking care of a biological need and nothing more.

I shook my head because none of that shit mattered. Even if I wanted to start something with Nathan – and I didn't – it wasn't even an option. Not with the life I led.

And most certainly not with his.

The man stood for everything I hated.

So why wasn't that enough to have me calling up Ronan and telling him to get someone else to figure all this shit out? It certainly would have been the smart thing to do.

I placed my hands flat against the tile and let the water slide over my back. My skin stung where Nathan had scratched me as he'd clung to me. It hadn't been enough to draw blood or anything, but I'd seen the angry red marks up and down my back and even on my ass where he'd grabbed onto me. The man was incredibly responsive, but damn, when he wanted something…

I cursed the smile that crept across my mouth.

I was so preoccupied that I didn't even notice the cool air at first. When I did, I knew where it was coming from and I knew there was no threat to me.

At least not the kind that I knew how to handle.

I looked over my shoulder and saw Nathan standing just outside the shower door, his hand still on the handle. His eyes were plastered to my back. He was still a mess with his hair sticking up all over the place and his body covered in stains. I should have been horrified to know I'd gotten some blood on him, but the sight turned me on.

God, I was a sick bastard.

I waited to see what he would do, because truth be told, I was stunned to see him standing there, completely naked and very much turned on if his hardening dick was anything to go by. His eyes shifted to mine and I slowly turned around. I'd already been hard, but seeing him standing there with the proof of how well I'd loved him still lingering on his body, sent me to a whole other level. I was certain he'd run when he got a look at me, but the hunger in his eyes had me second-guessing myself. I'd been so sure he'd go hide out in his room like I was, and we'd pretend this whole thing had never happened.

We both hung there for several long seconds and then he was stepping into the shower, a look of determination in his eyes that had all my cylinders firing.

The shower door snicked into place as he held there for a moment and then he was pushing into my arms, his mouth seeking out mine. Despite the promise I'd made to myself that I wouldn't touch him again, I instantly wrapped my arms around him.

"Everything's changed," he whispered against my mouth. "Can't go back...don't want to," he added, and then his tongue surged past my lips. I kissed him hard and pulled him flush with my body.

I didn't care what he was saying or why he was there or that I should be sending him back to his room. I didn't listen to my brain warning me that doing this would just cause more problems between us.

No, I let my hands slide up and down his body, trying to memorize the feel of him as if I hadn't just spent the past hour lost in his body.

Hell, I'd need a lifetime to get my fill of him.

Except I didn't have a lifetime. I barely had tonight. So I needed to make use of every second. I let my hand slip between our bodies and then I was taking us both in hand. I kept kissing him as I gripped our dicks in my fist and brought us to a quick and pleasurable end. Nathan cried out against my mouth as he came, and I followed mere seconds later. I reveled in the way his arms went around my shoulders as we rode out our orgasms. At some point, his fingers gently began toying with one of the large scratches on my shoulder blade.

"Sorry," he murmured against my skin.

"Unless you're sorry they're not deeper, shut up," I said softly as I kissed him and then gently pushed him so his back was flush with the wall. I reached up to adjust the showerhead so most of the spray was hitting him and then I took my time washing his body. Most of the blood and grass stains washed away instantly, but I was shocked to find I'd left bruises all over his body where I'd pressed my fingers into him just a bit too hard. I didn't even remember being that rough with him.

"Nate, I'm sor-"

His finger came up to press against my lips. "Unless you're sorry there aren't more of them, shut up," he said with a smile.

I chuckled and then leaned in to kiss him. He took his turn cleaning me up and by the time we were done, we were both hard again. When Nathan's fingers tentatively searched out my dick, I showed him exactly how much pressure to exert as I closed my hand around his throbbing length. This time I came first and Nathan was the one to follow. When we were once again clean, we got out of the shower and dried off. Nathan hadn't brought any clothes with him, so he wrapped a towel around his hips. I didn't bother with a towel or any other clothing. Nathan's body flushed a pretty shade of pink as he took in the sight of me, and then he swallowed hard and turned to leave the bathroom.

He hesitated once he reached my bedroom, and I didn't miss the way his eyes settled briefly on my bed and then the door to the room. Considering the balls it had taken to walk into my room and then my bathroom uninvited, I fully expected him to head for my bed. But insecurity must have taken over because he began heading towards the door. It would have been easier to just let him go, but I wasn't interested in easy…at least not tonight.

I snagged his hand and led him to the bed. I heard the tiniest sigh of relief escape his lips as he followed me, and when I pulled back the covers and got rid of his towel, he crawled between the sheets.

A momentary twinge of guilt went through me at what I was about to do, but I quelled it and climbed in after him.

I hadn't shared this house or even this bed with David, but I'd also never spent the night with another man since his death. And since I'd only ever been in a relationship with David, that meant I'd never actually *slept* with another man. And here I was about to do it for the second time with Nathan.

I didn't know what that meant, but none of it was good for me…or him.

God, this was so fucked up.

But that didn't stop me from pressing my front to Nathan's back as I curled my body around his. My arm went around his waist and I didn't relax until his fingers covered mine where they were resting on his chest. I could feel his heart pounding beneath my hand. My dick was lodged against his ass and though I was turned on, my body had finally had enough and my cock remained only half-hard.

"Did I hurt you?" I asked as Nathan played with our fingers where they were linked over his chest.

He was quiet for so long that I was sure he wasn't going to answer. But then he whispered, "I think you broke something inside of me, Vincent." I felt my insides clench at that until he lifted my uninjured hand to his lips and pressed a gentle kiss against my palm. "Thank you," he said so quietly, I barely heard him. He clenched my hand with his and then he was out, his breathing evening out to indicate he'd found some peace in sleep.

Lucky bastard.

Because those few words had pretty much ensured I wouldn't be as fortunate tonight.

CHAPTER 19

NATHAN

A cold, wet nose was pressed against my neck while a soft, hairy tail was flicking against my mouth. It wasn't the best way to wake up, but certainly not the worst, either. The best would have been to feel Vincent's lips on the back of my neck and his thick cock buried deep inside of me. Despite my sore ass, I would have welcomed him sliding into my body again. Less than twelve hours had passed since he'd pushed his thickness inside of me, and I was feeling the loss. I'd come more in the last few hours than I had in the last year, but it wasn't enough. Even if he'd just gotten me off with his hand like he had in the shower or in the early morning hours as he'd slid his dick between the crease of my ass and humped against me as he'd jerked me to completion, I would have been more than happy. But it had been far too long since I'd felt that sense of satisfaction come over me.

I knew without looking that Vincent wasn't in bed with me anymore. I used my hand to push Mickey's tail out of my face so I could check the clock on the nightstand. It was barely after nine in the morning. Not particularly late, but late for me. I couldn't allow myself to get used to this – the long nights of pleasure, the sleeping in, the not needing to answer Preston's endless calls or prepare myself for the next interview or speech.

Even though certain parts of my life could never go back to the way they'd been, I still had a life to get back to. It had just become a hell of a lot more complicated in the past twenty-four hours.

I let my fingers slide through Mickey's fur for a moment as I thought about the young man who'd likely named the cat and his sister. I still hadn't seen any pictures of David, but I was more than curious now to know what kind of man had held Vincent's heart for so long. Of course, part of me didn't really want to know, because I'd never be able to compete with what they'd had.

And the fact that I was even thinking about it that way – like I was competing for something that belonged to a dead man – was too fucked up to consider for too long.

I carefully sat up, forcing the cat to move away. He gave me an irritated look and then jumped off the bed and stalked from the room, his tail high and proud. I glanced around the bedroom, admiring it in the light of day since I'd barely noticed it the night before when I'd stormed into Vincent's room, not caring about his privacy in the least. I still couldn't believe the sight that had greeted me in that shower.

I could feel the color rising in my cheeks as I once again saw all the scratch marks I'd left on Vincent's back…and farther south.

I chuckled to myself as I remembered how Virginia used to always accuse me of being cold in bed.

If she only knew…

Vincent's room, like the rest of the house, had a certain sterility about it. Mostly because it lacked anything personal. It was done in mainly white and black colors, and there were no pictures on the walls or any of the furnishings. He had a huge bookshelf along one wall that was stocked full of books to the point it almost looked messy. I got up and went to look at some of the titles and then smiled to myself as I realized what they were.

Children's novels…old ones. The classics.

There were endless copies of books from the *Hardy Boys* series, *Nancy Drew*, and *The Black Stallion*. They were carefully organized in order and most of then looked old and worn, like they'd been read dozens and dozens of times. There was a shelf with some more modern mystery and horror books, but most of the bookcase had the older, children's collections. I carefully pulled one of the *Hardy Boys* books out and flipped it open. The inside cover had a short missive scrawled inside of it.

For David.

Always...Vincent.

My heart broke at the short note and when I checked a few more books, I saw the same message. Not in all of the books, but in many of them.

I quickly returned the books as they'd been. What had started off as simple curiosity left me with mixed feelings, and I hurriedly made my way back to my room to get dressed. I could smell the telltale signs of bacon cooking and coffee brewing, so I pulled on a pair of sweats and a T-shirt from my bag. I'd really need to do laundry soon, because most of my clothes were either covered in grass stains or the proof of my sexual awakening.

I smiled to myself as I hurried to the bathroom to use the toilet and brush my teeth. I still looked a mess, but in a well-used kind of way, and I had no particular desire to change anything about my mussed-up hair or flushed skin. It wasn't like Vincent didn't know what he'd turned me into. God knew he'd had me begging for release often enough in the past few hours as he'd jacked me off while spewing his cum all over my ass. I hadn't even been functional enough to participate in him cleaning me up with a washcloth.

But the second I stepped into the kitchen, I realized I most definitely should have taken the time to get cleaned up. Because standing at the stove was not the dark-haired, hard man who'd somehow wormed his way beneath my skin in the span of a matter of days.

Nope, I was staring at the now familiar back of my idol.

"Ah, Nathan, good morning," Everett said when he turned around. He was wearing a simple black apron that was protecting his dress clothes from the bacon that was sputtering in a pool of grease on the stove.

"Mr. President," I said as I quickly ran my fingers through my hair.

"What did I tell you about that Mr. President nonsense last night?" Everett chided as he began searching out a couple of plates.

Two plates.

Damn. Where was Vincent?

"Where is he?" I asked before I could think better of it.

Everett's sharp eyes held mine for a moment. "He had some things to do this morning and asked me to stop by and keep you company." Everett's eyes went past me and I turned to spy Nash standing in the hallway leading towards the garage. The younger man's eyes met Everett's, but I couldn't discern the expression in his gaze as they stared at each other. My eyes fell to the gun sticking out from Nash's jacket.

I swallowed hard. Vincent had let the man into his house armed.

Even after all the crap that had gone down yesterday when Nash had refused to put his weapons in the trunk.

"Where is he?" I asked again, hating the twinge of worry that seeped into my voice.

"I don't know," Everett said with a sigh, and then he was turning off the stove and reaching for the coffee pot. "He just said he had some place to be and that if he wasn't back tonight, to take you back to my house with me. It isn't like this place," Everett said as he waved his hand in the air. "But Nash can call in some more agents if needed."

The fucking bastard had left me.

And I knew exactly why.

All that shit he'd spouted about me being an equal participant…

Anger went through me and I was half-tempted to chuck the mug Everett slid in my direction against the wall. Right after the fury came the stark fear. What if the guy who'd tried to kill me got the drop on Vincent somehow?

"Call him," I said.

"He won't answer," Everett said as he filled his mug with coffee. "I already tried."

I didn't know what that meant, nor did I care. But I could tell Everett wasn't exactly thrilled with the circumstances.

"Bastard," I muttered. "Not you," I said as I glanced up at Everett.

Everett smiled and then went to fill my mug. "That he is."

I put my hand over the top of the mug before he could pour and Everett immediately pulled back. "You said he won't answer, right?" I asked.

Everett shook his head. "When he's working…"

I nodded in understanding. I glanced at the watch on my wrist and then quickly took it off. "You might want to go home, Mr. President," I said as I put the watch on the counter and then reached for the mug.

"I'm pretty sure I don't," he said with a smile, and then he leaned back and put the coffee pot down. He grabbed his own mug and took a sip as I proceeded to use my mug to pound the watch into oblivion. Once both it and the mug were destroyed, I went around the island and got a new mug. "Looks good," I said as I looked at the food Everett had been cooking.

Everett chuckled and said, "I think you'll do fine, Nathan Wilder. I think you'll do just fine."

~

"Ignore it," Everett said for the third time to Nash as his phone began ringing. The man had declined to join us for breakfast, though I'd been the one to extend the invitation, not Everett. I had the clear feeling that Everett and his Secret Service agent were at odds, but for whatever reason, Everett hadn't fired the man after yesterday's fiasco.

Nash's phone went silent and Everett's began to vibrate again. He'd turned it to silent after the first three times Vincent had called, and he'd resorted to turning it over on the table so he wouldn't have to read the texts that kept pinging on the phone. After smashing the watch, I'd used a chair to reach the singular security camera in the kitchen and had tossed a dishtowel over the thing. I figured if we didn't move around, whatever motion detectors Vincent had in the house wouldn't alert him to our presence. I knew I was courting trouble, but I didn't give a shit. Vincent might have a lot to say to me when he got back, but he was going to get an earful, too.

"Did you ever meet my father?" I asked Everett as I pushed my plate away from me. Despite my certainty that I'd done the right thing, knowing I was going to be confronting a very angry Vincent soon had my appetite diminishing.

"Once," Everett said. "The White House was hosting this event honoring a young solider who'd been killed saving his unit from an ambush attack. Your father was invited because the young man had been from South Carolina."

I nodded. "Private First Class Geoffrey Waters," I said.

"Yeah," Everett said sadly. "We were honoring him posthumously with the Medal of Honor."

I felt sick to my stomach because I knew very well what my father had done at that event. After the service had ended, he'd gone to the young man's family to thank them for their sacrifice and then had proceeded to ask if their son, who'd been rumored to have been gay, had sought absolution before his death so he'd get to sit at his heavenly father's side in the afterlife. While my father had left the event when he'd politely been asked to do so, he'd used the cameras of the reporters waiting outside to suggest that the young soldier would still be alive if he'd followed the path of God.

It was the first time I'd questioned my father…and my faith. I just hadn't had the guts to go against him, and when he'd gotten home that night crowing about his success, Brody and I had both sat on the couch, silent as church mice as we'd listened to our father call it a victory for good Christians. A few months later, Brody had come out to me, and I'd gone running to my father to tell him his own son had been possessed by the lure of the devil.

"Can I ask you what made you do it, son?" Everett asked.

I flinched because my first thought was that he was talking about what I'd done to Brody. But then he said, "What made you switch sides?"

I had the stock answer on the tip of my tongue, but I couldn't give voice to it.

Because it just wasn't true anymore, no matter how hard I'd worked to convince myself I'd done what I had for Brody and others like him.

I met Everett's eyes. "Because I'm gay."

It was the last thing he expected me to say. That much was clear.

I'd expected the words to be harder to get out, but it was surprisingly easy, and the fact that Nash would have been able to hear the admission didn't bother me in the least. Vincent had most definitely broken something inside of me, but in the best way. He'd broken something that had healed wrong after all those years of pretending I'd done the right thing by Brody when I'd betrayed him.

Everett studied me for a moment and then held up his coffee cup. I lifted mine and clinked it gently against his. "Bet that felt good," he said softly.

I laughed and said, "You have no idea."

He watched me sadly for a moment and then said, "Yeah, Nathan, I do."

It took me a really long time to get what he was telling me. I shook my head in disbelief. He couldn't be...

"How?" was all I could ask, though I wasn't even sure what I was really asking. "You...you were married! You have a son."

Everett smiled patiently and lowered his mug. "A son who won't talk to me anymore," he said quietly.

"Everett, I'm sorry," I began, but he waved me off.

"I knew something was wrong when I married Eleanor, but I didn't know what it was. I was in denial for a really long time. When Reese came along, I put everything that was wrong with the marriage behind me because I needed to make it work for my son. And we managed it for a lot of years – making it look like we were the perfect, happy couple."

"What changed?" I asked. I'd seen the president and his wife together hundreds of times in the years Everett had been in the White House, and I'd never seen even a hint that something was off between them.

"I met someone who made me realize I'd been hiding who I really was. He...he was the worst possible person for me to fall in love with, and it came at one of the most inopportune times in my life, but none of that mattered. I knew as soon as I saw him that he was going to change everything for me. And for once, I didn't care."

The sadness that overtook Everett made my heart hurt. I glanced over my shoulder to see if Nash was still listening, but was surprised to find he'd left the room at some point.

"It's okay, Everett," I said as I reached my hand across the table and covered his. "We don't have to talk about this."

But he continued like I hadn't spoken. "He was in the army, so he wasn't free to be with me, either. I still had a few years left in my second term...so we settled for stolen moments whenever we could. My marriage to Eleanor had been over for a while, but we'd agreed to keep pretending the marriage was real until my term was finished. We didn't even tell Reese."

"Your son joined the military the year you became president, right?"

Everett nodded.

"Reese was how I met..."

Everett's voice dropped off briefly. "Reese got hurt in combat. His mother and I flew to Landstuhl to be with him. His commanding officer came to visit him one day..." Everett shook his head. "I couldn't take my eyes off him...he was just so damn beautiful. And when he shook my hand..."

I nodded in understanding. I knew exactly what he was talking about.

"I think it surprised him, too," Everett continued. "He'd always known he was gay, but he'd been careful not to be open about it. Not after his younger brother was discharged from the military when it came out that he was gay."

I stiffened at that and pulled my hand from Everett's. "No," I whispered.

Everett's gaze shifted to the window, but I knew he wasn't really seeing anything outside of it. I could see Nash walking back and forth across the driveway, his sharp eyes on his surroundings.

"Pierce?" I asked. "You...you were in love with Vincent's brother?"

"Love," he whispered. "God, that word doesn't seem like enough to describe what that man did for me...the things he made me feel."

I felt like I was going to be sick because I understood everything he was saying. Jesus, was that what was happening to me? Were the feelings I had for Vincent more than just the emotion that came with finding a piece of myself I'd been denying for so long?

My thoughts drifted to the story Vincent had told me about his brother. I felt tears sting the backs of my eyes as I realized what it meant. Vincent had lost his brother, but Everett...he'd lost so much more.

"Everett, I'm sorry," I croaked.

His sad eyes returned to me. "All those months I'd worried about losing him in combat," he murmured. He dashed at his eyes. "He'd decided to leave the army so that once my second term was up, we could be together. I was going to come out once I'd left office. I waited too long."

Everett sucked in a breath and tore his eyes from the window. "Pierce and I got to be together a few times, but it was a lot of work to keep our secret. Eleanor suspected what was going on, but Reese had no idea until he walked in on me and Pierce one day in my private office in the residence. Eleanor had been out of town visiting her mother, and I'd dismissed my Secret Service detail so I could have some time with Pierce. Grady was the only agent who knew about us, and he worked really hard to keep my secret and to help me find a few moments here and there for me and Pierce to be together. We didn't know Reese was stopping by."

"What happened?" I asked.

"What didn't?" Everett said softly. "He blamed Pierce, he blamed me...he didn't care that I loved Pierce or that his mother and I had been over for a long time. He saw it as a betrayal and that was it. I've only seen him once since that night...at his mother's funeral a few years ago. He left the military and I lost track of him for a while."

"Do you know where he is now?" I asked.

Everett nodded. "He refused any kind of Secret Service protection.

Which meant he pretty much had a target painted on his back. Lots of agencies and individuals that would love nothing more than to get their hands on the son of a former president. A man I met a couple of years after I lost Pierce reached out to me last year to tell me he had intel that Reese was in danger. I knew Reese wouldn't accept my help, so I asked the man to do what he could for Reese, but to keep my name out of it."

"And did he?" I asked.

Everett nodded. "Reese is working for him in Seattle. I get regular reports that he's doing well...seems happy."

"That's good," I said encouragingly, just because Everett looked so damn broken. Before I could say anything else, I heard the rumble of an engine and the squealing of tires. My insides dropped out and my eyes met Everett's over the table.

"Let the games begin," Everett said with a smile, and then he was standing. "I'll..." he began as he looked at the dirty dishes. Raised voices came from outside...well, Nash's raised voice. Probably throwing me under the bus.

Which was what Everett did when he said, "I'll just let you take care of this," as he motioned to the table and then snatched his jacket off the back of his chair.

I climbed to my feet as Everett hurried past me. He stopped long enough to settle his hand on my shoulder. "Don't be afraid to fight for what you want, son," he said, and then he was gone. I couldn't hear what he said a second after the front door slammed open, but the fact that Vincent didn't respond probably wasn't a good sign.

At least not for me.

A moment of regret went through me when I glanced at the broken watch on the kitchen island, but it didn't last long because Vincent stepped into the room, his gun hanging loosely by his side, his face twisted into a mask of fury. And just like that the reason he'd left me in the first place came roaring back, along with the terrible fear that I could have lost him.

Before he could even say a word, I was in his face. "Say the wrong thing to me right now, Vincent, and see what happens," I warned. "If the next words out of your mouth don't start with an apology-"

That was as much as I got out before his lips came crashing down on mine.

It wasn't a kiss. No, it was way too brutal for that.

It was him claiming me...punishing me, even. But that didn't make me love it any less. Or not return the treatment.

I was barely aware of him dropping his gun onto the island behind me, and then both his arms wrapped around me in a brutally tight hold. We each fought to control the kiss, but when Vincent won out, I gladly gave him my mouth. My back hit the island behind me and a second later, cool air greeted my skin as my sweats were pushed down.

Vincent kneaded my ass as he maneuvered me backwards past the island. It wasn't until I heard the sound of dishware breaking that I realized we'd reached the table and he'd cleared it with one sweep of his arm. The edge of the table bit into my ass as Vincent consumed my mouth. Neither of us had spoken a word, but we didn't need to.

I knew what he wanted...it was the same thing I wanted.

No, needed.

My cock throbbed as Vincent's jeans brushed against it. I let out a harsh cry, and then I was frantically trying to get his pants undone. I'd barely gotten the zipper down when he spun me around and forced me face-first down over the table. I grabbed onto the edges of it as Vincent began humping my ass. At some point his pants were gone and his bare cock was pressing against me.

Hungry.

Seeking.

Desperate.

Vincent's fingers clawed at my shirt as he pushed it up, and then his nails were raking gently down my back. He kept rocking against me, his dick working its way into my crease. I bucked back against him.

"Vincent," I called out, my voice rough and needy. When he

suddenly pulled away from me, I cried out in protest and rose enough so I could look over my shoulder.

But he hadn't gone far.

Only the few feet it had taken him to reach the counter next to the stove. He swiped a bottle of olive oil off the countertop and ripped at the top. The cap went sailing and he carelessly dumped some of the oil on his fingers. My eyes fell to his angry, flushed cock as he covered it in the slick substance. The bottle of olive oil hit the floor but didn't shatter as he closed the distance between us.

Vincent was back on me within seconds. His mouth covered mine as his fingers pressed between my ass cheeks and then he was pushing an oil-covered digit deep inside of me. I gasped at the burn as he stretched me and moments later, another finger was joining the first. My body began trembling so bad, I had no choice but to drop my chest back down to the table.

"God, Vincent, fuck me…please!" I cried, not caring at the picture I must have made.

His finger nudged my gland and my whole body jerked. But the pleasurable sensation didn't last because suddenly his fingers were gone and his cock was sliding into me. The pain was intense, but it wasn't enough. I pushed back against him, trying to take him deeper.

And luckily, he gave me exactly what I wanted.

I let out a hoarse shout as he surged into me, bottoming out in one hard thrust. I reached behind me to grab his thigh.

But not to stop him.

No, just to hold onto him.

Because it felt so damn good I was sure I'd float away into nothingness if I didn't have him to ground me.

He began fucking me hard. The table rattled beneath me and I desperately clung to it as his body pushed mine forward. His dick was hot and hard inside of me and his fingers were digging into my hips as he held me for his pummeling.

After just a few strokes, Vincent draped himself over my back and his hands covered my wrists, pinning my arms to the table. "Mine," he growled into my ear as he ruthlessly fucked me.

I wanted to tell him yes, but I was too overcome by the pleasure that was scorching up my spine. The orgasm was coming hard and fast, and I both welcomed it and was terrified of it at the same time. I was completely powerless and at his mercy, but I'd never felt safer.

He kept repeating the word "mine" over and over as he rammed into me. I might have managed to agree with him, but I wasn't sure. I felt one hand sift through my hair as he tangled his fingers in my locks. He held me that way, one hand pinned to the table, the other holding my head at an angle so he could kiss me, and his entire weight holding me down against the unforgiving table as he ravaged my body in the best way. I managed to use my free hand to reach above me to hold onto his head. It was the only movement he granted me, but it was enough.

"So close," I choked out as I desperately reached for the orgasm that was just beyond my grasp. Vincent's teeth closed over the sensitive lobe of my ear, and then the hand from my hair disappeared and suddenly wrapped around my painfully hard cock.

"Come for me, Nate," he said softly, his voice so very different from the brutal way he was claiming me.

My name on his lips was enough to send me over. I cried out in relief as I came. My body jerked and bucked uncontrollably beneath his as he stroked me through the climax. Seconds later, he roared in my ear and shoved ruthlessly into me and held there. I moaned as the heat that began to burn my insides set off another orgasm.

It was then that it finally registered that he'd taken me without a condom. That the warmth I was feeling was his release filling me up. The knowledge had me shuddering in disbelief.

And excitement.

Vincent's body continued to jerk against mine for several long moments before he finally relaxed and settled all his weight on me. But it didn't take long before he was pulling free of me. I was too exhausted to move. I sensed rather than saw him standing just behind me, and it took every bit of strength I had to turn my head to seek him out. His eyes were on my ass.

And I knew why.

Even now, I could feel his semen seeping out of me and down my thigh.

Vincent lifted his eyes to mine and I saw the confusion there. He reached down to quietly pull his pants up, and then he was gone.

I managed to get myself to my feet. As I pulled my sweats up, I shook my head at the sight that greeted me.

Broken dishes and half-eaten food on the floor, a pool of olive oil spreading over the tile. Vincent's discarded gun still sitting on the island next to the watch I'd broken.

My body continued to tremble as I stepped around the mess and left the kitchen. Part of me said to give Vincent some space, but I couldn't do it. That look in his eyes as he'd stared down at my ass had scared me.

Like something big had been happening in his head as he'd watched me.

Something I wouldn't like.

I hurried up the stairs and went directly to his room. He was sitting on the edge of his bed, his head hung. His hair was damp, and I suspected it was because he'd washed his hands and then run them through his hair at some point.

"Not now, Nathan," Vincent ground out.

I ignored him and went to stand in front of him. "Yes, now," I said.

He shook his head and then got up to step past me. But he didn't leave the room. Instead, he went to the set of glass French doors that led out to a small balcony. "Do you have any idea what you put me through?" he asked quietly.

Too quietly.

I was used to pissed-off, reactive Vincent.

Emotionless Vincent.

I knew how to handle *him*. This Vincent...this Vincent was a different story altogether.

"Do you have any idea the things I thought were happening to you? The things I was thinking about if I couldn't get to you in time?"

In truth, I hadn't given it much thought. I'd been pissed and scared, and I'd reacted in the only way I'd known to get him back here. Guilt tore through me as I remembered the story he'd told me about his brother.

Never in a million years would I have thought he'd be feeling that same terror...not for...me.

"I'm sorry, Vincent-"

"Don't be sorry," he interjected. "Go pack your shit. You're getting your wish."

Heat washed through me. "What...what wish?"

But he didn't answer me.

And he didn't need to, because I already knew the answer.

CHAPTER 20

VINCENT

"So that's it?" Nathan murmured. "You get to decide this, too?"

I wasn't *deciding* anything. I was doing what I needed to do to keep my fucking sanity.

I still couldn't believe what I'd let happen downstairs. I'd fucked the man like an animal on my kitchen table, and I'd done it without a condom. The only other man I'd ever gone bare with had been David, first as dumb kids who hadn't known any better, and then as grown men who'd been in a committed relationship.

I wasn't either of those things with Nathan, yet when I'd realized I hadn't put another condom and packet of lube in my wallet after the previous day's encounter, instead of stopping the whole damn thing, I'd grabbed a bottle of fucking olive oil, ignored the voice of reason in my head, and buried myself inside his perfect body before he or God or anyone could have stopped me.

And I'd fucking loved it.

Even now I was getting hard just thinking about how good it had felt. How much hotter and tighter he'd felt gripping my dick. The moans that had fallen from his lips, the way the table had creaked under our weight as I'd pinned him to it…

Jesus.

I willed my dick to settle down as I tried to make plans. I'd call Ronan and tell him to get one of his guys to meet me for the hand-off. When Ronan had talked to me earlier this year about Ethan's broken phone, he'd mentioned having operatives in D.C., Virginia, and Maryland, so any one of them should be able to meet me and take over Nathan's case.

I ignored the panicked feeling that went through me at the prospect of not having eyes on Nathan anymore.

He wasn't my responsibility, damn it. He was a fucking favor, nothing more.

A favor that had gone wrong from the second I'd met him.

"Go pack your stuff," I murmured again, not daring to look at Nathan. I was sure that if I did, I'd be dealing with a repeat of the encounter in the kitchen. Only this time I could finally fuck him in a soft bed.

It shouldn't have surprised me that instead of following my order, Nathan stomped to my side and grabbed my arm. Hell, I'd pretty much been expecting it.

Because the man never did what he was told.

Unless he was naked beneath me.

"I'm sorry, Vincent," he said, his voice going calm and even. "I *didn't* think about what might be going through your head when I broke that watch. I was thinking about what was going through *my* head."

Even though he was standing right in front of me, my mind still went back to the vision that had been tormenting me from the moment I'd received an alert on my phone that his signal had gone offline.

Nathan bound to a chair, blood running down his body and pooling on the floor beneath him. His beautiful head hung with sheets of blood clinging to his light hair.

I'd tried calling, of course, as soon as I'd gotten the alert, but there'd been no answer either from Everett or Nash, who I'd finally agreed to let into my house so that Nathan would have someone protecting him in my absence. It wasn't that I completely trusted the man, it was that I'd feared for Nathan's safety more than the prospect of having the armed agent in my home. When they hadn't answered, I'd checked the security cameras one by one, using my phone, until I'd gotten to the kitchen one which had been dark.

And just like that, it was the room that had become Nathan's torture chamber.

I'd barely even given much thought to Everett and Nash, because my entire focus had been on what the assailant had been doing to Nathan. Had he been finishing what he'd started with that knife, or had he simply put a bullet in Nathan's brain and moved on? Or had he taken Nathan somewhere that I'd have no hope of ever finding him?

I'd probably broken every single traffic law getting back to the house at that point. Luckily, I'd only been about an hour from the house and with the speed I'd been going, I'd made it in half that time.

Only to find Agent Nash calmly waiting for me in the driveway.

But even then, I'd needed to see Nathan. My brain had processed what the agent's presence had meant, but it hadn't meant a goddamn thing until I'd seen Nathan for myself. And as pissed as I was at Nash and especially Everett, I'd been glad they'd left, because after seeing Nathan, the most important thing had been getting my hands on him.

"You're not the only one who was scared, Vincent," I heard Nathan say. "Who *is* scared."

"Nathan, go-"

"Right after I realized you'd broken your word about me being an equal participant in this, I started seeing things…"

His voice cracked, and that had me turning to look at him. His eyes were on the ground. "I kept seeing your body on the floor in some fucking motel room in the middle of nowhere, and I knew I was too late."

"Nathan-"

"And don't ask me to fucking explain why I even care, since you're such a complete and total asshole."

I wanted to smile at that. Not the words themselves, but the way he said them. Like he truly was exasperated by the whole thing. Yeah, well, he wasn't the only one. I could count on one hand the number of guys I'd been with more than once and I'd only need one damn finger.

Well, two now.

"And you've fucked up my entire life..." There was still no anger in his voice as he lifted his eyes. "Tell me I've fucked up your life, Vincent. Tell me that what happened down there" – he pointed towards my bedroom door – "wasn't just because you were pissed." He sucked in a breath. "Tell me that leaving me this morning was hard for you...that lying to me was hard for you."

I knew what he wanted, and I knew no matter what I said, I was going to end up hurting him. I could lie and tell him every kiss, every touch, every second I'd spent lost inside his body was nothing more than me getting my rocks off with someone who represented all the people who'd ruined David's and my life.

Or I could tell him the truth and then try to explain to him why none of it mattered...why it changed absolutely nothing.

So I settled for something that had served me well in the past.

I kept my mouth shut and turned away from him and let him believe whatever the hell he wanted. It was the coward's way out, but for once, I didn't care. I kept my eyes on the expansive view of my backyard. I ignored the urge to look at the spot by the pond where everything had changed...where I'd slid into his body for the first time and had been certain it had been made just for me.

But of course, that was exactly where my gaze took me.

And all the while, Nathan remained where he was. I wanted to scream at him. To tell him to look around him...that this was my life. A life I couldn't condemn him to.

Or myself.

That was the crux of it.

Even if I thought there was something between us worth exploring beyond the intense chemistry, I couldn't go through even another minute like the thirty I'd spent in my car racing back here. I couldn't obsess over Nathan's whereabouts every second of every day and wonder if today was the day my enemies made the connection...that I finally had a vulnerability I couldn't protect.

The mere thought of putting Nathan in danger had me forcing coldness into my voice as I said, "Nathan, go pack. We're leaving in ten minutes."

He didn't respond and I didn't dare look at him. But it wouldn't have mattered because he was pushing into my arms a moment later, his strong fingers reaching up to clasp the back of my neck. "No," he said firmly. "You broke our deal when you left me. I don't take orders anymore." He yanked me down for a hard kiss. I tried to keep from kissing him back, but it was like trying to stop the coming tide. But it wasn't until he whispered, "Only place you get to order me around is in that big bed of yours, Vincent" and nipped at my lips and then licked over them with his tongue, that I knew I wasn't going to win this one.

"What do you want?" he asked huskily.

I knew that physically, he was no match for me. But that didn't matter, because he'd said the right words. He'd flipped that switch inside me that had lain dormant since I'd lost David.

David, who'd been the only one I'd ever trusted enough to show him what I needed.

Until now.

"Get on your knees," I growled.

Nathan's breath came out in a rush and his eyes went dark. He slowly sank to his knees in front of me. I could tell he knew what I wanted and that, despite everything I'd done to him, he was nervous. It was exactly the reason I'd given the order.

But I wasn't sure if I wanted him to go.

Or stay.

He made the decision for me when he lifted his eyes to meet mine and waited. His hands were resting on the outside of my thighs.

"Open my pants. Take me out."

His fingers shook as he did what I said, and it took him longer than it probably should have. But all that did was turn me on. I loved this side of him...this side where he confronted his fear, despite the fact that it made him so open and vulnerable.

I let out a groan as his fingers grazed my skin as he carefully worked my dick free of my pants. My eyes were fastened on him as he stared hungrily at my cock. His fingers were gently gripping my base. I could see my own juices still clinging to my dick since I hadn't had a chance to clean up after the encounter in the kitchen beyond washing my hands.

Nathan didn't even wait for my next order. Instead, he leaned in and pressed his nose against my groin and inhaled deeply. His thumb toyed with my skin briefly, and then his warm breath wafted over my flesh as he tentatively licked the shaft. He'd already tasted himself the night before when I'd shared the essence of his release with him, but he lingered over my flavor for a brief moment before taking another lick.

And another.

Over and over he tongued my shaft, licking up the remnants of my cum. Then his mouth was closing over the head and he gave me a gentle suck.

"Harder," I groaned as I let my fingers slide through his soft hair.

His eyes lifted to mine even as he took me back into his mouth. He sucked harder, then harder still, carefully gauging my reaction. I'd intended to use the encounter to test how far he was willing to go, but I had my answer pretty quickly because within a minute, he was eagerly trying to take me to the back of his throat. It didn't work, of course, but my body didn't give a shit about his inexperience. Nor did he seem embarrassed by it, because despite the fact that he couldn't figure out how to deep throat me, he kept working my dick between his mouth and his hands until I was ready to blow.

I tried to warn him, but the orgasm was on me before I could stop it and then I was unloading down his throat. He sputtered and jerked his mouth in surprise, causing some of my cum to hit his chin and neck. Just as quickly, he drew my dick back into his mouth and swallowed as much of my release as he could. By the time the orgasm had started to wane, his skin was glistening from my release and his pupils were blown. I yanked him to his feet and crushed my mouth against his, and then lapped up every drop of cum I could find as I walked him backwards towards the bed. His back hit the mattress as I shoved him down, and in one move, I was on my knees and pulling his sweats down. I swallowed him down before he could say anything, and when he came in my mouth moments later, he cried out my name.

We were both breathing hard by the time I flopped down on my back on the bed next to him. I had no clue where to go from here, because I hadn't yet managed to catch up to the fact that Nathan was blowing all of my expectations out of the water.

He rolled over on top of me and then his mouth was on mine. I managed to kiss him back, though in truth, my limbs felt like jelly.

"Was that okay?" he asked, a hint of insecurity seeping into his voice. It would have been the perfect time to feed into that insecurity with the intent of driving him away, but when his amber eyes met mine, I couldn't do it.

"Perfect," I whispered.

"Liar," he said with a grin. He kissed me and said, "But practice *does* make perfect." He waggled his eyebrows at me in such a way that I had no choice but to laugh. The emotion felt foreign to me, as did the way Nathan looked longingly at me as soon as my chuckling died down.

"Don't end this yet, Vincent," he murmured, all humor gone now. I couldn't help but reach up to cradle his cheek with my hand. My throat felt too tight to speak.

It wouldn't have mattered anyway, because I couldn't have told him the words I should have said, anyway. I couldn't have given voice to the truth that this would never work and that he was only going to get hurt in the long run.

No, I couldn't do any of that because I was a selfish fucking asshole who wasn't ready to let go yet.

So I didn't answer him at all.

Well, not with words, anyway.

But I did let my lips do the talking as I pulled him down for a searing kiss that would let him know he wasn't going anywhere.

Yet.

"Here," I said as I handed the bottle of beer to Nathan. He was sitting on the far end of the lounger on my deck, staring off into the distance. The sun was just starting to fall, so the sky above us was lit up with swirls of fiery orange and red. The air had turned cool, and while I'd pulled on a long-sleeved shirt after my shower earlier, Nathan was still wearing a T-shirt.

"Why don't we go inside?" I said as I let my fingers drift over his cheek.

I hated how quiet he'd gotten since this morning. After the encounter in my bedroom, we'd each gone to our own bathrooms to get cleaned up. I'd joined Nathan in the kitchen to clean up the mess we'd made...that I'd made. There had been an awkward tension between us ever since then, and Nathan had spent most of the day in his room with one of my laptops. When he'd tried to show me the emails he'd written to get my approval before sending them, I'd waved him off because I trusted him not to put either of us in danger by revealing his location.

I'd spent the day in my office trying to track down Nathan's assailant, but hadn't had any luck. Whoever the guy was, he was good at not leaving an electronic footprint behind.

"Not yet," Nathan murmured. I liked how he leaned into my touch.

I swung my leg over the lounger just behind him and then sat down. I settled against the lounger's back. "Come here," I said softly as I closed my fingers over Nathan's elbow. He glanced over his shoulder at me and then got up. He settled himself between my legs and pressed his back against my chest. The intimate embrace should have felt awkward, but it just felt...right.

I settled my arm around his waist and then put my beer on the ground next to me. Reaching into my pocket, I pulled out the new watch I'd programmed for Nathan. He didn't object when I fastened it around his right wrist. In fact, when I was done, he grabbed my fingers and laced them with his and then pulled my hand around to his chest.

"Nathan, we need to talk about what happened this morning," I began. "I didn't use a condom. I'm sorry…it was incredibly irresponsible."

He didn't respond at first. When he did, it was merely to pull my fingers to his mouth so he could press a kiss against them. "I trust you, Vincent. I know you would never put me in danger."

"I wouldn't," I confirmed. "But I should have told you beforehand that I've been tested and I'm negative."

Nathan nodded. "Me too. My last girlfriend wasn't exactly faithful, and even though I always used protection with her, I wanted to be sure." After several beats, he went on to say, "I liked it…knowing part of you was still with me."

Fuck, this man was going to be the death of me. How had I ever thought he was like the others in his business? The man seemed incapable of telling a lie.

Nathan settled more heavily against me, and I gladly wrapped my arms around him when I felt his body tremble.

"I told Everett I was gay," he whispered.

I settled my mouth against his temple. "How did it go?"

"It was scary as fuck."

I nodded in understanding, even though he couldn't see me. I figured he could feel the motion.

"I can't stop thinking about Brody…how scared he must have been to tell me. He was so young…"

"You were, too," I reminded him.

He shook his head. "I was his big brother. I was supposed to look out for him. He…he'd barely even gotten the words out when I told him he wasn't…that he couldn't…"

Nathan's voice broke, but he pressed on. "I told him he couldn't be a fag and that he'd go to hell." Nathan's hand reached up to wipe at what I assumed were tears. "But he refused to take it back. I called him a sick pervert, and then I went straight to my father and told him what Brody had said. I betrayed my own brother."

A sob tore free from him, and when he curled his body so he could press his wet face against my chest, I gladly held onto him. I dropped a kiss to his head. "It's okay, Nathan."

He shook his head. "No. My father...he threatened to send Brody to one of those places where they pray the gay away..."

I stiffened at that. "Conversion therapy?" I asked.

Nathan nodded. "Brody begged my father not to. He promised he'd overcome it. My father was paranoid that it would somehow be leaked to the press, so he agreed to have our minister meet with Brody. It lasted weeks. Brody met with him night after night for hours at a time. He...he never told me what happened during the sessions, but I didn't even recognize him when he was deemed cured. It was like he was just this shell of himself. We barely talked after that. The plan had always been for us to go to college and law school together, but he convinced my father to let him go to Yale while I attended Princeton. He came out again to our entire family a couple months after graduating from law school. I cut him out of my life after that. Told him he was a sick fuck and we were no longer brothers."

I sucked in a breath. It was hard to link the man in my arms to such a cold act of cruelty.

"It should have been harder," Nathan murmured. I could feel moisture seeping through my shirt and realized Nathan was likely still crying, but silently.

"What should?" I asked.

"Coming out for the first time. It should have been to my father or someone like him."

"Is that what you think Brody would have wanted? For you to suffer like he did?"

"No, Brody's too good of a man for that."

We both fell silent for several minutes until Nathan said, "Everett told me about him and your brother." Nathan shifted enough so he could sit up. His wet eyes connected with mine. "Will you tell me about him? Your brother, I mean."

I wanted to tell him no, because I knew what talking about Pierce would do to me. But I found myself nodding my head instead and when I opened my arms again, Nathan settled himself back against my chest.

His weight on my body and the feel of his heartbeat against where our hands were joined on my chest made it much easier to open my mouth and start talking.

CHAPTER 21

NATHAN

"From the time I was old enough to say his name, I wanted to be just like Pierce. I idolized him and literally followed him everywhere. My mom used to love to tell everyone the story about how she came into my room one morning to find me missing from my crib. She and my dad had already called the cops by the time they found me asleep on the floor next to Pierce's bed. From that moment on, wherever Pierce was, I was. Even as he got older, he spent more time with me than he needed to. If he was going to meet friends to shoot some hoops or whatever, he took me along. When I was old enough to play, he let me join in. If I had to choose between hanging out with my own friends or Pierce and his, I always chose Pierce," Vincent explained, his voice soft and reverent.

I knew exactly what he was talking about because I'd had that kind of closeness with Brody. But knowing that there'd been a pretty sizeable age gap between Vincent and his brother made it all the more amazing that Pierce would have been so devoted to Vincent.

"Our father had been grooming us for the army from day one and even though I wasn't in the same unit as Pierce, I had aspirations to achieve the same rank as him and in the same timeline."

"He was a colonel, right?" I asked.

"Yeah…he was well on his way to becoming one of the youngest generals in the military. Which was why it didn't make sense when he told me he was leaving the army instead of re-enlisting when his tour ended."

Vincent's finger began stroking against mine where I was holding his hand against his chest. I wondered if he was even aware of the self-soothing gesture.

"I thought maybe he'd done it as some kind of tribute to me."

"Because of what the army did to you and David?"

I felt Vincent nod before he said, "Yeah. David had been gone for a few years by then and I had no interest in re-enlisting, even if the army would have made that offer. So I was actually pretty pissed at him for throwing away his career."

"He didn't do it for you," I murmured. "He did it for Everett. So they could be together."

Another nod, but this time Vincent didn't say anything.

"Did you know about them?" I asked.

"Not until after Pierce's death. I'd known Pierce was gay…he came out to me after I was kicked out of the military. But I didn't find out about Everett until I went to the cemetery a few days after Pierce's funeral."

"What happened?" I asked.

"Pierce was buried at Arlington National Cemetery. When I got there, there were Secret Service agents everywhere. They wouldn't let me past a certain point at first. When I told them who I was and that I was visiting my brother's grave, they let me through. I'd figured some bigwig was visiting a loved one who happened to be buried near my brother, but it turned out to be Everett and he was standing over Pierce's grave."

I felt my throat tighten at the thought of Everett saying his goodbyes to the man who'd meant so much to him. The man he'd been ready to change his entire life for.

"That must have been surreal," I murmured. "Seeing the President of the United States at your brother's grave."

"Yeah…I couldn't figure out why he was there. Pierce had been given a military funeral with all the honors, but he hadn't been high up enough to know the president, let alone have a personal enough relationship with him to explain the man's presence."

"He told you the truth about them?" I asked.

"He did. I was..."

I felt rather than saw Vincent shaking his head. "I was completely floored. And then I just fucking lost it. Knowing my brother had finally found the love of his life only to die protecting me-"

Vincent's voice cut off sharply as a strangled sob left his throat. I immediately sat up and turned so I could face him. His eyes were closed and I could see him struggling to contain his emotions.

"C'mere," I whispered as I pulled him forward against my chest. "It wasn't your fault," I murmured against his head as he clung to me. He didn't respond, and I knew why.

He'd blame himself no matter what. And even though I knew it wasn't his fault, he'd told me enough that I knew the perpetrators *had* been after Vincent, and Pierce had just been in the wrong place at the wrong time.

"He never blamed me," Vincent said softly. "Everett."

"Because he knew it wasn't your fault. And because he knew your brother would have done anything to keep you safe."

Vincent nodded and pulled back. He wiped at his eyes and then searched out his beer and took a long draw on it, presumably so he could pull himself together.

"So you became best friends with the President," I mused, hoping to interject some lightness into our conversation.

Vincent smiled. "You'd think it would come with all kinds of benefits, but I usually end up feeding his cheap ass and watching whatever reality show he's obsessed with."

I chuckled and reached up to cup his cheek. "I'm glad you have each other."

"Me too," he murmured.

He leaned back against the lounger and just stared at me, and I found myself doing the same. I was at a loss as to what to do next. I was in completely new territory. Sure, I'd been in relationships before, but I wasn't sure that was even what Vincent and I had. He hadn't brought up the issue again of me leaving, but it felt like it was right there on the tip of his tongue. If I said or did even a single thing wrong, this could all be over.

And I didn't know why that mattered so much.

It wasn't like we had anything we could build a future on. I still knew next to nothing about the man, but what I did know was that he hated politics and pretty much everything I stood for. Our chemistry was off the charts, but I knew that wouldn't be enough to sustain this thing between us.

But that was just it.

There was something more between us than just sex.

Wasn't there?

I certainly hadn't been scared shitless this morning when I'd discovered he'd left to go after my assailant on his own because I would have missed the sex if something had happened to him. And I couldn't fathom that he'd let me stay just so he could keep fucking me.

Fuck, why was this shit so complicated? With Virginia, I'd never had to wonder about this kind of stuff. Of course, with Virginia, all I'd felt was trapped.

"What's going on in that head of yours?" Vincent asked as he took another sip of his beer.

"Nothing," I said with a shake of my head. "Just tired."

He eyed me for a long time, but didn't say anything.

"What happens now?" I asked. "With finding the guy," I clarified, since I sure as shit wasn't ready to hear Vincent tell me this thing between us needed to come to an end.

"My plan this morning was to draw him out, but someone blew that out of the water with his little stunt."

I was surprised to see a small smile grace Vincent's hard mouth, proof that he was no longer pissed at me for what I'd done this morning to get him back here.

"We can still do that," I said. "Draw him out."

Vincent opened his mouth to say something, so I quickly continued before he could protest. "I'm scheduled to speak at a rally on Saturday. Maybe if this guy sees that I'm getting back to my normal routine, he'll come after me again."

"No, it's too dangerous," Vincent said before the last syllable had even left my mouth.

"There will be security there. And you can blend in with the crowd. I can tell the security team that you're my bodyguard...it's not unheard of for political candidates to have them."

The fact that he didn't cut me off again was a good sign. "You said we could make it look like I was staying in a hotel in Charleston..."

He took another long draw of his beer. The fact that he hadn't shot me down was proof that whatever he'd been doing on his own hadn't been working.

"Vincent, he needs to see me...he needs to see that he hasn't stopped me." I was about to continue my argument when Vincent suddenly stood. His jaw was hard as he studied the backyard for a moment and then, without a word, he turned and strode into the house. I grabbed my own beer and followed, waiting long enough for Mickey and Minnie to follow me into the house before shutting the patio door.

I found him in the kitchen pouring himself a drink. There was a glass for me, but he didn't fill it up. He merely slid the bottle and glass towards me and then snatched his glass off the island and went to stand by the kitchen table so he could stare out the window. I poured a small amount of the whiskey into the glass and downed it in one swallow, then capped the bottle. As much as I would have liked another drink, I needed to keep my wits about me for whatever was to come.

"What do you want, Vincent?" I finally asked when he remained silent. "This morning you seemed eager to finish this thing – I'm assuming because you wanted to get me out of your life sooner rather than later. But now that I'm giving you a surefire way to do that, you won't take me up on it."

"It's what I don't want that's the issue, Nathan," he said without turning around.

"Okay, what *don't* you want?" I asked.

"For you to get too comfortable. For you to start thinking there's something here...between us."

His words stung, even though I'd suspected as much. But even though I'd wanted to force him to talk to me, now I just wanted him to shut the hell up. I felt weak and foolish for thinking there might even be a chance he was feeling a fraction of what I was feeling.

"I get it," I mumbled as the alcohol in my belly began to sour. "I'm sorry...I shouldn't have pushed this on you. I'll go pack. If you'll lend me a car, I can drive myself to the nearest police station, or you can drop me off there yourself. I'll report the attack..."

I didn't wait for him to respond. I hurried to my room and searched out my bag. I wanted to laugh at the fact that I still hadn't managed to do laundry, so I had nothing clean to change into. But I supposed it didn't matter if I showed up at the police station in sweats and a T-shirt. My political career likely wouldn't survive any of this anyway, so potentially having a picture snapped by reporters in the casual attire seemed pretty irrelevant at this point. As soon as the story got out that I'd been attacked in my own home, my opponents would make sure the public was wondering what skeletons in my closet had triggered the incident. The good news was that if I dropped out of the race now, my party could still nominate someone to put on the ballot in my place. It wasn't ideal, but they'd still have a chance of running a successful campaign against the Republican candidate.

I waited for the disappointment to hit me as I considered what giving up my career in politics would mean, but surprisingly, all I felt was a lingering curiosity about the whole thing. Like what my life would have been like as a U.S. Senator. But along with that feeling came an odd and completely unexpected sense of freedom.

I didn't even know how to process that.

Before I could give it much thought, I sensed a presence and turned to see Vincent standing in my doorway, his hard eyes on the bag I had in my hand.

"I'm almost ready," I said as I wondered if I'd been dallying too long. The man hadn't actually barked out a time limit like he usually did, but the hard set of his jaw was telling me he was pissed just the same.

I turned to head towards the bathroom to grab my toiletries, but just as quickly I was spun back around as Vincent wrapped his hand around my elbow.

"Vincent-"

"Shut up," he snapped, and then he took the bag from my hand and flung it to the floor. Then his fingers curled around my hand and he led me from the room. I held my tongue as I realized our destination.

His room.

I hated the shimmer of hope that went through me at the prospect of getting to be with him one last time. It was pathetic that I would take even the crumbs he threw my way, but I wasn't going to try to deny it. Or pretend I was somehow strong enough to say no. Or that I had enough pride left.

Because I didn't.

I expected him to lead me to the bed, but he surprised me when he shoved me up against the wall next to the door and pinned my arms next to my head. The move hadn't actually hurt me, but it had caught me off guard.

"Vincent, what-"

"If this thing is going to work, Nathan, you need to stop assuming things and actually stop running long enough to give me time to think…and speak."

I wanted to laugh at that, because the man had never had an issue with telling me what he thought before.

"You had plenty to say downstairs," I reminded him.

He eyed me for a moment, and then he released me and dragged me over to the bed. I was on my back beneath his heavy body in one swift move. He ground his very hard cock against mine and I cursed the fabric that was separating us.

"Maybe now you'll shut the fuck up and listen," he groused. His lips fell to mine, but he didn't actually kiss me. "This is the only place you said you'd take orders from me, right, Nate?" he drawled.

I nodded, though he knew very well what kind of orders I'd been talking about. The *get naked* kind. I thought back to the very inexperienced blow job I'd given him this morning. Maybe I'd get a chance to improve on my earlier score.

"Nathan, focus," Vincent growled, and I realized I'd dropped my eyes to where our hips were grinding together.

"Stop humping my dick and I will," I bit back. "Or shut the hell up and just kiss me already."

He did neither of those things. Just continued to hold me pinned to the bed as he studied me.

"You're not the only one I don't want reading too much into what all this means," he finally admitted. His words were enough to help me focus on what he was saying instead of what his body was doing to mine.

His lips finally brushed over mine and he settled more of his weight down on me. "I knew the second the words left my lips this morning that I wouldn't be able to do it, Nate."

"Do what?" I whispered.

"Let you go."

Heat lanced through my body and my chest felt insanely tight.

"Vincent-"

He kissed me to shut me up again and then he was pressing his forehead against mine. "I can't want this, Nathan. Do you understand me? Not don't...*can't*."

I nodded and squeezed my eyes closed because I *did* understand. "You won't lose me, Vincent. I promise," I whispered desperately.

He kissed me again. "Baby, you know it isn't about making me that promise."

I wanted to cry because I knew he was right. And I wanted to curse whoever was hunting him that had taken his ability to choose me away. I wanted to tell him it wasn't fair, but he'd had his share of not fair. His career stolen, his lover lost to him forever, his brother brutally murdered...I didn't hold that same station in his life, but maybe I could have.

"Nate, open your eyes."

I did as he said, and furiously blinked back the tears that were threatening to fall. But I knew he could tell what I was doing because he shook his head slightly and let out a soft sigh. Fortunately, he didn't comment on it. Instead he said, "We'll go to the rally on Saturday and try to draw the fucker out. But when you're safe, Nathan…when this is all over, I need you to promise me you'll walk away. I need you to do that for me."

I wanted to rant at him that it wasn't fair for him to ask that of me. But the fact that he'd had to make the request in the first place told me where he was at. And as good as it felt to know he was in this thing as deeply as me, I still cursed the unseen circumstances that were bent on keeping us from figuring this thing out between us.

"Promise," I said hoarsely.

His lips found mine and he kissed me reverently. He spent an endless amount of time worshiping my body with his mouth and hands as he plucked my clothes from me piece by piece. I was boneless when he stood up and pulled his own clothes off. By the time he slid into me, I was desperate to come, but Vincent tortured me with slow, deep thrusts meant to keep me on the edge. Only when I was begging him to send me over the edge did he shift his hips so he could hit my gland on every stroke. As the orgasm crashed over me, he ordered me to keep my eyes on him and I was helpless to do anything else. But instead of following me over, he began his sensuous torture all over again, and when I came for the second time, he was right there with me.

I couldn't say how long we lay there trying to catch our breath, but when we were finally forced to move, it was only long enough to take a quick shower where we washed each other, and then he was leading me back to his bed.

As I curled into his side, my eyes fell on the bookshelf opposite the bed.

"Will you tell me about him?" I asked as I ran my hand up and down Vincent's chest.

Vincent didn't need to ask who I was talking about. "What do you want to know?" he asked after a few moments.

"The books – they were his?"

I motioned towards the bookshelf with my chin.

"Yes. He started collecting them when we were kids. He had a learning disability that made it hard for him to read, so his teachers suggested his parents find books that really captured his interest. As hard as it was for him, he was always reading. When I would spend the night at his house, we'd lie in his bed and I'd spend hours reading to him."

Vincent fell silent for a moment before saying, "When we got kicked out of the army, he started selling some of his older books that were worth money because they were first editions. It broke his heart, but we were desperate for the money. So when I started working again, I began buying them back for him. The look in his eyes every time I brought him another one…"

I pressed a kiss against Vincent's shoulder when his voice cracked. "It's okay, you don't have to go on," I murmured.

He shook his head. "No, he…he deserves to be remembered more often." Vincent's fingers trailed up and down my back as he continued. "Even after he died, I kept buying the books for him. I only have a few more to find. Not sure what I'll do then."

The heartbreak in his voice tore at me. I sat up and leaned across him to turn on the light next to the bed. I let my fingers skim over his cheek. "Which one was his favorite?" I asked.

"The Outsiders."

I glanced at the bookshelf. "Can I read it to you?"

Vincent sucked in a breath and then nodded. I didn't care that I was naked as I climbed out of the bed and went to the bookshelf.

"Right side, third shelf. All the way to the right," Vincent said.

I found the book and returned to the bed. I leaned back against the headboard. Vincent sat up and did the same as I flipped the book open. I was about to start when he put his hand on my wrist. I watched as he reached over into the second drawer of the nightstand and pulled out a small picture frame.

I knew without needing to ask that the picture was of David. Vincent handed it to me and I studied the smiling face looking back at me. He was a beautiful young man with bright green eyes, light blond hair and a wide grin that lit up his entire face. I couldn't even fathom the demons that had consumed him.

"That smile," I said softly.

"Yeah," Vincent agreed and then he was taking the picture back. He held it reverently for a moment before standing it up on the nightstand. He straightened and then nodded at me. As I began reading, Vincent's fingers curled around my free hand which I had resting in my lap. When it came time to turn the page, he did it for me.

My heart skipped a beat as I realized how easily I could get used to this.

Except that I'd promised him I wouldn't.

How the hell was I ever going to be able to keep that promise?

CHAPTER 22

VINCENT

I'd just turned on the stove when my watch vibrated. I'd assumed it was Nathan getting up, but a glance at the display showed my guest wasn't the man I'd spent the entire night making love to. I kept pulling ingredients out of the refrigerator, but turned the stove back off. By the time I'd searched out a second mug and filled it with coffee, Everett was entering the kitchen. He didn't say anything as he pulled out one of the island bar stools and sat down. Once I'd finished preparing the coffee the way he liked it, I slid it across the island to him.

"Thanks," he murmured.

He looked tired and, for once, he seemed to carry the weight of all his fifty-eight years.

"I'm sorry, Vincent. I shouldn't have participated yesterday. Nathan didn't know any better, but I did."

I knew what he was talking about, of course. If anyone would have known what I was going through as I'd raced to get back to the house, it would have been Everett. He'd seen the police report. He'd known the torture Pierce had been forced to endure.

"Why did you?" I asked.

He shook his head. "I wanted him to rattle your cage."

"Nathan?" I clarified.

A quick nod, then, "He's good for you, Vincent. You've been... different these past few days. Except for yesterday. Leaving without telling him. Refusing to answer our calls, even knowing he'd be worried about you."

"I didn't consider that," I interjected. Everett's eyes lifted to meet mine. "I knew he'd be pissed, but I thought that would be the extent of it."

"He was terrified," Everett murmured. "He hid it well, but it wasn't until my phone rang that first time that he relaxed."

I nodded. Nathan had admitted as much yesterday when he'd told me he'd imagined my body lying in a motel somewhere. "We're good, Ev," I said as I took a sip of my own coffee.

Everett relaxed somewhat, but the smile I was so used to seeing didn't return. I'd known the man for more than ten years, and he nearly always had a smile on his face.

But it had been that fake smile he'd worn for the cameras for so many years. On the rarest of occasions, he'd let me in enough to let me see the man who'd fallen in love with my brother. And it was usually when he was talking about Pierce that I got to see that piece of him. Like when something came on television that he thought Pierce would have liked, or when the military had finally repealed Don't Ask, Don't Tell years earlier. For those few moments, he'd let himself think of my brother and his reaction to something, and he'd be the Everett I should have met one day when my brother had been ready to introduce me to him.

"Nathan told me what you two talked about yesterday."

Everett's fingers played with the handle on the mug. "He shouldn't make the same mistake I did," the older man murmured. "I wanted him to know what waiting even a day too long could cost him."

I knew what he was talking about. On the few occasions Everett would have a little too much to drink, he'd get nostalgic and start talking about how he would have done things differently. Not a day went by that I knew he wasn't regretting not coming out while he was still in office. It would have caused a stir, but he would have been able to acknowledge his relationship with Pierce. And whatever firestorm he would have had to face, he'd have had my brother at his side when he'd done it. The fact that Pierce had left the military was a sign that he'd been all-in and ready to expose himself to the world as the man the leader of the free world was in love with.

As for Nathan, I had no idea what his plans were for when his life got back to normal. He'd embraced his sexuality here in the safety of my home, but out there in the real world? I shook my head as I thought about what he'd have to face.

And how he'd have to do it alone.

"Nathan will do what's best for him," I said.

"You're what's best for him."

Pain radiated through my chest at Everett's declaration. They were words I hadn't allowed myself to admit.

For the same reason I'd made Nathan promise he'd walk away when this was all over.

Because I was terrified that I wasn't strong enough to let him go.

"I'm not having this discussion with you," I said as I began preparing breakfast.

"It's been years since the last attempt..." Everett said as I turned my back on him to get the stove going.

"We both know there's no expiration date on revenge," I muttered. "Let it go, Everett."

"So what, Vincent? You're going to live like this for the rest of your life?" he asked, his voice uncharacteristically heavy with anger.

"Yeah, Everett, I am," I snapped as I turned back around. "Because there's no getting out for me! And he'll pay the price," I ground out as I pointed towards the stairs. I froze when I saw Nathan standing in the entryway to the kitchen. I held his startled gaze for a moment, and then turned back to the stove and tried to focus on getting the omelets going.

"Morning," Nathan said as he entered the room.

"Morning, Nathan," Everett said.

I stiffened when Nathan came around to my side of the island. I expected him to confront me about what I'd said, but instead, he leaned in and kissed me softly on the mouth. "Morning."

"Morning," I managed to say back. He grabbed the coffee pot and a mug and then went to sit next to Everett.

Nathan and Everett made small talk as I cooked, but when I asked Everett if he was staying for breakfast, he waved me off with an excuse about having already eaten. I didn't believe him, but I kept my mouth shut. I watched as he and Nathan said their goodbyes. I hated how worn down my friend looked, but I wasn't sure what to say, so I kept my mouth shut. He came around the island to give me a quick hug and then he was shuffling out the door.

"I'm worried about him," Nathan murmured as he came around the island and began picking at some of the diced ham I'd set aside for the second omelet.

I nodded. "He's usually better at hiding it."

"Hiding what?" Nathan asked.

"The fact that he's still in mourning."

"Have you ever talked to him about it? About trying to move on?"

"Yeah, a couple of times. Keeps saying he's too old and he'll only ever love one man in his lifetime. It's the reason he never bothered coming out."

"What do you mean?" Nathan asked as he leaned against the counter.

"I think it's his way of hanging on to my brother's memory, you know? Like coming out means he's starting a new chapter...one without Pierce."

I glanced at Nathan to see him studying the spot where Everett had been sitting. "What about his son?"

"He told you about Reese?" I asked in surprise.

Nathan nodded. "He said Reese accused him of having an affair. He said Pierce was his commanding officer."

I nodded because I'd heard the story from Everett about Reese walking in on him and Pierce so many years ago. "It probably ate Pierce up," I mused.

"He said Reese works for someone in Seattle…it's not your friend, is it? Beck's uncle?"

I stilled at that and lifted my eyes to meet Nathan's. "What?"

Nathan tensed. "You didn't know?"

I shook my head as things finally fell into place. Everett had always been tight-lipped around me about how he and Ronan had met, and I'd accepted that. But I'd had no clue Reese had somehow ended up working for Ronan. And I had no doubt that he was the man Nathan was talking about, not Dom. I'd known enough about Reese before he'd disappeared to be aware that he'd hooked up with some mercenaries after leaving the military. The mercenaries had been less interested in being patriots and more interested in making some easy money. If Reese had made one wrong move with guys like that, it would have spelled disaster.

I shook my head. "No, I didn't." I thought back to his first question. "No, it's probably not Beck's uncle. There's another guy out there who does some security consulting work," I hedged.

Nathan eyed me. "Security consulting," he said skeptically, his eyebrows raised. "Is that what they call it?"

I smiled at that. "Anyway, Ronan – that's the guy's name – I suspect he did it as a favor to Everett…to keep an eye on the kid."

"You think Reese knows what Everett did for him?" Nathan asked.

I shook my head. "Probably not. He'd shoot himself in the foot to spite his father. If he found out Everett was involved, he'd likely disappear again like he did after his mother's death."

"How did Everett and this Ronan guy meet?"

"I actually don't know," I admitted. "Everett's never told me the details about that."

I finished the first omelet and slid it onto a plate and handed it to Nathan. "Thanks," he said as he took it and went to the table. He paused before sitting down and letting his finger gloss over the table.

Right where I'd held him down as I'd fucked him the day before.

When he looked at me, color flooded his cheeks, and he smiled knowingly. I laughed and shook my head. Yeah, I'd never be able to look at that damn table the same way, either.

I finished getting my own food ready and went to sit down across from him. The second I did, his foot pressed against mine beneath the table. It was subtle, but it rocked me to my core. Knowing that he needed that physical connection with me, despite the fact that I was literally two feet away, made something tear open inside of me.

Something I'd buried along with David's body years earlier.

I knew my feelings for Nathan were growing exponentially with every minute I spent in his presence, but I was helpless to stop it.

"So the plan is to head to Charleston tomorrow?" Nathan asked as he practically inhaled his food. My mouth felt dry, like it had been stuffed full of cotton.

"Uh-huh," I managed to get out as I reached for my coffee and took a healthy swallow. When it felt like I could breathe again, I said, "I'm going to have you send some emails today confirming your appearance at the rally. I'll make it look like the emails are coming from an internet café in Charleston. We want it to look like you're still being careful, but that you're starting to feel more comfortable with coming out of hiding."

"And we'll stay in a motel the night of the rally?"

I shook my head. "No, I've decided we're going to go back to your house."

"Won't that be harder to secure? I mean, there are so many ways for him to get into the house."

"Ronan's got some men in the Metro D.C. area. I'll have them help me secure both the rally and the house."

Nathan nodded and turned his attention back to his food.

A wave of uncertainty went through me. It was an unfamiliar and hated sensation, and I could feel the edges of another episode of panic creeping in.

"Nathan," I said, and waited until he was looking at me.

"When we're there, you do everything I say. Without question."

He must have sensed something in my expression, because he quickly nodded and then he reached his hand out to cover mine where it was resting next to my plate.

"I will, Vincent. I promise."

It wasn't until he began stroking his thumb over my skin that I felt any measure of relief.

Fuck, I'd always been so confident about my decisions, but knowing what was at stake - that it wasn't just my own life on the line – had me on edge. And on edge people made stupid mistakes.

I forced myself to finish the omelet, even though it tasted like sandpaper going down. When I was finished, I reached for my plate, but Nathan waved me away. "Go do your thing. I'll take care of this," he said as Mickey appeared and then jumped on his lap. I automatically searched out Minnie and was surprised to see she was sitting on the floor next to Nathan's leg, rubbing up against it.

The strangest sensation of rightness came over me as I watched him sitting there at my kitchen table, eating my food, playing with my cats.

God, what I wouldn't give to go back in time and tell Dominic Barretti I would take him up on his job offer. I had to believe that even if things had been different all those years ago, my life still would have led me to this moment...to this man. I knew it was unfaithful to David to not be thinking about him as part of that life after I'd chosen what Dom had been offering, but in my gut, I knew I would have lost David to his demons no matter what. I'd lost him the moment the military had rejected us.

"You okay?" Nathan asked.

I nodded and pushed my chair back. "Just have a lot to do," I said.

"Let me know what you need me to do, okay?"

"I will," I agreed and then, like it was the most natural thing in the world, I leaned down and kissed him. Because even if it was only temporary and we were just playing house, I was damn well going to pretend it was real for as long as I could.

I'd deal with the consequences later...once Nathan was gone and I had to go back to the way things were.

The way they'd always be.

"No, tell me you're not...a channel flipper," I groused as I watched the image on the TV screen switch a mere second after the channel was changed. Not even long enough to figure out what show was on the screen.

"Shut up," Nathan murmured as he elbowed me.

Somehow, we'd ended up sitting side by side on the couch, despite there being several different pieces of furniture for us to spread out on, and we'd migrated toward one another until Nathan was leaning against my side.

Just before dinner, Nathan and I had sent out the agreed-upon emails to his assistant, campaign manager, and the rally organizers, telling them Nathan was feeling well enough to attend the rally on Saturday. I'd embedded code into each email that would allow me to tell anytime it was opened and by whom, so we'd know if Nathan's assailant was watching them or not. So far only his campaign manager and the rally organizer had viewed the email, so I'd settled in with Nathan to watch something on TV while we waited for the final email to be viewed before heading to bed. Our plan was to leave for Charleston in the morning. We'd spend the day at Nathan's house getting Ronan's men installed so that some were watching the house from the outside while one secured the inside. I'd have a couple more men backing me up at the rally. As soon as I'd told Ronan what I'd needed, he'd gotten it for me within a matter of minutes. Even with five men at my disposal, he'd told me he could get more to me within a matter of hours if I thought it was necessary.

I didn't.

But it sure as hell felt good to know Nathan's safety now lay in the hands of several capable men instead of just mine.

"How about this?" Nathan asked.

I glanced at the TV and barely refrained from rolling my eyes. "Please tell me you're kidding."

"What? It's cool to see how much they're able to sell the house for after they fix it up."

"Pass," I said.

Nathan made a rude sound, but changed the channel anyway. He began flipping again, but stopped suddenly on a news channel. He stiffened against me and then sat up.

"And I think the fact that Mr. Wilder hasn't been seen or heard from in nearly a week should have the good people of this state wondering if he's fit for the demanding challenges of this office."

I knew who the man was – Lawrence Braxton, the incumbent Republican Senator for the state of South Carolina. The same man whose seat Nathan was running for. The arrogant-looking asshole had a smug look on his face as he spoke with the reporter interviewing him.

The reporter, an older woman, said, "Mr. Wilder's campaign has said he's been battling the flu this week. Do you believe it's something more, Senator Braxton? Do you believe he's starting to crack under the pressure?"

The man let out a raucous laugh. "Now don't you go putting words in my mouth, young lady," he said with his best Southern drawl. "But I do have to wonder if someone with no political experience and who seems to volley on every position you all ask him about...well now, should he really be given the responsibility of speaking for our great state in the mire of Washington?"

The interview ended and the anchor in the news studio began talking about another story, so Nathan changed the channel, but stopped flipping through them. I sat up and used my fingers to brush some hair behind his ear, even though it didn't need it. It was just an excuse to touch him.

"You okay?" I asked.

Nathan nodded. "I think that's part of the problem. I *am* okay."

"What do you mean?"

He was silent for a moment as he stared at the TV. Then he turned to me and said, "In the past, I would have been on the phone to Preston strategizing a response. But...I just don't care. What does that say, Vincent?" he asked. "About me? About my campaign? About why I'm really doing this?"

I shook my head. "I don't know what you mean, Nathan," I admitted.

He sighed. "Yeah, me neither, I guess. I just…"

"Just what?" I prodded.

"Everything's changed so much and so fast."

"Things will be clearer when life gets back to normal," I offered. But my words seemed to agitate him more. He didn't respond. Just nodded and settled back against my side and began flipping channels again.

"Did you always know you wanted to go into politics?" I heard myself asking. It was a topic we'd both worked hard to avoid, but I found myself avidly interested in the subject now. Of course, I was interested in everything there was to know about this man.

"No," he said. "It was more like I accepted it."

"What do you mean?"

"Brody was the one with big dreams. When people would ask him what he wanted to be, he'd have those stock answers like being a fireman or an astronaut."

"And you?"

"I was too afraid to answer."

"Afraid? How so?"

"Growing up in the Wilder household was about one thing and one thing only. Having the right answer. And by right, I mean the answer my father wanted you to have. I got that early on. Brody struggled with it. It was harder for him to accept that our lives had already been decided for us. I tried to help him by taking the attention off him…by doing things so well, he'd maybe have a chance to be the things he wanted. It didn't really work, though. I think he resented me, and my father just saw him as a failure and a disappointment. I guess in the end, I just made things worse."

"You were trying to protect him," I said softly.

"Trying and doing aren't the same thing," he responded. "Brody was always the brave one. He was the one who had the guts to ask why things were the way they were. I just did what was expected. Straight A's in school, captain of the football team, dated the most popular girl in school...I never broke the rules. Brody, he was always finding ways to stretch them."

"So why stay in politics after you decided not to run as a Republican?"

"I thought I could undo some of what I'd done."

"To Brody?" I asked carefully.

He nodded. He was still staring at the TV, but I knew he wasn't watching what was on the screen anymore.

"Knowing people would never leave Brody alone to live his life... that he'd carry this label around that somehow made him less than human...I couldn't just stand by and let that happen. This whole time I had myself convinced it was just about Brody and people like him. I don't know why it was so hard to admit the truth to myself."

"Not many people seek out being different, Nathan. I sure as shit didn't want to be gay," I admitted. "I knew I wanted to be with David, but I think if I'd had a choice in the whole thing, I would have chosen the path that ensured I could have everything I wanted. Military career, family. I mean, who wants to have to fight for things that should just be a given? It shouldn't have been about me fighting to be allowed to love whoever I wanted. But that's what it became - that's who I became. Not a soldier, not a man, not a brother. Gay. I'm gay first and everything else second. It shouldn't be that way, but it is."

"You don't think things can change?" Nathan asked as he straightened and turned to look at me again.

"Over time, maybe. But do I think in my lifetime, or even yours, that that label will go away? No, I don't."

"But that doesn't mean we should stop fighting. Maybe the battle we win today is one less battle that needs to be fought tomorrow."

I sighed and nodded. "Maybe. But I'm damn tired of fighting," I murmured.

Nathan nodded and settled back against me. "Here, you old geezer," he said as he handed me the remote.

I took it and let my free hand slide down his abdomen until it lingered just above the button of his jeans. "Geezer, huh?" I said softly as I gently bit down on his earlobe. Nathan shuddered, and then his hand was covering mine and trying to urge it south. "Maybe you need a repeat of what I did to you on that kitchen table?"

The sounds coming out of his mouth had no meaning, but it was clear what his bobbing head was saying. Then he was turning to seek out my lips. Unfortunately, an alert on my phone beeped, and I was forced to pull my mouth from his. "I gotta check this, baby," I said as he tried to follow me with his mouth. He let out a growl and dropped his head to my chest. I grabbed my laptop off the side table and opened it up.

"Someone besides your assistant opened the email," I said.

"Can you trace it?" Nathan asked.

I spent several minutes tracking the guy's trail, but just like the others, it began hopping from one IP address to another. I shook my head and closed the laptop.

"At least we know he's still watching," Nathan murmured.

"Yeah. Just be nice to know who it was we're looking for," I said in frustration. I had a general idea of the guy's build from the night he'd attacked Nathan, but that was it.

"How do you know how to do all this stuff?" Nathan asked as he motioned to my laptop. "Did the army teach you?"

"Some of it. I was always into gadgets and stuff when I was a kid. My dad liked to fix old radios, so that was how it started. As I got older, I just liked figuring out how things worked. I suppose if I hadn't gone into the military, I would have been an engineer or something."

"So you taught yourself?" Nathan probed.

I knew what he was really asking me. I sighed, and Nathan immediately shifted back. "I'm...I'm sorry. I shouldn't-"

I grabbed his hand when he tried to stand. "Sit," I said gently. He settled back on the couch and I turned so I was facing him. I studied him for a moment and shook my head. "I keep telling myself I'm not telling you because I'm worried it'll get out, but that's bullshit," I admitted. "I know you'd take my secrets to your grave."

He nodded, but remained silent, his whiskey-colored eyes holding mine.

"Truth is, I'm afraid it will change how you look at me."

"It wouldn't-"

I pressed my thumb against his lips to silence him. "I can't tell you everything…"

Nathan nodded and when I dropped my hand, he remained silent.

"After the military discharged me and the contracting work started to dry up, the Department of Defense came calling with a job offer. One of my commanding officers worked for this unit that worked with other groups…FBI, CIA, NSA. The department ran top secret missions all over the world, usually as part of small teams of men, all former military. The work seemed legit at first…saving high-value hostages, doing recon on targets, that sort of thing. But then everything changed."

CHAPTER 23

NATHAN

I tried to keep up as Vincent spoke, but the deeper he got into his story, the harder it was for me to understand what he was telling me. It was the shit that didn't exist in real life, only on the big screen in high octane action movies. But as he told me about the first man he'd killed when he'd been sent out on his own for his first solo operation, I knew it was true.

He was an assassin.

There was just no other way to describe what he was telling me. He'd been given a target with orders to pull the trigger, and he'd done it.

That simple.

Except that it wasn't, because I knew this man. I knew in my bones that he wasn't capable of cold-blooded murder.

"How many?" I interjected.

"How many what?" he asked, his voice solemn.

"How many people have you killed?"

Vincent straightened and hardened his jaw. "I lost track after the first twenty or so."

I managed a nod. "Go on," I said, because I knew in my gut there was more to his story. He was a hard man, but he wouldn't just pull the trigger and end a life for no reason.

"About three years into the job, I knew something had changed. I'd trusted the man in charge of the unit, so we'd always had really good intel about our targets and why they were being terminated. But when the guy retired, the unit got a new director, and I knew pretty much right away that things were different. I was assigned to take out this twenty-something-year-old grad student, but something about the whole thing was wrong to me. So instead of completing the job, I followed the kid and tried to learn as much about him as I could. Turned out he was this genius who was designing a guidance system that he was hoping to present to NASA for their space program. Only, the government decided they could put the guidance system to better use on their ICBMs."

"ICBMs...those are intercontinental ballistic missiles," I murmured. "They carry nuclear warheads."

Vincent nodded. "The kid wasn't interested in giving his technology to the government, so they took it. When he discovered the theft, he threatened to go to the press. That was when I was called in."

"They wanted you to silence him."

"Only they didn't sell it that way. The kid's parents were Middle Eastern, so they sold me on the angle that the kid was trying to sell the guidance system to the highest bidder."

"What happened to him?" I asked. "Were you able to save him?"

Vincent stiffened and sat back a little. "You're so certain I didn't do it?" he asked in confusion.

I shook my head in disbelief. "Vincent, I know you," I whispered. "You're...you're not like that. Whatever you did early on, you did it because you believed it was the right thing. And because you had proof."

He studied me for a long time before continuing. "I didn't do it, but I knew my handler would just send someone along who would do the job without question. I helped get the kid and his parents set up in another country with new identities. But doing that painted a target on my back."

"They came after you," I said softly as things began to make sense.

"The team they sent found Pierce instead of me that night."

I swallowed hard as I remembered the gruesome details he'd shared with me about his brother's murder.

"What did you do?" I asked.

"I became the hunted," Vincent responded. "So I got smart. It was that or face a lifetime of running." He settled back against the cushions. "Three years of killing people for the government taught me who the power players were. So, while they played cat and mouse with me, I did the same with them. I convinced those in power that killing me wouldn't safeguard their precious secrets."

"That worked?" I asked.

"Not at first. I had to prove that I was in the game until the end. Every team they sent after me I sent back in body bags. And every time they tried to take me down, I leaked some of their secrets. Not enough to bring any one person down, but enough to make them uncomfortable. I became known as *The Ghost.*" Vincent waved his hand. "I know, it's a stupid nickname, but I was more interested in what it meant."

"What did it mean?"

"It meant anyone who came into contact with me should be scared. That I could appear and disappear whenever and however I wanted. That I could take someone down as easily with information as I could with my gun. Eventually the powers that be figured it was safer just to leave me be."

"But…you still live like this," I murmured as I motioned to the house.

"Because I'm not foolish enough to believe anything those fuckers tell me. You remember that child's fable about the scorpion and the frog?"

"Yeah. The frog agrees to give the scorpion a ride across the river in exchange for the scorpion not stinging him, and the scorpion agrees, but then stings him anyway and they both die."

Vincent nodded. "And the frog asks the scorpion why he did it and he says, 'Because it's my nature.'"

He fell silent, so I said, "You think they'll keep coming after you. That they can't help themselves."

"I've built up enough relationships that I've got most guys running scared who will do their best to ensure I'm left alone, but there will always be that asshole who doesn't like knowing I'm out there…that with a few words I can take him and everyone around him down. Add in the guys who want revenge for the loved ones I took out over the years, and there's always someone waiting for that moment when *The Ghost* exposes a vulnerable spot."

I nodded as things began to make more sense. "I'm a vulnerable spot," I murmured.

Vincent's hand came up to clasp my neck so he could force my eyes up. "Baby, you're not a spot – you're my goddamn jugular."

I wanted to cry, because while his words were proof that he was getting in as deep into this thing as me, he'd also sealed our fate. Being with me would put him at risk. Maybe not today or tomorrow, but there'd come a time when the next guy would come along and use me to get to him.

"When was the last time…that someone tried?" I asked.

"Three years ago."

"But you're…you're out of the business?" I asked.

"I've been out for more than ten years. I have good relationships with a few guys that I'll help out once in a while if they need it."

"Like who?"

"Director of the FBI. Head of the NSA…that's on account of Everett."

"So Everett knows about you?"

"He does. He's helped get the word out as much as he can that I'm off limits. He also has enough contacts that he can help me out on occasion – like getting your house cleaned up without a lot of questions after we left that night. He also hooked me up with Ronan, who's the one who asked me to take your case."

"I thought Beck's uncle was the one who asked you."

Vincent shook his head. "Beck's uncle and his father are friends with Ronan, but I didn't know that going into all this. I ran into Dom by chance when I was meeting with Ronan and one of his men. Dom told me about Beck. He was the reason I agreed."

"You didn't initially want to do it?" I asked.

Vincent smiled. "Let's just say I wasn't your biggest fan when Ronan told me what you did for a living."

I chuckled. "And now?"

Vincent's expression turned serious as he held my gaze. "Definitely a fan," he whispered, and then he was pulling me forward for a long, sweet kiss. When he tried to pull back, I followed until I was straddling his lap.

I grabbed his face to make sure he was focused on me when I said, "Thank you for telling me. Doesn't change a thing," I said softly. "But thank you for trusting me."

Vincent nodded and then he was kissing me again. His hands drifted down my ass so he could grind our cocks together. It was a struggle to stop kissing him long enough for him to get my shirt off. It wasn't until his hand snaked down my pants and gripped my cock that I tore my mouth from his and let out a guttural groan. He gave me several long strokes that had me bucking against his hand. My breath was coming in hard pants as I said, "Do you…do you have anything?"

I hoped like hell he knew what I was talking about, because I couldn't get the damn thought out beyond those few words.

"Uh-huh," he murmured against my mouth. "Pants off," he ordered as he pulled his wallet out of his jeans and began rifling through it.

I stumbled to my feet and practically ripped my pants off. By the time I'd kicked them aside, he had his pants shoved down his hips and he was lubing up his dick. I waited for him to tell me what position he wanted me in, but when he snagged my wrist and dragged me back down onto his lap, I lost all train of thought. His slick dick rubbed up against mine and then his hand was there.

"Lift up a little," he said. I used my knees to lift off him and let out a hoarse moan when his finger found my hole. I braced my hands on his shoulders as he pressed his finger inside of me in one swift move, and as he finger-fucked me, I tried grinding my erection against his body.

Then his dick was there and he was urging me back down. It wasn't until his crown nudged up against my hole that I realized he was going to take me just like this – with me straddling him.

Riding him.

"Oh God," I cried out as he began to sink inside of me. I dropped all my weight down onto him in my eagerness to get him fully inside of me.

"Slow, baby," he whispered.

I shook my head. I didn't want slow. I wanted fast and hard and hot.

The position gave me more control than I'd ever had before, which I eagerly took advantage of. Even as Vincent tried to grab my hips to slow me down, I let gravity work in my favor. The stretch bordered on painful as he bottomed out inside of me. I sat there, heart thudding inside my chest, breaths seesawing in and out of me as I tried to adjust to how full the new position made me feel. It wasn't until Vincent murmured, "Your show, baby," against my lips that I realized he was really going to let me have this.

He was going to let me control our pleasure.

I lifted up a little and dropped back down, but true to his word, Vincent's hold on my hips was merely to steady me and not urge me on either way. I found the rhythm I wanted after just a couple of minutes. I could feel Vincent's pants scraping my ass every time I lowered myself onto him, but the sensation just ratcheted my need higher.

I began to frantically ride him as I wrapped my arms around his neck. "So good, Vincent," I growled as I chased my orgasm. "So close," I told him, hoping he wasn't far behind me.

"Take what you want, Nate. Wanna watch you come."

It was the permission I needed. I lost all interest in where he was at and just used his body to my benefit. I was dimly aware of him urging me on with his voice and his hands, but I was too far gone to care. My one and only goal was to come.

I reached between our bodies and began desperately jerking myself off as the friction of his dick sliding in and out of me began to dictate how I moved.

"That's it, baby. Shoot it all over me."

Vincent's voice broke through the haze of pleasure, and I looked down to see my hand furiously stroking my dick over the hard muscles of Vincent's abdomen. Our bodies were slick with sweat, and I used my free hand to clasp his neck as the orgasm raced up my spine. I came hard and fast, but luckily, I managed to keep my eyes open long enough to see a jet of cum splatter across Vincent's open lips. Another shot of semen grazed his cheek. I was so turned on by the sight that I kept riding Vincent as I leaned over and ran my tongue up his cheek to collect the fluid. His chin was next, and then I was kissing him and sharing my taste with him. He eagerly lapped at my mouth as he took everything I gave him. I felt his dick pulsing inside of me, signaling the end. He shouted into our next kiss as he came, and I hung onto his shoulders as he jerked his hips upwards so he could press himself as deep inside of me as he could get.

When it was all over, we hung there in blissful silence as we both came down.

Reality intruded, and I realized that tonight very well could be one of my last nights with him.

And for the first time since I'd been attacked in my own home, I wasn't eager to find the assailant.

How fucked up was that?

CHAPTER 24

VINCENT

"Everybody clear?" I asked as I took one last look at the map laid out on the table.

The men around the table nodded, and then they were leaving the room. The long-haired one, Jace, patted me on the shoulder. "We've got your back, Vincent. Nothing will happen to him."

I wasn't sure what surprised me more - the physical contact or the realization that Jace had figured out what Nathan meant to me, despite the fact I'd only known the operative for a short time.

As caught off guard as I was by the reassurance, it was still oddly comforting. I'd literally met these guys an hour ago, and yet I was putting Nathan's life in their hands. Ronan had sent me background on each man, so I knew they were the best of the best. Jace, for his part, was considered one of the best snipers in the world.

A skill that would come in handy when he was perched on top of one of the buildings surrounding the park where the rally was being held. He'd be able to keep eyes on Nathan through his scope and take out anyone the rest of us couldn't reach on foot as we worked the crowd while Nathan was giving his speech.

"Thanks," I murmured as I watched him leave. Two of the men would sit outside the house overnight and a third would be staying inside the house with me and Nathan to keep watch while we slept. That same man would keep the house secure the following day while the rest accompanied us to and from the rally.

Even though Ronan's guys would be enough for the job, I'd decided to take it a step further and cash in my chips with the head of the NSA. The man had agreed to send some of his agents to cover the rally in place of the standard security guards. They'd also look the other way when it came to me and my men being armed on the premises. So, between the men I was bringing with me and the Secret Service agents, Nathan would be one of the most well-protected men in America tomorrow.

I glanced up at the repaired picture window and shuddered at the memory of Nathan's assailant standing behind him with a knife.

Too fucking close.

I switched off the lights and did a quick check of the first floor to make sure everything was locked up before heading upstairs.

Things had gotten a little awkward when we'd arrived at the house. Nathan had seemed uncomfortable as he'd babbled on about me using a guest room if I wanted, or sharing his room. I'd attributed the whole thing to a mix of nerves about tomorrow, as well as us no longer being in the privacy of my own home, but in truth, I was a little on edge about the whole thing. I'd ended up agreeing to a guest room just to put him at ease, but there was no way in hell I had any intention of actually sleeping in it.

Not after having spent the last several nights with Nathan snuggled up against my side.

In theory, I should have welcomed the opportunity to get some distance from him, but between the danger tomorrow would bring, and the realization that tonight could very well be my last night with him if tomorrow went our way, I sure as hell wasn't spending the night apart from him.

I snagged my bag off the bed in the guest room and went to Nathan's room. The door was closed, but I didn't bother knocking. He wasn't in the room, but I could see a plume of steam coming from the open bathroom door. I dropped my bag on the floor and reached into it to search out my shaving kit and toothbrush.

As I neared the bathroom, I saw Nathan standing in front of the vanity, his eyes on his reflection in the huge mirror. His hair was damp and he had a towel wrapped around his hips. His eyes met mine in the reflection and held them as I stepped up behind him and put my shaving kit and toothbrush down on the counter.

Neither of us spoke as we watched each other.

We didn't have to.

I knew exactly what he was thinking, and I suspected it was the same for him.

I let my hand skim over his beautiful back as I dropped my lips to his shoulder. His skin was warm and damp. I lifted my other hand to clasp his waist as I trailed my lips up his neck. When my mouth found his, he straightened and his hand reached behind him to tangle in my hair. The kiss was raw and carnal, with each of us trying to gain control of it.

I won, but only because I chose that moment to release his towel. As he gasped, I took ownership of his mouth and then the rest of him. My hands roamed all over his body as I began pumping my hips against his. When I finally reached his dick, Nathan whispered my name.

"What, baby?" I asked as I began giving him short, jerky strokes that wouldn't give him the satisfaction he was seeking.

"Fuck me," he begged as he thrust his ass against me. The fabric of my jeans did nothing to hide my erection.

"Look in the mirror," I ordered. It took him a moment to follow through on the command. He pressed both hands on the counter to support himself as he looked in the mirror. But his eyes were on me, not himself.

"Look at yourself," I said.

When he did, I leaned in to nip at his ear. "Now beg me to fuck you again," I murmured. "See what I see when you're begging for my cock."

Nathan's body trembled at my words. His eyes remained on his own reflection. "Vincent, please…please fuck me," he managed to get out.

I rewarded him with a hard stroke on his dick and then I fondled his balls. He let out a whimper of protest when I released his cock. I kept humping his ass as I reached behind me and tugged my shirt off. Nathan's eyes were plastered on me in the mirror as I put my hands on his hips and began to pump my erection against his ass, mimicking the hard fucking I was going to be giving him.

"Yes," he cried out. "More."

Sweat started forming on his body, making his tanned skin glow beneath the soft overhead lights.

I stepped back enough to admire his gorgeous backside, but when he tried to turn around, I smacked his ass hard enough to get his attention. "Don't move," I said firmly.

He let out a little moan, but managed a nod. His upper body had collapsed onto the countertop, his weight supported by his forearms as he buried his face in his hands.

I continued to toy with him for a few minutes by letting my hands slide all over his body, but ignoring the parts of him that were most desperate for my touch. Then I was dropping to my knees behind him.

"Vincent?" Nathan whispered uncertainly as I split him open, but I gave him no time to consider what I was doing. The second I licked over his opening, he let out a harsh shout and slammed his hand against the glass to brace himself. He tried to jerk away from me, but I grabbed his hips and licked him again, then gently sucked. All of his struggles ceased and within seconds, he was pushing his ass backwards, trying to get more.

I toyed with his hole a little and then slid my tongue down his crease until I reached his balls. I took each one into my mouth, and then I lavished attention on his leaking dick. When I returned to his hole, I felt his hand reach around to slide into my hair, presumably to try and force me to give him more of what I was already giving him.

I worked his opening with soft licks and kisses until it began to relax, and then I stiffened my tongue and pushed it between the tight muscles. Nathan let out a keening cry as I began fucking him with my mouth.

"I'm going to come!" he shouted.

I grabbed the base of his dick to keep him from coming and pulled my mouth from his fluttering entrance.

I quickly stood and leaned over his back and kissed him, forcing his head into an awkward angle as I owned his mouth. There wasn't even an ounce of hesitation on his part to kiss me back, despite where my mouth had just been.

"You don't come until I tell you to, do you understand me?" I growled.

Nathan let out a soft groan, but nodded.

I reached down to find the lube I kept in one of the side pockets of my shaving kit. I kept bumping my hips up against Nathan's ass as I worked to open the small bottle. I undid my pants and released my rock-hard cock, but instead of slathering it with lube right away, I grabbed Nathan's ass cheeks and separated them so I could spear my dick between his crease over and over again until he was writhing beneath me. None of the words he spoke made any sense.

I quickly covered my dick with lube and then swiped some over his pink hole. I tossed the lube aside and wiped my hand on a nearby towel before grabbing his hips and guiding my cock to his opening. His body, still relaxed from the rimming I'd given him, didn't fight me as I pushed into him. I was seated fully inside of him in just a few thrusts.

Nathan braced his hands on the counter again as I began moving in and out of him.

"Look at us," I told him, and his eyes quickly went to the mirror. "Look how perfect we fit together," I bit out as I began to increase the pace. Nathan's body was hot and tight around me and I knew I wouldn't last.

"Do you see it?" I demanded.

Nathan managed a nod. "See it," he whispered. "Beautiful."

Hell yeah, it was. I leaned over him to kiss him hard as I fucked him. He returned my kiss eagerly.

"Remember, I come first," I said. "Want you to see what you do to me."

He nodded frantically.

I quickly pulled out of him and turned him around. My mouth slammed down on his as I lifted him so he was sitting on the counter. I dragged his ass to the edge and he automatically wrapped his legs around my waist. I shoved into him hard. He let out a keening cry as I nailed his prostate, and I quickly slapped my hand over his mouth so the guy guarding the inside of the house wouldn't hear him and come running.

I shuttled in and out of Nathan's hot body as my orgasm hovered just out of reach. Nathan's fingers bit into my arms where he was hanging onto me. I replaced my hand with my mouth and kissed him, absorbing his cries of pleasure.

"So beautiful," I told him as I pounded into him. "Mine, Nate. You're mine."

Nathan nodded in agreement. "Mine too, Vincent," he managed to get out. "You're mine…always."

His claim of ownership was enough to send me over the edge. He clasped my face in his hands so he could watch me as I came deep inside of him. I didn't manage to stifle the snarl of satisfaction that was caught in my throat as my orgasm washed over me in waves. I hung there as my balls emptied and my release bathed my dick in heat. I could barely breathe as explosions of pleasure continued to detonate under my skin. My harsh breaths mixed with Nathan's whimpers in the silence of the bathroom. I glanced down to see he'd heeded my warning not to come, but his dick was flushed an angry shade of purple and his abdomen was covered with lines of sticky pre-cum.

"Do you need to come, my beautiful boy?" I asked as I leaned down to gently kiss him.

He nodded, because he didn't seem capable of anything else.

"Keep hanging onto me, okay?" I said softly as I began to slowly pump in and out of him. I closed my hand around his dick and gave him a few gentle tugs before I added pressure. I could hear my release squishing inside of him as I began to thrust into him harder and harder. Nathan's fingers dug into my skin as he hung onto the backs of my upper arms. I kept working his dick as I increased my pace, shuttling my half-hard dick in and out of his ass. His inner muscles began to pulse around me and his throbbing cock swelled. Cries of delight escaped his throat, and I covered his mouth with mine to swallow the sound.

"Come for me, baby," I whispered against Nathan's lips as I changed the angle of my hips and pressed against his prostate. He shouted my name and then he was coming all over my hand, my chest, even my chin. I loved the feel of his warm cum coating my skin as he came apart in my arms. His body jerked and thrashed beyond his control until the orgasm finally eased. When he began to relax, I pulled him upright and wrapped my arms around him, not caring about the cum stuck between our bodies or still covering my hand. All I cared about was the feeling of Nathan's body lined up perfectly with mine and the way he clung to me, like he would never let me go.

For those few moments, everything was right in my world.

Until he said the words that I'd never expected to hear again in my lifetime.

"I love you, Vincent."

~

I love you, Vincent.

The words had been playing on an endless loop in my head all morning, and I'd only managed to escape them once Nathan had taken the stage to give his speech. At that point, I'd been all business as I'd worked the crowd and coordinated with Ronan's men and the plain-clothed Secret Service agents to identify anything unusual. I'd barely listened to Nathan as he'd spoken, but I hadn't missed how charged the crowd was when he took the stage. Or that he was a natural in the way he spoke to them. I almost wished I could have just stopped and listened to him speak, because he was mesmerizing.

His speech lasted a mere twenty minutes. I returned to his side when he was departing the stage and kept my eyes on all the men and women who pressed forward to give him their well-wishes. He worked the crowd like he'd been doing it his entire life. I supposed, in a way, he had been. The close proximity gave me a chance to study his reactions as he spoke to his constituents.

And there was most certainly something off.

I doubted the average person would notice, but I wasn't just some person.

I was the man Nathan was in love with.

Jesus, how the hell had this happened?

I hadn't responded when he'd said those words to me. I hadn't had any clue *how* to respond. What did you say when someone literally changed your entire world with three little words?

I'd merely hung onto him, and then I'd led him into the shower where we'd lovingly cleaned each other off. He'd fallen asleep quickly once we'd gotten into bed, but I'd spent most of the night awake, wondering how I'd let all of this happen.

And not just the part about him loving me.

He may have been the only one brave enough to admit his feelings, but he wasn't the only one feeling them.

I forced myself to focus on the crowd as we worked our way back to my SUV. One of Ronan's men had stayed with the car to make sure it hadn't been tampered with. He opened the door for us when we got to the vehicle. A couple of pushy reporters kept yelling questions at Nathan, including ones about whether or not there was a heightened security presence at today's rally and why, but he steadfastly ignored them. I climbed into the car after him and shut the door. We were moving within a couple of minutes. I pressed the communication device in my ear.

"Anything?" I asked.

One by one, the men reported in that no one was following the SUV.

I was both relieved and disappointed.

So far, Nathan's assailant hadn't taken the bait.

When I glanced at Nathan, he looked at me questioningly. I shook my head. He nodded and his eyes fell. I reached over to link my fingers with his.

"We'll get him," I murmured.

Nathan squeezed my fingers. "I know."

I leaned back against the seat and wasn't surprised when Nathan pressed into my side. I loved how tactile of a person he was. I wondered if it was just because he was with me, or if it was something he was feeling the need for after a lifetime with parents who likely hadn't shown him and his brother any kind of affection.

Since we had a thirty-minute drive back to Nathan's house, I began gently massaging the back of his neck in the hopes he'd fall asleep. Despite the fact that he'd been eating well and sleeping through the night while he'd been staying with me, he still seemed overly tired. It probably hadn't helped that I'd woken him up in the middle of the night to make love to him again.

After just a few minutes, I felt Nathan's body relax against mine, but it didn't last because my phone rang. Nathan sat up so I could reach for the phone. I removed the com from my ear when I saw who the caller was.

"Hey, Ronan," I said as I answered. "We're all good here," I said, assuming he'd called me to see how the rally went.

"Are you with Nathan?" Ronan asked.

I stiffened when I heard the tension in his voice.

"Yes," I said. "What's wrong?"

At that, Nathan's hand came to rest on my arm. "What is it?" he asked, his eyes going from relaxed to full-on worried just like that.

"Something's happened…to Brody," Ronan said.

I glanced at Nathan, and he must have seen something in my eyes because he began shaking his head. "No," he whispered.

I grabbed his hand and put the phone on speaker. "Ronan, you're on speaker. Nathan's here."

"Is it Brody?" Nathan asked, his voice thick with emotion.

"He's alive, Nathan," was the first thing Ronan said. Nathan's fingers squeezed mine so hard I was sure they'd break.

"What happened?" I asked.

"There was a fire at the house Brody, Quinn, and Beck are renting. Beck and Quinn had already left for work. The guy I had watching Brody got Brody out, but the house exploded when the fire reached the propane tank."

"Was Brody hurt?" I asked.

"His injuries from the explosion are minor. But as soon as he and my guy got out of the house, they came under fire."

"Under…under fire…what does that mean?" Nathan asked.

"Someone started shooting at them," Ronan said. "Brody was hit while he was helping my guy get to cover."

"Where was he shot?" I asked.

"Shoulder," Ronan said. "Nathan, he's okay, I promise you. The injury isn't life-threatening."

Nathan nodded, but that was all he could manage.

"What happened with the shooter?" I asked.

"My guy managed to hold him off until backup arrived. The shooter got away…my guys are looking for him now."

"I need to be there," Nathan said to me.

"I'm sending a plane for you. Vincent, I'll have the pilot call you when he's ready to submit his flight plan so you'll need to be able to tell him where you want him to land."

"Got it," I answered.

"With the shooter still on the loose, I'm sending Brody, Quinn, and Beck to Seattle."

"Is Brody okay to travel?" Nathan asked.

"He is. But Vincent…"

"Yeah?"

"The guy who was protecting Brody…it was Reese."

I sucked in a breath at that, and Nathan's fingers clenched mine.

"Is he hurt?" I asked.

"Yeah…it's not good. Some debris from the explosion hit him, and he took a couple of shots, too. Brody treated him on the scene until they could get him to the hospital. I'm on my way there now. My plane should be landing within the hour."

"Have you called Everett?" I asked.

"I just got off the phone with him. He'll be flying up there with you guys. The plane will drop him off in Missoula, and then you and Nathan will fly to Seattle."

"Okay, thanks, Ronan."

"Yeah," was all Ronan said. "I'll call you as soon as I hear something."

I hung up the phone. Nathan had released my hand at some point. He had his face buried in his hands and his elbows were resting on his knees.

"It's not your fault," I said.

"It's most certainly my fault," he whispered.

When I tried to reach for him, he pulled away from me. "Don't," he said softly. "Please, just don't."

"Fuck that," I bit out, and pulled him against my chest. He let out a harsh sob and struggled against me, but when I refused to release him, he quickly gave up and his fingers curled into my shirt. He began to cry, so I settled my lips against his ear. "He's okay, Nathan. They're all okay and I'm going to find this guy and I'm going to end him. Do you hear me?" My voice was harsh – too harsh, probably, but I didn't care. I'd meant what I'd said.

I'd find the fucker and I'd tear him limb from limb before he got another chance to take anything from my man.

My Nate.

CHAPTER 25

NATHAN

It was just starting to get dark by the time the plane landed at a small airstrip in the San Juan Islands. I'd only half-listened as Vincent had explained to me that we were going to Dominic Barretti's vacation home where Brody, Beck, and Quinn were staying, along with a couple of Ronan's men.

My fear for my brother had pretty much kept me paralyzed for the entire trip, despite the constant reassurances from Vincent that Brody was okay. Add on the unbearable guilt of knowing the man who'd tried to kill me had nearly succeeded in taking the life of Everett's son, and I was barely able to function. We'd at least gotten some good news when we'd landed in Missoula. Reese had gotten out of surgery and was expected to make a complete recovery, though he'd been badly burned in the attack. Everett had been a mess on the flight to Montana, but once he'd gotten the news that Reese was alive and doing well, he'd told Vincent and me to continue onto Seattle instead of escorting him to the hospital like we'd wanted to. It was only after Vincent had gotten Everett to promise that he'd send updates every hour that we'd finally agreed.

As with much of the trip, as soon as we were in the SUV that was waiting for us when we got off the plane, Vincent pulled me against his side and I happily went. As raw as I felt, he'd become my balm, and that made it possible for me to put one foot in front of the other.

The drive took about fifteen minutes, and then we were pulling into the expansive driveway of a huge estate on the water's edge. I'd never been to Seattle and if the circumstances had been different, I would have taken the time to admire the beauty of the mountains and water. But I just didn't have it in me.

My legs felt shaky as I climbed out of the SUV. Vincent's hand was at my back as we began the short walk to the front door. We both came to a stop when it opened and my brother stepped through it. Something inside of me ripped wide open at the sight of my twin. It felt like every terrible thing I'd said and done to him came crashing down on me in that moment, and I wasn't sure I had the strength to stay upright. I couldn't move forward as sob after sob tore through my body, and soon the tears blurred my vision to the point I couldn't even make out my brother anymore.

But I knew it was his arm that went around me a moment later and it was his voice that whispered in my ear, "I'm okay."

I nodded against his neck. "Sorry!" I cried out, since I couldn't manage any words besides the one I'd wanted to say to him for so long.

"It's okay, Nathan," Brody said softly as he held onto me. I was dimly aware of his left arm in a sling so I was careful not to cling to him like I wanted to. But his hold on me, even with the one arm, was firm and unrelenting.

He held me for as long as it took for me to settle, and then he was pressing his forehead against mine. "Missed you so much, Nathan."

I nodded. "Love you," was all I was able to get out.

"Love you too, big brother."

The endearment threatened to send me to my knees again, but Vincent's hand on my back steadied me in a way nothing else probably could have. We hadn't talked about how I would introduce him to Brody, but in that moment, I knew what needed to happen. Maybe it was because I'd already felt stripped so raw that it wouldn't matter, or maybe I just wanted to get everything out in the open so my brother could turn his back on me now before I had the chance to really sit down and talk to him.

I wasn't sure.

But life had just sent me a stark, brutal wake-up call that I refused to ignore.

I pulled back from Brody. "Um, Brody, this is Vincent," I began. I threaded my fingers through Vincent's and was glad when he didn't hesitate to hold my hand. "My boyfriend." I knew I was reaching with the title, but I was going for all or nothing with Brody. I just hoped like hell it didn't bother Vincent, because if Brody did let loose on me like I deserved, I'd need Vincent more than ever.

Brody's eyes widened slightly, but he recovered quickly and then he was reaching out his hand to Vincent. "Nice to meet you. I'm Brody Wilder."

I was holding Vincent's left hand, so he was able to reach out his right to shake Brody's hand while still holding onto mine.

"Wish the circumstances could have been better," Vincent murmured.

"Yeah, me too," Brody said.

"You're okay?" I asked Brody as I looked at his arm. He was wearing a regular T-shirt but I could see the outline of a bandage beneath the fabric just above his left pectoral muscle.

"I'm good," he said. "Come on inside. I've been holding off on taking my pain meds until you got here, but I wait too much longer and Quinn and Beck are going to use their powers of persuasion on me," he added with a smile.

It wasn't until Brody motioned over his shoulder that I realized we were no longer alone. I remembered both Beck and Quinn from when I'd met them the previous month when I'd gone to see Brody in Dare. Quinn had his arm around Beck, but the second Brody turned to head towards the doors, Beck hurried down to him and put his arm around him. I saw Beck say something to Brody, who nodded and then kissed his forehead.

Vincent didn't release my hand until we were in the house. A couple more men were waiting inside, along with a small brown dog that I remembered seeing with Beck, Brody, and Quinn in Dare.

"Vincent," one of the men said as he smiled and stepped forward. I bit back the tendrils of jealousy that flared to life when Vincent released my hand so he could hug the other man.

"Ethan," Vincent said with a nod. Then he extended his hand to a large blond man standing just behind the man he'd called Ethan. "Cain," he said as they shook hands. "Surprised to see you here."

"Ronan asked us to help keep an eye on things," Cain said.

"Nathan, this is Dr. Ethan Rhodes," Vincent said as he introduced me. I liked that he put his hand on my back again. "Ethan, this is Nathan Wilder."

"Nice to meet you,'" Ethan said. "This is my fiancé, Cain," he added as he motioned to the blond. I extended my greetings to both men.

"Ronan thought it might be a good idea to have a doctor around to keep an eye on Brody's injury," Quinn said to me. "Since he wanted to be with Reese."

"Is…is there anything to worry about?" I asked Ethan.

He shook his head. "No. The shot was a through and through, and only damaged tissue and muscle. It didn't hit the bones and there's no sign of nerve damage. I'm just here to keep an eye out for any signs of infection, which is a very minor possibility."

I nodded as I took in a deep breath. My body ached from the stress of it all, but it was nothing compared to what Brody and Reese had been through.

"Nathan, you remember Beck and Quinn," Brody said.

I nodded and shook both their hands. When Vincent introduced himself, I saw Beck automatically take a step back. My brother put an arm around his lover and murmured something in his ear that had Beck relaxing. Vincent, for his part, sensed the younger man's tension and bypassed him to shake Quinn's hand and then stepped back.

A couple more men entered the room, and I felt Vincent stiffen next to me.

"Major St. James," I heard the dark-haired man say as a huge grin spread across his handsome features. I guessed him to be a little younger than Vincent.

"It's just Vincent these days, Gamble," Vincent said with a smile as he stepped forward to embrace the other man.

"Better not let my husband hear you calling me that. I'm a Barretti through and through now," the man said as he slapped Vincent on the back.

"Fair enough," Vincent said with a chuckle and then he was hugging the other man. "Dom," he murmured.

"Glad you guys made it," the bald guy said as he returned the embrace.

"Nathan, this is Cade Barretti, Beck's father," Vincent said as he motioned to the dark-haired man. "And this is Dom Barretti, Beck's uncle."

I recognized Dom's name immediately. I shook both their hands. "Thank you…for helping me."

Dom nodded and then slapped Cade on the shoulder. "Thank this one here. He was the one who got Ronan and Memphis involved."

Cade glanced at his son and then reached out to pat his shoulder. "We do what we need to do for family," he said softly. Beck smiled, his eyes glistening with unshed tears as he stepped into his father's side. "Isn't that right, Nathan?" Cade asked as he glanced at me.

His sharp eyes seemed to be looking straight through me…like he knew more than he was saying. I merely nodded, because I was feeling completely overwhelmed.

"Baby," Quinn said as he stroked his fingers over Brody's cheek. "You need to take your pills."

Brody nodded, and I finally noticed how pinched his expression had become.

"I'll get them," Ethan offered. "Maybe you want to go lie down?" he asked Brody.

Brody nodded.

"I'll get you something to eat, okay?" Beck said as he returned to my brother's side. Brody kissed his forehead.

"Thanks." My brother's eyes landed on me. "Would you come sit with me for a bit?" he asked.

"Yeah," I said, thankful that I got to spend some more time with him. Even if now wasn't the time to say everything I needed to say to him, the fact that he wanted me around was a good sign that maybe I'd get the chance to make amends.

As Beck, his father, and his uncle went with Cain and Ethan towards what I assumed was the kitchen, the little dog trailing in their wake, Quinn and Brody headed for the stairs. I turned to look at Vincent. For some reason, I was unreasonably afraid he wouldn't be here when I came back down. In theory, I didn't need his protection anymore since I was surrounded by men who were clearly in the same line of work.

"You'll be here when I come down, right?" I asked, hating how insecure I suddenly felt. The attack had left everything up in the air and I hadn't had the energy to ask Vincent what was going to happen now.

"Not going anywhere," Vincent said softly just before he brushed his mouth over mine. "Go spend some time with your brother."

I nodded and then hurried to catch up to my twin and his lover. I didn't miss how Brody was looking at me.

He definitely had a lot of questions for me.

I was just hoping I had the answers.

It was the least I owed him.

CHAPTER 26

VINCENT

"Thanks for the update, Ev," I said just before hanging up the phone.

"How's Reese doing?" Dom asked as he slid a cup of coffee across the kitchen island to me. Cade was standing on the opposite side of the island, coffee in hand. Beck had finished making a sandwich for Brody a few minutes earlier and had gone with Ethan to take it and the pain medication upstairs. Cain had excused himself to check the perimeter of the house. I hadn't expected to see either Cain or Ethan again, but it was comforting to know both men were here to watch out for Brody, his men, and Nathan. I'd been caught off guard when Ethan had hugged me, but I had to admit, it had felt good – like reuniting with an old friend. And considering all the abuse Ethan had suffered at the hands of his vengeful ex, he looked really good. He'd put on some weight, and that constant fear that had seemed to be a permanent part of his expression had been nowhere to be seen.

"He's in recovery. Still groggy so they don't know the full extent of the damage," I murmured. "One of the bullets was lodged near his spine, so they're worried about possible paralysis," I said with a sigh.

Everett had sounded gutted when Ronan had handed him the phone. The older man hadn't managed more than a few words, not that I could really blame him. I was glad that he at least had Ronan and Nash to lean on while they waited for more news. If the damage turned out to be permanent, Nathan would never forgive himself.

Hell, he'd likely never forgive himself as it stood now.

Even though he'd done nothing wrong.

"I should have seen this coming," I said as I scrubbed at my face with my hands.

"None of us did," Dom said. "To go from half-hearted threats to this," the man said with a shake of his head. "The guy's obviously not right in the head."

"I need to talk to Ronan about getting some guys on Nathan and Brody's parents. I doubt he'd go after them, but who knows," I said.

Cade spoke up. "Ronan mentioned sending some guys down there to sit on their place in Louisiana. I think he made the call before he got on the plane to Missoula."

"Good," I said with a nod.

"Major Fucking St. James," Cade said with a grin as he looked me over. "What are the odds?"

I chuckled and shook my head. Cade had always been the kind of guy who said exactly what he was thinking. "About as good as you getting married, I guess."

Dom snorted and Cade shrugged. "If you saw my husband, you wouldn't be saying that."

"Jesus, Cade, are you ever going to remember that's my little brother you're talking about when you say shit like that?" Dom said.

"What about you?" I said to Dom. "You said you were married and with kids, no less."

Dom nodded. "Four kids," he confirmed. "Eli is our oldest, then Tristan. Tanner's almost ten and Sylvie's five. Logan and I have been together for almost eleven years now."

"And if I'm not mistaken, there's talk about maybe another baby on the way," Cade remarked casually.

Dom took a swipe at his brother-in-law. "Just trying to keep up with you and your brood. Five kids," Dom added as he jerked his chin towards Cade.

I shook my head as I watched the two men. I hadn't even known them to be friends in the military before I'd been discharged, but looking at them now, they were so much more than that. I hated the regret that lanced through me as I once again considered how different my life would have been if I'd said yes to Dom all those years ago.

"What about you?" Dom asked. "You and Nathan, that's…unexpected."

I laughed. He had no idea.

"Yeah, didn't really see it coming," I admitted.

"Ronan told us what happened to your…to David," Cade said quietly. "And your brother."

I nodded. Since I hadn't told Ronan about either man, I had to assume he'd heard it from Everett at some point. Surprisingly, it didn't anger me.

"Things didn't quite work out as expected," was all I said.

"They rarely do," Dom murmured. "When I lost my wife to cancer, I figured life was about waiting until my own number came up so I could be with her again. But life decided to throw me a curveball and sent me Logan. Not everyone's lucky enough to get a second soulmate," he said. His eyes pinned mine. "Hopefully you're smart enough to recognize it when it happens to you."

I sighed, because it didn't take a genius to figure out what he was saying. "Second chances don't do you a bit of good if you aren't in any position to accept them."

"Vincent-" Cade began, but I put up my hand.

"Not all choices can be undone. I know that better than anyone." Before either man could say anything, I straightened and said, "I should go check on Nathan."

I was glad when they didn't try to stop me. As I reached the front foyer where we'd entered the house, I saw Ethan coming down the stairs. He smiled at me and stopped when he reached the bottom step. "Wasn't sure I'd ever get the chance to thank you," he said softly.

"No thanks necessary," I automatically said.

He cocked his head at me, but didn't say anything.

"I watched the trial. You were amazing," I said.

Ethan had been forced to testify in open court about the abuse he'd suffered at the hands of his ex-boyfriend. I'd suspected the man had traumatized Ethan when I'd met the fucker after Ethan had begged me to take him to stop Cain from killing the man. We'd arrived in time for the asshole to spew his hateful shit at Ethan and threaten to keep pursuing the young doctor. Ethan had talked Cain out of killing the man, but I'd been less interested in allowing the courts to deliver a message that I could send the man just as easily.

So I'd shot him in the dick.

Message received, loud and clear.

Just before I'd blown a hole in his groin, I'd made sure the former cop knew what would happen to him in prison if he so much as even breathed Ethan's name.

The move hadn't stopped him from trying to come up with some lame-ass defense when he'd been arrested for beating and raping Ethan on multiple occasions. He'd been convicted, of course. And I'd seen recent reports that he'd been charged with murdering another police officer and the man's wife, a crime that carried the death penalty.

"I'm just glad it's finally over," Ethan said as his fingers automatically began toying with the ring on his left hand.

"When's the big day?" I asked.

"Next month. And now that you're back, Cain and I expect to see you and Nathan there. No arguments," he said as he pointed his finger at me and gave me a stern look.

I nodded, but didn't say anything.

What was I supposed to say?

That Nathan and I would have long gone our separate ways by then? "He still with Brody?" I asked.

"Yeah. Second door on the left. Quinn and Beck went outside to get some air so Brody and Nathan could talk."

"Thanks," I said as I began climbing the stairs.

"Vincent."

I looked over my shoulder at him.

"Thank you," he said, his voice going soft.

I held his gaze for a moment and saw the seriousness there. "You're welcome, Ethan," I finally said. Satisfied, he turned away, and I continued up the stairs. I knocked on the door I assumed was the one Ethan had been talking about, but when there was no answer, I carefully pushed it open.

Brody was asleep in the bed, so my eyes quickly searched out Nathan. He was sitting in a chair next to the bed, but at some point, he too had fallen asleep. His hand was covering his brother's on the bed. I was half-tempted to wake him so he could get some real rest, but decided against it. I went to the room Dom had directed me to and found both mine and Nathan's bags sitting on the bed. Between the events of the day and the lack of sleep the night before, I was wiped out, and within minutes of lying down and closing my eyes, I was out. I didn't wake up until a familiar weight pressed against my side.

I curled into Nathan's body and pressed my lips against his temple. "You okay?" I asked.

He nodded against me.

"What time is it?" I asked.

"After nine. Brody, Beck, and Quinn went to bed already. Dom went home – said he'd be back in the morning. Cade's keeping an eye on things so Cain could get some sleep."

"Did you and Brody get to talk?" I asked.

"A little. The pain pills knocked him out pretty fast, so I told him to sleep and we'd talk more tomorrow. Ronan called Dom to give us an update. Reese is starting to wake up, but he's still too out of it for them to determine if there's any permanent damage. He said Everett is hanging in there."

"He'll be okay," I murmured.

Nathan nodded as his hands began skimming over my body. It didn't take much to get me going, so when Nathan pushed me to my back and covered my mouth with his, I gladly complied. There was a certain franticness to his moves as he began tugging at my clothes. I understood where it was coming from, though, so when he grabbed his shirt and yanked it over his head and then went to work on his pants, I grabbed his wrists.

"Baby," I said as I rolled him beneath me and ground our hips together. "Let's change things up a bit, okay?"

He nodded. "Yeah, okay," he said impatiently. "Just…fuck me really hard, please."

The desperation in his voice didn't surprise me at all. Everything had spiraled out of his control in the last twenty-four hours and he was feeling rudderless. But as badly as he needed to not feel those emotions, I knew there was something he needed even more.

I brought his palm to my mouth and gently kissed the stitches I'd placed there what now seemed like a lifetime ago, but had really been only a week. Fortunately, the injury didn't seem to be bothering him anymore, other than the dull pain that came with that kind of wound.

"I want *you* to fuck *me* tonight," I said slowly as I ran his hand down my neck and over my chest.

He stiffened at my words, but not surprisingly, his dick jumped against mine, despite the clothes separating our bodies.

"What?"

I kissed him slow and deep and only when we were both panting did I say, "Want to feel you inside me."

"Have you ever…?"

I nodded. "A few times with David. It wasn't his thing so it wasn't often, but I loved it. I loved being with him that way, and I want that with you." I sipped at his lips until he was squirming beneath me. "Tell me you want that, too."

"Yes," he whispered. "Yes," he repeated and then his instincts and need took over as he rolled me to my back. His hands roamed all over my body as he undressed me, and then his mouth was everywhere. I certainly didn't need the extra stimulation when his mouth closed around my dick, but I wasn't about to argue with him about it. I did have to force him to stop, though, when the orgasm began to creep up my spine.

"Want you inside me," I moaned when I pulled him back up to my mouth.

He nodded as he kissed me hard. I sat up to help him get his clothes off and the lube on his dick, because his hands were shaking so badly that he was struggling to get the cap off the bottle. I kissed him gently and nuzzled his ear as I smoothed the lube over his hardness. "It'll be perfect," I reminded him. "Being with you is always perfect."

Nathan sucked in a breath and finally relaxed somewhat.

"What position do you want me in, baby?" I asked as I wiped my hand on the bedspread before clasping his face between my fingers.

"Just like this," he murmured. "Wanna see you."

I nodded and pulled him down on top of me. He gathered some of the lube from his dick onto his fingers and then began probing me with them. His nerves kicked in as he fumbled to get his finger inside of me, but once he realized he wasn't hurting me, he seemed to relax and began exploring my reactions to his touch. When he found my prostate, I nearly bowed off the bed.

And he used that to his advantage as he teased me mercilessly at the same time that he sucked my dick to the back of his throat.

"Yes!" I called out as I closed my hands over his head and began fucking his mouth. When he added a second finger, I was done and I gently pulled him off my dick. "Now," I ordered right before I kissed him.

"Bossy to the end," Nathan said with a smile, and I couldn't help but laugh.

But all jokes ended when his cock replaced his fingers and he began to push inside of me. I held onto his arms which were braced alongside me as he worked himself deeper and deeper inside of me. The pressure was intense, and I couldn't remember a time I'd ever felt so full before. I hadn't lied when I'd said I'd enjoyed the few times David had taken me, but I couldn't remember it being this good before. I couldn't remember this need to crawl out of my skin and bury myself under his so we'd never have to be apart again.

Once Nathan was all the way inside of me, he settled his weight down on top of me and I curled my legs around his ass. He kissed me over and over until the worst of the pain eased and changed over to a delicious burn.

"Need you to move," I grated as heat began to engulf my body in heady anticipation.

Nathan pulled out slowly and then slid back into me in one slick move, then did it again. Over and over again, he drove into me. I wrapped my arms around his back and hung on as he sent me higher with every agonizingly deep thrust. When it became too much, I told him so and he kissed me hard and picked up the pace. The bed rocked and creaked as Nathan's instincts took over and he began ramming into me. His fingers sifted through my hair to hold me in place as he fucked me mercilessly, while his lips pressed gentle kisses to my forehead.

"So close," I called out as I reached for my dick and began jerking myself off. I loved the feel of Nathan's hard abdomen brushing over the backs of my fingers as I worked myself over to match the rhythm he'd set with his body.

"Gonna come," he growled as he pressed his mouth against my throat and wrapped his arms around my shoulders, lifting my upper body off the bed and holding me tight against his chest.

I ended up coming first, but he was literally just seconds behind me. I cried out in relief as the orgasm washed over me, and the sensation of his hot cum filling me up sent a violent aftershock through my entire system. We clung to each other as we came down from the high. I settled my hands on Nathan's ass to keep him inside me a little longer as he placed soft kisses on my lips.

"Did I hurt you?" he asked.

"In the best way possible," I said drowsily, which caused him to smile.

"We're definitely doing that more often," he said.

"Agreed," I returned before I realized what I was saying.

Because we didn't have that many "oftens" left. But I didn't say that. I just let him hold me and when he suggested a shower together, I agreed without argument and followed him into the bathroom.

CHAPTER 27

NATHAN

"Can I get you anything? A blanket? Something to drink?" I asked as I watched Brody carefully ease himself into one of the deck chairs on the large patio that overlooked a gorgeous infinity swimming pool.

"Nathan, relax," Brody said. "You're worse than Mom when you broke your arm when you fell out of that tree at Grandpa's farm."

"I wouldn't have been in that tree if you hadn't convinced me you'd seen a monkey in it," I reminded him.

He laughed. "Yeah, you were so gullible."

"I was seven," I said with a roll of my eyes as I sat down in the chair next to his. "And you seemed intent on getting me in trouble that summer."

Brody smiled, but didn't comment.

And I knew why.

At that age, we'd still been too naïve to understand what the future had in store for us. We'd just been a couple of innocent kids playing silly games and trying to best one another.

We both sat in uncomfortable silence for a moment before Brody said, "I don't know where to start."

"Me either," I admitted. "So many things I need to say to you, but I can't think of a single one of them right now."

"Okay, let's start with something easy," Brody said as he shifted so he was facing me. I did the same. "Vincent."

I laughed and shook my head. "What happened to easy?" I asked as I ran my fingers through my hair.

"I saw the way you two looked at each other, Nathan. Admitting that part should be pretty easy, since you clearly suck so bad at hiding it."

I took in a deep breath because I knew he was right. "I'm in love with him. I know it's crazy and it's too soon and I only admitted to myself I'm gay like five minutes ago…but there it is. I'm in love with him."

"See? Easy!" Brody said with a smirk.

I took a swipe at him, but made sure not to make contact since I didn't want him jerking away and hurting himself.

"He hasn't said it back," I admitted as I let my eyes connect with Brody's. I knew it was selfish to dump that on him considering everything that had happened, but I literally had no one else to talk to about it, and the fact that Vincent hadn't said the words back to me was messing with my head.

"Even if he hasn't said it, Nathan, he's not doing a lot to hide it."

I nodded. Every time we were together, it felt like Vincent was saying things to me without the use of words, but I couldn't be sure.

I let my eyes drift to the scenery around us. It really was a gorgeous view, and although there were a few puffy white clouds in the sky, I didn't see even a hint of the rain that Seattle was famous for.

"Brody, you have to believe me that I didn't really know until I met him. I mean, maybe deep down I did, but I got so good at denying it that I was just able to pass it off as being related to stress."

"You mean being gay?"

I nodded. "And my problems with women. I just never…I never associated one with the other. I mean, when we were kids, I was so certain that some of the thoughts I had were the devil trying to get inside of me. If I thought some guy was good-looking, it wasn't really me…it was the sin of the devil trying to lure me away from the side of the righteous."

Even now, saying the things that had been drilled to us in sermon after sermon made me want to throw up. The fact that I'd actually believed them…that I'd thrown my brother aside in favor of believing the lies I'd been fed since birth…

"I'm so sorry, Brody," I said with a shake of my head. "I wanted to protect you and that night when you told me that, I thought the devil was trying to steal your soul and-"

I fisted my hair in the hopes the pain would keep me from throwing up all over the place as my cruel words rang in my ears.

"I know, Nathan," Brody said, and I felt his hand close over one of mine. He gently pried my fingers free of the death grip I had on my hair. "Believe me, I thought the same thing about myself. I didn't want it to be true."

"I should have talked to you…I should have listened instead of going to Dad."

Brody's fingers squeezed mine hard. "Nathan, please look at me."

When I did, he said, "I know why you did it. You always did your best to protect me, and that's what you thought you were doing that night."

I dashed at the tears that threatened to fall. "I wish I could go back to that moment. I wish I could do it differently…there are so many things I wish I could have done differently."

"Me too," Brody murmured. "But I ended up where I was supposed to, Nathan. Just like I think you did, too. I don't…I don't want to live in the past. I don't want to wonder how things could have been different, because every outcome I can think of would mean I never would have met Quinn or Beck. And the idea of not having them in my life…"

"I know," I said quickly when Brody's voice caught and he dropped his eyes. I forced his chin up. "I'm so happy for you. I couldn't have dreamed up a better life for you."

Brody smiled and nodded. "Nathan, I hope all this means you're back in my life for good."

"It does," I said with a nod. "If you want that."

Brody's fingers closed around mine. "More than anything."

I felt something inside of me ease at his words. I hadn't been sure that was something he wanted, but knowing he did…it put me on cloud nine.

"I'm okay with us revisiting the past if and when we need to," Brody murmured. "But today, I want to talk about the present…and the future."

"I'd like that," I said as I wiped a stray tear from my eye. "I'm sorry," I whispered as I glanced at the arm that was in the sling. "I really thought he'd leave you alone if I stayed away."

Brody gently opened my hand to reveal the line of stitches. "Did he do this?" he asked, his voice uneven.

I nodded. As much as I didn't want to tell him about the attack, I knew I had to. He deserved my honesty, even if it was something that would be hard for him to hear.

He held my hand as I recounted the night of the attack. I heard him choke back tears at times, but he remained quiet. When I was finished and he still didn't speak, I gently gripped his fingers and said, "I'm safe, Brody. Vincent won't let anything happen to me."

Brody nodded and wiped at his eyes. "Promise me you won't go back there until this is resolved," he said. I figured he was talking about my house, since that was where I'd been attacked.

"Promise," I agreed.

"You said it was Beck's father and uncle that asked Ronan to find someone to watch out for you."

I nodded.

Brody chuckled. "Bastard's been torturing me and Quinn for weeks."

"What?"

Brody shook his head. "Cade. You know, playing the overprotective dad role. Making me and Quinn sleep in a different bedroom when we come for a visit. Sending us threatening looks and having some of the guys at family dinner give us subtle warnings."

I must have looked startled because Brody quickly said, "It's all in fun, Nathan. I think it's some kind of family ritual with these guys... razz the newest members."

The concept was both odd and comforting at the same time. Our own family had always been so serious that I couldn't even imagine the banter Brody was talking about. But to know he'd been accepted into a family so different from our own...

"So things are good for you," I clarified. "Here?" I asked as I looked around the big house.

"It's an amazing family, Nathan. We're not even the only guys in a threesome. Beck's uncle and his husbands have been together for ten years now. They've got two daughters. And Beck's cousin, Tristan, is in a relationship with two other men. So not only do we fit in, we don't even stand out."

I chuckled at that. "Well, I'm glad you've got a future father-in-law who's looking out for you."

"It could be the same for you, Nathan. Even if things don't work out between you and Vincent, there's still a place for you...with us. In Dare."

My throat felt too thick to speak, so I nodded. Even though I knew I was going to lose Vincent at some point, hearing Brody actually say it somehow made it hurt even worse.

"Everything's so fucked up right now, Brody," I admitted. "I don't know what I want anymore."

That wasn't quite true. I did know one thing I wanted, but it was the one thing I couldn't have.

"You're not locked into anything, Nathan. There's still time to make changes."

I knew what he was talking about. Of all the people in my life, he was probably one of the few who suspected the profession I'd chosen to pursue wasn't a choice I'd made with my heart, but rather with my head.

"Fuck, Nathan," Brody whispered as he suddenly stood up and wrapped his free arm around me. He bent over me and pressed a kiss to my head. "I hate what this is doing to you."

"Sorry," I said softly, even as I wrapped my arms around his waist and pressed my head against his stomach. "You can feel it, can't you?" I asked, since I couldn't fathom that he'd picked up on my distress just from my words alone. He had to be picking up on my emotions through the bond that came with being twins.

"Yeah, I can. And I promise, we'll figure it out. Okay?"

"Nathan?"

Vincent's worried voice had me pulling away from Brody and climbing to my feet. He was walking towards us, his concern clear as day.

"I'll give you two a second," Brody said as he took a few steps away from us.

"You okay?" Vincent asked when he reached me.

I nodded. "Yeah, just...memories, you know?" I murmured.

"Yeah," he replied before he pulled me into his arms for a quick hug. "Ronan called."

I pulled back. "Is it Reese? Is he okay?"

"He's awake. He's lost feeling from the waist down, but his doctors are hopeful that the paralysis they're seeing is temporary."

I managed a nod, even though I felt sick to my stomach.

"Listen, Ronan was also calling me to tell me his guys caught the shooter."

"What?" I asked, not sure I'd heard him right. They'd gotten the guy who'd attacked me? It was over?

"One of the shots Reese fired at the guy hit him, and he eventually passed out from the blood loss and crashed his car into a ditch just outside Dare. Ronan's guys found him before anyone else could, and they've moved him to a secure location. I'm flying out there to question him myself. I want to find out if he was a lone wolf or if he was working for someone. I need you to stay here, okay?"

"Okay," I said as my head spun with all the information he was throwing at me.

"Don't leave the property, do you understand me?"

"I won't, I promise."

Vincent brushed his mouth over mine. "I'll call you when I land."

I nodded and kissed him again. "Be careful."

"I will." One more kiss, and then he was gone.

I sank back down on the chair I'd been sitting in. I wasn't surprised when I felt Brody's hand on my shoulder. I reached up to grab it, grateful he was there.

It was a lot more than I deserved.

But I'd definitely take it.

CHAPTER 28

VINCENT

It was early afternoon by the time I arrived in Missoula. As eager as I was to question the man who'd tried to kill Nathan and who'd hurt Brody and Reese, I needed to check on Everett first. I hadn't been completely honest when I'd given Nathan an update on Reese's condition. I'd heard the despair in Everett's voice, and while I knew he had some support in the form of Agent Nash and Ronan, I knew it wasn't enough.

The hospital was quiet and the man who'd picked me up from the airport – another of Ronan's men – led me past the information desk and straight to the third floor. I'd expected him to take me to Reese's room, but instead, he showed me to what looked like a small conference room. Nash was standing stiffly outside the door.

Ronan's man bid me farewell, leaving me and Nash alone.

"What's going on?" I asked. "Is Everett in there?"

Nash nodded. "He is."

I glanced around us. "Why isn't he in Reese's room?" Panic flared in my belly. "Did something-"

"No," Nash quickly interrupted. He dropped his voice. "His son asked him to leave."

"What?" I asked, not sure I'd heard him correctly.

"When Reese woke up and saw him..." Nash hesitated and dropped his eyes. "It wasn't pretty."

Anger simmered through me. "Thanks," I said to Nash as I opened the door. Everett looked up at me from where he and Ronan were in deep conversation. My steps faltered as I took in Everett's disheveled appearance. His rumpled clothes were the same ones he'd been wearing yesterday and his hair was all over the place, like he'd been running his fingers through it over and over. His eyes were swollen and red, proof he'd been crying.

I walked over to him and instead of sitting down next to him, I crouched in front of him. I put my hand on his arm. "Talk to me," I murmured.

The only time I'd ever seen Everett like this had been the few times he'd gotten drunk and allowed himself to truly mourn the loss of my brother. He'd always hidden his grief behind closed doors otherwise.

"They...they aren't sure if he'll be able to walk again," Everett whispered, his voice hoarse.

"He's strong, Ev. Look at everything he's been through. Gets that from his father," I said softly.

Everett nodded and wiped at his eyes.

"What about his other injuries?" I asked. "The burns."

"They're mostly on his chest and arms," Ronan said. "He'll need skin grafts. It's going to be a long recovery process."

My stomach rolled violently, but I managed to quell the urge to vomit. "He's going to make it, Everett. You're going to get him home and take care of him."

Everett began shaking his head. "He won't let me see him, Vincent. He's...he's so angry."

Frustration went through me as I climbed to my feet. I was heading for the door before I even realized what I was doing.

"Vincent, don't!" Everett called.

But I ignored him as I left the room. I had one goal in mind.

"What room is he in?" I asked Nash, my voice cold.

"315."

It took less than a minute to find the room. The curtains on the glass walls were drawn, so I couldn't see inside. I took a deep breath to calm myself before opening the door. I stilled at the sight of the young man in the bed. His upper body and arms were wrapped in layers and layers of white bandaging. There was another bandage around his forehead. His face was turned away from me at first, but when I stepped farther into the room, he slowly turned to look my way.

"Can I help you?" I heard someone off to my right say.

I glanced at the man I hadn't noticed at first. I guessed him to be in his early forties or so, with a head of thick, gray hair. He was heavily built. In his hand, he had a cup of water with a straw sticking out of it. He put the pitcher in his other hand down and approached the bed.

"Vincent!" I heard Everett call, though his voice was low. A second later, he was pushing into the room.

Just like that, Reese's eyes went from pain-filled and tired to sharp and pissed-off.

"Get out," he said, his cold eyes on his father. "I told you I didn't want to see you."

The young man shifted in the bed and immediately stifled a cry of pain. The older man put his hand on Reese's bandaged shoulder. "Stay still," he said softly.

"I'm...I'm sorry," Everett stammered, his voice shaky and uneven. Watching my best friend, one of the most confident, powerful men I'd ever met, transform into an insecure, uncertain man practically before my eyes reminded me why I'd come here.

"Reese, I know you're hurting-"

"Vincent," Everett said, but I ignored him.

"Vincent," Reese repeated. His mouth pulled into a tight frown. "I know you," he said. "You're *his* brother." His eyes shifted back to his father. "You fucking him now?"

Everett let out a little gasp, and I was striding forward before I even realized what I was doing.

"Don't," the man with the gray hair said as he stepped into my path. He was my size and probably had a few extra pounds of muscle on me, but I didn't care. But it was the calmness in his voice that had me stopping my forward movement.

"He's in pain," he said softly. "And he's scared to death," he said so quietly that I was likely the only one who'd heard him.

I managed a nod because I knew he was right. My instinct to protect Everett had overridden my common sense. I stepped back and let my eyes settle on Reese. "I'm sorry," I said. "Thank you for what you did for Brody. It took guts, and because of you, we caught the guy."

Reese seemed caught off guard by my words. He hesitated for the briefest of moments and then gave me a slight nod. "Please leave," he said after a moment, before turning his face towards the window again. "All of you."

The gray-haired man followed us from the room and slid the door closed behind him.

"Gage, this is Vincent St. James," Ronan said as he motioned to me. The gray-haired man, Gage, shook my hand.

"Thanks for that," I said as I jerked my chin towards the room.

He nodded. "I've partnered with Reese a few times now, so I'm starting to figure out what makes him tick."

"And this is Everett Shaw," Ronan said to Gage.

Gage turned his attention to Everett. "Mr. President," he said quietly as he extended his hand. "I'm sorry, I know how difficult this must be for you. But your son is one of the strongest men I know. He'll beat this."

Everett nodded and shook the man's hand. I noticed that Gage didn't release Everett's hand until the older man looked up at him and their eyes connected for several long beats. Only then did he let go of Everett's hand.

"Gage is going to take you to question the suspect," Ronan said. "We're holding him in a warehouse on the outskirts of the city," he said in a low voice.

I nodded and then looked at Everett. "You going to be okay?"

It took a moment for Everett to respond. He looked dead on his feet. "Fine," he mumbled.

"Ev, you need to go get some rest. Let Nash take you to a hotel," I suggested as I glanced at the Secret Service agent whose watchful eyes shifted between our surroundings and Everett.

"Can't," Everett said tiredly. "My boy might need me."

My heart broke for my friend, but before I could say anything, Gage said, "Mr. President, you won't do Reese any good if you make yourself sick. He may not act like it, but he's going to need you, sir. He's going to need you to be strong for him when he can't."

Everett was quiet for a moment before he finally nodded. "Okay," he murmured. "Maybe for a few minutes."

Ronan nodded to Nash who immediately came up and put his hand at Everett's elbow, as if to steady him. The agent's gaze connected with Gage, and I swore I saw a flash of something between them.

Everett allowed Nash to lead him away, but he stopped long enough to say to Gage, "Thank you, Gage. Call me Everett."

"You're welcome…Everett," the other man said with a nod.

Once Everett and Nash were out of sight, Gage turned to me, his expression hardening. "You ready to go?" he asked. "Been waiting all morning to get my hands on the fucker."

A man after my own heart.

"Lead the way," I said with a smirk. I cast Ronan a nod over my shoulder as I followed Gage.

Time to do what I did best.

~

All my cylinders were firing when I walked into the small room that Ronan's men had stashed the guy in. He was tied to a chair by both his hands and feet. A small amount of dried blood was caked on his forehead, probably from where he'd hit the steering wheel when his car had crashed into the ditch. A considerably larger swath of blood had stained his shirt on the right side of his body, just beneath his armpit. Since they'd caught the guy hours ago, I had to assume the injury wasn't life-threatening.

But it sure would work in my favor.

Gage followed me into the room and went to stand against the far wall. We'd agreed on the ride over that it was my show, though Gage had made it clear he wanted a piece of the man.

Vengeance for Reese, probably. I had no clue what his relationship with Reese consisted of, but I suspected it didn't go beyond friendship considering the way he'd looked at Everett. It was a development I just didn't have the time to deal with at the moment.

"What's your name?" I asked as I took my time taking off my watch and sticking it in my pocket.

"It's fuck you, what's yours?"

I guessed the man to be in his early twenties at the most. There was a thin gash on his left cheek, presumably from when Nathan had cut him with the broken glass the night of the attack. He was wearing camouflage clothing, and I'd had a chance to look at his weaponry before I'd entered the room. He'd definitely come prepared to do some damage, because he'd had enough firepower in his car to take out a small platoon...or a rural police department. It had left me wondering if his intent had been to hunt down Brody's men once he'd taken care of Brody. It wouldn't have been unreasonable for him to have watched Brody for a while to learn all he could about his movements. And what better way to inflict as much emotional damage on Nathan as he could by taking out his brother *and* a slew of innocent people as well?

I stepped forward and studied the young man for a moment before slamming my fist into his jaw. His head whipped to the side and blood went flying as I knocked at least one tooth loose.

"Now, let's try that again. What's your name?"

"Fuck-"

Another punch cut off the response and two more to his gut had him gasping for breath. I didn't wait for him to catch his breath before I grabbed him by the hair and wrenched his head back. "Name," was all I said. I took my gun out and pointed it at his groin to let him know I wasn't playing.

He remained silent, but when I pulled the trigger, unloading a bullet into the wood between his legs, he let out a bark of fear and yelled, "Clint!"

"Clint," I said in satisfaction as I stepped back. "Clint what?"

He began shaking his head. Before he'd even finished the motion, I shot him in the knee. He screamed in agony as his body jerked in the chair. "Yates!" he shouted when I aimed for his other knee.

I glanced at Gage, who nodded and left the room. He was pulling his cell phone out as he walked through the door. I knew Ronan had a lot of resources at his disposal, so we'd likely have the basics on Clint in a matter of minutes.

But I wanted more than just the basics.

"He's going to kill you," Clint growled between pants as he tried to control the pain.

"Oh yeah?" I asked casually. "Who is?"

Clint remained stubbornly silent, so I shot him in the foot. He bellowed in pain and let off a string of curses. I strode forward and snagged him by the hair. "Did you think this was a game?" I asked coldly. "Did you think we'd dance around with this? That I'd try to be your friend or that I'd toss you some empty threats to try to get you to talk?"

Clint wisely didn't answer. Sweat was pouring off his brow and he was struggling to catch his breath. I took my gun and jammed it against the bullet wound Reese had inflicted earlier. Clint cried out in pain and tried to twist away from me.

"Why were you after Nathan Wilder?"

Only when Clint looked like he was going to pass out did I relieve the pressure on the injury. When he didn't answer me, I aimed for his other knee.

"My pocket!" he screamed. "Check my back pocket!"

I hesitated and then stepped around him to check his pockets. There was nothing in the first, but when my fingers grazed a piece of paper in the second, I carefully worked it free and stepped around to Clint's front again.

Gage returned to the room and said, "Our girl's working on pulling his info."

I nodded as he stopped beside me. His eyes impassively took in Clint's moans of pain before he looked at the piece of my paper in my hand.

Except it wasn't exactly a piece of paper.

It was a check.

I opened it and flinched when I saw Nathan's name on the signature line. The check was made out to someone named Megan Yates. The amount was for five thousand dollars. I glanced at the account information and realized the check had been drawn on Nathan's campaign fund account.

"What is this?" I asked as I turned the check over. The check had never been endorsed and there was no indication it had been deposited or canceled.

"The cost of penance," he snarled.

Pure fury went through me. I put the gun to the guy's head. "What the fuck did I tell you about this not being a game?" I snapped. "Who is Megan Yates?"

"My sister!" Clint yelled.

"What's the money for?" I asked.

"I told you-"

I aimed my gun at his other knee and pulled the trigger. Clint screamed as tears streaked down his face.

"What is the fucking money for?" I asked again.

It took several moments for Clint to speak. His voice was choked as he tried to deal with the pain. "Abortion!" he cried out. "He knocked her up and told her to get rid of it."

I was so stunned, I actually lowered my gun and stepped back. It wasn't fucking possible.

"You're saying Nathan got your sister pregnant and paid her to get an abortion?" Gage asked.

"Fucker told her he loved her! That they were going to be together. She was eighteen goddamned years old!" Clint sucked in several harsh breaths. "She killed herself when he told her all she'd been was a good fuck!"

"You're lying!" I snarled.

"No!" Clint shot back. "Look at the goddamn evidence! It's right there in your fucking hand!"

I looked at the check again.

"Why not go to the press?" Gage asked. "You could have destroyed him politically."

"I don't give a fuck about his career," Clint growled. "I want him to know what it's like! To lose that one person that means everything to you!"

"Why go after Nathan in his house, then?" I asked.

Clint managed a smirk. "Couldn't pass up the opportunity," he said. "Him sitting there, not knowing what was coming."

Gage's phone beeped. He glanced at it and then handed it to me. The screen showed Clint's military record. He was ex Special Forces.

Which explained his skill with a gun.

But not his ability to hack Nathan's accounts. "Who helped you?" I asked.

Clint's eyes went wide before he quickly shook his head. "No one, I work alone."

Gage took the phone back and scrolled through it. "His father," Gage murmured as he showed me the screen.

I shook my head. "William Yates, retired FBI agent specializing in Intelligence," I said softly. I handed the phone back to Gage and glanced at the check again. "Where is he?" I asked.

"Fuck you," Clint bit out.

"We're back to that again?" I asked calmly as my eyes caught on Nathan's signature.

I stared at it for so long that Gage asked, "What? What is it?"

I shook my head as I tried to figure out what was wrong with it. I searched my memory for that fleeting piece of information that was trying to elude me. Finally, it hit me.

"It's not his signature," I said.

"What?" Gage asked.

"It's not his signature," I repeated, louder this time. "I've seen his signature...but this handwriting," – I tapped the signature on the check – "I've seen it too."

I searched my pocket for my phone, and then remembered I'd left it outside the room after sending Cain a text asking him to let Nathan know I'd made it to Montana okay. I left the room with Gage right behind me.

"It's his mother's handwriting," I said as I looked at the check again. "When I was researching Nathan, I saw a handwritten letter she'd sent the press. They posted a picture of the letter. It was in response to Nathan switching parties. She was telling the press how disappointed she and her husband were in losing both of their sons to the devil, and she was asking people to pray for them."

I found my phone on a small table next to the cache of weapons Ronan's men had found on Clint. But as soon as I turned the phone over, I saw a flurry of notifications for missed calls…all within the last five minutes.

They were from Cain.

Panic went through me as I scrambled to unlock my phone. Gage's phone rang just as I was starting to dial.

"It's Cain," Gage said as he put his hand on my arm. He hit the speakerphone.

"Cain, I'm with Vincent," Gage said.

"What happened?" I asked, my heart in my throat, because there was only one reason Cain would be calling me so often.

"I'm sorry, Vincent. Nathan's gone."

CHAPTER 29

NATHAN

"Get up!" a voice snapped as I felt a hand dig into my hair and yank me to my feet. Pain ratcheted through my body as searing agony fired up my arms which had been bound behind my back for hours. I stumbled as my numb legs tried to hold my weight. The hold on my hair was unforgiving, and I winced when I received another sharp yank. Then, blessedly, hard fingers closed around my upper arm instead.

My vision was fucked up because I'd been punched repeatedly on the right side of my face. My assailant was definitely a leftie.

I wanted to spit out the blood that had collected in my mouth while I'd been passed out, but I couldn't find the strength to do even that, so I had no choice but to swallow it. My captor dragged me maybe a hundred feet or so before he shoved me to the hard cement floor. My knees buckled as soon as I hit the ground, and with my hands bound, I had no way to break my fall. I tried rolling on my shoulder and barely stifled a cry of pain as a booted foot hit me in the middle of my back.

"Not so tough when it's not an innocent girl you're toying with, huh?" another voice said as heavy footsteps headed my way. *That* voice I did know. I'd heard it for the first time several hours earlier when I'd answered Brody's phone while he'd been asleep. I'd been in his room talking to him while he'd waited for his pain meds to kick in. I'd grabbed the phone to put it on vibrate when it had started ringing, but when I'd recognized my mother's phone number, I'd answered it instead.

The memory came back in a rush.

"Brody?"

My mother's voice was uncharacteristically shaky.

"No, Mom, it's Nathan."

"Oh, Nathan, thank God," she said, and then I heard a muffled squeak just before a man's voice had come on the line.

"Mr. Wilder, for someone who likes the cameras so much, you've proven awfully difficult to find lately."

I stiffened as I realized who I was talking to. And what it meant that he was talking to me using my mother's phone.

"Please don't hurt her," I said softly so Brody wouldn't wake up. I took the phone and went into the attached bathroom.

"Your parents will be just fine if you do what I say," he said.

Parents.

Jesus, he had both my mother and my father? If he was with my parents, who the hell was Vincent questioning?

"Mr. Wilder," the man repeated impatiently, and I realized I'd been quiet for too long.

"Yes, okay, anything," I quickly said. "I'll do anything."

As much as I hated my parents, I still loved them.

"Your one job, if you want your parents to get through this thing in one piece, is for you to make it to the mainland. Alone."

The fact that he'd referenced the mainland had me guessing he knew exactly where I was. I could only assume he'd tracked Brody's phone or something.

"My associate will be waiting for you at the Anacortes ferry terminal."

"I...I can't leave. People are watching the house," I said frantically.

"You seem like a resourceful young man, Mr. Wilder. I suggest you figure it out, and quickly. You have three hours. And if you're followed..."

I didn't even let him finish the threat. "I'll be there," I said. "Alone."

"No phones. My associate will be searching you," he warned.

"Yes, okay."

"Three hours," the man said again, and then he hung up. Panic seared through me as I checked the watch Vincent had given me. I stared at it as I realized it would be the first thing Vincent checked when he found out I was gone. And if Cain realized I was missing quickly enough, Vincent could tell him where I was and he'd intercept me before I could make sure my parents were safe. But if I left the watch behind, I had no hope of Vincent finding me. I took the watch off and studied it. It took me several precious seconds to finally figure out how to open the back of it. My eyes fell on the battery. Removing it would mean Vincent couldn't track me, but I couldn't be sure that putting it back in would somehow magically link the watch back up to the app Vincent used to monitor it.

It didn't matter; I didn't have a choice.

I sent Vincent a silent apology and then pulled the battery out.

"I don't know what girl you're talking about," I managed to get out as the guy behind me pulled me upright so I was on my knees. Tears pricked the backs of my eyes as pain washed over my entire body. The man who'd called me had also been the one who'd beaten me as he'd kept throwing questions at me about a girl named Megan. All I'd managed to figure out was that the girl was his daughter and he clearly blamed me for whatever had happened to her.

But I'd never heard of her before.

The man grabbed my chin. "You're lucky I promised Clint he could have you," the man snarled. "He'll kill you fast."

He shoved me hard, but I managed to stay upright. "My...my parents," I mumbled, though my tongue felt thick in my mouth. Nausea had my stomach rolling back and forth, and I prayed I wouldn't pass out again.

I'd ended up stealing Dominic Barretti's boat to escape the property. I'd managed to figure out how to get to the ferry dock only because I'd seen a ferry making its way towards the mainland. Just before I'd reached land, I'd put the battery back into my watch. I'd been relieved when the time showed up on the normal-looking dial, but there'd been no way to know if the watch had reconnected with Vincent's app.

I'd docked the boat in the harbor, certain that I'd run into one of Dom's or Ronan's men, but it had been a guy in black jeans and a dark T-shirt that had appeared at my side and pressed a gun between my ribs. After searching me for a phone and thankfully leaving me with the watch, we'd driven for a good two hours before the car had turned onto a narrow dirt road that had led to some kind of singular building. Inside had been a few pieces of large machinery. I'd been led to a back room where a guy with silver hair had been waiting, and I'd barely gotten the question out about my parents before he'd hit me. I'd lost track of things after the fourth blow.

"Your parents are the least of your concerns," the man said. "You-"

The man's words dropped off suddenly when there were a series of loud pops coming from outside the building. The man snagged my arm and dragged me to my feet. To the other man who'd been covering me he said, "Go check it out."

I was dimly aware of more popping sounds, and I sensed the man behind me getting more and more agitated as he kept turning us around to face the direction of the sounds. There was enough light from the overhead lights that I could make out more of the inside of the building. I suspected it was some kind of outbuilding for a farm, because the few pieces of farm equipment inside of the building looked used.

The popping sounds stopped and the man began calling out different names. When the door on the far end of the building opened, he jammed a gun against my temple. "Don't move," he warned me.

I wanted to tell him I couldn't promise anything because I was so dizzy. I tried to focus on the figure at the far end of the building.

Several figures.

I thought it was his men at first, but when the guy yelled, "Stop right there!" I knew they weren't his guys.

Which meant only one thing.

"Vincent," I whispered, though I knew there was no way he could have heard me.

Knowing he was here helped clear the fog in my head, and I managed to make him out, along with another man with gray hair. Between them was a third guy. It looked like Vincent and the other guy were holding the third guy up.

"You lose something, Yates?" Vincent called.

I heard the man behind me suck in a breath when Vincent and the other guy released the third guy and he fell to his knees between them and let out a scream of pain.

"Clint!" he shouted. The man's hold on me eased a little and I felt the hard metal of the gun ease back from my skin. "What did you-"

That was all he got out as I watched Vincent raise his gun in one fluid move. Warm liquid hit my skin as the man behind me crumpled to the floor. My knees refused to hold my weight anymore and I unceremoniously fell onto them. I managed to look over my shoulder at the guy's lifeless body, blood leeching all over the floor from a gaping hole in the middle of his forehead.

"Nathan, baby," Vincent called as he reached me. He caught me just as I started to fall over.

"Knew you'd come," I managed to say as he stroked my face.

"Always," he whispered, and then his mouth was brushing gently over mine.

That was the last thing I was aware of before I let the darkness claim me.

CHAPTER 30

VINCENT

The first thing I saw when I entered the room was Nathan sitting on the edge of the bed, his back to me. I quietly shut the door behind me and went around the bed.

"You should be lying down," I murmured as I sat down in the chair next to the bed. My belly rolled at the sight of the bruises covering Nathan's face. Since I'd helped Ethan undress him so he could examine him, I knew his sides were also covered in black and blue marks. It made me want to kill William Yates all over again.

Nathan's uninjured eye shifted to me. "I need to take a shower. I...I can still feel the blood on me."

I knew he was talking about Yates's blood. I'd used a washcloth to clean it off Nathan as best I could, but it was still in his hair and I was sure he was still remembering the warm spray of it on his skin. It was something that couldn't have been avoided, since Yates had given me the perfect opportunity to take him out when he'd been distracted by his son's condition.

"Will you help me?" Nathan asked. "Ethan said it was okay if I had help."

I nodded and reached out to put my arm around his waist. Ethan had given him something for the pain, but I knew it was only taking the edge off. We took it slow as we made our way to the bathroom. I sat Nathan down on the small bench that was tucked up beneath the vanity. As I began undressing him, he said, "Is it true? Are they dead?"

I knew he was talking about his parents because Brody had broken the news to him shortly before I'd entered the room to check on him.

"It's true," I confirmed. "Yates had his men kill them as soon as his guys picked you up at the marina."

Nathan nodded. "Brody said you found proof that the girl...Megan...that she knew my father."

"She went to church with your parents. Your father approached her to see if she wanted to help with your campaign...it was while you were still planning to run on the Republican ticket."

Nathan nodded in understanding. "I don't remember meeting her," he murmured.

"You didn't. There's no record of her having ever worked on the campaign. Your father used it as an excuse."

"To seduce her," Nathan said.

"Yeah," I acknowledged. "She got pregnant and went to your father. At that point, his mental health had started to decline. Your mother found out about her and paid her off using a forged check from the funds left over in your campaign. Clint and his father found the check among Megan's belongings along with a suicide note that said she didn't want to live if she couldn't be with the father of her baby. They assumed she was talking about you because of the check."

Nathan shook his head in disbelief. "All the lives he destroyed," he murmured.

I figured he was talking about his father, but I didn't comment.

"Brody said Aunt Verona is okay, right?"

"Yes, your aunt was out of town visiting a friend at the time. Yates had his guys attack your parents and had them do a conference call with Brody to make it seem like he was with your parents when he spoke to you. Since he couldn't reach you, he figured Brody would tell him where you were, or he'd get his hands on Brody and force you out of hiding."

I helped Nathan stand so I could work the sweats off his body. I tried to ignore the bruising on his body, since all it did was piss me off that I hadn't gotten to him sooner. Not to mention it made me want to hunt Clint down and put a bullet through his head. If Nathan hadn't needed me, I probably would have done it right there in the warehouse. But the man was Ronan's problem now, and since he'd nearly killed one of Ronan's men, I doubted he'd get off easy…or at all.

"I knew you'd find me," Nathan murmured as I straightened and helped him get his shirt off.

"I'll always find you when you need me," I said softly, right before I kissed him.

His arms went around me and I just held him for a while. But when his body began to get heavy, I sat him back down and then quickly undressed myself. I got the shower going and waited for the water to warm up before I helped Nathan to his feet and got him in the shower. I held him against my body as I carefully washed his body, and when it came time to wash his hair, I sat him down on a small bench in the shower. When I was finished cleaning him, I put my arms around him and just held him under the hot spray of water for a while.

I was still reeling from the close call myself.

After Cain's call, I'd immediately checked my app to figure out where Nathan was, but when I'd gotten an alert that the watch was offline, I'd completely lost it. It was Gage who'd managed to keep it together long enough to get me and Clint to the airport. We'd been airborne with the intent of going back to Seattle when the app had alerted me that the watch was back online. By the time we'd crossed the border into Washington state, we'd had to veer south to follow the signal to a remote area in Central Washington.

Nathan's injuries had been pretty bad, but not enough to warrant a trip to the hospital. I'd gotten him on Ronan's plane and headed back to San Juan Island, leaving Gage to deal with the authorities. I'd had to call in another favor with the FBI director to let him know I'd left another body in my wake. Like he'd done with the shooting when we'd gone after Ethan's ex, the man had smoothed things over with the local authorities. While I still needed to give my statement, it was nothing more than a formality at this point.

I pressed kisses against Nathan's neck as I held him. The relief at having him back in my arms was bittersweet, and my heart ached at what I needed to do.

"I love you, Nathan," I whispered into his ear. I heard him let out a harsh sob and felt him nod against my neck. I had a feeling he knew exactly why I was telling him here and now because he wrapped his arms around me even tighter, a move that I was sure cost him what little strength he had left.

"Love you," he said as he pulled back a little and kissed me. He pressed his forehead against mine. "Please, Vincent, we can figure this out."

Pain exploded in my chest at his plea and I felt tears stinging my eyes. "Baby, remember your promise," I said, my voice catching on the last word.

He let out a whimper and then crushed his face against my neck. I held him a while longer, and then got him out of the shower and dried him off. We didn't speak again until I'd tucked him under the covers. "Go change the world, Nathan," I said softly, right before I kissed him again. He closed his eyes after that.

Probably so he wouldn't have to watch me walk away.

I barely made it out the bedroom door before the tears began to fall. I wiped them away and straightened. I came to an abrupt halt when I saw Brody watching me from the top of the stairs.

"Take care of him," I told him, but I didn't give him time to say anything back. I hurried down the stairs and grabbed my bag, which I'd left at the base of the stairs.

"Vincent."

I turned to see Dom hurriedly walking towards me.

"I've got to go," I said as I discreetly wiped at my eyes some more to get rid of the lingering tears. "My cab will be here any second."

"I know. I sent it away."

"What? Why?"

"Because if my old friend insists on running away, the least I can do is give him a goddamn ride," he said impatiently.

He opened the door for me.

I eyed him warily as I left the house. My chest felt tight as I climbed into the SUV. It wasn't until we were well on our way that Dom said, "So you're really going to leave it like this?"

"Let it go, Dom," I bit out.

"Just explain to me why you're doing this," he said.

I was already so raw that I didn't even think about my words before I snapped, "Because it's the only way to keep him safe!" I looked at him and said, "You want to know the truth, Dom? It hurts so fucking bad to know that one choice fifteen years ago brought me to this point!"

"What choice?"

"Your choice!" I snapped. "If I'd had the sense to pick your offer over the one I got, my brother would still be alive and I wouldn't have to fucking live in Fort Knox and I'd have that amazing man" – I pointed in the direction of Dom's house – "waiting for me when I got home every night!" I knew I wasn't making sense, but I didn't care. "But no, I had something to prove! I had to show those assholes how they fucked up when they sent me and David packing! All that fucking pride, and what did it get me? Nothing. Fucking nothing!"

I shook my head as I cast my eyes out the window. "It's too damn late. I had my chance."

Awkward silence flooded the SUV. God, I just needed to get the fuck out of here. The sooner I got back to normal, the better.

"If you had another one, would you take it?" Dom asked.

"Another what?" I bit out tiredly.

"Chance. Another chance."

"What difference does it make?" I murmured.

"My friend, you have a lot to learn about us Barrettis," he said with amusement. "We wrote the book on second chances. The question is" – he waited until my eyes met his – "how bad do you want it?"

CHAPTER 31

NATHAN

"Ladies and gentlemen, please have a seat. Mr. Wilder will make a statement and then he'll take a few questions."

Preston patted me gently on the shoulder as he leaned down to speak into my ear so the microphone in front of me wouldn't pick up the sound. "It's been an honor, Nathan."

I put my hand on his and sent him a nod, hoping he got my silent message. He returned the smile and then went to stand off to the side of the small raised platform. Flashes from several cameras continued to go off as the reporters took my picture, and I waited until they died down before speaking. I rested my hands on the podium in front of me, but didn't bother looking at the notes I'd prepared. Preston had helped me with the cookie-cutter speech explaining my withdrawal from the race, but I had no interest in the written statement anymore. I was tired of playing it safe.

"Thank you all for coming," I said. My voice felt dry and rusty, like I hadn't used it enough in the past two weeks.

Which was probably true, since I hadn't had much to say after Vincent had left me. Even the mere thought of the man threatened to derail me, so I forced myself to focus on the crowd of eager reporters.

"I'd like to start by confirming the rumors that have been circulating about me leaving the race for the U.S. Senate seat. As great of an honor as it would have been to represent you and the great state of South Carolina in our nation's capital this January, I've decided I need to face some realities in my own life before I'm ready to be a voice for others."

There were a few muffled murmurs, but the crowd quickly fell silent again.

"First and foremost, I am looking forward to rebuilding a relationship I never should have forsaken to begin with. I've been fortunate enough to spend the last couple of weeks with my brother, Brody, but all it's done is prove to me that I should have put him first, and I haven't always done that. I have a chance to remedy that, and I'm going to take it. Secondly, the recent attack on me and my family has been a stark reminder of how quickly life can change, how it can be snatched from you in the blink of an eye. I'm not going to ever take that for granted again."

I took in a deep breath to steady myself. "But I think what I've learned these past few weeks that's been the real eye-opener is that there are so many ways I can speak for myself and others, and it isn't necessarily limited to holding public office. It was a path I was set on from an early age, but one that, in my heart, I never really wanted. It took someone very special to make me realize that it was just one of many lies I'd been telling myself for a long time. Which leads me to my last point...a topic that I wish I didn't have to address, but I know will not be put to rest unless I do it myself."

I steeled myself for what was to come as I said, "For whatever reason, my sexuality has been brought into question on multiple occasions by my opponent, as well as by many of you here in this room. I wish it was something that held no weight when it comes to my ability to do this job, but the reality is that it has weight because you've given it that. You've made who I love a factor in my ability to speak for the people I wanted to represent. You've decided that who I go home to each night is more important than my desire to see that all Americans are equally protected under the law. You spend time pondering what label to attach to me rather than questioning my commitment to the people I was seeking to serve. So because I want the focus to be on my replacement's qualifications rather than me after today, I'm going to share something that isn't anyone's business but mine. Yes, I am gay."

I waited for the clicks of the cameras to die down and the rumble of conversation to cease before I continued. "No, I wasn't attempting to hide my sexuality or deny it. It was something that I simply didn't know how to deal with, so I chose to ignore it. I'd been raised to believe that being gay meant I wasn't equal in God's eyes anymore…or in society's. I don't believe the former, but sadly, the latter is still true and will continue to be true until labels like gay or straight aren't needed anymore because It. Doesn't. Matter." I shook my head slightly. "I just hope that that day comes in my lifetime and going forward, I'm going to do everything in my power to make sure that when the next generation is sitting up here announcing their candidacy for one of the greatest jobs in the world, their sexuality won't even be a blip on the radar. Questions?"

Predictably, several hands shot up at once and everyone began yelling questions. I pointed to a young woman in the first row. "Barb," I said with a nod.

"Mr. Wilder, you haven't mentioned what role, if any, your parents' brutal murders and the subsequent scandal surrounding them played in your decision."

"The loss of my parents did not factor into my decision. And to be clear, it isn't a scandal. Authorities have found concrete proof of *both* of my parents' roles in Megan Yates' death. They will both need to answer to the sins they so often accused others of being guilty of. Beyond that, I don't have much to say on the matter."

I pointed to the next reporter. It went on like that for a good twenty minutes before I glanced at Preston, who nodded and then called a halt to the press conference. Not surprisingly, many of the reporters followed me out of the building, but luckily, Preston had been prepared for that likelihood and had arranged for a cab to be waiting for me. Since I knew the reporters would be congregating at my house, I'd decided to spend a few days at a hotel until the worst of it had died down.

After giving the driver the address, I sank back against the seat and pulled out my cell phone. The press conference had been a live telecast, so I wasn't surprised to see a text from Brody congratulating me on a job well done. More texts from Ethan and several of the Barretti members I'd met over the past couple of weeks followed. It wasn't until I saw a text from Everett that I felt the tears start to gather.

Proud of you.

The three simple words were my undoing, and I found myself dialing Everett's number without even thinking about it. I'd talked to him a few times over the past two weeks. Luckily, Reese had started to get some sensation back, and doctors were certain that after physical therapy, he'd be able to walk again and would eventually completely recover. The treatment for his burns would be ongoing for a while, and Ronan had decided it would be best for Reese to be moved to Seattle so Ronan could oversee his recovery. Even though Reese still wasn't on speaking terms with Everett, the man had decided to spend the foreseeable future in Seattle to be there if and when Reese finally came around.

If he ever did.

"Nathan, how are you holding up?" Everett asked as soon as he answered.

"Good," I lied, since I figured the endless crushing pain in my chest didn't really count as "holding up."

Luckily, Everett didn't seem to pick up on anything in my voice because he said, "So you're headed to your brother's place soon."

"Yeah," I murmured. "Once the shit with the reporters dies down, I'll get my stuff packed up."

Brody had invited me to stay with him and Beck and Quinn indefinitely, but I wasn't sure if that was what I really wanted. I wanted to be closer to him, but since I had no clue what I wanted to do for a living, I wasn't sure if Montana would be the best place for me. In any case, I'd agreed to go for an extended visit while I figured out what to do next.

"Nathan, you haven't by chance heard from Vincent, have you?"

Even the man's name caused an unbearable ache in my chest. I was so fucking pissed at Vincent for telling me he loved me right before he'd walked away from me. But as hard as the words had been to hear, knowing what had been coming, I still clung to them like they were a lifeline of sorts.

"Um, no," I said. "Why?"

"Oh, nothing…I just haven't heard from him in a while and he's not returning my calls. Just has me a little worried, that's all."

I sat up. Well, Christ, now he had me worried.

"He's not returning your calls?" I asked as I glanced at the watch I had yet to take off.

"No," Everett said. "Not even to check up on how Reese is doing."

That wasn't like Vincent at all. My throat felt tight as I managed to say, "I'm sure he's fine."

"Yeah, you're probably right," Everett said, though I could hear the worry in his voice. "Hey, listen, I have to go but I'll check in with you soon, okay?"

"What?" I asked distractedly. "Um, yeah, of course."

Everett hung up, leaving me to stare at the phone. I didn't even have Vincent's number to check on him myself. Not that he'd answer or return my calls.

Fuck, what if something had happened to him?

My thoughts drifted to that damn house of his and all the protective measures it had. What if something had failed and he was in trouble? What if…fuck, what if his body…

"Um, sir," I said to the cabbie. "I need you to take me someplace else."

"Sure. Where to?"

"West Virginia."

∽

Fear shimmied through me as I approached the first gate. What if my watch didn't work? I'd have no way of getting into the house. I'd already sent the cab away after charging the obscenely high fare to my credit card, along with a generous tip. I had my phone so I could always call for help.

I held my breath as I put my watch against the keypad next to the gate. Relief flooded my nerve endings when it opened, but the feeling was temporary as I hurried through the second gate and then ran to the front door. Blessedly, it too opened.

"Vincent!" I called the second I was inside. The house wasn't in lockdown mode, so that had to be a good sign, right?

I ran past the garage and into the kitchen, which was empty. There was no sign of Mickey or Minnie as I darted up the stairs. "Vincent!" I shouted again, and just as I rounded the corner at the top of the stairs, I slammed against a hard body. I sagged in relief as familiar hands came up to grab my arms.

"Nathan, what the hell-"

I cut him off with a hard kiss. "Thank you, God," I whispered just before I kissed him again. Vincent kissed me back, and then he was pressing me back against the wall as he consumed my mouth.

"Fuck, no time for this," he said as he grabbed my hand. I saw him snag a black duffle bag off the floor. He dragged me down the stairs. "Is your car in the driveway?" he asked impatiently.

"What?"

"Your car?" he repeated.

"I didn't drive. I took a cab."

"Good," was all he said, and then he was leading me to the garage. "Get in," he said as he motioned to his car.

"Vincent-"

"There's no time. In the car." His eyes caught mine briefly as he went to the trunk. "Please, Nate."

I held my tongue and climbed into the front passenger seat. I was immediately greeted with two distinct meows, and I turned to see Mickey and Minnie watching me from separate pet carriers in the back seat. The trunk slammed closed and then Vincent was climbing into the front seat. He hit the garage door opener as he started the car up. It took less than a minute to get out of the driveway. Vincent pulled the car to a stop by the end of the curving road leading to his driveway. As far as I knew, it was the only one in or out. I watched as he glanced at his watch.

"What...what are we doing?" I asked in confusion as we sat there.

"Need to make sure no one comes up the road," Vincent murmured.

"Why-"

That was all I got out before I heard a huge booming sound. I jerked my attention to the right and saw a black plume of smoke along with a huge fireball shoot into the air.

In the same direction where Vincent's house was.

"Oh my God," I said. "Was that your house?"

Before I could even process what was happening, Vincent was dragging me into his arms and his mouth was closing over mine. I forgot all about the explosion, the cats, and everything in between as he kissed me.

"Missed you," he said softly against my mouth.

I knew I needed to figure out what the hell was happening, but at the moment, I didn't care. "Me too." I practically crawled across the console to get to him. He eventually pulled back from the kiss and urged me back into my own seat.

"Buckle up," he said with a wink, and then he was getting the car on the road.

I did as he said. "What's going on, Vincent?"

"What are you doing here, Nathan?" he asked, ignoring my question.

"I talked to Everett. He said he hadn't heard from you in a while and I started to worry-" I stopped talking when Vincent began shaking his head.

"Meddling bastard," he said with a smile.

"What?" I asked in confusion. "What are you talking about?"

"He pulled a broken watch on you, baby."

"What?" I had entered the Twilight Zone, because nothing was making sense to me.

"I talked to Everett this morning...and every day for the last two weeks," Vincent explained.

"You did? Then why did he..."

My brain registered what Vincent had said about the broken watch. The watch I'd broken weeks ago to scare Vincent into coming back to check on me.

"That bastard," I said in disbelief. "He conned me."

"Yeah, he did," Vincent said with a laugh. "Saved me a trip to Charleston, though." He motioned to the watch on my wrist. "That asshole knew the first thing I'd do after leaving the house was figure out where you were – probably assumed we'd pass each other on the way."

"Huh?" I shook my head. "Was that your house that blew up?"

Vincent curled his fingers with mine and pulled my hand up to his mouth. "I promise I'll tell you everything when we get to where we're going, baby." He pressed a kiss to my skin. "Why don't you get some rest? That press conference had to have worn you out."

"You saw it?"

He nodded. "You were amazing." He kept our hands joined as he dropped them to his thigh. "Get some sleep, Nathan. We've got a lot to talk about."

His words gave me an odd sense of comfort...and hope. "You'll tell me everything?" I asked, even as I laid my head back on the headrest.

"Yeah, I will."

I was sure I wouldn't be able to sleep, but I closed my eyes anyway. A couple of hours later, Vincent was gently shaking me awake. "Baby, we're here," he said.

I sat up and tried to clear the cobwebs from my brain as I looked around. "Are you kidding me?" I said when I realized where we were.

It was the motel we'd spent the first night together in after he'd saved my life at my house. The tacky one with the heart-shaped bed and mirror on the ceiling.

Vincent smiled and kissed me. "It's our special place. I knew the second you pressed that hot body of yours against mine that morning that you were going to fuck everything up for me." His mouth brushed mine. "You did…in the best way."

I groaned as I put my hand behind his neck and held him to me for a deeper kiss. When we finally separated, he got out of the car and reached in to get one of the pet carriers. I grabbed the other. The room was the exact same one, and while I got Mickey and Minnie out of their cages, Vincent went back to the car and returned with his bag and a litterbox for the cats. He got the cats some food and water while I put the carriers aside. The animals were unsettled at first, but once they found the window, they sat on the small ledge in front of it so they could look outside.

And just like that, I was back in Vincent's arms as his mouth descended on mine. I wrestled with his clothes as he walked me backwards towards the bed, but he grabbed my wrists before I could reach for his pants. He pushed me down on the bed and kissed me hard. "Talking first," he said, his breath coming in heavy pants.

I tried to sit up so I could pay better attention to him, but he shook his head. "Nope, like this. I've been waiting weeks to get you underneath me again and now that I have you here, you're not going anywhere."

I was about to remind him that he could have had that this whole time, but I held my tongue. I'd rather hear what he had to say.

"Yes, I blew up my house."

"Why?" I asked, completely floored.

"Because for me to really live, Vincent St. James had to die."

I shook my head, not understanding, but he kissed me to silence my next question. "If Vincent St. James no longer exists, there's no reason to hunt him…there's no revenge to be had. They called me *The Ghost* for a reason, Nate. It was because I was good at not being seen. The men I worked with years ago haven't seen me since then. They know where I live because I never tried to hide that, but that's it. No friends meant no links to the outside world. No lovers meant no one else they could target."

"But Everett," I said.

"Everett is going to mourn the loss of his friend. He'll likely be the only one who will attend my funeral. He'll handle my estate. He'll make sure to spread the word that Vincent is gone...died tragically when a natural gas leak caused his house to explode."

"You can't do that to him, Vincent..."

"He's in on it, baby. He knows all about it." He ran his fingers down my cheek. My bruises had mostly healed, but he seemed to linger on the spots they'd once been. "My enemies won't have any way of tracking me because I won't be me anymore. Turns out Ronan and Dom have some skills even I don't possess."

"Like what?"

"Like finding a body at a morgue in Chattanooga that fit my general description. Like giving me a whole new identity. Social security, employment history, the works."

It was almost too much to believe. "Why?" I asked.

"You know why," he whispered, just before he kissed me.

"For me?" I asked. "You did this to be with me?"

"I thought I'd have to wait until you finished your first term in the Senate to beg you to make some changes for me." He shook his head. "But when I saw the press conference...it was like my second chance and third chance all wrapped up into one." His eyes held mine. "Nate, it wouldn't be safe for me to be in the public eye in any kind of way, but if you decide to run for office at some point, we can make it work."

"You mean like what Everett and Pierce had? Sneaking around? Hiding?"

"I know it's not ideal, but I would do anything for you...but standing by your side in front of news cameras...it would just be too dangerous."

"No," I said with a shake of my head.

Vincent froze and then he was lifting off me. I grabbed his arm because I knew exactly what he was thinking.

"I mean no to the hiding and sneaking around, Vincent." He stopped his upward motion and sat back down on the bed next to me.

"If we do this, we're all in. Both of us." I leaned in to kiss him. "Don't you know, Vincent?"

His eyes met mine as I pulled back just a little. "You're it for me. I don't need anything else."

His arm snaked around my waist and then he was pulling me flush with his chest. "Just us," he murmured.

"Just us."

"Sounds perfect, Nate."

I let my hands stroke over his face, hardly able to believe he was really here and that he was mine.

"That's because it is." I put my arms around him and held on, certain I'd never be able to let him go again. "It really is."

EPILOGUE

VINCENT

One month later

"Three," I said impatiently.

"Two," Nathan countered. "Keep arguing and it'll be one."

"Not one," I said with a shake of my head. "Impossible."

Nathan shrugged his shoulders. "Two. Take it or leave it," he said.

"Fine," I grumbled as I wrote it down on the piece of paper in front of me. "I'm sure there are plenty of places that have more than two locks on the damn front door."

"Yeah, they're called prisons," Nathan said.

He leaned back in the chair as I scanned the plans in front of me. He'd vetoed most of the security measures I'd wanted to put into place in the new house we were building. Logically, I knew most of his vetoes made sense, but I was having trouble giving up the habits of the past. Just this morning I'd finally managed to not check for tampering beneath the hood of my car after we'd stopped to get coffee. I'd been a nervous wreck about the whole thing, but I'd managed it.

"I want you to carry a gun."

"Absolutely not. Veto. Next."

"I'd give you lessons on how to shoot it," I said.

"Only kind of gun I'm interested in learning how to shoot is a paintball gun…maybe. What's next?"

I sighed. "Escape hatch."

Nathan rolled his eyes at me. "Did you seriously sneak that on the list?" he asked.

"It'll be like a panic room," I insisted.

Nathan merely shook his head. Mickey jumped up onto his lap. "I gave you the fence," he reminded me.

"A regular fence," I said. "Not even a single watt running through the sucker."

Nathan sighed and put Mickey on the floor. He stood and came to my side of the table. I automatically moved my chair back because I knew what his plan was. He straddled my lap and closed his hands around my neck. "Take deep breaths, baby," he said. "I'm safe. You're safe. Vincent St. James is gone."

I nodded. It was something he had to remind me of often. Even having seen the pictures from my own funeral hadn't been enough to always convince me that Dominic Barretti's crazy plan had worked. And crazy was exactly what I'd thought of it when he'd suggested it to me. But the more he'd talked, the more I'd listened.

And hoped.

Ironically, it had been the reclusive lifestyle I'd been living for so long that had made the whole thing possible. While I'd been "alive," I'd been a threat to countless agencies and individuals. But "dead" Vincent was a harmless Vincent. Undoubtedly, there were some who'd waited to see if any of the countless secrets I held would die with me or rise up from the dead, but over time they'd forget all about me.

If only it was as simple for me to forget about them.

And the threat they'd posed to me for so many years.

It hadn't been hard in the least to give up all the associations I'd forged over the years, even the beneficial ones. Although the director of the FBI had gotten me out of a couple of jams in exchange for the many jobs I'd done for his agency off the books over the years, there'd been no exception for him or anyone else. Every single person I'd ever worked or interacted with were led to believe I was dead. The only ones who knew better were Everett, Ronan and his men, and the Barrettis.

All people who would take my secret to the grave.

The new identity Ronan and Dom had created for me had allowed me to keep nothing of my former life except for my first name. Surprisingly, there'd been little else to leave behind. The only thing I'd lost that had really hurt had been some of David's stuff, including his treasured books and the motorcycle he'd loved. I'd ended up walking out of my house with a few changes of clothes, David's picture, and the well-worn copy of The Outsiders that had a special place on my nightstand. I'd thought Nathan might have a problem with my attachment to the book, but he'd surprised me when he'd not only invited me to read the book to him on the nights I was feeling nostalgic, but had found a special place in our bedroom to hang David's picture. He hadn't relegated my lover's memory to a drawer like I had for so many years. No, he'd welcomed him into our lives, and he'd continued to pry stories out of me about when David and I had been children. It was his way of helping me make sure I never forgot my first love.

Undoubtedly because Nathan knew *he* was, and always would be, my last love.

In addition to the new identity Dom had procured for me, he'd offered me a chance to buy into his and his brothers' business. I'd been hesitant at first, but once I'd met all four Barretti brothers, along with their partners, I'd realized they were all gladly willing to sell equal shares of the business to me. They'd taken it a step further and welcomed me and Nathan into their lives, too. We spent nearly every Sunday at Dom's house on San Juan Island as part of their family dinner celebration that had gotten so big, they needed an entire day to enjoy it. Our plan was to drive or fly out to Dare to spend the weekend with his brother and the extended family out there at least once a month. Brody, Quinn, and Beck similarly traveled to Seattle nearly as often for the family get-together as well.

Everett continued to struggle with Reese, who hadn't warmed up to the idea of letting his father back into his life, but Gage had been trying to smooth Reese's rough edges. And while I suspected part of that had to do with being Reese's friend, I had to wonder if the man didn't have an ulterior motive, since he seemed to have an awfully hard time taking his eyes off a certain former Commander-in-Chief whenever they were in the same room together.

Which seemed to irritate Agent Jon Nash to no end.

It was a dynamic that I still hadn't made sense of, and I wasn't sure Everett had even noticed, since he'd long ago dismissed the idea that anyone could take Pierce's place in his heart. I hadn't bothered to try to explain to him that it wasn't about replacing one love with another. Not when there were men out there who were strong enough to love you and that piece of your heart that would always belong to another.

Men like my Nate.

"How about we finish this another time, Vincent Dorfmeyer?" Nathan said as he rubbed up against me.

"Fuck, I hate when you call me that," I said.

I still wanted to kick Dom's ass for the ridiculous last name he and Ronan had come up with for my new identity, but, of course, each man had pointed to the other when I'd asked about it.

"I had some thoughts about that, too," Nathan murmured as he placed soft kisses all around my mouth, but never landed on it.

I snagged the back of his head and held him in place so I could take what he was teasing me with.

"You were saying?" I asked when I pulled back. The cocky grin faded and Nathan's hungry eyes met mine.

He toyed with my hair. "Although Dorfmeyer has a certain ring to it," – he yelped when I pinched his ass – "okay, okay." He wriggled his ass against my palm when I went to rub the sore spot.

"Nate?"

"What?" he asked as his breath got heavy and he began to grind his cock against mine.

"You going to finish your thought?"

"What? Oh, right." He began chewing on his lip, a sure sign he was nervous. "I was thinking…Wilder might be a better fit."

I stilled at that.

"Vincent Wilder," Nathan said softly. "What do you think?"

Was he…fuck, was he actually asking me to…

"Don't fuck with me," I said. "That better not be a hypothetical-"

"It's not," Nathan cut in. He kissed me hard. "It's me asking you to marry me."

"This is me saying yes," I snarled as I slammed my mouth down on his and lifted him up. "Yes," I repeated as I swept the blueprints that were spread out on the table to the floor.

"What are you doing?" Nathan asked with a laugh as I lowered him onto his back on the table.

"Christening our new table, what does it look like?" I asked as I skimmed my lips over his pulse point. He moaned and pushed up against me.

"The furniture's rented, remember?" he said hoarsely.

"Not anymore, baby. Any piece I make love to you on goes in our new place."

Nathan smiled and kissed me. "Well then, you better get busy. We've got a big house to furnish."

I chuckled. "On it."

"Love you, Vincent," Nathan whispered.

"Love you too," I said as I sank my fingers into his beautiful hair. "My Nate," I said firmly.

His gorgeous eyes held mine. "Always," he said simply.

And it was true. Whether he was my husband, my lover, my boyfriend…didn't matter. He was and always would be, first and foremost, *My Nate*.

The End

Turn the page to check out a sneak peek from Unexpected, Everett, Gage & Nash's story!

SNEAK PEEK

UNEXPECTED (THE PROTECTORS, BOOK 10) (M/M/M)

PROLOGUE

EVERETT

THIRTEEN YEARS EARLIER

"It's an honor, Mr. President."

The silky-smooth voice slid through me like the finest whiskey and all I could do was stare at the large hand that was extended in my direction. I tried to draw in a gulp of air as I suddenly felt light-headed.

What the hell is happening to me?

I was dimly aware of the fact that we weren't alone, but we might as well have been the last two people on earth – his hold on me was that absolute. I was inarguably the most powerful man in the world, but I couldn't stop shaking and I was sure I was going to fucking pass out from the lack of oxygen.

God, he was beautiful.

There was just no other way to describe him.

Closely cropped black hair, dark blue eyes, heavily built body that filled out his uniform.

His uniform...

God, right, because he was a fucking soldier.

In the military that I commanded.

And not just any solider, but my son's commanding officer.

Oh, and of course, he was a goddamn man. What the ever-loving hell was wrong with me?

"The honor's mine, Colonel St. James," I somehow managed to get out as I reached for his hand.

And immediately regretted it.

Because that one touch – that sensation of his rough, warm skin sliding over mine answered every question I'd ever had about myself – every question I'd tried to sweep under the rug since I'd been a little boy and my mother had grabbed my arm in a painful hold and dragged me away from my own birthday party and into a darkened corner of the house after she'd caught me and my best friend, Joseph, holding hands after I'd blown out the candles on my cake. My mother had forced me to my knees right there in her sewing room and then she'd dropped to her own next to me and we'd done the only thing that she'd said could save me from eternal damnation.

We'd prayed.

And prayed.

And prayed.

My knees had hurt so badly I could barely climb to my feet by the time my father had come looking for us to ask why there were half a dozen twelve-year-olds running around the house unattended. I couldn't remember what my mother had told him, but thankfully she hadn't told him about Joseph.

Because my father's response would have been so much more painful than bruised knees.

Joseph had gone away after that, but the feelings he'd stirred in me hadn't. And no amount of prayer or my father's heavy hand would have been able to make me forget the spark of energy that had flowed through me so strongly that I'd finally felt truly alive for the first time in my life.

The spark that had nothing on the current inferno of need that was pulsing just beneath the surface of my skin as the man held my hand in his, long after he should have released it.

Or maybe after I should have released his.

I didn't really know.

"Pierce," was all the man said.

I couldn't call him by his first name. I just couldn't. But that was exactly what I did.

"Pierce," I whispered. A small smile of satisfaction slid across his beautiful lips and my entire body went tight with desire.

Right there in the fucking hospital room where my twenty-one-year-old son was recovering from wounds he'd sustained in an insurgent ambush. My only saving grace was that Reese was asleep and my wife was off somewhere hassling the staff about our son's room not being on the side of the hospital that overlooked the large man-made pond and nicely landscaped grounds.

But that didn't mean we were alone.

I quickly dropped Pierce's hand and glanced over my shoulder at my perpetual shadow, Grady.

William Grady was one of the Secret Service agents who'd been assigned to me shortly after I'd taken on the role of vice president. He'd been the only agent to transition to the team protecting me when I won the presidency eight years later.

Grady's eyes weren't actually on me and Pierce, but I knew that didn't mean anything. The man was trained to see things even when he wasn't looking. I knew that fact should freak me the fuck out, but for some reason it didn't. Maybe because I knew Grady would take anything he knew about me – and he knew a lot – to the grave with him.

Or maybe it was because his presence meant I couldn't do what I'd been trained to do practically from birth.

Pretend.

I returned my gaze to Pierce and then dropped my eyes to his hands, which he had pressed together in front of him.

"Mr. President—"

"Everett," I said without thinking as Pierce's voice washed over me like the gentlest of caresses.

Fuck, what the hell? I couldn't let him call me by my first name. It was beyond inappropriate. I was this man's superior. There were rules to be followed...

I was both grateful and disappointed when Pierce didn't say my name. I tried really hard to listen as he outlined what had happened with the ambush, but it wasn't until he said Reese's name that I felt my insides clench and I turned to look at my son. He'd gotten lucky that the only injuries he'd sustained had been a bullet wound to the leg and a concussion. I knew I was supposed to see a hardened soldier in that bed, but all I saw was the little boy who'd made life bearable. To the outside world, I was the epitome of success, but Reese was the only thing I'd ever gotten right.

Though in truth, I was giving myself more credit than I deserved. I'd sired him, but I hadn't been the father he'd needed.

No, there'd been too many things I'd needed to accomplish first. Too many things I'd needed to prove to people who didn't matter.

Regret seared my bones and I felt the need to curl in on myself until I was no longer visible to the outside world. Maybe then I wouldn't feel like such a fucking fraud.

"He'll be okay," Pierce murmured from behind me. I couldn't mistake what the heat along my back was.

His body.

His big, beautiful body that was just inches from mine. The body that I wanted so badly to close the inconsequential gap between us and just fix everything.

Me.

Reese.

My farce of a life.

I closed my eyes and pretended I could feel Pierce's strong arms wrapping around me from behind. I imagined how it would feel to sink into his hold and never have to worry about someone telling me it was wrong. I practically shook with the need to feel his lips on my neck as he urged me to let go – to let him take care of everything for a while.

I could escape to a place where I didn't have the eyes of the world watching my every move.

I could pretend I wasn't a colossal failure at being a husband... or father.

And I could dream of how things would have been different if I'd just been a little bit braver when I'd been a kid and my entire life had been laid out before me.

A life that looked perfectly lived on paper.

But was nothing more than a sham.

How the hell could one fucking handshake tear apart the entire fabric of my world? And why couldn't I focus on anything but the fact that one handshake wasn't enough?

It would never be enough.

I couldn't do this. I had to keep it together. I'd chosen my path and there was no going back. Whatever this man had done to me in the past few minutes was a fluke – the crazy sensations were just a result of the stress I was feeling at the near loss of my child. None of what was happening to me was real.

Before I could even call myself a liar, Pierce did it for me.

But not with words.

No.

Not even close.

He did exactly what I'd wanted and closed that little bit of distance between us. Not enough to touch me, but enough that my body went haywire. The need screaming through me was impossible to ignore. But it wasn't until his mouth dropped close to my ear so that only I could hear him that I knew my life was about to irrevocably change.

And just like that, with just a few softly spoken words, Pierce St. James stole away the last of the lies that had protected me for so very long.

"Everything will be okay... *Everett*. Trust me."

CHAPTER 1

NASH

PRESENT DAY

I didn't like when he got like this.

I mean, I didn't like the guy, period, but I really didn't like when he got like this.

He was quiet... too quiet. And not the kind of quiet that meant he was planning something, like trying to ditch me again.

No, it was the kind of quiet that he sometimes got when he was in the middle of doing something unimportant and his mind just wandered off.

Wandering wasn't the right word, because that made it sound like he was just preoccupied. No, when he got like this it was so much... more.

What the fuck do you care, Nash? It's not like this is a real gig.

I couldn't deny the voice in my head was right. After all, babysitting a former president who lived in Bumfuck, Nowhereland, wasn't exactly the highlight of my career.

The familiar bitterness that washed over me just served to piss me off. In the first half-dozen foster homes I'd been placed in, I'd tried so many variations of being the perfect kid that I'd easily lost myself in the process. By the time both my age and the count of foster homes hit double digits, I'd accepted that life wasn't going to hand me a fucking break, and I'd reacted accordingly.

So, it wasn't like I shouldn't be used to being thrown a curveball every now and again. Or at just about every opportunity, since Fate seemed to enjoy fucking with me.

I forced the negativity away and focused on my charge. Of course, all that did was piss me off again as I remembered the day before. Babysitting Everett Shaw, former leader of the free world, had been meant to knock me down a couple of pegs, and hell if it hadn't worked. The man was a fucking pain in my ass – a fact that had been proven yet again the day before when he'd taken off on me after sending me on a fool's errand to track down a magazine he'd supposedly left in the gazebo that he spent so much of his time in.

I'd returned with said magazine – which had turned out to be nothing more than a prop in a carefully planned act of rebellion – only to find the man had taken off in his 1941 Cadillac Series 61. He'd gone so far as to employ his housekeeper and the groundskeeper to help him make his escape, but fortunately my predecessor had warned me that the man had a habit of ditching his Secret Service agents. I'd gotten the impression that Shaw and Grady had formed some kind of friendship in the years they'd been together, but Grady had done his duty and shared the tidbit anyway.

A clear sign the agent had never forgotten he was honor bound to first and foremost protect the former president.

It was a fact I was grateful for, because if I hadn't planted a tracking device on the man's car, I never would have found him and I'd have paid for it with my superiors. At this point, the assholes were looking for any excuse to can my ass, and losing track of my charge was sure to make that happen.

So I'd been in a carefully veiled rage by the time I'd tracked Shaw down at his friend Vincent's house. Grady had warned me all about Vincent St. James and his fanatical rules about not allowing armed agents onto his property, but I'd already made the decision that despite Grady's loyalty to Shaw, he'd been too damn lenient with the man. My intention had been to show Shaw and his friend that there was a new sheriff in town, but I'd let my irritation get the better of me and had made my decision based on emotion rather than reason.

Despite doing my homework on Vincent, I'd truly thought Grady was just over-exaggerating the mysterious man's attitude and all it would take was a little bit of my own to show the former soldier who was really in charge.

I'd underestimated the man big time.

Big time.

Even when the tall asshole had come striding out of his garage, rifle in hand, I'd been slow to react. Probably because I couldn't have even imagined the balls it would take for someone to approach a federal officer so blatantly armed. I'd told myself the weapon was just for show even as I'd scrambled to pull my own firearm from the holster, an awkward feat considering I'd still been sitting in my car at the time, which had been trapped between two gates leading onto the property.

But the weapon hadn't been for show, and I'd barely gotten the first few words of warning out for Vincent to put the gun down when he'd shot out my tire.

Shaw had managed to diffuse the situation with his friend, but then he'd laid into me about not following Vincent's ridiculous rules.

As someone who'd always prided himself on his ability to stay cool in any situation, something about having Everett Shaw talking down to me like I was nothing more than a misbehaving child had really done a number on me. In that moment, I hadn't given a shit that my words would likely end up costing me my job. I'd gotten in Shaw's face and practically told the man who'd once commanded the world's most powerful army that he was acting like a spoiled brat. Then I'd turned my fury on Vincent St. James, a man who'd already proven he wasn't exactly the most reasonable of guys. Fortunately, he'd surprised me again by seeing reason and had allowed me to inspect his property while he'd given me a rundown on the security measures he'd taken to secure the fortress-like home. I hadn't been allowed to go inside and I hadn't asked to, since I'd garnered enough information from Grady to know that whoever the mysterious Vincent was, he cared a great deal about Shaw and wouldn't let anything happen to him when he was in his presence.

Shaw and I hadn't spoken again until several hours later when he'd been ready to go home.

Well, I'd spoken, he'd pretended to listen.

Vincent had helped me replace my tire with the spare, so I'd been ready to leave when Shaw had exited the house. I'd expected for him to try and rake me over the coals again, but he'd barely made eye contact with me.

A fact that should have been okay with me.

But it hadn't been.

Just like it wasn't sitting well with me now as I watched him stare off in the distance, a pair of gardening shears forgotten in his hand. It was early in the morning and the sun was just starting to rise, but he'd been at work in his garden for more than an hour. It wasn't overly cold, but I still fought the urge to insist he come inside with me. At fifty-eight, Everett Shaw was in good shape, but there was just something about him when he got like this.

He always looked so... frail.

Yeah, I didn't like it.

I'd rather have him in my face acting like the confident leader I'd seen so many times on television when I'd been dreaming of the day when I'd protect his successor. I refused to acknowledge the other reason that I couldn't get that moment when he'd been standing so close to me as he'd berated me for breaking Vincent's rule out of my head.

The early morning silence was broken by the muffled ringing of a phone. I watched as it took Shaw several beats to even seem to acknowledge the sound. His moves were slow as he searched the phone out and put it to his ear. I couldn't hear him talking, but it didn't matter because a moment later, he was climbing to his feet. When he turned, he actually seemed surprised to see me, though I had to wonder why, since I was practically glued to the man's ass all day.

The only time we ever managed to get away from one another was at night and on my days off when another agent took over, though the lucky bastard rarely had to spend any time in Shaw's company, since the older man was usually asleep by eleven each night.

Shaw studied me for a moment, his expression unreadable. Then he was walking my way, his hands in his pockets. The former president lived on a small estate just east of the Jefferson National Forest in Virginia. The closest town was a good twenty minutes away and didn't have much more than half a dozen shops and a single gas station. Additionally, the surrounding land was sparsely populated, so when it came to threats against a man like Shaw, they were few and far between. Yeah, there were always fanatics out there, but unlike many of his predecessors, Everett Shaw had kept a low profile since leaving office and that had served him well when it came to things like privacy.

Too well, it sometimes seemed.

Because besides Vincent and the married couple who served as his only staff and lived in a guest cottage on the property, there seemed to be no one in Shaw's life. No dog to greet him when he came home or a cat to curl up against at night. It was just him and his roses and the television shows that kept him company night after night.

"I need to go to Vincent's house," Shaw murmured as he neared me.

"Of course, Mr. President," I said as he passed me. He paused briefly when I addressed him by his title, and I swore I saw him flinch, but then he was moving again. It took him just a few minutes to get cleaned up and changed, and when we headed outside, he didn't even argue about driving himself. He simply walked to my agency-issued sedan and climbed into the back seat.

It was all so very perfectly routine.

And it irritated the fuck out of me.

God, what the hell was wrong with me? The man was behaving exactly as he should, especially considering the bullshit he'd put me through the day before.

Neither of us spoke as we made the forty-five-minute drive to

Vincent's house, which was deep within the same forest Shaw lived near, but on the West Virginia side. Vincent was waiting for us in the driveway and unlike the day before, the two gates were already open, so I drove straight through. Vincent definitely looked on edge. I scanned the property for the second man I'd seen him with the day before, but I didn't see him. I'd heard him referred to as Nathan, and although there was something familiar about him, we hadn't been introduced, so I hadn't had the chance to do any research on him.

I stayed near the car as Shaw got out to talk to Vincent. He finally began to show some animation when he began arguing with the other man.

"Don't do this, Vincent," Shaw said.

Vincent ignored him and went to the trunk of his car. He placed a large black duffel bag in it before slamming it closed. I could hear Shaw's muffled voice as he seemed to be pleading with Vincent. But it wasn't until Vincent turned and began striding toward me that I stiffened. I hadn't removed my firearm, so I was fully expecting the man to go to battle with me over it. But his eyes only briefly strayed to my gun where it was resting in a holster under my jacket.

"I need you to watch them both while I'm gone," Vincent said. It wasn't a request. The man's jaw was tight.

"Them?" I asked.

"I've asked Everett to hang around for a bit. Nathan is still asleep."

A sudden awareness went through me when Vincent said Nathan's name. There was a slight tick in his jaw, but it was his eyes that gave him away.

They softened just the littlest bit.

God, were he and Nathan...?

"If I'm not back by tonight, take Nathan with you back to Everett's house. Don't let him leave. Under any circumstances."

I should have bristled at the way the man was ordering me around, but I was caught up in the edge of fear I heard in his voice.

Yeah, he definitely had feelings for Nathan.

Was scared for him.

An unexpected shard of pity for Vincent went through me and I found myself nodding before I could think better of it.

Vincent turned to walk away, then paused and said, "You can go inside. Keep your gun with you."

He didn't wait for me to respond. He just hurried back to his car and climbed into it, barely sparing Shaw a glance. The engine roared to life and then the car was tearing out of the driveway. Shaw's worried eyes met mine, but he remained silent. I wanted to ask what the hell was going on, but had the sense not to.

The agent in me didn't want to know.

Once inside, Shaw got to work making breakfast after finding a black apron in a drawer near the stove. I stationed myself in the hallway between the kitchen and the front door. Less than thirty minutes later, I heard footsteps on the staircase. A mussed-looking Nathan appeared in the door.

No, not mussed.

Well-loved.

I knew I was likely reaching, but my suspicions that there was something going on between Vincent and Nathan were confirmed when I saw Nathan's face fall at the sight of Shaw. He managed to recover long enough to exchange pleasantries with Shaw, but it abruptly ended when he spied the two place settings on the table.

"Where is he?" Nathan asked.

Shaw's gaze connected with Nathan's. "He had some things to do this morning and asked me to stop by and keep you company." His eyes landed on me and then Nathan's gaze did the same.

Well, not on me, exactly.

But my gun, which was visible beneath my jacket.

"Where is he?" Nathan repeated, his voice going a tad higher.

"I don't know," Shaw said tiredly, then he was turning off the stove and getting the coffee pot.

Because my eyes were on Nathan, I only half-listened as Shaw explained that Nathan would be coming with us if Vincent didn't return by nightfall. I couldn't see his face, but I didn't really need to, since the tension in his body gave him away.

He was fucking terrified.

For Vincent.

I tried not to feel sorry for the man, because I could have told him that no good came of tying yourself to one person the way he'd so clearly tied himself to the mysterious Vincent, but I couldn't deny the pity that I felt.

Or the little spark of envy that went along with it.

I shoved the errant emotion aside and trained my eyes on the small set of monitors along the wall that gave me a picture of what was happening outside. But when I heard a crunching sound, I turned and watched in disbelief as Nathan used a mug to destroy the watch he'd been wearing.

Vincent had explained the importance of the watch that was exactly like the one Shaw wore. It was no ordinary wristwatch. No, it was its own tracking device, and destroying it was so much more than Nathan letting out his rage.

Predictably, Shaw's phone started ringing about two minutes later, but instead of answering it, he turned it off. I watched in shock as Nathan and Shaw casually chatted as they sat down at the table, plates of food in hand.

"Nash?"

I jerked to attention at Nathan's voice. "What?" I asked stupidly. I could hear Shaw's phone vibrating, but he didn't answer it.

"Would you like to join us?" He motioned to the table.

"No, thank you," I said as I took in Shaw's expression as Nathan extended the offer. I knew for a fact that Grady had often shared a meal with Shaw, but it wasn't an invitation the man had ever extended to me.

And he sure as hell didn't look pleased about the prospect now.

I had to admit, he looked more engaged than he had earlier this morning, but I doubted it would last, especially when his phone continued to vibrate off and on for several minutes.

Then my phone rang.

"Don't answer that," Shaw ordered before I could even reach for the phone.

I reached for it anyway.

"Nash," Shaw said in warning. Since I wasn't about to ditch protocol, not to mention fuck with a guy who could likely rearrange my internal organs with one punch, I ignored him.

"Nash," Shaw repeated, but this time his voice was different. Gone was the no-nonsense tone. I looked up at him and felt something go through me at the way he was looking at me.

He'd looked at me in a lot of different ways over the past week since I'd first arrived at his home, but he'd never looked at me like he was now.

"Please," Shaw murmured softly, and I could tell it killed him to do it.

A shiver of awareness seeped into every nerve ending as I held the man's gaze. His bright blue eyes were alight with some emotion I couldn't quite name. I held my phone hard enough to potentially break the damn thing.

Follow fucking protocol, Nash. This man is not your friend!

"I have to at least check who it is," I finally said.

Shaw sent me a nod. I quickly flipped the phone over and saw that it was an unknown caller. The need to answer it was great, but for some reason, the need to see the life stay in Shaw's eyes for a while longer was greater.

Jesus, Nash, get a fucking grip.

I put the phone away and tried not to enjoy the spark of warmth that went through me when a small smile graced Shaw's lips.

My phone rang a couple more times over the following few minutes, and I did as Shaw asked and ignored the calls. I only half-listened as Nathan and Shaw began talking, but it took everything in me to keep my eyes on the security monitors in front of me when Nathan flat-out admitted to Shaw he was gay.

"Bet that felt good," Shaw said.

Nathan let out a little laugh and said, "You have no idea."

"Yeah, Nathan, I do," Everett murmured.

I couldn't stop myself from looking over at Shaw as his quiet words sank in.

No way.

No FUCKING way.

Heat flooded my entire system as Nathan expressed the disbelief I was feeling. I managed to catch Shaw saying something about his son not speaking to him when Nathan pointed out he'd been married, but I couldn't really process what exactly that meant.

Everett Shaw, former president of the United States, is gay.

Everett Shaw is gay.

Shaw is gay.

Holy fuck.

"I knew something was wrong when I married Elanor, but I didn't know what it was. I was in denial for a really long time…"

That was as much as I could bear to hear. Not only were his words hitting just a little too close to home, I felt like I was violating the man's privacy by being there. Yes, he knew I'd overhear him, but still, it wasn't right.

I quietly turned and hurried down the hall and out the front door. I began sucking in big gulps of air.

Everett Shaw is gay.

I told myself my body was shaking because of the shock, but I knew it wasn't true. But I refused to give words to the real reason. Instead, I busied myself with walking the fence line. Twenty minutes later, I heard rather than saw the proof that all hell was about to break loose.

As Vincent's muscle car roared into the driveway a moment later, the tires squealing as he hit the brakes just in time to keep from plowing into the garage door, my nerves got the better of me.

"They're okay!" I shouted as Vincent got out of the car, since I was still a good hundred yards away from the house. With his gun in hand, he sent me what could only be classified as a deadly look and then strode into the house. Concern for Shaw had me running toward the house. I was almost at the door when it opened. I nearly slammed into Shaw as he came out and he quickly put his hand up and flattened it on my chest to stop my forward movement.

"Hold on there, son," he said.

Something about him calling me son pissed me off, though I wasn't sure why. And I couldn't give it too much thought because heat and electricity were spiraling out from the spot where his hand was resting on my chest.

All that sensation and it was... fuck, it was going straight to my balls. My dick hardened in my pants as Shaw lifted his eyes to meet mine. I couldn't make sense of what I was seeing, especially since he quickly shuttered his eyes and then dropped his hand. He pushed past me and said, "We should go."

I heard muffled sounds coming from inside the house, then what sounded like dishes breaking. My instinct to make sure Nathan was okay warred with my need to escape this whole fucked-up mess.

Everett Shaw was gay and my body had decided to pick this exact moment to rejoice over that fact.

"Let's go, son," Shaw called to me. "Those boys will be just fine now," he added with a smirk over his shoulder.

I caught up to him right before he reached the car. For the life of me, I couldn't figure out what possessed me to do it, but I grabbed his arm and turned him so his back was practically pressed up against the side of the car. "I'm not your son," I murmured. I'd meant to say the words angrily, but they definitely didn't come out that way.

No, they came out the way I'd been feeling them.

Not pissed that he'd been talking down to me, but more like I was desperate to make sure he in no way thought of me as his kid.

I had my body practically mashed up against Shaw's, but I couldn't force myself to ease off.

"I'm not your son," I repeated.

Shaw, for his part, seemed confused at first, then something switched. I would have missed his reaction if I hadn't been standing so close to him.

Ticked-up breathing.

A slight tremor snaking through his body.

His fingers tightening on my forearm where he'd grabbed me at some point.

Lips parting just a little.

God, those lips…

Shaw managed a nod. "The things you heard in there," he began, his eyes shifting briefly toward the house.

"Aren't any of my business," I finished for him. There was no missing the relief in his eyes. Desperate to get us back to where we were supposed to be, I added "Mr. President" and forced myself to step back.

He tensed up at the title and dropped his hand from my arm. His jaw tightened and he turned his head away from me so he wouldn't be forced to look me in the eye. "I'd like you to take me somewhere, Agent Nash."

Agent.

That was new.

"Yes, sir," I said as all the warmth I'd been feeling evaporated. I stepped back enough so I could open the back door for him. "Where to, Mr. President?"

Shaw straightened his clothes and then walked around me and the door. His next words were so soft, I barely heard him.

"Arlington National Cemetery."

ABOUT THE AUTHOR

Dear Reader,

I hope you enjoyed Vincent and Nathan's story. And yes, Everett, Gage and Nash's story is next in the series.

As an independent author, I am always grateful for feedback so if you have the time and desire, please leave a review, good or bad, so I can continue to find out what my readers like and don't like. You can also send me feedback via email at sloane@sloanekennedy.com

Join my Facebook Fan Group: Sloane's Secret Sinners

Connect with me:
www.sloanekennedy.com
sloane@sloanekennedy.com

ALSO BY SLOANE KENNEDY

(Note: Not all titles will be available on all retail sites)

The Escort Series
Gabriel's Rule (M/F)
Shane's Fall (M/F)
Logan's Need (M/M)

Barretti Security Series
Loving Vin (M/F)
Redeeming Rafe (M/M)
Saving Ren (M/M/M)
Freeing Zane (M/M)

Finding Series
Finding Home (M/M/M)
Finding Trust (M/M)
Finding Peace (M/M)
Finding Forgiveness (M/M)
Finding Hope (M/M/M)

The Protectors
Absolution (M/M/M)

Salvation (M/M)
Retribution (M/M)
Forsaken (M/M)
Vengeance (M/M/M)
A Protectors Family Christmas
Atonement (M/M)
Revelation (M/M)
Redemption (M/M)
Defiance (M/M)
Protecting Elliot (M/M)

Non-Series
Letting Go (M/F)

Printed in Great Britain
by Amazon